### *So this was Penny Sue Paine? Guardian to Lucky, the multi-millionaire dog?*

She stared at Vic with huge, chocolate-brown eyes fringed with thick, dark lashes. Her features were almost too perfect. Small, tip-tilted nose. Full luscious lips. Oval face. Flawless olive complexion. And a mane of dark, auburn-brown hair that flowed around her slender shoulders.

And her body. Holy hell. The body was to-die-for. No more than five-four, with an hourglass shape. Tiny waist, rounded hips and high, full breasts.

"Are you all right, Mr. Noble?" she asked.

"Uh...yeah, I'm fine."

"Then perhaps we should get started. What would you like to do first?" Penny Sue asked.

What would he like to do first?

*I'd like to make love to you, Miss Penny Sue. That's what I'd like to do.*

Dear Reader,

Like my heroine, Penny Sue Paine, I was born into a fairly typical Southern family, with predecessors ranging from highly respected doctors and wealthy landowners to a notorious outlaw who died on the gallows. And like Penny Sue, I am blessed with a group of marvelously eccentric relatives, a writer's treasure trove of unique characters.

Did I draw from real life to create Penny Sue and her family? You bet I did. Is any one character based on a real person? No, of course not. Doesn't everyone have kinfolk who've squabbled over a sizable (and even a not-so-sizable) inheritance? I think most of us have relatives that we both love and hate, that we're sometimes ashamed of and occasionally frustrated and angry with, but when push comes to shove, we stand by them when they need us. For a lot of us Southerners, that Scots-Irish clan mentality is an inherited trait. Without a doubt, there is a little bit of Penny Sue in me and many of my female cousins. From childhood, we were taught good manners, good taste and a strong sense of responsibility. We steel magnolias take care of our own.

Warmest regards,

*Beverly Barton*

# BEVERLY
# BARTON

*Penny Sue Got Lucky*

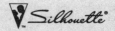

**INTIMATE MOMENTS™**

Published by Silhouette Books

**America's Publisher of Contemporary Romance**

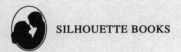 **SILHOUETTE BOOKS**

ISBN 0-373-27469-6

PENNY SUE GOT LUCKY

## BEVERLY BARTON

has been in love with romance since her grandfather gave her an illustrated book of *Beauty and the Beast*. An avid reader since childhood, Beverly wrote her first book at the age of nine. After marriage to her own "hero" and the births of her daughter and son, Beverly chose to be a full-time homemaker, aka wife, mother, friend and volunteer. The author of over thirty-five books, Beverly is a member of Romance Writers of America and helped found the Heart of Dixie chapter in Alabama. She has won numerous awards and has made the Waldenbooks and *USA TODAY* bestseller lists.

To my cousins, Sue Elkins and Penny Von Boeckman.

There is a little bit of Penny Sue in both of you, in me and in so many of our other female relatives, steel magnolias every one. Here's to all true Southern belles, past, present and future. Sometimes gentleness is the greatest strength of all.

## *Prologue*

Did you ever want to disown your entire family? I mean every last one of them. Or at the very least trade them in for another family? It's not as if I don't love them, although lately they've tried my patience almost to the breaking point. And I'm not an impatient person. Just ask anyone who knows me. Even my worst enemy—if I had one—would tell you that Penny Sue Paine has the patience of a saint. But I swear a saint would lose patience with this bunch. Of course, I'm not a saint, not by any stretch of the imagination. I am, however, a good person. I always— and I mean always—send thank-you notes. I give blood on a regular basis. I teach a Sunday-school class for preschoolers. I never wear white shoes after Labor Day or before Easter. I would not be caught dead in public without my makeup on and my hair fixed. I don't curse. Unless you count saying "Lord have mercy!" as cursing. I never destroy anything of worth when I'm finally pushed to my limit and start breaking things. Except once—I accidently shoved my hand through the glass front door at Grandmother Paine's house. Of course I was only three at the time and hadn't learned to control my temper. And I do not throw hissy fits in public, which is no small feat, let me tell you, because the Paine women are known throughout the county for their royal hissy fits. Well, there was that one time when the Country Kettle was out of glazed carrots and I got a tad upset. After all, who ever heard of a restaurant that specializes in vegetable plates running out of carrots before the dinner crowd arrives? But I'm getting off the subject, aren't I? I was explaining why I've had it up to my eyeballs with my family, wasn't I? Aunt Lottie always said digression was one of my weaknesses.

"Get to the point," Aunt Lottie would say. "Stop digressing." Then she'd glance over at Aunt Dottie and say, "It's a weakness you inherited from her, the silly goose."

Aunt Dottie would giggle and reply, "I'm not a silly goose. I simply have an effervescent personality. And giving all the details when telling a story is a family trait I inherited from Daddy, so it has to be a good trait, doesn't it, since Daddy was such a good man."

Aunt Lottie would roll her eyes and mumble something unintelligible.

God love 'em both. Lottie was the elder twin, born five whole minutes before Dottie. Although they were identical, no one had ever mistaken one for the other. Grandmother Paine never dressed them alike, not even as toddlers, which set a precedent in their lives, allowing them to be individuals. Lottie was the brains, Dottie the beauty. Lottie was serious-minded, Dottie was frivolous. Lottie took a nice little inheritance from her parents and turned it into millions by making shrewd investments. On the other hand, what money Dottie didn't spend on clothes, cars, fancy vacations and cosmetic surgery, she lost to a conniving swindler who stole not only her money but her heart. So, in their old age, Lottie financially supported her younger sister.

Oh, dear me. I'm digressing again.

Back to the current situation with my family.

I suppose the problem began when Aunt Lottie passed away. Well, actually, the problem began when Uncle Willie—that's Wilfred Hopkins, Aunt Lottie's lawyer, who isn't actually a blood relative—read the will. His wife, Aunt Pattie, is dog-tail kin to us, of course, her mother having been a first cousin to Grandmother Paine. And in case you don't know what dog-tail kin is—it's when you're distantly related, enough so that if you had a mind to, you could actually marry each other. That is if one was a man and the other a woman.

But as I said, the will is what caused the problem. We were assembled in the front parlor of Aunt Lottie's Victorian house on First Street—Aunt Dottie, Uncle Douglas, all the cousins and me—when Uncle Willie dropped the bombshell. Even I was surprised, but I shouldn't have been. After all, I knew better than anyone how much Aunt Lottie had loved Lucky.

You know, come to think of it, the root of the current problem actually began nearly four years ago. And I'm not digressing again. Really I'm not. To fully understand why Aunt Lottie did what she did, you have to understand things from the beginning. Well, not actually the beginning, since I wasn't there when Lucky was born, but… Okay, I was digressing there a bit, wasn't I?

It all started when Topper died. Topper was Aunt Lottie's black cocker spaniel. If you look up the term *spoiled rotten* in the dictionary, you'll find a picture of Topper right there beside the definition. I suppose having no husband and no children would make a woman love her pets more than most people did. And from childhood, Aunt Lottie had been a dog person and Aunt Dottie a cat person. When I was a child, Skippy had ruled the roost. He was Aunt Lottie's feisty little half feist, half Chihuahua. He went to puppy-dog heaven when I was eighteen and my father, the younger of the twins' two brothers, had promptly purchased Topper as a Christmas gift for his grieving sister. Within days, Topper had become top dog in every way, and until his dying day, he lived a life most humans would envy. Even Daddy often said that when he died, he wanted to come back as one of Lottie's dogs. And truth be told, on more than one occasion, I've wondered if maybe at least part of Daddy's spirit hasn't returned in Lucky. I've never told a living soul about that. We Paines are considered the town eccentrics as is. No need to add fuel to the flames.

I know. I know. I'm digressing again.

When Topper died, Aunt Lottie was inconsolable. She hadn't carried on half as bad when Daddy had died two years before, and he was her favorite brother. She loved Uncle Douglas well enough, but she'd said it herself, "Percy can be counted on. Douglas can't be."

One of my favorite charities is Animal Haven. It's Alabaster Creek, Alabama's equivalent to the dog pound, I suppose. Although Animal Haven shelters all sorts of animals, cats and dogs make up the bulk of their residents. I volunteer one afternoon a week at the shelter and back about four years ago, this precious little puppy, who had been abused by his previous owner, was dropped on the doorstep, the pitiful thing half-dead. The minute I told Aunt Lottie about the mongrel pup, she not only paid the vet's bills, but after taking one look at the puppy, she adopted him that very day.

After Doc Stone had given him a clean bill of health, Aunt Lottie had lifted the puppy into her arms, stroked his little head and said, "Well, mutt, you're one lucky dog. I'm taking you home with me." And that's how Lucky got his name.

Now, I'm not saying that Aunt Lottie loved Lucky more than any of her previous dogs, but there's something special about Lucky. He's not just smart, he's super-smart. And he's gentle and loving. Real friendly. And he adored Aunt Lottie. Actually the only flaw Lucky has is his intolerance of Puff, Aunt Dottie's cat. But then again, nobody likes that darn cat except Aunt Dottie.

Now, this brings me back to when Uncle Willie read Aunt Lottie's last will and testament, two months ago. I can still see Aunt Dottie swooning over in a dead faint. And Uncle Douglas's face turning beet-red as he struggled for words. I'm not sure who whined the loudest or the longest, but I think it was probably Cousin Valerie. She and her hubby, Dylan Redley, were counting on inheriting a sizable chunk of Aunt Lottie's fortune. They and their demon child, Dylan III—whom they call Trey—even moved home to Alabaster Creek two years ago so they could suck up to Aunt Lottie.

One little thing you should know about Dylan Redley. He was my high-school sweetheart and my fiancé. Yes, he's the one who ran off with the preacher's wife right before our wedding. And yes, my second cousin, Valerie, was the preacher's wife.

I know, I know. I'm digressing again. I can almost hear Aunt Lottie saying, "Stop rattling and get to the point, Penny Sue."

Well, the point is that Aunt Lottie left her entire twenty-three million dollars to Lucky. That's what I said. My aunt left her very sizable fortune to her dog. I was surprised. The other family members were shocked. Some were outraged. And the whole town of Alabaster Creek found the turn of events quite amusing. Most folks are still laughing—behind our backs—about nutty old Lottie Paine leaving millions to a dog-pound pooch.

Now you understand, I don't need Aunt Lottie's money. My father, God rest him, left me well off. I'm not a multi-millionaire, not rich enough to have men beating a path to my door, but if I chose never to work another day in my life, I'll still be financially secure. Percy Paine, like his sister, Lottie, had not squandered his inheritance. So, I suppose that was one reason Aunt Lottie made me executor of her will and Lucky's legal guardian. That and the fact she knew I loved Lucky, that I love animals in general and dogs in particular. That's one trait I did inherit from her.

The other heirs complained—loud and long. They shouted that they would protest the will, to which Uncle Willie immediately replied, "No point wasting your time. At Lottie's request, I saw to it that her will is iron-clad. No judge in the country would overturn it."

Now, you'd have thought that would be that, right? Oh, no. To a person, they—even Aunt Dottie—hired lawyers. Didn't do them a darn bit of good. They should have listened to Uncle Willie and saved themselves the time and the money. All the heirs would inherit someday, of course—but only after Lucky died.

Like I said, I love my family, at least nearly all of them. I can't say I've entirely forgiven Valerie for running off with Dylan. But I don't hate her. And seeing what a good-for-nothing Dylan turned out to be, I suppose I should be grateful to her. Every family has its faults, its idiosyncrasies, its skeletons in the closet, etc., etc., and the Paine clan is no different. But all in all, we're good people. God-fearing, flag-waving, all-American Southerners. So just imagine how totally traumatized I was when a member of my family tried to kill Lucky. I don't know who did it, but I'm convinced it was a disgruntled, disappointed heir who is willing to kill a poor little innocent dog for money. And in retrospect, I realize that this latest attempt might not have been the first, just the closest to successful.

After being shot, Lucky is recovering nicely over at Doc Stone's veterinary clinic and he's due to be released tomorrow. Since I have been unable to convince the police that Lucky is in danger, that he needs protection—when I'm elected mayor, I'll definitely be looking into local law-enforcement practices—I was left with only one choice. It's what Aunt Lottie would have wanted, what she would have done herself.

I hired a bodyguard for Lucky.

# *Chapter 1*

$V$ic Noble got off the elevator on the sixth floor of the downtown Atlanta building. He had finished his most recent assignment for the Dundee Private Security and Investigation agency two days ago and had hoped for a bit more downtime before being reassigned. No such luck. Daisy Holbrook, the office manager, had phoned him this morning to tell him that the CEO, Sawyer McNamara, had contacted her from his vacation home in Hilton Head, South Carolina, with the details of Vic's new job.

As he approached Daisy's desk in the heart of the Dundee agency office complex, she apparently sensed his presence. Glancing up, she offered him her usual pleasant smile. Daisy was a sweetheart. A cute, plump little brunette the staff referred to as Ms. Efficiency. Every agent thought of her as a kid sister. Even he did, and there weren't that many people Vic took a shine to, especially women in general. Oh, women had their place in his life, but only on a temporary, mutually satisfying yet non-emotional basis. Having been a loner since childhood, he liked his solitary, uncomplicated life. He'd been involved once, maybe even in love, but the experience had been bitter-sweet, to stay the least.

"Good morning, Vic," Daisy greeted him when he stopped at her desk. "Sorry to cut your down-time short, but you're the only available agent. We've been working shorthanded for quite some time, ever since Frank, Kate and J.J. all left us this past year. Mr. McNamara told me to thank you for taking this assignment."

"No problem," Vic said, but a peculiar glint in Daisy's eyes warned him that something wasn't quite right. "Or *is* there a problem?"

"Not that I know of."

Her smile widened, going from warm and friendly to forced and phony. Not a good sign. Vic smelled trouble with a capital *T*.

"You're not a very good liar," he told her.

"I'm not lying. There is no problem." She picked up a file folder and held it out to him. "You're booked on a flight leaving early this afternoon. I've arranged for a rental car and everything else you'll need. You'll be flying into Huntsville, Alabama, and driving from there about sixty miles to Alabaster Creek."

"What's going on in Alabaster Creek, Alabama, that requires a Dundee agent?"

With her fake smile in place, Daisy cleared her throat. "Mr. McNamara did ask me to explain that we're taking this case because the client is a relative of a friend of a friend, if you know what I mean."

Vic leaned over her desk and looked directly into her eyes. "Whatever it is, just tell me. It can't be that bad."

"I have no idea what you're talking about."

"Who's the client? What's the job?"

"The client…the lady who hired us is Penny Sue Paine."

Vic grinned. Penny Sue Paine? Could that name actually belong to a real person? It sounded more like the name for a cartoon character. "Why does Penny Sue Paine need a bodyguard?"

"She doesn't."

"Then why does she need an investigator?"

"Well…Ms. Paine needs you to find out who's trying to kill the…uh…the client she is hiring you to protect."

"I thought Ms. Paine was the client."

"She's the person who has hired Dundee's, but she hired us to protect someone else, someone who is recovering from a gunshot wound."

"And this someone is?"

"Uh…" Daisy hesitated, then said in a rush, "His name is Lucky. Lucky Paine. He's a four-year-old mixed-breed dog who just inherited twenty-three million dollars."

Vic pulled away from Daisy's desk, squared his shoulders and took a deep breath. "Let me get this straight—I'm traveling to Alabaster Creek, Alabama, this afternoon to guard a dog?"

"Twenty-four/seven." Daisy's fake smile returned.

"Send somebody else."

"There is no one else. Every agent is already on an assignment."

"Then call somebody in. I'll swap places with any agent who's—"

"I'm sorry, Vic, but nobody is willing. Mr. McNamara figured you wouldn't want this assignment and asked me to see if I could find another agent willing to swap places with you. Of course, he really wanted to hand this one over to Lucie. She was his first choice. You know how that would have pleased him, getting her all riled up over an assignment. But she's out of the country and there's no way she can come back right now, even if she wanted to take this job."

Vic cursed under his breath.

"If you'll go to Alabama today, I promise that the minute another agent works off, I'll get down on my hands and knees and beg him to relieve you."

Vic considered the situation. If he took this job, the other agents would never let him hear the end of it. He wasn't exactly known for his sense of humor and although he was on friendly terms with the other agents, he kept his distance on a personal level. He was a guy who traveled alone, traveled light. No ties that bound, no entanglements weighed him down. In his former line of work, as a CIA operative, he'd been known as the lone wolf.

"Call Sawyer and tell him I'll go to Alabama until another

agent is available. I want time-and-a-half pay and two weeks' paid vacation when I come in."

"I'm sure he'll agree."

Vic grabbed the file folder Daisy held. "Call him anyway. And once he's agreed, call Ms. Paine and let her know I'll phone her when I arrive in Huntsville." He fanned the file folder at Daisy. "I assume her phone number is in here."

"Her home phone, her business phone and her cell phone."

"Just what business is Ms. Paine in?"

"She owns her own business. A shop called Penny Sue's Pretties. It's a specialty gifts and home-decorating shop."

Vic groaned. Oh, God, she was one of *those* women.

"She's also running for mayor of Alabaster Creek, population 5,437. I understand it's a part-time job that pays about fifteen thousand a year."

Vic groaned again.

He knew, right this minute, before he ever left Dundee headquarters here in Atlanta, that this would turn out to be the assignment from hell.

"Do you really think pink will work in our bedroom?" Hazel Carruthers studied the pale-pink satin material. "Alton's not big on anything too feminine. He likes navy blue and green and red and brown."

Penny Sue sighed. "This is your bedroom, too, isn't it? You shouldn't have to do all the compromising. Pink is your favorite color."

"I know, but I have to live with that man, and if I use pink as the dominant color in our bedroom, he'll sleep on the sofa."

Penny Sue knew Alton Carruthers. If he were her husband, she'd rather have him sleep on the sofa than in her bed. The man was as ugly as homemade soap, with a grumpy disposition and an I'm-head-of-the-household mentality. He'd chosen wisely when he married Hazel, a plain, skinny redhead with a sweet, gentle temperament and a willingness to please. Although Penny Sue wished the woman would grow a backbone, she liked her nonetheless.

"Paint the walls beige. A light beige with just a hint of pink," Penny Sue suggested reluctantly. If she pressed Hazel to go against Alton's wishes, she would be doing her client a disservice. And the client always came first. "Use navy blue as the dominant color in the drapes and bedding, then use pink in the throw pillows and small accent pieces. How does that sound?"

Hazel's blue eyes brightened. "One pink pillow and maybe some pink candles. Surely Alton can't complain about that."

Although every feminist instinct in her groaned, Penny Sue smiled. "Why don't you look around and see if you can find something you like. I'll make some notations in my notebook and work up a complete plan for your bedroom."

Hazel gazed longingly at the pink satin drapery material, then sighed heavily before walking away to search for a pink pillow.

Penny Sue was of the opinion that men should stick to things they know—like hunting and fishing, cars and trucks, sports and beer—and leave home-decorating entirely in the hands of the women in their lives. If she had a husband, which she didn't and possibly never would, she'd tell him straight away that if she wanted a pink bedroom, then by golly she'd have one and he'd just have to get used to it. Now it wasn't as if she was opposed to catering to a man, to making him feel special and building up his ego, but there were limits to what a woman should have to do.

Just as Penny Sue headed toward her desk, tucked away in the corner of Penny Sue's Pretties, the bell over the door tinkled, informing her that a customer had either entered or exited her shop. Since Hazel was the only person in the store, other than herself, that meant she'd have to postpone working on Hazel's bedroom plans and see to the needs of the new customer. After laying her notebook on the antique French desk, she retraced her steps and headed toward the front of the store. The minute she saw her cousin Valerie marching toward her, Penny Sue came to a dead stop. She could tell from the look on Val's face that her cousin was in a snit.

Valerie Redley, with her silky blond hair and slanted green eyes, glared at Penny Sue. Model-thin, long-legged and bosomy, her cousin had "that look." You know, the look that tells men she's not only hot, but also available. "That look" came from the other side of her family, not from the Paines. The Paine women were known for their modesty and ladylike manners.

"Are you out of your mind?" Val asked, her voice loud enough to be heard throughout the store.

"I beg your pardon?"

"Don't you play innocent with me. I just came from Doc Stone's, where I'd gone to check on Lucky, and Tanya told me what you've done."

Penny Sue stood her ground, putting the most defiant look on her face she possibly could. But when a person had small, soft features, the way she did, it wasn't easy. Killer stares were better accomplished by people with chiseled features.

"And just what did Doc Stone's receptionist tell you I've done?"

"You're wasting Aunt Lottie's money on the most foolish notion I've ever heard of," Val said. "Hiring a bodyguard for that stupid dog is outrageous. Whatever were you thinking?"

Sticking her nose in the air, hoping for a snooty look since she couldn't quite pull off defiant, Penny Sue replied, "I was thinking that Lucky needed protection from whomever is trying to kill him."

Val groaned. "Nobody is trying to kill that mutt. You have no right to spend Aunt Lottie's money—"

Penny Sue stuck her index finger right in Val's face. "It's not Aunt Lottie's money anymore. It's Lucky's money." Val's expression hardened, putting wrinkles in her forehead and between her eyes. Val wasn't aging well. Another trait she must have inherited from the other side of her family. The Paines always aged well. "Have you forgotten that someone shot Lucky and nearly killed him?"

"It was an accident. All the men around Alabaster Creek own guns and many of them target practice in their backyards, so it's not that big a stretch to think a stray bullet might hit something other than its intended target. Even the police think that Lucky was just in the wrong place at the wrong time and—"

"Hogwash."

"What?"

"You heard me—hogwash. One of my relatives—" she looked pointedly at Val "—is willing to murder Lucky in order to inherit his money."

Val huffed, then sucked in her cheeks and pursed her lips.

Penny Sue wondered if Dylan had ever noticed that his wife was not a pretty woman. Sexy. Yes. Attractive in a floozie kind of way. Yes. But pretty. No. And as she grew older, the good Paine genes she had inherited from her father—a first cousin to Lottie, Dottie, Douglas and Percy—were being ravaged by the less-favorable genes she had inherited from her mother. Valerie's mother had not been a pretty woman either. None of the Goodwins in and around Alabaster Creek were good-looking.

"You should know that I've called a meeting for this evening so that we can discuss what you've done," Val said. "Even Aunt Dottie is upset with you."

In her peripheral vision, Penny Sue caught a glimpse of Hazel Carruthers cautiously coming up the aisle, her eyes wide, her attention focused on the loud disagreement. "Call all the meetings you want. I've done what I thought best for Lucky and there's really nothing you can do about it."

"I think someone other than you should be named executor of Aunt Lottie's will and made Lucky's guardian."

Penny Sue took a step toward her cousin, who took a step back, her eyes rounded in surprise. "I'm not going to hit you, even though a part of me would like to slap you silly. You're such a twit. Aunt Lottie chose me for good reason. And Uncle Willie made sure there's little chance of her wishes being overturned in any court of law. Lucky inherited Aunt Lottie's money and I'm her executor and Lucky's guardian and I intend to see that Lucky lives to a ripe old age. He's only four. He could easily live another ten or twelve years."

"Do you intend to throw away millions on a private bodyguard for the next ten years? If you do, you'll be certifiably insane and we might be able to have you committed."

Penny Sue grinned. "Get real, will you? I'm a Paine. I'm *supposed* to be eccentric. And as for keeping a bodyguard indefinitely—I don't think that will be necessary. Once we find out who tried to kill Lucky, Uncle Willie says it's possible that we can legally remove that person from the list of heirs."

"You can't do that!"

"No, I can't, but Uncle Willie probably can. There's a provision in Aunt Lottie's will that speaks to that issue."

"I don't remember Uncle Willie reading anything about—"

"It was worded in legal jargon and everyone was so upset and making all kinds of threats that day that I seriously doubt anyone was listening when he read the specific provision concerning disqualifying heirs."

"Well, I can assure you that Dylan and I would never harm a hair on Lucky's head," Val said. "And I really don't think anyone else in the family tried to kill Lucky, but if they did, then they should definitely be removed from the list of heirs who will inherit when Lucky dies."

Penny Sue's grin widened. Valerie had changed her tune rather quickly. No doubt she was calculating how much more money she would inherit if the list of heirs was cut by one. That meant either she was not the would-be killer or she was trying to figure out a way to frame someone else.

"I'll let the others know that this bodyguard you've hired for Lucky is only a temporary thing," Val said. "However, since you're the one who hired him, I think you should be the one to pay him—out of your own pocket. It's not fair to take money away from the rest of us, now is it?"

Penny Sue glowered at Val. The bell over the entrance door chimed again. Since Hazel stood only a few feet away, that meant someone new had entered the shop. Momentarily taking her eyes off Val to check on the newcomer, Penny Sue saw her cousin Eula, who had retired from her job at Alabaster Creek Utilities last year, at the age of sixty-two. Eula worked part-time at Penny Sue's Pretties now. And today was one of her three half-days, which included Wednesdays, Saturdays and Fridays.

Val turned and smiled when she saw Eula. "I'm glad you came in before I left. I'm phoning everyone in the family to let them know I'm hosting a meeting tonight to discuss Penny Sue's decision to hire a bodyguard for Lucky. Telling you in person saves me a phone call."

Eula's faded brown eyes glanced from Val to Penny Sue. "You hired a bodyguard for Lottie's dog?"

"An expensive bodyguard who'll watch Lucky twenty-four hours a day, seven days a week," Val said. "Isn't that a ridiculous waste of money?"

Frown lines wrinkled Eula's forehead as her narrowed gaze confronted Penny Sue. Eula was a true Paine in looks and personality. A first cousin to Penny Sue's father, Eula possessed the same dark eyes, hair and complexion as Lottie and Dottie, as well as the high-strung, opinionated and eccentric nature for which all the Paine women were infamous. And, she, too, was an old maid.

"You still think one of us tried to kill Lucky, don't you?" Eula asked.

"I know one of the heirs shot Lucky and it's my job to protect him," Penny Sue said.

"Then you've done the right thing by hiring someone to guard him around the clock." Eula moved past her cousins and headed toward the back of the store.

"Eula!" Val shrieked the name.

Eula stopped, turned and said, "Valerie, did your mother not teach you that it's very unladylike to scream?"

Scowling, Val walked toward Eula. "I believe Penny Sue should cover the cost of the bodyguard herself and not take the money out of our inheritance."

Eula cocked her head to one side. "Hmm…" She cocked her head to the other side, then sighed dramatically. "No, that wouldn't be right. Lucky is Lottie's dog, so Lottie's money should pay for protecting him."

Val fumed. You could practically see the steam rising off the top of her bleached-blond head. "Since you're apparently on Penny Sue's side in this matter, there's no point in your being at tonight's meeting. I'll tell the others—"

"That won't be necessary," Penny Sue said. "Eula and I are family. We're two of the heirs who will inherit when Lucky goes to puppy-dog heaven, so we will most certainly want to be present at the meeting. As a matter of fact, I'll even bring Lucky's bodyguard with me so y'all can meet him."

Val's eyes grew large as saucers and her mouth gaped into an outraged oval.

"Close your mouth, dear," Eula said, "before you start catching flies."

Val shut her mouth, then opened it again, wide enough to speak. "Seven o'clock, at Aunt Dottie's. She's graciously agreed to allow us to meet in her home since my house is rather small."

"How very gracious of Aunt Dottie to offer her home, especially considering that she's living in Aunt Lottie's house, which, by the way, is now my home. Mine and Lucky's."

"But I thought you moved back to your place after Lucky was shot," Val said. "I naturally assumed—"

"Never assume," Penny Sue told her. "I simply took the opportunity to go back to my place and start packing in order to make the move into the Paine mansion permanent."

"Oh, I see."

Penny Sue barely managed to hide the smile beginning to curve her lips. Every member of the family had wanted the house, but Aunt Lottie, who had owned it free and clear, had left the house to Penny Sue, with the provision that both Lucky and Dottie be allowed to live there for the remainder of their lives. The Paine mansion was the biggest and best house in town. Built in the early 1880s, the three-story Victorian house boasted wide porches, two circular towers and a profusion of elaborate gingerbread trim. Aunt Lottie had chosen to paint the place in various shades of green and pink. Nothing gaudy, just colors that were appropriate for the style and design of the house. Original paint colors, true to the Victorian era.

Eula reached out and patted Val on the shoulder. "We'll see you tonight then, dear. At seven. At Penny Sue's house."

Val forced a smile before jerking around and stomping out of the shop.

The minute the bell over the door chimed, Hazel Carruthers rushed toward Penny Sue and Eula.

"I...uh...I'll come back later and discuss redecorating the bedroom. I do apologize for being present while y'all discussed family matters. But I swear not a word of what I heard will go one bit further. I know how to keep my mouth shut."

Penny Sue and Eula exchanged yeah-sure-tell-me-another-one glances. Hazel hurried out of the shop, as if her butt was on fire. The first person she met once outside on the sidewalk was Stella Lowrance, the owner of the Cut and Curl beauty salon.

Penny Sue groaned, then shook her head and laughed.

"Well, the family's personal business will be front-page news by suppertime tonight," Eula said. "The two biggest busybodies in town are Hazel and Stella. Everybody's going to know that you've hired a bodyguard for Lucky and that most of the family members aren't happy about it. We'll be the talk of the town."

Penny Sue shrugged. "Everybody in town would have known anyway. It seems Tanya over at Doc Stone's is telling everyone she sees. Besides, what do we care what other people say about us? The Paines have been the talk of Alabaster Creek for several generations. I can't imagine what the good citizens would find to talk about if not for us."

Vic slowed the rental car, a mid-size black Chevy, as he entered the downtown area of Alabaster Creek. Apparently a recent renovation of the area had restored many of the old buildings to their original splendor, giving Main Street the look of a bygone era. Underground utilities, trees and shrubs on every corner and gas-lamp-style streetlights added to the ambience. He drove slowly up the street, glancing at the shops on his left. He passed a bakery, a drugstore/ice cream parlor, a hardware store and—Penny Sue's Pretties. He whipped the car into a parking place, the only empty one on the block, at the very end of the street. He should probably take the time to read over the file folder Daisy had given him on Ms. Paine, but there should be time enough for that tonight. He could have read the file on the plane from Atlanta, but the flight had lasted less than thirty minutes, so he'd opted for a quick nap. When he'd phoned Ms. Paine from the Huntsville airport, she'd told him that they wouldn't be picking up Lucky until tomorrow, so he wouldn't be on official bodyguard duty until then.

"The family is having a meeting tonight," she'd said. "Some of them disapprove of my hiring you. I intend for us to be there and I want you to make it clear that you'll be investigating the crime and bringing the person who shot Lucky to justice."

Vic grunted as he got out of the car and stepped up on the sidewalk. It wasn't that he didn't like dogs. He did. As a boy, raised in the backwoods of Kentucky, near the Tennessee border, he'd known men who thought more of their hunting dogs than they did their wives. He'd even had a dog himself when he was a kid. But Old Beau had slept outside and eaten scraps from the table. In the dead cold of winter, he found a spot under the floor near the gas furnace to stay warm. People of Vic's acquaintance didn't pamper dogs, didn't treat them like they were humans. And they sure as hell didn't leave them twenty-three million dollars.

He paused before entering Ms. Paine's shop, a two-story structure painted pale yellow, with a bright blue awning over the entrance and two huge display windows flanking either side of the glass door, the wooden trim also a bright blue. Hanging on the brick wall at the second-story level were large bright blue wooden letters that spelled out Penny Sue's Pretties. As he glanced into the display windows, he noted a variety of items, from an antique chair covered in a floral material to scented candles and an assortment of toiletries. Scattered throughout the other items on display was an assortment of Easter items, such as baskets, hand-painted porcelain eggs and toy bunny rabbits.

Just the thought of going inside this store made him shiver. He avoided "girlie" places like the plague. His idea of hell on earth was going shopping with a woman. Any woman. He appreciated seeing a woman in a sheer silk teddy and lying on satin sheets as much as the next man, just so long as he didn't have to go with her to shop for her undies or her bed linens.

Drawing in a deep, you-can-do-this breath, Vic reached for the door handle. The minute he opened the door, he heard a bell tinkling. Oh, God! Looking up, he saw the little silver bell attached to the facing over the door so that any entrance to or exit from the shop would trigger the chime. After stepping into the shop overflowing with wall-to-wall "pretties," Vic scanned the interior. There were half a dozen shoppers, each carrying a yellow straw basket approximately twelve-by-twenty inches in size. Then he saw the person he assumed was Ms. Paine standing with one of the customers, pointing out the superiority of soy candles over wax candles.

"These are a new line of candles that we just started carrying a couple of weeks ago," Ms. Paine said. "They're clean-burning and soot-free. You must smell this one." She picked up a glass container, popped off the lid and held it under the customer's nose. "Cinnamon. Isn't it heavenly?"

Vic cleared his throat. Both women looked at him.

"Yes, sir, I'll be with you in a moment." Ms. Paine smiled at him.

Vic nodded, then tried his best to be as inconspicuous as possible, which wasn't easy for a guy who stood six-four. For a couple of minutes he stared down at the wooden floor, then he hazarded a glance to the right and then to the left. In both directions, he saw women staring at him, sizing him up, whispering about the stranger in town. At least he figured that was what they were whispering about. Cutting his gaze sharply toward the ceiling, he tightened his hands into fists. He released, then tightened, then released again.

How long did it take to sell a woman a damn candle? When he glanced in Ms. Paine's direction, he noted that she was leading the customer toward the glass counter at the front of the shop where a computerized cash register waited to ring up the sale. Ms. Paine looked older than she'd sounded on the phone. Her voice had been bubbly. And soft and slightly sexy. He'd imagined her to be in her twenties or thirties. But this lady had to be in her fifties. In her younger days, she'd probably been pretty. Even now, with short gray hair and tiny wrinkles framing her eyes and mouth, she was attractive, in a neat and orderly sort of way.

Vic headed for the checkout counter just as Ms. Paine rounded the corner and came toward him.

"Yes, sir, how may I help you?" She smiled pleasantly.

Maybe this woman wasn't Ms. Paine. She could be an employee, couldn't she? "Ms. Paine?"

"Yes."

He didn't know whether to be relieved or disappointed. Relieved, he told himself. "I'm Vic Noble."

She stared at him quizzically, as if she'd never heard the name before in her life. How was that possible? He had spoken to her only an hour ago.

"Vic Noble, from the Dundee agency," he told her.

"The Dundee agency?"

"Dundee Private Security and Investigation."

"Oh!" Her mouth formed a wide-open circle. "You must be Lucky's bodyguard."

"Yes, ma'am. We spoke on the phone. I called you from Huntsville."

She laughed. "Oh, my dear young man, you didn't speak to me. You spoke to—"

"You spoke to me, Mr. Noble." The syrupy-sweet voice came from behind him.

He turned, took one look at the lady and felt as if he'd been poleaxed. The woman smiling at him as she came forward took his breath away. He didn't know any other way to describe how he felt. As a rule, women either turned him on or they didn't. This woman did a lot more than turn him on. She turned him inside out, and he sure as hell didn't like the feeling.

She held out her small, delicate hand. "I'm Penny Sue Paine. It's so nice to meet you, Mr. Noble."

He stared at her hand for a split second, then took it, shook it a little too hard and released it as if it were a red-hot poker. Say something, he told himself. Don't just stand here looking at her. But his male libido told him to look all he wanted, to appreciate every lovely curve of her body, every feature of her pretty face.

So this was Penny Sue Paine? Executor of Lottie Paine's will and guardian to Lucky, the multi-millionaire dog.

She stared at him with huge, chocolate-brown eyes, fringed with thick dark lashes. Her features were almost too perfect. Small, tip-tilted nose. Full luscious lips. Oval face. Flawless olive complexion that probably tanned easily. And a mane of dark auburn-brown hair that flowed around her slender shoulders.

And her body? Holy hell. The body was to die for. No more than five-four, with an hourglass shape. Tiny waist, rounded hips and high, full breasts.

"Are you all right, Mr. Noble?" she asked.

"Uh...yeah, I'm fine. I was just surprised there for a minute. I thought the other lady—" he inclined his head toward the older Ms. Paine.

"That's my cousin, Eula," Penny Sue said.

"I see."

"Now that you're here, we can go to Doc Stone's so you can meet Lucky or we can go to the house so you can settle in or— have you had lunch? If not, we can go over to the Country Kettle. What would you like to do first?" Penny Sue asked.

What would he like to do first? The one and only thought that popped into Vic's mind was *I'd like to screw you, Miss Penny Sue. That's what I'd like to do.*

## Chapter 2

Penny Sue walked alongside the Dundee agent she had hired to protect Lucky and wondered exactly what kind of man this Vic Noble was—other than being a devastatingly attractive male specimen. The first moment she'd seen him, she had instantly gone weak in the knees. And that wasn't something she did all that often. It had only happened a couple of times in her entire life. The first time had been when Dylan Redley French-kissed her when she was fifteen. The second time had been when she'd met Mr. Tom Selleck in person.

"I hope you don't mind walking," Penny Sue said. "I always walk to and from the shop. It's good exercise and gives me a chance to do a little politicking when I see my neighbors on their porches or in their yards."

When he didn't respond, she cut her eyes in his direction to see if he'd even heard her. Since they had turned his rental car in, at her suggestion, over at Burns's Service Station and Mini-Mart, the man hadn't said ten words to her. She'd had to explain to him that Burns's was also the automobile and moving-van rental place in town. Old Man Burns had believed in diversifying and his two sons, Dwight and Dwayne, were following in his footsteps.

"You won't need a car," Penny Sue had told Vic. "You can use either my car or Aunt Lottie's car while you're here."

As she glanced at Lucky's protector, Penny Sue noted how very tall he was. She was five-four and he stood a good foot taller than she. Without being too obvious, she let her gaze travel over him, from his thick, dark hair, down his proud nose to his wide, hard mouth. Didn't this man ever smile?

Several times, he had walked a few steps ahead of her, but when he'd realized she couldn't keep up with his long gait, he'd slowed and got in step with her. As they left the commercial blocks of downtown Alabaster Creek and moved on to the first residential street—Maple Avenue—she began searching for any voters who might be out and about this afternoon. So far, she'd paused to speak to half a dozen people in town, but Maple Avenue seemed deserted, not a person in sight.

"Alabaster Creek is one of the oldest towns in north Alabama," Penny Sue said, just making conversation, which wasn't easy with this man. "We were actually a town before Alabama became a state."

Vic Noble didn't say a word. With his black vinyl suitcase in hand, he marched alongside her. Tall, dark and silent.

"Most of the houses here on Maple Avenue were built post-War Between the States, but there's one—see, right up there, the two-story white wooden structure—that was built in 1838. It's the Rutland house. And would you believe descendants of the family who built the house still live in it today. As a matter of fact, Tommy Rutland is running against me for mayor. His father was once the mayor, but then again so was my father and my grandfather."

"Hmm…"

Most people found the history of Alabaster Creek interesting, but not this man. What was his problem? Didn't he know that not keeping up your end of a conversation was considered bad manners?

"You aren't much of a talker, are you, Mr. Noble?"

"No, ma'am, I'm not."

He didn't bother even to look at her, which irritated her no end. This man might be big and macho and terribly attractive in a caveman sort of way, but his dour personality wasn't the least bit appealing. But perhaps she shouldn't judge him too harshly. After all, they'd just met and it took some people more time than it did her to warm up to others. Also, there was his profession to consider—he was a bodyguard and a private investigator. Lord only knew what kind of life this man had lived and what sort of cases he'd worked on over the years. It could be that he'd seen too much of the dark side of life. She'd heard that tended to make men somber and introspective.

"I suppose most of your cases are different from this one," Penny Sue said, hoping that by talking business, she could encourage him to open up a bit.

"Yeah. Very different."

Aha, he could talk. "Have you ever guarded a dog?"

"No, ma'am, I haven't. This is a first for me."

"You'll like Lucky. He's precious. Everyone adores him."

"Not everyone."

"What? Oh, yes, you're right. Not everyone. Not the person who shot him."

"Do you have any idea who that person might be?"

She shook her head. "One of the heirs. But there are eight of us and other than knowing for sure that I didn't shoot Lucky, I can't imagine who did. And I shouldn't have said everyone adores Lucky. I should have said most people do. Even Aunt Dottie, whose cat, Puff, hates Lucky, admits that Lucky is a dear."

"Ms. Paine, why would your aunt leave twenty-three million dollars to a dog?"

When she stopped on the sidewalk in front of the Kimbrew house, he paused and looked at her for the first time since they'd left Burns's. Her stomach did a naughty flip-flop when he settled his gaze on her, his pensive hazel-and-blue eyes incredibly sexy. She'd always thought only brown eyes could be referred to as bedroom eyes, but now she knew better.

Penny Sue sighed. "You might as well know before you meet everyone tonight. The Paine family is…well, we're the town eccentrics. You know, slightly peculiar. Just a bit off center. We tend to do things our own way. And the women in our family are the worst. I suppose that's why so many Paine women die old maids. It's not that we don't want husbands, it's just that we seem to intimidate most men.

"We're all considered beauties and we can attract men like bears to honey, but we can't seem to keep a man once he realizes how independent and opinionated we are. Even Aunt Dottie, who is the sweetest thing, wasn't able to land a husband. And one of her fiancés turned out to be a swindler who ran off with a large chunk of her money and broke her heart to boot. And then there was *my* one and only fiancé—he didn't leave with any of my money, but he did run off with the Baptist preacher's wife only a couple of weeks before our wedding. And what made it even more of a scandal was the fact the woman was my cousin.

"Valerie's last name might have been Paine, but she takes after her mother's side of the family, which means she's not a true Paine. You'll meet her tonight. If you're like most men, you'll take one look at her and think she's easy, if you know what I mean. And you'd be right. She gets that from her mother's side of the family, too. The Paine women are known for their modesty and their ladylike manners. Aunt Lottie and Aunt Dottie, Cousin Eula, Cousin Stacie and—"

He dropped his case to the sidewalk and then grabbed her by the shoulders. For half a second she thought he was going to shake her. He didn't. The very instant she stopped talking, he released her. But not before every nerve ending in her entire body had gone to full alert. She'd been startled by his abrupt action, but not afraid. His touch had been firm yet gentle and the feel of his large, strong hands had sent a tingling sensation through her whole body.

She gazed up at him, into those stern hazel-blue eyes. "Is something wrong?"

"Ms. Paine, all I asked was why your aunt left her fortune to a dog."

Penny Sue laughed. "Oh, my, so you did. You'll have to forgive me, Mr. Noble—by the way, may I call you Vic? I'd like it if you called me Penny Sue. Everyone does. Well, not everyone in the whole world because I don't know everyone in the whole world, but everyone in Alabaster Creek and—"

He grabbed her shoulders again and this time he did shake her. Once. A very gentle shake, but enough to quiet her. She gazed up at him and smiled. "I was doing it again, wasn't I? I tend to get off track. It's another family trait—giving too many details. Aunt Lottie always scolded me for digressing."

She glanced at his big hands still clutching her shoulders. He released her immediately.

"Do you suppose you could manage to answer my questions in two sentences or less?" he asked.

"I'm not sure. But I could try." She reached up and smoothed his wrinkled brow with her fingertips. He jerked back as if her touch had burned him. "You really should smile more, Vic. You're a very good-looking man, but frowning all the time isn't very attractive."

"Ms. Paine—"

"Penny Sue."

He heaved a deep, exasperated sigh. Was he annoyed with her? Probably. Just a tad. Silly of him, of course, to get so bent out of shape over nothing.

"Penny Sue," he said. "How about we try yes and no answers?"

"All right. Does that mean you'll ask me a question and I'll say either yes or no?"

"That's what it means."

"All right. Now that we've got that settled, let's go on home. If we stand out here in front of the Kimbrew house for much longer, Oren Kimbrew will come out here and ask us what we're up to. He grows prize-winning roses and for the past two years, Aunt Dottie's roses have won first place in every contest in which they competed against each other. So when he sees any member of the Paine family near his house, he accuses us of trying to sabotage his roses."

Vic picked up his case with one hand and using the other hand, grabbed her arm and spurred her into motion, leading her up the block in an all-fired hurry. If she hadn't been so perturbed by his actions, she'd have noticed sooner that once again her body was tingling all over just from his touch.

"Vic?"

"Hush, will you?" After drawing in a deep breath, he added, "Please."

"What's wrong?"

"Nothing."

"I know better. Tell me."

Without looking at her, but holding on to her arm and keeping up their fast pace down the sidewalk, Vic said, "I've never met a woman who talked so much and said so little."

Penny Sue balked. He yanked on her arm, but she wouldn't budge. He let go of her.

"That wasn't a very nice thing to say," she told him.

"You're right. It wasn't. I tend to say exactly what I think. If you want an apology, then I'll apologize."

"No, don't bother. It wouldn't be sincere. And an insincere apology is worse than no apology at all."

"If you say so."

"I do say so." Penny Sue pursed her lips into a little pout. Tears moistened her eyes. Her chin trembled. There was no excuse for being rude. Well, maybe one. If Vic was a Yankee, she might be able to overlook his comment. But she could tell by his accent that he had been raised somewhere in the South, probably farther north than Alabama. Virginia or Kentucky. But even in those states, people were taught good manners, weren't they?

He studied her for a couple of minutes. "I didn't mean to hurt your feelings."

She sniffled. "Would you please put that into a question I can answer by either yes or no."

He glared at her. She glanced away, refusing to look at him. Since they were going to be spending a great deal of time together during the next few weeks, he needed to learn right now that she would not tolerate bad manners, especially not from an employee.

"Did I hurt your feelings?" he asked, his manner downright surly.

"Yes."

"Will you accept my apology?"

"No."

"Why the hell not?"

She gasped. It was a fake gasp, but he didn't know that.

"Don't tell me—you're offended by my saying hell?" he asked.

"Yes."

He blew out an irritated huff. "Look, lady, I'm a man. I occasionally use profanity. And my manners aren't all they could be. But you didn't hire me because I'm a gentleman. You hired me because I'm a professional. Can we agree on that?"

"Yes."

"Then will you accept my apology?"

"No."

"Why not?"

Lifting her head just enough to indicate indifference, she glanced right and then left. He needed to be taught the proper way to deal with a Paine woman. And the sooner, the better.

"You're not answering because you're sticking with the yes or no responses I asked you to give," he said. "Is that it?"

"Yes."

"I didn't mean it so literally," he told her. "I just wanted to find a way to cut your never-ending explanations to a minimum of words. Feel free to elaborate beyond yes and no." When she opened her mouth as if to speak, he held up a restraining hand. "Brief elaboration."

"No."

"Ms. Paine!"

She glared at him.

Then he said, "Penny Sue?"

She softened her gaze just a little, enough to let him know she was considering the possibility of being agreeable. "Yes?"

"I'm going to be perfectly honest with you. Is that all right?"

"Yes." She crossed her arms over her chest and waited.

He glanced from her face to her bosom, then swallowed hard and looked her right in the eyes. "I didn't want this assignment. I consider it frivolous and silly. My background qualifies me for just about anything the Dundee agency can throw my way, however, I think I'm just a little overqualified to guard a millionaire dog. But I'm here until another agent can take my place, so that means you and I have to work together on a daily basis. I think it will be to both your advantage and mine if we can be civil to each other. Do you agree?"

"Yes."

"Then will you start saying something other than yes and no?"

"Maybe."

When he grunted and rolled his eyes heavenward, Penny Sue grinned, then walked off and left him standing on the corner of Elm Avenue and First Street.

Penny Sue Paine hadn't said anything else to him on their walk to 413 First Street. He had taken his cue from her and remained silent. He'd never been very good at having to deal with a woman on a personal basis. Usually the female clients he worked with on Dundee assignments were normal women, often either a woman in jeopardy herself or the wife of a man in trouble. And when he was physically attracted to a client, he never made the first move and always waited to see if the attraction went both ways. On a couple of occasions, he'd had a brief affair with a client, but as a general rule, things remained strictly business. Any woman he encountered knew up-front that he wasn't interested in anything beyond a physical relationship.

But this drop-dead-gorgeous, Southern-belle chatterbox was unlike any woman he'd ever known. One minute he wanted to gag her and the next minute he wanted to kiss her.

Would he like to make love to Penny Sue Paine? Damn right he would. Any red-blooded man would want her. But after spending less than an hour with her this afternoon, he understood why she was still single, why, as she had told him, most of the Paine women died old maids. If all the others, past and present, were or had been anything like she was…

"This is it," Penny Sue said.

Surprised that she'd spoken, he snapped his head around and looked at her. She was gazing at the house at the end of the sidewalk. Three stories high and covered with elaborate wooden trim, the pink-and-green Victorian structure looked like something from the past. A grand old lady who was well preserved.

Penny Sue reached for the handle on the fancy black iron gate attached to the decorative iron fence that surrounded the large triple lot on which the Paine house sat. Vic slipped his arm alongside hers and flipped the latch, then moved to her side and opened the gate for her. She smiled, tilted her head in an I'm-pleased-with-you gesture and sauntered up the brick walkway in front of him. Following several feet behind her, he watched the seductive sway of her hips and wondered if she realized that with every move, her body was flirting, sending out come-here-big-boy signals. If she was as modest and well-mannered as she'd said the Paine women were, then she probably didn't know. The fact that she was a sexy woman who wasn't fully aware of just how sexy she was made her all the more desirable.

Desirable, yes. But off limits to you, he reminded himself.

He followed behind her like an obedient servant—or a devoted lap dog. Inwardly he cringed. Was this how his next few weeks would be spent? He and Lucky traipsing along behind Miss Penny Sue?

He had every intention of calling Daisy first thing in the morning to tell her he wanted out of this job ASAP. He'd forego any overtime pay if she could get him out of Alabaster Creek and away from Penny Sue. If the woman didn't drive him crazy first, he'd wind up dragging her off to a dark corner somewhere and having his way with her. And if their relationship reached that stage, there would be hell to pay. This was no one-night-stand kind of gal. No, this one would want orange blossoms and wedding bells. As far as he was concerned that was too high a price to pay for a piece of ass, no matter how shapely that ass might be.

When they approached the front door, it flew open and a gray Siamese cat zipped out onto the porch and past them, pausing long enough to hiss at them before running into the yard.

"Get back here, you naughty boy," the woman standing in the doorway cried. "That cat will be the death of me. His antics play havoc on my poor nerves." She looked Vic over, studied him admiringly and smiled. "Well, hello. Who are you?"

"Aunt Dottie, this is Mr. Noble," Penny Sue said. "He's the bodyguard I hired for Lucky. He'll be staying with us for a while."

The woman's keen black eyes opened wide. "You've hired a bodyguard for—"

"Don't play dumb with me," Penny Sue told her aunt. "Val stopped by the shop earlier and told me all about the meeting here tonight."

"Oh, dear, you aren't angry with me, are you? Val can be so persuasive. And I didn't see what harm it would do for the family to get together and discuss things."

Vic wondered just how old Aunt Dottie was. Past sixty, maybe even past seventy. She was tiny, no more than five-one and possibly a hundred pounds soaking wet. Her hair was short, stylish and jet-black. Her face was as smooth as a baby's butt, the skin drawn tightly over her cheeks and forehead. He'd bet his last dollar that the lady had undergone more than one facelift. Even with the changes age and cosmetic surgery had done to her face, it was obvious that Dottie Paine had once been a young beauty and there was a strong family resemblance between her and her niece.

"There really isn't anything to discuss." Penny Sue confronted her aunt, who backed down immediately and eased into the foyer. "I've hired a bodyguard for Lucky, to protect him from a potential killer. And I'm using the money Aunt Lottie left Lucky to pay for Mr. Noble's bodyguard duties as well as his investigative skills."

"He's an investigator, too?" Dottie asked.

"Come in, please, Vic." Penny Sue motioned for him to enter the house, so he complied with her wishes.

Just as Penny Sue started to close the door, Dottie cried out, "I can't leave Puff outside. He's liable to run off and Lord knows what would happen to him. He's not accustomed to life on the street."

Penny Sue shut the door. Dottie gasped.

"Oh, pooh. That spoiled cat isn't going anywhere," Penny Sue said. "He'll be scratching on the door in a couple of minutes."

Dottie eyed Vic. He tried to ignore the old woman's scrutiny.

"Do you think it proper for him to stay here in the house with us?" Dottie asked. "After all, he's a man and we're two single ladies. You know how people talk."

"Ruby and Tully live here, too," Penny Sue said. "Besides, what do we care about wagging tongues?"

"Who are Ruby and Tully?" Vic asked.

"They're the housekeeper and her husband," Dottie replied. "He's the gardener and does all the upkeep around the place. They have two rooms in the back. They used to live in their own house, but once their children grew up and moved away, we agreed it would be nice all the way around to have them living in."

"Oh." A high percentage of Dundee clients were wealthy and therefore had servants. Some servants were treated like members of the family, while others were treated little better than serfs. His mother, who'd cleaned houses for several well-to-do families back in Lafayette, Kentucky, had been treated like trash.

Turning to her aunt, Penny Sue asked, "Did you let Ruby know we're having guests over this evening?"

"Of course," Dottie replied. "I told her just coffee and tea, along with some little sandwiches and perhaps some homemade cookies or tarts."

Penny Sue glanced at Vic. "We would normally serve wine, too, but Cousin Clayton is a minister and he frowns on liquor of any kind."

"Believe me, Mr. Noble, Clayton would preach us all a sermon if we served liquor." Dottie tsk-tsked. "The man's a fanatic, if you ask me. Can you imagine anyone being rude enough to tell me that I shouldn't dye my hair and wear so much makeup because it's pure vanity and vanity is a sin?"

"Clayton was a real hell-raiser when he was a boy, but when he went off to college he met Phyllis, whose father and brother were both ministers, and before we knew what was happening, Clayton got religion and up and joined that Unity Church," Penny Sue explained. "Generations of Paines turned over in their graves when that happened. We've been Methodists since the first Paine set foot on American soil."

"Valerie married a Baptist preacher, the first time," Dottie said. "That was another disappointment for the family. But she got a divorce and remarried. Dylan is a good Methodist boy. He used to come to church every Sunday with Penny Sue, back when—" As if suddenly realizing she had said something inappropriate, Dottie hushed immediately. Her rouged cheeks darkened. She cleared her throat and changed the subject as she looked at her niece. "Perhaps you should show Mr. Noble up to his room. Douglas's old room should do nicely."

God, yes, Vic thought, show me to my room. He needed some time alone after listening to these two chirping Paine women rattle on and on about nothing.

"I asked Ruby to air out both Uncle Douglas's old room and Daddy's as well," Penny Sue said, "so Mr. Noble can choose which he would prefer."

Both women looked at him and smiled. He forced the corners of his mouth to lift in a hint of a smile.

"What a good idea." Dottie patted Vic on the arm. "They're both lovely rooms. And very masculine." Suddenly the old woman gasped. "Did you hear that? I believe it's Puff."

They all listened to the mewing and scratching sounds coming from outside the front door. Dottie rushed out of the room and into the foyer.

"We might as well go on up," Penny Sue said. "As soon as she brings Puff inside, she'll take him out to the kitchen and give him a treat of some kind. And while she's in the kitchen, she'll have Ruby fix her a cup of tea and they'll talk about dinner tonight."

Vic nodded.

Penny Sue stared at him as if expecting him to respond in some way. He didn't know what to say, had no idea what she wanted from him.

"I asked Ruby to prepare stuffed pork chops tonight," Penny Sue said. "Do you like—"

"Yes," he replied.

"If you have any special dietary needs—"

"I don't."

"Do you prefer your coffee black or—"

"Black."

"Can't you let me finish a sentence!" She glared at him, her chocolate-brown eyes focused on his face and her full, soft mouth closed in a frown.

Without giving any thought to what he was doing, he reached out and brushed his fingertips over her forehead. "You're a beautiful woman, Ms. Paine, but frowning isn't very attractive."

His fingertips lingered a little too long, edging across and down to her cheek. She sucked in her breath. Her eyes widened as their gazes locked. Suddenly she smiled and it was as if everything wrong in the world suddenly became right.

Vic snatched his hand away. What the hell was the matter with him?

"Nothing like having your own words come back to condemn you," she said.

Doing his best not to look right at her, he nodded. "How about showing me to my room?"

"Certainly. Follow me."

She led him up the wide wooden stairs covered with a plush burgundy carpet runner. The banisters were intricately carved and had been stained a dark walnut to match the steps and the flooring in the foyer and upstairs hallway. Although the house was old and the furniture antiques, the interior had a warm, homey feel to it.

"Did you grow up in this house?" he asked when they reached the landing.

"As a matter of fact, I did. My mother died when I was four and Daddy and I came here to live at the old homestead with my aunts."

"So your aunts were your surrogate mothers?"

"Most definitely. I suppose that's why I'm a real Paine, through and through. Although my auburn hair and my full figure came from my mother. She was a Bailey from over in Tishomingo, Mississippi. Her daddy, my granddaddy Bailey, was a pharmacist and her mother a teacher. I used to visit them often when I was growing up, but they both died before I turned twelve. They'd been older when they married and had my mama. She was an only child.

"I was very fortunate that my daddy had two old maid sisters who both doted on me. It was like having two mothers. Although I have to admit, sometimes I felt a bit like a bone being tugged on at both ends by a couple of determined dogs. Aunt Lottie was the disciplinarian whereas Aunt Dottie let me get away with murder. I suppose it all evened out in the end, but—"

"TMI," Vic blurted out, his head spinning from listening to this chattering woman.

"I beg your pardon?" She cocked her pretty little head and stared at him questioningly.

"Too much information, Ms. Penny Sue."

"Oh."

He couldn't take his eyes off her mouth. Wide. Full. Moist. His body hardened instantly when he thought about what her soft, moist mouth could do to him.

Then she licked her lips, running her tongue in a circular motion. "Is my lipstick smeared?" she asked. "Or do I have something in my—"

"Just show me to my room, okay?" He hadn't meant to snap at her, but damn it, she unnerved him. "I need to check in with headquarters, unpack, and read over the file folder on Lucky."

"Yes, of course. The rooms are this way." She indicated left, then took several tentative steps down the hallway.

"Where does Lucky sleep?" Vic asked.

"What? Oh, Lucky used to sleep with Aunt Lottie. Now, he sleeps with me. If he's not with me, he whines and cries all night."

Lucky was a damn lucky dog to sleep in Penny Sue's bed every night.

"And where is your room?"

She looked in the opposite direction, to the rooms on the right. "First door, down that way. It used to be Grandmother Paine's room. It's the largest room in the house and has a small attached room in the turret. That used to be the nursery."

"Is there a bed in the turret room?"

"Yes, a day bed."

"I'll sleep there."

"You can't."

"Why can't I?" he asked.

"Well, it wouldn't be proper, that's why. There is a connecting door between the old nursery and my bedroom. Besides, you wouldn't have your own bathroom and—"

"Okay, okay." He held up a restraining hand. "No need to elaborate. Tonight, I'll sleep in one of the other bedrooms.

Down there." He motioned toward the rooms on the left. "But if I'm still on this assignment tomorrow night, after we bring Lucky home—"

"What do you mean, *if* you're still on this assignment?"

Vic groaned. "Dundee sent me because there was no other agent available. I've been promised a replacement as soon as possible, which I'm hoping will be tomorrow."

Penny Sue tilted her chin and stuck her cute little nose up in the air. "I take it that you don't like Alabaster Creek."

"It's okay. I just don't want this job."

"Am I the reason you're in such a hurry for your employer to send in a new agent? You don't like me, do you?"

"Don't put words in my mouth."

"Then you do like me?"

He huffed. "Yes, I like you."

"Then what's the problem?"

"My liking you is the problem."

"Oh."

"Now that we have that settled…"

"The second and third rooms down the hall. Take your pick," Penny Sue said, a self-satisfied look on her face. "I have things to do myself, to get ready for tonight. But if you need anything, just let me know. I want your stay, however brief, to be a pleasant one."

"Thanks."

She turned and walked away, but then she stopped midway down the stairs and called back to him. "I like you, too. And I hope Dundee never sends another agent."

## *Chapter 3*

"Get me out of here. I don't care how you do it, just get me the hell out of Alabama. And the sooner, the better."

"Things can't be that bad, can they?" Daisy asked, amusement in her voice. "After all, you just arrived there a few hours ago."

"Are you laughing?"

"Laughing? Me?" She smothered a giggle. "I'm simply amazed that you're this uptight about an assignment. I've never seen you flustered."

"I'm not flustered," Vic growled.

"Oh, no, of course not. You're upset because—"

"I'm not upset. I just want off this stupid assignment."

"What happened?"

"Nothing happened." *I've got the hots for Penny Sue Paine, that's what happened,* he thought, but he wasn't about to confide that embarrassing bit of information to Daisy. After all, he had a reputation to uphold, didn't he? Everyone at Dundee thought of him as Mr. Cool.

"Before you left Atlanta today, I promised you a replacement at the earliest possible moment," Daisy told him. "Lucie should be back in the country next week and Dom's latest assignment might end early and he could be available within ten days."

"Next week is too long." Vic groaned inwardly. He couldn't stand a week of walking around with a hard-on, caused by the most talkative, irritating, gorgeous, irresistible woman he'd ever met. If they'd met in a social situation where he could walk away and not look back, he would do just that. He'd done it before when he'd been physically attracted to the wrong kind of woman. And God knew Penny Sue Paine was about as wrong as you could get. Wrong for him, that is. She'd make some local yokel a great little wife. The kind of wife who baked cookies, attended PTA meetings, took the kiddies to Sunday school and would appease all her husband's needs in and out of the bedroom.

Now where had that last thought come from? From below his belt, that's where.

"Vic? Vic, are you still there?" Daisy asked.

"Huh? Yeah, I'm still here. And I expect you to perform a miracle and get another agent to swap assignments with me. If you can do that, I'll owe you big-time."

"I'll see what I can do, but it could take several days."

Several days? Just how long would his resolve to not make a move on Penny Sue last? "Yeah, sure. Okay. I should be able to make it for a few days."

"I'm sure you can. Whatever's got you running scared can't be that bad."

"Who says I'm running scared?" Vic practically shouted the question.

"Sorry. I just meant—"

"No, I'm the one who should be apologizing. It's not your fault that I got stuck with this assignment. It's not anyone's fault. Just the luck of the draw, I guess."

"Vic, I promise I'll get someone to replace you just as soon as I possibly can."

A soft knock sounded on the closed bedroom door and then a sweet, sexy voice called, "Vic, supper's ready. It'll be just you and me and Aunt Dottie. Come on down whenever you're ready."

"Be right there, Penny Sue," Vic replied, then said into the phone, "Thanks, Daisy. I've got to go."

"Hmm…already on a first-name basis with Ms. Paine, huh?"

"Don't go there," Vic warned.

Daisy laughed. "Enjoy your supper." Then she hung up before Vic could say anything else.

He closed his cell phone, inserted it in the belt holder, walked to the door and opened it. Penny Sue stood there smiling at him. Pretty Penny Sue. He tried to concentrate on her beautiful face so he wouldn't react sexually to her, but despite his best efforts, he let his gaze travel over her quickly before refocusing on her face. His body stirred to life, reminding him how attracted he was to this woman. Instant attraction. It happened to people. Even to him. But only a couple of times in the past. And never with a nice girl like Penny Sue.

Maybe she's not so nice, an inner voice suggested. Could be she knows exactly what kind of vibes she's putting out. It's not as if she's a teenage virgin. A woman her age had to know the score. Right?

"Are you all right?" she asked.

"Huh?"

"You're acting mighty peculiar," Penny Sue said. "You're not sick or anything, are you?"

He willed his libido and erring thoughts under control, then cleared his throat. "I'm fine." Smile at her, he told himself, but he couldn't quite manage it. He wasn't the kind of guy who went around grinning like an idiot.

"Supper's ready. I imagine you're hungry. Flying always makes me ravenous. I don't know why. Come to think of it, traveling of any kind makes me hungry. And wears me tee-totally out, too. Some people can drive hundreds of miles and it doesn't affect them, but if I drive to Huntsville and back, I'm wiped out. What about you? Are you one of those…"

He wanted to tell her to shut up, to remind her that she was rattling, that she talked way too much and about absolutely nothing of any importance. But instead he simply concentrated not on what she was saying, but the way her mouth moved and the way her dark eyes sparkled.

He followed her along the hallway and down the stairs, nodding occasionally and saying uh-huh a couple of times as if he were actually listening to her instead of struggling not to grab her and kiss her to make her shut up. When they reached the dining room, she turned to him and said something, then waited for a response. Okay, his goose was cooked. He had no idea what she'd asked him.

"Would you repeat that?" He made direct eye contact with her, hoping she would take that as a sign of interest.

"I said I want us to have a big Christmas wedding and I'd like to be pregnant with our first child when we return from our honeymoon," Penny Sue said, her expression dead serious.

"What!"

"When I asked you to marry me, you said uh-huh. Didn't you mean it? Are you saying now that you're having second thoughts?"

Despite the earnest expression on her face, Vic realized she was joking, paying him back for his lack of attention. "No second thoughts. Only I'd prefer waiting until New Year's Day to get married. Start the year off right."

Penny Sue's lips spread into a tentative smile. "You haven't listened to a word I said. You just tuned me out, didn't you?"

"Yeah, I'm afraid I did."

"Why?"

"Why?" He stared at her, wondering if she truly didn't know. "Because you talk too damn much, that's why."

Her smile vanished. "You can be so rude."

"Sorry. But I have a tendency to be blunt-spoken."

"You must hurt people's feelings a great deal."

"Not intentionally."

As he followed her into the dining room, she said, "I really don't understand your lack of manners. I can tell from your accent that you're from the South." When she stopped dead still just beyond the open pocket doors, he skidded to a halt, barely preventing himself from barreling into her. She whipped around and glared at him. "You *are* from the South, aren't you?"

"Born and bred in Kentucky. Lafayette, Kentucky, to be exact."

"Didn't your mother teach you how important good manners are?" Her big brown eyes bored into him, demanding a response.

"My old lady was too busy trying to keep food on the table and a roof over our heads to worry about unimportant things like good manners."

"Oh. Oh, dear, Vic, I'm so terribly sorry. You were...*poor*." She whispered the word as if saying it aloud would breach some idiotic code of etiquette.

"Nah, honey, I wasn't just poor. I was white trash." The only reason he decided to be so specific was because he hoped that knowing his background would warn her off, just in case he did make a move on her later. He figured the Paines didn't associate with people of an inferior social class.

"Well, you certainly seem to have overcome your upbringing," Dottie Paine said as she strolled into the dining room, in a flowing hot-pink jacket and matching slacks in some sort of silky material. "In my experience, self-made men are far superior to the ones who were handed everything on a silver platter."

Forcing himself to ignore Penny Sue completely, he turned to her elderly aunt and smiled. "Why, thank you, ma'am." Without so much as a by-your-leave to Penny Sue, he headed straight for Miss Dottie, pulled out her chair at the antique Duncan Phyfe dining table and assisted her in sitting. She looked up at him and batted her long black eyelashes. He chuckled inwardly. The old gal was actually flirting with him. He'd bet she'd been a real firecracker in her younger days. Not easy. No sir, not by any means. But the kind of woman who knew how to make a man glad to be a man.

Casting a sidelong glance at Penny Sue, he wondered if perhaps she possessed that same ability. Maybe it was a gift with which all the Paine women had been blessed. But you won't be finding out for yourself, an inner voice reminded.

"We often eat in the kitchen or the breakfast room," Dottie said. "But tonight, with a gentleman visiting, I thought it appropriate to dine in here. I hope that meets with your approval." She glanced at her niece. "After all, it isn't all that often that we have a man around the house. Not since dear Percy passed on."

"Percy was my father," Penny Sue explained as Vic pulled out a chair for her, being careful not to touch her.

Avoiding eye contact, he nodded, then took the seat opposite her.

Miss Dottie picked up a small silver bell and rang it. A tall, thin woman with short white hair, a straight back and a pleasant look on her plain face entered the room. Vic guessed her to be in her early sixties. She carried a silver tray laden with three salad plates.

Penny Sue made the introductions, which surprised Vic. In his experience, most people didn't introduce their servants to a guest. "Ruby, this is Mr. Noble. He'll be staying with us for a while. He's the bodyguard I hired for Lucky."

The housekeeper's sharp blue eyes sparkled with good humor. "Nice to meet you, Mr. Noble."

"Nice to meet you, too, Mrs….?"

"Just Ruby." She sized him up, then said, "I hope you like banana pudding."

"I do," he told her.

"If you've got any special requests while you're staying here, just let me know," Ruby said. "Tell me how you like your coffee, your eggs—"

"I don't want to be any trouble," Vic said. "I'm sure however you prepare things will be just fine."

"Black coffee would be my guess. And scrambled eggs." Ruby looked him over a second time. "No starch in your collars, right? You're not a suit-and-tie kind of man."

"Goodness, Ruby, stop giving him the third degree," Dottie scolded.

"Kind of nice having a man about the place again, isn't it, Miss Penny Sue?" Ruby winked at her as she set a salad plate in front of her. "Especially such a good-looking one."

The minute Ruby disappeared into the kitchen, Penny Sue said, "You'll have to forgive Ruby. She's rather outspoken. And rather determined that I won't die an old maid."

"She never did learn her place," Dottie said. "Then again, Mama and Daddy weren't sticklers about servants keeping their place. A good servant is worth his or her weight in gold, Daddy always said."

"And Grandmother Paine taught me that everyone should be treated the same," Penny Sue added. "Treat people the way you want to be treated."

These two Paine women were oddities, Vic thought. Old-fashioned Southern-belle types, but without the snooty superiority he'd grown accustomed to seeing in the women for whom his mother had slaved year in and year out.

From the salad through the entrée, dinner conversation hardly lulled for more than a minute or two, and during those brief lulls he supposed he'd been expected to contribute his input. But barely missing a beat when he didn't respond, either Dottie or Penny Sue kept the chitchat going. Neverending, actually. Talk, talk, talk. And about nothing. Absolutely nothing. Apparently this ability was another Paine trait.

Just as Ruby served dessert—large bowls of banana pudding topped with thick meringue—the doorbell rang.

"It seems that somebody's early for tonight's family meeting," Ruby grumbled. "It's barely six-thirty."

"Well, never mind," Dottie said. "Go see who it is and show them into the front parlor."

"Don't bother. I'll do it." Penny Sue shoved back her chair and hopped to her feet. "I shouldn't eat dessert anyway. It goes straight to my *hips*." Emphasizing the word hips, she planted her hands just below her waist on either side and slid her open palms down over the smooth material of her tan suede skirt.

There was nothing wrong with her hips, Vic noted. They were perfect. Wide, rounded and totally feminine. He swallowed hard. Everything about Penny Sue was ultra-feminine, from her beautiful face to her great body to her soft laughter and the sexy way she moved. Unconsciously sexy, which was far more captivating than a blatant display.

"It's probably Eula," Dottie said. "She's always early. Comes from having too much time on her hands since she retired."

Penny Sue hurried from the room, her tan heels tapping on the wooden floor. Vic's gaze followed her out into the hall, but from where he was sitting, he couldn't see all the way to the front door.

"My niece is a lovely girl, isn't she?" Dottie held a small, delicate hand to her throat and played with the short strand of pearls she wore.

"Yes ma'am, she is."

"Are you married, Mr. Noble?"

A tight knot formed in the pit of Vic's belly. "No ma'am, I'm not."

"A man your age should have a wife."

He wanted to ask her how she knew his age, but instead said, "I'm not good husband material. Too set in my ways."

Just as Miss Dottie opened her mouth to reply—and Vic was certain the old lady would have had an excellent comeback—they heard Penny Sue screaming.

Loud, frightened screams.

Vic knocked over his chair as he jumped to his feet. If anything had happened to her, if anyone had dared to harm her… With his heart racing, he ran out of the dining room and into the foyer. Penny Sue stood at the open front door, her body trembling, her right hand drawn into a fist and pressed against her lips. Vic reached her in seconds, not knowing what danger she faced, but realizing that he would lay down his life to protect her. After he grabbed her around the waist and pulled her to his side, she shut her eyes and pressed her body against his. While holding her, he maneuvered her around so that he could see whatever lay beyond the door. That's when he saw what had made her scream. A small, open pet carrier had been placed on the porch, directly in front of the entrance. Inside the carrier lay a medium-size stuffed dog, a menacing butcher knife stuck through its body and what Vic assumed was fake blood of some sort oozing from the wound.

"It's okay, honey." He stroked her back soothingly. "It's not a real dog. This is just somebody's idea of a joke. A very sick joke."

Penny Sue lifted her head and looked up at Vic, moisture glistening in her eyes. "I realize it's not a real dog, but at first… for just a minute…I thought it was Lucky." She eased away from him and turned to glare at the pet carrier. "I'm sorry about screaming. It's just seeing him—that—" she nodded toward the gruesome sight "—was so totally unexpected. I don't usually act like such a ninny."

"You were frightened. It's perfectly understandable that you'd react the way you did." And he meant exactly what he'd said. It *was* understandable that on first glance she'd think the stuffed dog was Lucky and that she would scream. But what wasn't understandable was why Penny Sue reacting in a typical female way didn't irritate the hell out of him. As a general rule, he preferred his women sophisticated, even jaded. He avoided silly women who giggled or screamed or cried or talked too much.

"What the hell is that?" a man's voice called from outside the gate at the end of the sidewalk.

"Oh dear, that's Uncle Douglas," Penny Sue groaned.

"Well, what's all the ruckus about?" Dottie came up behind them, doing her best to see around Vic and Penny Sue. "That's Douglas and Candy, isn't it? Why on earth did Penny Sue scream?"

Reaching down to grasp Vic's hand, Penny Sue took a deep breath. "Would you please get rid of it—all of it—right now?" Her words were whispered, for his ears only. "I'll take care of Aunt Dottie and explain things to her and Uncle Douglas."

"We should call the police first," Vic told her.

"It won't do a bit of good. Chief Miller isn't going to waste his time on a stunt like that," Penny Sue said. "The police aren't the least bit interested in protecting Lucky."

Vic nodded. In a way, he understood the police chief's reasoning. Not many law enforcement officers would take threats on a dog's life seriously and they'd do little more than laugh at the stuffed dog, even one that had been mutilated in such a grotesque fashion.

"I'll take care of it," Vic assured her. "Are you sure you're all right?"

Nodding, she offered him a closed-mouth, forced smile.

He squeezed her arm reassuringly, then headed out the front door just as a gray-haired man and a woman of no more than thirty came up on the front porch. Penny Sue circled around Vic and met the visitors.

* * *

"Why on earth would somebody do such a darn fool thing?" Douglas Paine nursed a crystal tumbler half full of whiskey. Penny Sue had poured her uncle the drink herself, after she had calmed Aunt Dottie with soothing words and a hug.

"Don't you think maybe somebody is just making fun of Penny Sue?" Candy Paine positioned her skinny behind on the arm of her husband's chair and laid her hand on his knee. "It's obviously just a joke. One of the family poking fun at the fact that Penny Sue thinks someone's trying to kill Lucky."

Penny Sue glared at Candy. "Someone did try to kill lucky."

"So you keep telling us." Candy rubbed her hand up and down Douglas's leg. "But you're the only one who believes such silliness."

Eyeing Candy's caressing hand, Aunt Dottie cleared her throat disapprovingly. Uncle Douglas grasped his young wife's hand and lifted it in his. The whole family had been mortified when Douglas had married for the fourth time, more because of who he married than the fact it was his fourth walk down the aisle. Redheaded, bosomy Candy Coley had been a wannabe Vegas showgirl, someone Douglas Paine had met at a convention two years ago. After a whirlwind courtship, they'd been married in some shabby Vegas chapel by an Elvis impersonator. It hadn't taken the family, including Douglas's two children by his first wife, very long to realize Candy considered her new husband a real sugar daddy. However, despite his lucrative dental practice in Alabaster Creek, Douglas was not a millionaire—not yet. But when he inherited his share of Aunt Lottie's fortune that fact would change immediately.

"Candy, dear, why don't you come sit on the sofa by me?" Aunt Dottie asked. "You'll be so much more comfortable than you are perched there on the arm of Douglas's chair."

Before Candy could reply, the doorbell rang.

"Let Ruby get it," Dottie said.

Penny Sue nodded. Where was Vic? What was taking him so long? All he had to do was take the pet carrier and dump it in the garbage can in the detached three-car garage behind the house.

Eula Paine showed herself into the front parlor. "Am I late?" she asked.

"No, no," Dottie said. "Douglas and Candy are early."

The doorbell rang again. Ruby called from the foyer, "I might as well keep the front door open at this rate."

Within five minutes, the front parlor filled with Paine relatives. Aunt Lottie's heirs. And last, but not least, coming in at seven o'clock on the dot, was Uncle Willie. Since this was, for all intents and purposes, a business meeting as far as Uncle Willie was concerned, Aunt Pattie hadn't come with him tonight as she usually did to Paine functions. After all, she, not he, was the blood relative.

Penny Sue kept glancing out into the foyer, wondering what had happened to Vic. Where is he? Why isn't he here? He'd known she wanted him present for this meeting.

Once she had made the rounds and welcomed everyone, taking her hostess duties seriously, Aunt Dottie came over to Penny Sue and clutched her hand. "Perhaps he has decided to forego this family meeting."

"What?"

"You're concerned about Mr. Noble, aren't you?"

"Not concerned, just wondering where he is."

"The natives are getting restless." Dottie squeezed her hand. "Why don't I have Ruby see what everyone wants to drink. It might keep them pacified. In the meantime, you go find Mr. Noble. I'm sure he can convince the others that Lucky needs a bodyguard."

"What about you, Aunt Dottie, are you convinced?"

"It's not my decision to make. It's yours. And I support you in whatever you do. Haven't I always?"

Penny Sue sighed. "Yes, of course you have. Even when Aunt Lottie…well, we both know she could be rather stern at times."

"Lottie loved you, my dear, and trusted you more than anyone in the family," Dottie said. "She wouldn't have entrusted Lucky to anyone else. That says a great deal about how much faith she had in you. And although I think it was rather foolish of her to have left her money to her dog, I do think she made the right choice in naming you the executor of her will. I've done the same, you know."

"You've done what?"

"I named you executor of my will," Dottie replied. "Of course, I won't be leaving such a sizable fortune, but—"

"Oh, my...my goodness." Penny Sue hugged her tiny, fragile aunt. As her father used to say, "Dottie's so thin that she looks as if a strong wind would blow her away."

"When are we going to start the meeting?" Stacie Paine asked. She was Uncle Douglas's eldest child, an old-maid schoolteacher, who had turned forty her last birthday.

"It's already past seven," Valerie said as she stood up and took a prominent position in front of the fireplace. "I see no reason to delay things. If everyone is ready—"

"We should begin the meeting with a prayer," Reverend Clayton Dickson proclaimed loudly in a voice that singled him out as a preacher of the gospel.

Clayton was Penny Sue's first cousin once removed, her father's first cousin. Clayton's mother had been one of the few Paine women to snag herself a husband. Since marrying Phyllis and getting religion, Clayton had become a fanatic, totally obsessed with sin and salvation.

Chris Paine, Stacie's younger brother, groaned loudly and rolled his dark eyes toward the ceiling. He and Clayton had once been best friends, back in their teens when they'd both been hell-raisers. But in recent years, their friendship long dead, Chris took every opportunity to ridicule his cousin.

"A prayer never hurts," Eula said. "Get on with it, Clayton."

To everyone's dismay, except his wife Phyllis's, Clayton dropped to his knees, right there in the front parlor on Grandmother Paine's Persian carpet. He lifted his folded hands in front of him, closed his eyes and beseeched his maker for mercy on his sinful soul.

While the others sat quietly and at least pretended to listen to Clayton's prayer, Penny Sue slipped out of the parlor as quietly as possible. Taking the downstairs rooms, one by one, she searched for Vic. When she entered the kitchen, Ruby paused in her preparations and glanced at Penny Sue.

"Did you come to help me get these drinks out to the parlor?" Ruby asked. "I'm getting too old to be lifting such heavy trays."

"I'll be glad to help you," Penny Sue replied, "but not right now. I'm looking for Vic. For Mr. Noble."

"He's out there on the back porch with Tully," Ruby said. "He's going over that stuffed dog and the carrier it was in, searching for something."

"What's he searching for?"

"How should I know? And I need help now with these drinks, not later."

"Why don't you just make two trips to the parlor with those drinks," Penny Sue said. "Or ask Stacie or Cousin Eula to help you. I really need to speak to Vic."

Ruby grunted and mumbled to herself.

Just as Penny Sue opened the back door and took her first step onto the porch, Vic glanced up from where he sat beside Tully in old, identical wicker rockers.

"The family meeting is ready to start," she told Vic. "I'd like for you to come and meet everyone."

Without hesitation, Vic rose from the rocker. "See you later, Tully."

The old man nodded.

Vic took Penny Sue's elbow and turned her around, then escorted her inside before she had a chance to say anything else.

As they walked out of the kitchen, she asked, "Why were you looking over the pet carrier and stuffed dog? What were you searching for?"

He paused, eyed her quizzically and grunted.

"Ruby said you were—" she continued.

"Nothing in particular," he told her. "Just some general checking. Not really any scientific testing. After all, I don't have the equipment, but I would like to send everything to the Dundee lab first thing in the morning."

"Why is that?"

"Because that red stuff on the toy dog was real blood."

## *Chapter 4*

Vic led Penny Sue into the front parlor, then paused just past the threshold. A horde of Paine relatives buzzed about inside the room like a swarm of busy bees, all with a common goal, some with their stingers ready to strike. But which family members were deadly and which totally harmless? Who had shot Lucky? Who wanted to kill the millionaire dog? And who had left the little surprise package on the front porch tonight? The answer to all four questions could well be the same, but what if there was more than one perpetrator, more than one heir willing to kill Lottie Paine's dog in order to receive their inheritance now instead of waiting for old age to claim Lucky's life?

"Should I call Dr. Stone's office and check on Lucky?" Penny Sue asked Vic. "You don't think that might have been Lucky's blood on the stuffed dog, do you?"

"My guess is that Lucky's fine. Otherwise the vet's office would have contacted you," Vic told her. "As for the blood—it's probably animal blood, but I doubt it's Lucky's."

"Oh look, everyone," Dottie Paine said exuberantly. "Here's our

Penny Sue and she has Mr. Noble with her. Come on in, you two."
Dottie waved them forward with a sweep of her hand, as if presenting a royal couple to their subjects.

All heads turned in their direction. Instinctively Vic slipped his arm around Penny Sue's waist. On some basic, primeval level he sensed she needed protection from these people. Just a gut reaction, but heeding his instincts had saved his life in the past. Everything within him sensed danger.

*No one is going to harm Penny Sue,* an inner voice said.

But she's not the one in danger, he reminded himself. The victim is Lucky. So why was it that he felt so strongly that Penny Sue needed him?

"We're ready to start the meeting." Dottie fluttered about like a nervous butterfly, bestowing smiles on everyone. "Penny Sue, dear…"

"I believe Valerie called this meeting." Penny Sue glowered at the long, lean blonde sitting on the sofa beside a stocky, rosy-cheeked man Vic assumed was her husband. "Since everyone is here, why don't you start things off by telling the family why you're so concerned."

Valerie rose to her full five foot eight, scanned the faces of everyone assembled and paused on Vic. She let her gaze linger for a moment too long, her mannerisms sending out sexual signals. The woman might be married, but he figured that didn't stop her from flirting with other men. And she was well aware of what she was doing, unlike Penny Sue, to whom flirting came as naturally as breathing and was as genuine as her smile.

"As we all know, Lucky was the victim of a terrible accident," Valerie said, then looked away from Vic. "But Penny Sue has convinced herself that one of us tried to kill him."

A roar of protest rose quickly.

"Penny Sue hasn't accused anyone," Dottie reminded the others. "She simply feels—"

"I can speak for myself," Penny Sue said. "I believe that someone with something to gain if Lucky dies took it upon himself—or herself—to dispose of the only thing standing between all of us and rather sizable inheritances."

Penny Sue looked pointedly at Valerie, who gasped silently and glanced around so that the others could see the shocked expression on her face.

Some grumbled angrily while others sat quietly, as if afraid that speaking out might cast suspicion on them. Vic studied the group, one by one. Valerie and her husband protested the loudest and Eula Paine appeared to be the least agitated.

An elderly, rather distinguished gentleman standing in the corner of the room cleared his throat loudly, then spoke up. "For what it's worth, I agree with Penny Sue. Someone, probably someone in this room, tried to kill Lucky."

More grumbling ensued, the family members jabbering among themselves, complaining that they'd been lumped together as possible dog-killers.

"Who is he?" Vic asked, keeping his voice low so that only Penny Sue could hear him.

"That's Uncle Willie. Wilfred Hopkins, Aunt Lottie's lawyer."

"Hmm…"

"I need to make it perfectly clear that if anyone is caught trying to harm Lucky, that person will not inherit one cent from Lottie," Wilfred said.

Various people responded, all of them talking at once. Vic picked up on more than one voice saying, "*if* the person is caught." Why was it that people intent on perpetrating a crime—be it armed robbery or the murder of a millionaire dog—always thought they could get away with it, that they were too smart to get caught?

Valerie waved her hands frantically, trying unsuccessfully to gain everyone's attention. Finally, exasperated, she let out a long, loud whistle.

Dead silence.

"Whether or not someone intentionally shot Lucky is not why I called this meeting," Valerie said. "Well, perhaps indirectly it is, but it's not the main reason."

"Just what is?" another elderly man asked.

"That's Uncle Douglas," Penny Sue told Vic. "He's my father's brother."

Vic nodded. He was beginning to feel as if he needed a scorecard. Not counting Dottie, Penny Sue and him, there were ten people present. Wilfred Hopkins, Lottie's lawyer, Valerie and Dylan Redley, Eula Paine, Clayton and Phyllis Dickson, Douglas Paine and his wife Candy and his two adult children, Stacie and Chris.

As he studied Douglas Paine, he saw a strong family resemblance between him and his sister Dottie. Where Dottie kept her hair dyed black, Douglas had allowed his to go salt-and-pepper, but their facial features were almost identical—the dark, sparkling eyes, the naturally tan complexion, the lean build, the wide mouths and prominent chins.

"Penny Sue has hired a very expensive bodyguard for Lucky," Valerie told the others. "I assume that's him. The man Aunt Dottie called Mr. Noble."

Everyone turned and stared at Vic, some hostilely, others simply curiously. He had the oddest notion that he should take a bow.

"And she intends to use Aunt Lottie's money to pay for this man's services," the stocky, red-faced man said, an indignant look on his face.

"That's Dylan Redley," Penny Sue whispered. "He's Valerie's second husband and my former fiancé."

That bit of information settled in Vic's stomach like a lead weight. Without responding to her comment, he focused on the man in question. The guy looked like a former jock who'd allowed easy living and the approach of middle age to turn his once muscular body into blubber.

By his ruddy cheeks, Vic assumed one of three things—either the guy spent a great deal of time outdoors or he was a heavy drinker or he was plagued by rosacea.

"Let me guess," Vic said. "He played high-school football. He was captain of the team and you were homecoming queen."

Penny Sue's mouth gaped open wide. "How did you know that?"

"Just a guess." Vic decided then and there that he did not like Dylan Redley.

Douglas Paine called out to his niece, "Penny Sue, is that true? Do you intend to waste our inheritance on a bodyguard for Lottie's dog?"

"Yes, that's exactly what I intend to do," she replied. "As a matter of fact, that's what I've done. And until whoever tried to kill Lucky is caught and disinherited, Vic—Mr. Noble—will be guarding Lucky around the clock."

"This is the most ridiculous thing I've ever heard." The comment came from a man in his mid-forties with a robust voice. "You have no right to—"

"That's where you're wrong, Cousin Clayton," Penny Sue said. "I have every right to do whatever is necessary to keep Lucky safe and that includes spending every dime of the money Aunt Lottie left him to see that he lives to a ripe old age."

"You can't mean that you'll keep a bodyguard for Lucky as long as he lives," the bosomy redhead practically sitting in Douglas Paine's lap said.

"Now y'all see why I'm concerned." Valerie smiled triumphantly. "Penny Sue has lost her mind. She shouldn't be in control of Aunt Lottie's fortune if she plans…"

Suddenly everyone started talking at once, each with a specific opinion, the majority apparently as upset with Penny Sue as Valerie was. When they started coming toward her, accusing her of being as loony as Lottie and demanding she rethink her position, Penny Sue stood her ground.

"If everyone would be quiet—" Penny Sue tried to talk above the incessant clamor.

"Hush…please…everyone…" Aunt Dottie's pleas fell on deaf ears.

"I have every legal right to take care of Lucky," Penny Sue told them in a loud voice. "As far as I'm concerned this meeting is over. If you have any complaints, take them up with Uncle Willie."

"Or with me," Vic said.

The room quieted. Everyone focused on him.

Now was the time for him to step in and lay down some ground rules. Although he hadn't been hired to defend Penny Sue Paine against her greedy relatives, that was just what he intended to do.

"I'm Vic Noble, with the Dundee Private Security and Investigation agency, based in Atlanta, Georgia. Be forewarned—I've been hired by Ms. Paine to guard her dog twenty-four/seven. And our agency will also be investigating Lucky's shooting. Each of you will be checked out thoroughly, everything from your where-abouts when Lucky was shot to any past history of abuse of ani-mals." Vic threw in that last comment for good measure. "I also plan to retrieve the bullet from Dr. Stone and have a ballistic test run on it. If we can find the weapon, we'll have our shooter. And the pet carrier and bloody stuffed dog left on the front porch to-night will also be gone over thoroughly at our Dundee lab."

Utter silence prevailed.

Utilizing his notorious make-my-day expression, Vic waited a couple of seconds for any rebuttal. There was none.

He leaned over and whispered to Penny Sue, "Now would be a good time for you to make yourself scarce, while they're digest-ing the information I just gave them."

"You aren't suggesting that I run off like a scared rabbit, are you? Believe me, that's not my style."

He tightened his hold around her waist. "You've had your say. Right? No use beating a dead horse. They might not like your de-cision, but there really isn't anything they can do except complain. You don't want to stick around and listen to everyone bellyache some more, do you?"

"What do you have in mind?"

"Let's take a drive. We can stop somewhere and get drinks—" when she frowned, crinkling her cute little nose, he corrected him-self "—or we could get some coffee and talk. You can fill me in on details about the suspects." Vic ushered her out of the parlor, down the hall, through the kitchen and out the back door, the two of them nodding to Ruby and Tully on their way out.

Once on the back porch, Penny Sue stopped abruptly. "Car keys. We don't have—"

Vic held up a set of keys she immediately recognized as the ones belonging to Tully's old Chevy truck. "When did you—"

"Tully gave me the extra set of keys to his truck so that I could use it when I take the pet carrier and stuffed dog to the nearest over-night shipping service tomorrow morning."

"Oh."

Vic tugged on her hand. "We'd better make our getaway before somebody comes looking for you."

When they entered the backyard, the night wind chilled her, reminding her that she hadn't bothered with a wrap. "It's cooler than I thought it would be."

I'll keep you warm, baby, was his first thought. But he said, "We'll be warm enough in the truck."

"I need chocolate."

Vic grunted.

"Chocolate reduces stress," she told him.

"If you say so."

"I think hot chocolate is in order tonight," she said when he opened the truck door and helped her up and into the passenger seat.

She looked at him, smiled and said, "Thank you."

"For what?"

"For being such a gentleman."

Her comment surprised him. He'd been called a lot of things in his life, but never a gentleman. "Only for you, Penny Sue." He spoke the words aloud before realizing he had vocalized his thoughts.

Her smile softened and she looked at him as if she wanted to wrap her arms around him. Vic cleared his throat, pulled away from her and closed the door. Damn! What was it about this woman that made him want to jump through hoops to please her? Pacifying a woman wasn't his style. Nor was feeling protective and possessive. Yes, he protected his clients. That was his job. But Penny Sue wasn't his client.

Vic rounded the truck, got behind the wheel and started the engine. As he backed out of the drive, he asked, "So where's the best place in town to get hot chocolate?"

Penny Sue explained to him about their destination before they arrived downtown. Alabaster Creek Bookstore stayed open until nine every night, but not because the townspeople were literary enthusiasts. No, the reason was that the owner had added a coffee shop in the back a couple of years ago. Now, people who'd never been in a bookstore before kept this one crowded from the time the doors opened at nine every morning until the last customer left in the evening. The menu consisted of a variety of coffees, including latte, cappuccino and espresso. And of course, hot chocolate. The bakery down the street provided an assortment of items, different each day, for the customers.

After ordering two large hot chocolates and two king-size chocolate chip cookies, Penny Sue led Vic up the wide wooden staircase to a sitting area on the mezzanine level to the right of the magazine racks and overlooking the front of the store. Two small tables, each flanked by comfy-looking chairs, nestled against the old brick outer wall.

After they sat down and relaxed in the leather chairs, Vic watched in fascination as Penny Sue munched hungrily on one of the cookies, like an eager child devouring a favorite treat. Even on their short acquaintance, he had formed an opinion about this beautiful lady. She possessed several childlike qualities, some that perhaps more adults should emulate, the least of which was exuberance. He couldn't help wondering if she displayed that trait in the bedroom. Would she be an enthusiastic lover?

Vic lifted his cup, brought it to his lips and sipped. Then he yowled. Hot! Too hot! He'd burned his tongue. He'd been so engrossed in thoughts of Penny Sue that he hadn't noticed the steam rising from the foam topping the cup.

"Oh, you've burned your tongue." Penny Sue looked at him with great concern. "I should have told you to be careful. They always serve their hot chocolate steaming hot."

Vic rubbed his burning tongue over the roof of his mouth, then ran the tip over his upper lip. "It was my own damn fault."

Penny Sue reached across the table and touched her index finger to his lips. "I know it hurts."

"I'll live," Vic said, then clamped his mouth shut and gritted his teeth. She had touched him as innocently as a mother soothing a child, but he had reacted the way a man reacts to a woman's seductive caress.

Apparently noticing the instant lust in his eyes, she removed her finger from his lips, then glanced down into her lap, as if slightly embarrassed.

They sat together quietly for several minutes, each allowing their drinks to cool from piping hot to drinkable hot.

"So, what do you want to know?" she asked.

"Pardon?"

"About the suspects. You said we would go for drinks and I could fill you in about the suspects."

"Yeah, so I did."

"So…?"

"Is there anyone in particular you'd put at the top of a suspects list?" he asked.

"Hmm… I don't think so. I find it difficult to believe that anyone in my family is capable of murder."

Vic's lips twitched. The way he'd been raised, killing an animal, even a pet cat or dog, wasn't murder. Of course, if someone had ever shot one of his daddy's hunting dogs, the old man would have gone after the culprit with his rifle. But he supposed to a woman such as Penny Sue, killing a pet would be murder.

"Greed does strange things to people," Vic told her. "It can turn an ordinary person into a monster."

"I wish Aunt Lottie hadn't left her money to Lucky. I'm not sure why she did. She had to have known that I'd take good care of him regardless."

"Maybe leaving her millions to Lucky was her way of rooting out the bad seeds. Could be she knew someone might try to kill him." When Penny Sue stared at Vic with an incredulous look in her eyes, he explained, "She did put a stipulation in her will that if anyone tried to harm Lucky, they'd be disinherited."

"You're right. She did. And I wouldn't put it past Aunt Lottie to have done just what you think she did."

Vic eyed his mug warily, then when Penny Sue lifted her cup to her lips and sipped, he did the same. The smooth, rich concoction was much too sweet for his tastes, but it was hot and wet and—

*Hot and wet.* The two words replayed over and over again in his mind. Don't go there, he told himself. He had to stop turning every thought in his head into something lascivious. Hell, it was Penny Sue's fault. Everything about her was alluring. Just look at those big brown eyes, that wide, full, pink mouth. That mane of flowing auburn hair. And those—he stared at her ample bosom, his imagination slowly peeling away the blouse and then the bra. He sucked in a deep breath.

"Are you all right?" she asked.

"Yeah, yeah. I'm fine." After taking another deep breath, he said, "Tell me about your cousin Valerie and how she wound up married to your ex-fiancé?"

"You've seen Valerie," Penny Sue said, as if that was explanation enough.

Vic shrugged. "So?"

"So, her first marriage was on the rocks and she looked around for solace and found it with Dylan. She's the kind of woman men can't refuse. And to be perfectly honest, I don't think she had to do much persuading with Dylan."

"Meaning?"

"I didn't realize it at the time, but in retrospect, I can see how dissatisfied he was with our relationship. I think he asked me to marry him because everyone expected it, even me. We'd been high-school sweethearts and everyone thought we were perfect for each other. We weren't. I found out after he ran off with Valerie—two weeks before our wedding—that he'd been fooling around with other girls the whole time we'd been dating."

"Then the man was an idiot," Vic said.

Penny Sue smiled. "That's very sweet of you to say, but...well, to be honest, Dylan and I didn't mess around in high school. I kept putting him off and I'm sure he was frustrated. And when we were in college and actually...well, you know—" she leaned over and whispered "—it wasn't all that good. I never...you know...and he got upset because I didn't and..." Her cheeks flushed bright pink. "I didn't mean to get so personal, but I wanted you to realize it wasn't all Dylan's fault."

"Is that what he told you?" Vic asked. "When he explained why he dumped you for your cousin? He told you it was your fault?"

"Something like that."

Vic groaned. "You don't still believe that, do you? I mean once you were with a man who…that you…you know—" Listen to yourself. You're babbling like an idiot and avoiding using normal terminology because you think it might offend Penny Sue. He'd never watched his language around a woman, so why now, with this one woman?

Penny Sue's cheeks flamed red. "That's just it. You see, I've never… I've been in love only once. Or at least thought I was. With Dylan."

Was she saying what he thought she was? "Only with Dylan?"

She nodded.

Holy hell! Penny Sue Paine was practically a virgin. How was that possible in this day and age? But that was just it—she was a throwback to another era, one where a girl didn't have sex with a guy unless she was in love with him.

"Honey, are you for real?" he asked.

She stared at him, a dreamy expression and a shimmer of unshed tears in her eyes. It was all he could do not to reach out, drag her into his lap and kiss her senseless. That was exactly what she needed. And what he needed, too. Only he wanted a lot more than a few heated kisses, but Penny Sue Paine wasn't likely to give it to him without a bunch of emotional strings attached.

"Vic…I…"

A loud voice cried out from below them, on the main level of the bookstore. "Oh, my God, Doc Stone's place is on fire!"

Other voices joined in, then the rumble of feet and the sound of the double front doors opening and closing.

"Somebody call the fire department," another person said.

Penny Sue jumped to her feet. "Come on." She grabbed Vic's hand and tugged.

Confused as to why they should join the curiosity seekers at a house fire, Vic hesitated, but gave in and stood up when he noted the frightened expression on her face.

Leaving their cookies and hot chocolate on the table, they raced down the stairs.

"Doc Stone's veterinary clinic is just across the street. That's where Lucky is. If the place is on fire…"

Now Vic understood Penny Sue's panic.

"You think somebody set the fire deliberately to kill Lucky?" Vic asked just as they reached the bottom of the stairs.

"Maybe," she replied. "I don't want to believe that anyone I know would be capable of doing such a terrible thing, but—"

Another bookstore customer cried, "If the fire department doesn't show up soon, the place will be a total loss. Just look at those flames, will you."

Penny Sue ran through the bookstore, Vic right beside her. Once outside, she pushed her way through the curiosity seekers gathered on the sidewalk in front, a safe distance from the burning veterinary clinic that sat in the middle of a back street. A vacant lot beside the burning building had been fenced in and was apparently used as an exercise area for the boarded animals.

When she started across the street, Vic grabbed her arm to stop her. "Where do you think you're going?"

"I'm going to see if there's anything I can do. I have to get Lucky and the other animals out of there, if I can."

"Honey, you can't—"

She jerked away from him and ran across the street. He raced after her, catching up with her quickly, but not before she had made her way to the front of the clinic.

"The fire seems to be contained in the front part of the building," she said. "At least for now. All the animals are kept in the back. If there was some way to get in the back door…"

"You aren't going anywhere," he told her. "We should wait for the fire department. They're trained for this sort of thing."

She confronted him, a don't-you-dare-try-to-stop-me expression on her face. "All the boarded animals could die from smoke inhalation before the firemen get here."

"How close is the fire station? It can't be that far away in a town this size."

"It's not. But every minute counts."

He grabbed her shoulders. "You stay here. I'll see what I can do." He couldn't believe he intended to risk his life to save a dog. But it was either risk his life or allow Penny Sue to risk hers.

"Let me help you." She pulled free and grabbed his hand.

"Are there any windows in the back where they keep the animals?" he asked.

"Yes, there are two."

"I'll try to break out one of the windows and go in that way."

She flung her arms around him and kissed him. When he pulled away, she said, "Please be careful."

Penny Sue followed him to the side of the building, even though he had told her to stay put. Removing his concealed Glock from his shoulder holster, he used the handle of the weapon to break the glass in the window. After removing his jacket and using it to swipe away the shattered glass and clear his path, he heard the whine of sirens. He tossed his jacket on the ground and laid his gun on it, then crawled inside the clinic through the window.

Penny Sue waited, her heart caught in her throat. Every passing second seemed endless as the fire continued to spread, the flames leaping closer and closer to the back area of the clinic. She was so absorbed in her fear for Vic and the animals he'd gone inside to rescue that she barely heard the thunder of feet and the shouts of the firemen as they surrounded the building. Only when someone spoke her name did she react.

"Penny Sue, what are you doing here?" Wayne Boggus asked.

"Oh, Wayne," Penny Sue cried, relieved to see the familiar face of the man she'd been casually dating as of late. "Thank goodness y'all got here so quickly. You have to put the fire out."

"That's why we're here. My men will have things under control soon, and I'll secure the area."

"Hurry, please."

"Oh…I just now realized. You must be worried about Lucky. Believe me, sweetie, we'll do everything we can to bring him out safe and sound, but—"

"Vic's gone in to save Lucky and the other animals. Please, go help him right now."

"Who's Vic?"

"Stop asking me questions and get in there and bring Vic and Lucky and—"

A sudden, loud crash stopped her mid-sentence. The front part of the roof caved in, making an ear-splitting noise. Penny Sue gasped.

"Get them out of there. Now!" she screamed

Dear God, what if she had sent Vic to his death? As much as she loved Lucky—loved all animals—she'd had no right to expect Vic to lay his life on the line to save him. He'd gone into the clinic, into the smoke and quickly spreading fire because of her.

"You'd better get back," Wayne said. "You shouldn't be this close. Go wait in the street."

"I'm not moving from this spot until Vic comes out of the clinic."

Wayne glared at her and repeated his question. "Who is Vic?"

He's my hero, Penny Sue thought, but said, "He's Lucky's bodyguard," as Wayne reached for her, pulling her out of harm's way.

## Chapter 5

Penny Sue stood her ground, refusing to move, even when Wayne threatened to pick her up and carry her to safety. Agonizing over what might be happening to Vic and the animals trapped inside the clinic, she watched in horror as the firemen aimed their large hoses and sprayed water onto the burning building.

What was taking so long? Was Vic trapped?

Please, God, please bring Vic out safe and sound. And if it's not asking too much, let Lucky and all the animals be spared, too.

As if in answer to her prayers—an immediate and positive response from the good Lord—the side door to the clinic, which had been locked from the inside, was flung open and a menagerie of animals came bounding outside. Three cats, four dogs—none of them Lucky—two rabbits and a raccoon.

"What the—" Wayne Boggus yelped. "Hey, somebody catch those critters."

Penny Sue kept her gaze riveted on the open doorway through which the animals had escaped, all of them appearing through a thick haze of dark smoke. *Vic, where are you?*

And then she saw him, down on all fours, crawling away from the burning building. Once outside, Vic bounded to his feet and stood. He had a cage filled with five little birds in one hand and tucked under his other arm was a small, squirming, short-haired dog. Lucky!

Penny Sue ran toward Vic, paying no heed to whatever Wayne was shouting at her. Vic headed straight for her, set the bird cage on the ground and caught her with his free arm just as she barreled into him.

"Oh, thank God you're all right." Looking up into his soot-covered face, she gulped and asked, "You are all right, aren't you?"

"Maybe a little smoke inhalation," he told her. "Otherwise, I'm fine."

She glanced down at Lucky snuggled against Vic's side and patted his little head. "You saved Lucky. Oh, Vic, you risked your life to save all the animals. You're a hero. A real hero." Tears she could no longer hold in check trickled down her cheeks. "You scared me half to death. I hope you know that. I kept thinking that I'd sent you to your death."

Vic tightened his hold around her waist and drew her closer. Her heart caught in her throat. Then reacting as naturally as taking her next breath, she stood on tiptoe and kissed him. Right on the lips. He tasted of soot and smoke—and life. Every nerve in her body came fully alert when he returned her kiss, his mouth firm and warm against hers. And when he traced his tongue across her bottom lip, her femininity tingled…and tingled…and tingled.

Wayne Boggus cleared his throat loudly behind them and said, "Penny Sue, your Mr. Noble should let the medics check him out."

She opened her eyes and gasped. What had she done? She had kissed another man in front of Wayne, as well as several of the Alabaster Creek firemen and a horde of concerned citizens gathered in front of the clinic. When she pulled away from Vic, he released his hold on her waist, but his pensive gaze kept her connected to him.

"Here, Miss Paine, you take Lucky." Vic held the little dog

out to her. "I'll go let the medics check me out and then I'll drive you two home."

She grabbed Lucky. "We'll go with you. I want to make sure you're okay. After all, it's my fault that you went into the burning clinic."

"And if the medics say I need some TLC, will you provide it?"

"Well, of course I will," she responded before fully comprehending the innuendo contained in his question.

"Receiving special care from you might turn out to be well worth having risked my life," Vic told her, a devilish glint in his eyes.

Wayne Boggus growled. "Sir, I take exception to the way you've treated Miss Paine and the way you're talking to her."

Penny Sue looked over her shoulder at her angry friend, suddenly realizing that he'd been listening to her conversation with Vic. Oh, dear, this wouldn't do. Why had Wayne eavesdropped anyway? Shouldn't he be spearheading the fire brigade's efforts to extinguish the blaze consuming the clinic?

"And just why is it any of your business?" Vic asked.

Penny Sue glanced back and forth between the two men. Five-foot-nine, round-shouldered and slender, with brown hair and eyes, Wayne was fairly nondescript, despite a cocky, self-confident attitude that sometimes bothered Penny Sue. And then there was Vic. Six-foot-four, lean and mean, with piercing hazel-and-blue eyes and a take-no-prisoners demeanor that she suspected came from past experience.

"Now boys," Penny Sue said, then cringed when she realized she had just referred to two men in their late thirties as boys.

She looked at Vic. "You go out there where the medics are and let them check you over, then we'll take Lucky home."

Vic hesitated.

"Go on." Penny Sue gave him a do-as-I-say glare.

Vic speared Wayne with a hard glance, as if warning him. Warning him about what? Penny Sue wondered. It wasn't as if Vic had any claim on her. But then again, neither did Wayne. A few dates certainly didn't give Wayne any rights where she was concerned. It wasn't as if they were engaged or anything.

Well, some folks in Alabaster Creek thought that more than five dates meant that two people were a couple. She didn't think that way herself.

Vic went over and picked up his gun and his jacket, slipped the gun into the shoulder holster and slung his jacket over his arm.

The minute Vic was out of earshot, Wayne said, "You let that man kiss you. Right here in public."

"Yes, I did," Penny Sue replied. "And to be perfectly honest, I kissed him first."

Wayne's gaze narrowed. "I realize you were grateful that he saved Lucky, but really, Penny Sue, don't you think that's carrying gratitude a little too far?"

"I was overcome with relief. Vic went into the clinic to rescue Lucky and the other animals because of me. I was so grateful to see him alive and well and all the animals safe and—"

Doc Stone came rushing up behind them, wringing his meaty hands and saying, "Mercy, mercy. How could this have happened?"

"Oh, Doc, it could have been much worse," Penny Sue told him. "All the animals are safe, thanks to Vic. He went in through a back window and let out every single animal."

"Yes, yes, I saw all of them when I arrived. A group of people rounded them up and are taking them across the street to Myers Feed and Seed. Joe Myers is going to put them up in his back storeroom until I can make other arrangements." Clasping his hands in a prayer-like gesture, Doc Stone turned to Penny Sue. "Who is this Vic you said rescued the animals? I certainly want to shake his hand and tell him how grateful I am. When I got the call that the clinic was on fire, all I could think about were my poor animals."

"Vic Noble is the bodyguard I hired for Lucky," Penny Sue said. "He and I were over at the bookstore when the clinic caught on fire. We rushed right over and Vic…" She paused in her rapid-fire explanation, caught her breath and spoke more slowly. "Vic went inside the clinic and brought out all the animals. He's a real hero."

"Indeed he is." Doc Stone glanced around, searching the immediate area. "Where is he?"

"Being checked out by the medics." Penny Sue glanced in the

general direction, seeing only the back end of the ambulance parked across the street.

"Then I'd appreciate it if you'd go with me to thank the man in person." Doc held out his arm to Penny Sue. "He's Lucky's bodyguard, huh? I'd say you chose wisely, my dear. It seems he's saved Lucky's life the first day on the job."

Thirty minutes later, after half the town had thanked Vic and made a big to-do over him rescuing the animals trapped in the clinic, Penny Sue and Vic arrived home. He parked Tully's old pickup in the driveway, then stepped down and out, but before he could open the passenger door, Aunt Dottie, Ruby and Tully came rushing out the back door, all three rapidly shooting questions at them.

"Are you both all right?" Aunt Dottie opened her arms when she came toward Penny Sue. "We've been worried sick." She looked at Lucky, nestled safely in Penny Sue's arms. "Well, he doesn't look any the worse for wear. A good bath and he'll be just fine."

"Lucky's not the only one who needs a good bath." Grinning, Ruby inspected Vic. "From the phone calls that have been pouring in for the past hour, I'd say you're quite a hero, young man."

"Yes, yes," Aunt Dottie added as she wrapped her arms around Penny Sue and smiled appreciatively at Vic. "If you hadn't been there, I have no doubt that Penny Sue would have foolishly tried to save the animals herself. This child would have leaped before looking. A terrible trait she shares with me. You no doubt saved her life as well as Lucky's." After taking Penny Sue's hand in hers, Dottie grasped Vic's hand, too. Then she looked him over from head to toe. "You *are* quite a sight, dear boy." She put Penny Sue's hand into Vic's. "You take Vic on up and see to it that he gets a bath and when you've got him all tucked in, Ruby can bring him up some nice warm cocoa." She glanced over at Tully. "You take Lucky, clean him up real good and then carry him upstairs later."

Penny Sue grinned at Vic, who simply looked at her, a soft expression in his eyes. She did so wish he would smile more. Perhaps in time, she could teach him the importance of a pleasant expression. She squeezed Vic's hand, then placed Lucky in Tully's waiting arms.

"Be very careful when you bathe him," Penny Sue said. "He's still recovering from that gunshot."

"I'll treat him like the baby he is," Tully assured her as he held Lucky against his chest. "We're old pals, aren't we?" Lucky licked Tully's cheek. "You've had a really hard time, haven't you, little fellow."

Penny Sue turned to Vic. "Now, you come along with me and we'll get you settled in for the night."

"I'm fine," Vic said. "A little smoke inhalation is no big deal."

"Of course you're fine, but I did promise you some TLC, didn't I?"

Vic gave in quite easily, following her into the house and up the back stairs like an obedient puppy. Something told her that Vic Noble never acquiesced that easily unless he wanted to, so why had he agreed to let her coddle him?

*Because he likes me. He likes me just as I like him. It's that simple. Or that complicated. Depending on how you look at it.*

He followed her into her father's old room. "Take off those nasty clothes," she said, then walked into the adjoining bath. "I'll turn on the shower for you and lay out a couple of fresh towels and—"

He came up behind her unexpectedly. She whirled around and when she saw him, her mouth gaped open. Having already removed his jacket, holster and shirt, he stood there naked from the waist up. Lord have mercy! The man had an incredible chest, fabulous shoulders and a washboard-flat belly. His skin was lightly tanned, a couple of shades darker than her own. His body was hard and muscular, yet lean. Dark brown hair covered his forearms and formed a V shape across his chest. A fine dark coating of soot covered his exposed flesh.

"What should I do with my clothes?" He held out his dirty jacket and shirt.

She gulped. "I—I'll take them." She grabbed both items.

He unbuckled his belt and unzipped his pants. Penny Sue stood there, frozen to the spot, her gaze fixed on his crotch. After bending down and removing his shoes and socks, he tossed her the socks, which thankfully landed atop his shirt that she had draped over her arm. He slid his pants down and off, then handed them to her. She grabbed at the pants, almost dropping them because she couldn't take her eyes off his body.

He seemed totally at ease standing there in nothing but a pair of tight black briefs that did very little to disguise how well-endowed he was. Penny Sue closed her eyes.

"Anything wrong?" he asked.

"No." Her voice squeaked. "It's just I don't think a gentleman would undress in front of me."

"Honey, I'm no gentleman."

Continuing to stare at him, her mouth gaped open.

"Are you planning on scrubbing my back?" he asked.

Her eyes flew open just as he stepped into the shower. The moment she caught a glimpse of his firm, round buttocks, heat spread through her body like fire through dry kindling. Her femininity tightened and released, signaling her arousal.

Suddenly realizing where she was and what she was doing, Penny Sue clasped Vic's dirty clothes to her chest and ran out of the bathroom, not even bothering to close the door. She didn't stop running until she reached the hallway. With her heart beating wildly and belated embarrassment overcoming her, she paused near the laundry chute, closed her eyes and took a deep breath. Why on earth had she just stood there and watched him remove all his clothes? What must he think of her? She opened the laundry chute and tossed his clothes inside, then leaned against the wall and sighed.

*Are you going to wash my back?* She heard his question echo inside her head. Had he been serious? Had he actually thought she would strip naked and join him in the shower?

"Oh, Lordy, Lordy…"

Images of the two of them together, both naked and in the shower, flashed through her mind. Warm water spraying over them. Soapy hands lathering. Caressing. Her hands on his body. His hands on hers.

Penny Sue inched over to the open bedroom door, peeked inside and listened to the water running in the shower. Quietly she reached out and closed the bedroom door, giving Vic the privacy he deserved.

"You should take a bath yourself, young lady." As Ruby arrived at the top of the stairs, she paused to inspect Penny Sue. "I've brought up some brandy for Mr. Noble. I figured he'd rather have some of Mr. Percy's brandy than warm milk or cocoa." She held the small tray containing a glass of liquor.

"You didn't bring me any?" Penny Sue asked.

"When did you start drinking anything stronger than wine?" Ruby eyed her curiously.

"I'm considering starting tonight."

Ruby lifted an inquisitive eyebrow. "I'll take this in and leave it by his bed, then pick up his dirty clothes and—"

"I tossed them down the laundry chute."

"You…" Ruby studied Penny Sue's face. "Did he hand them to you through the door?"

"Hmm…something like that."

"Penny Sue Paine, did you see that man naked?"

"What if I did? It's not as if I'm sixteen. I'm a grown woman of thirty-two with experience, thank you very much."

"Liked what you saw, did you?" Ruby's lips twitched.

"Why Ruby Cox, what a thing to say."

Ruby held out the silver tray. "Here, you take him his brandy. After he comes out of the bathroom."

With unsteady hands, Penny Sue took the tray. "I'll just leave it on his nightstand."

"A woman your age shouldn't waste any opportunities."

"What do you mean by that?"

"A man like Vic Noble doesn't come along every day of the week, you know."

"Lord, Ruby, you act as if there's something going on between Vic and me. I just met the man this afternoon. He's little more than a stranger."

"So, get to know him better. Try giving him a little sample of what he can look forward to…after a proper courtship, of course."

Ruby eyed the tray. "Probably wouldn't hurt if you took a sip of that yourself."

"If Aunt Dottie knew you were encouraging me to seduce—"

"Did I say one word about seducing?" Ruby shrugged innocently. "As for your aunt Dottie—don't think for one minute that she hasn't used her feminine wiles on more than one unsuspecting gentleman."

After soaping himself from head to toe and rinsing off the black grime coating his skin, Vic readjusted the water to barely lukewarm. He was already hot enough. Hot just thinking about Penny Sue and the way she'd looked at him. You'd have thought the woman had never seen a naked man before tonight.

Stop thinking about her, he told himself. She's trouble. And if you succumb to those big brown eyes, you'll be in deep.

She thought he was the big hero because he went into the burning clinic and saved Lucky and all those other animals. It would be so easy to use her gratitude as a means of getting into her pants. And God knew that's what he wanted. He wanted Penny Sue in the worst way.

Grumbling under his breath, Vic rinsed in tepid water, turned off the shower and stepped out onto the tile floor. Two huge fluffy white towels awaited him, one stacked on top of the other on the small vanity. He took the first one and dried his hair, then ran it over his arms and chest before moving downward to his belly and legs.

When the towel touched his erection, he groaned. He should have taken care of this problem while he'd been in the shower. But he had been trying damn hard to stop thinking about a certain beautiful chatterbox and if he'd touched himself, screwing Penny Sue would have been the only thing on his mind.

Hurriedly, Vic finished drying off, then walked into the bedroom and rummaged through his black vinyl case until he found a clean pair of briefs. When not on an assignment, he slept in his briefs only or buck naked, but he'd learned that when he was on duty, it was always a good idea to wear at least pajama bottoms.

Someone knocked softly on the bedroom door.

"Vic, are you decent?" Penny Sue asked.

He yanked on his pajama bottoms and trekked to the door barefoot and bare-chested, then eased the door open halfway. There she stood, cherry-pink cheeks, chocolate brown eyes and luscious creamy skin. She looked good enough to eat.

Vic groaned inwardly, forcing himself to focus on anything except how beautiful Penny Sue was. That's when he noticed the silver tray in her hand. "What have you got there?" he asked.

"Oh, this... Ruby thought you might like some brandy."

Vic picked up the glass from the tray, took a sip of the brandy and sighed. "Ruby was right. This is good stuff."

"The brandy was my father's. Aunt Dottie doesn't drink and neither did Aunt Lottie, so we've had the bottle just going to waste ever since Daddy died."

"Thank Ruby for me."

Penny Sue stood there smiling at him. Didn't she have any idea that his horny body was reading a lot more into her smile than she intended?

"Was there anything else?" Vic asked, wishing she'd either put him out of his misery or go away.

"I suppose you're worn to a frazzle and just want to go straight to bed."

Her big, beautiful, tempting breasts rose and fell as she sighed. Just how much was a man supposed to endure before reaching his breaking point?

"Yeah, I'm pretty tired, but since Lucky's home, I need to be on the job," he reminded her.

"Lucky? Oh yes, Lucky." She giggled. "I don't know where my mind is. Tully hasn't brought Lucky upstairs yet. I should go downstairs and get him." She motioned with her hands. He'd noticed that she couldn't talk without using her hands, which made him want to grab them and hold them. "I'm sure he's missed sleeping with me. He's such a cuddle-bunny. He curls up against me, right here—" she laid both of her crisscrossed hands just below her breasts "—and sometimes doesn't budge an inch all night, unless I roll him over."

"Can't say I blame him," Vic said without thinking.

Penny Sue's cheeks flushed. "I...er...I really should go get Lucky." She turned away from Vic.

He stepped over the threshold and out into the hall. "Since I'm his bodyguard, I should go with you."

"I think after what you've been through tonight, you should rest and begin your duties in the morning." She glanced back over her shoulder.

"Considering that somebody tried to kill Lucky again, I feel it's my duty to keep an eye on him. Starting tonight."

"Oh. Well, if you insist." She turned back around and looked at his bare chest. "Shouldn't you put on your robe—" she glanced at his bare feet "—and slippers?"

"Sure thing. Just wait here for me. Okay?"

He turned into the bedroom, unzipped his bag and tossed clothing out onto the bed until he found his slippers and robe. He hadn't originally packed either, but at the last minute he'd added them to the stack of clothing items he'd laid out on his bed at home.

After stuffing his feet into the black leather slip-on house loafers, he stuck his arms through the robe and hurried back to a waiting Penny Sue.

As they descended the back stairs together, he said, "I think I should go ahead and sleep on the daybed in the room next to yours."

"Do you think that's necessary? After all, it's highly unlikely anyone will try to harm Lucky in his own house and especially not when he's sleeping in my bed."

"Probably not," Vic agreed. "But did it ever enter your mind that someone would set fire to the veterinary clinic in order to kill Lucky?"

She stopped halfway down the stairs and confronted him. "Do you really think that's what happened? Do you think someone set fire to the clinic on purpose just to kill Lucky? I mean, it could have been an accident of some kind. Faulty wiring. A space heater—"

He grasped her shoulders. "Call your boyfriend and ask him. He's the fire chief, right? He might be able to tell you tonight if the fire was deliberately set."

"Wayne isn't my boyfriend. Well, not exactly. We have dated some, but…"

"But?"

"We haven't…we're friends. Our relationship hasn't progressed beyond a certain stage."

"Just how many dates have you had with this guy?"

"Five, maybe six if you count him coming here for Sunday dinner a couple of weeks ago."

Old Wayne had been on five or six dates with Miss Penny Sue and he still hadn't made it to third base with her. Hmm… So why should he care one way or the other? It wasn't anything to him if she had slept with half the men in Alabaster Creek.

Yeah, sure.

Why hadn't she slept with Wayne? Vic had picked up on some mighty possessive vibes from the fire chief tonight, which meant that he wanted Penny Sue. So if they hadn't had sex it was because she had said no. And he suspected he knew the reason.

"Vic?"

"Huh?" Until she spoke, he hadn't realized he'd been standing there gathering wool.

"I'll telephone Wayne first thing in the morning," she said. "And to be on the safe side, perhaps you *should* sleep in the old nursery tonight."

He nodded.

They continued down the back stairs.

"Mind if I ask you something?" He didn't slow down or glance her way.

"Sure. What?" She kept in step with him.

"Why haven't you slept with the fire chief?" Now why the hell did you ask her such a personal question, one that's none of your business?

Silence. For several seconds Penny Sue didn't say anything, then just as they reached the back hallway leading directly into the kitchen, she said, "I'm not in love with Wayne."

Her reply hit him like a sledgehammer, directly in the gut. He'd been pretty sure that was the reason.

This could go one of two ways—either he chose to see Penny

Sue as a challenge or he kept his hands off her until Daisy could send in another Dundee agent. The best thing that could happen for both of them was for him to leave town as soon as possible. Getting all hot and bothered over a woman like Penny Sue could lead to disaster.

Penny Sue had never discussed her sex life, or lack thereof, with a man. So why did she find it so easy to talk to Vic, to admit such intimate things about herself to him? Because he wasn't a permanent fixture in her life. Because he would come and go and she'd never see him again. Her stomach muscles knotted painfully at the thought. Silly girl, she scolded herself. She'd gone and fallen for a man she had just met. As she had pointed out to Ruby, she and Vic were practically strangers. And despite the undeniable fact that she found him attractive, she certainly wasn't in love with him. Was she? No. Definitely not. In lust, maybe. She didn't believe in love at first sight or even second sight for that matter. After what had happened with Dylan all those years ago, she wasn't sure she believed in true love at all. Mutual respect, commitment and deep caring. Those were things she believed in, the things she wanted with a potential mate. So, if that was all she wanted, why hadn't she encouraged Wayne? After all, he was considered quite a catch in Alabaster Creek. He was good-looking, self-confident, a basically good guy from a respectable family. And to top it all off, he held a position of respect and authority.

But Wayne didn't make her feel the way Vic did. All warm and fluttery and even giddy. Common sense told her that Vic wasn't the type to make a commitment, that he would run, not walk, away from any woman who tried to tie him down.

Before they reached the kitchen, Penny Sue heard voices and immediately recognized them. Aunt Dottie, Ruby and Wayne Boggus.

Penny Sue halted outside the open kitchen door. Vic came up behind her and laid his hand on her shoulder. Her body tensed. Her nerves rioted. This wouldn't do. She couldn't keep reacting like this every time he touched her.

She jerked away from his gentle hold and pranced into the

kitchen, putting a welcoming smile on her face as she approached the fire chief. "Wayne, how terribly sweet of you to come by to check on me."

She went right up to him and kissed him on the cheek. He grinned from ear to ear. Standing at Wayne's side, she faced the others, glancing first at her aunt and then at Ruby. Both women looked at her questioningly. She knew what they were thinking. They suspected she was making nice with Wayne in order to fend off her unwanted feelings for Vic Noble. Darn it, they knew her far too well.

Then she hazarded a glance at Vic. He stood just inside the doorway, his arms crossed over his broad chest. The lapels of his robe had slipped apart just enough to reveal the dark hair in the center of that very impressive chest. His cold, disgruntled expression told her nothing. He wasn't an easy man to read. Was he jealous? Did he see through her deception and was he upset with her? Or did he simply not care?

The back door opened and Tully came in with Lucky on a leash. "Here's our boy, all fresh and clean and ready for—" He stopped talking immediately when he saw Wayne. "Evening, chief. You're stopping by kind of late, aren't you?"

"Wayne came to check on Penny Sue," Ruby said. "And on Mr. Noble, too, of course."

"And to let us know that Doc Stone's clinic burned to the ground," Aunt Dottie said. "It was an old building and not even the new addition on the back where the animals were kept survived the fire."

Penny Sue moaned sadly.

"But all the animals are fine. Doc Stone checked them out and said not one of them is any the worse for wear." Wayne eyed Vic. "Thanks to Mr. Noble." He uttered the last comment rather begrudgingly. "But you were lucky, Noble. Being a civilian and all, you took a big risk going inside a burning building."

Vic didn't respond.

"If he hadn't risked his own life, Lucky and the other animals would all be dead." Penny Sue pointed out the obvious to Wayne, but deliberately didn't glance Vic's way.

"Possibly," Wayne said. "I might have been able to get some of them out. I'd certainly have tried."

"Yes, of course you would have," Aunt Dottie said. "No one is questioning your bravery, my dear boy."

Wayne flushed, then cleared his throat. "I…uh…I hate to be the bearer of bad tidings…"

"I thought you said all the animals were safe," Penny Sue said.

"They are."

"And Doc Stone had insurance, didn't he?" she asked.

Wayne nodded. "It's about the fire."

"What about the fire?" Aunt Dottie's gaze darted from Penny Sue to Vic.

"We found evidence that it was deliberately set," Wayne said. "The best we can tell, somebody doused kerosene on some old rags they'd put all the way around the clinic, then set fire to the rags."

"Why didn't the entire building catch fire at the same time?" Vic asked.

"Somehow the rags around the back side of the building didn't catch fire," Wayne explained. "Maybe a match blew out in the wind or just didn't make contact with the rags. We'll know more when the fire marshal—"

"Someone deliberately set fire to Doc Stone's clinic in order to kill Lucky." The truth hit Penny Sue hard, even though it didn't come as a surprise. She looked around the room, her gaze going from one person to the other. "Y'all see now, don't you, that I was right to hire a bodyguard for Lucky? Someone in our family is crazy and mean and greedy enough to kill a whole clinic full of animals in order to get rid of Lucky."

Emotion lodged in her throat. She bent down, picked up Lucky and cradled him in her arms. "Don't worry, sweetheart, I'm not going to let anyone hurt you." Feeling like a mother tiger protecting her young cub, Penny Sue turned to Vic. "I want to hire at least one more Dundee agent—maybe two—to come to Alabaster Creek and help out with the investigation. I want whoever shot Lucky and set the clinic on fire found as soon as possible before they wind up hurting Lucky and perhaps other innocent animals and people."

## Chapter 6

Someone was licking his face. In a half-asleep state, Vic tried to remember whom he'd gone to bed with last night. The only woman who came to mind was Penny Sue. He could see her clearly, smiling at him, her little pink tongue slipping between her full, moist lips. Vic sighed.

He opened one eye slowly and looked up. Sure enough, there stood Penny Sue, hovering over him. Both eyes popped open. Vic groaned.

Penny Sue reached for Lucky, who sat on Vic's chest. His wet tongue hung out of his mouth and his short tail wagged in a friendly gesture. She picked up the dog and tucked him under her arm.

"Good morning." Vic sat up. The covers dropped to his waist.

"I'm sorry Lucky woke you, but when I opened the door to check on you, he came racing in and straight to you. He likes you, which means you're a good person. Dogs have a sixth sense about things like that. They're often a lot smarter than we human beings are, especially when it comes to judging people.

"I had meant to let you sleep until at least eight. After all you went through last night, you certainly deserved to sleep in this morning. But now that you're awake, you might as well get up, get dressed and have breakfast with Lucky and me down in the kitchen, unless you prefer a tray up here in your—"

Vic grabbed Penny Sue's arm and dragged her down into the bed with him. As she toppled over, Vic maneuvered her around so that she wound up sitting on his lap. And there they sat, face to face, Lucky still in Penny Sue's arms.

"Why did you do that?" she asked guilelessly.

"If I tell you, promise not to get angry with me."

She eyed him speculatively. "I promise."

He didn't think she sounded very sincere, but she had promised so he felt obligated to come clean. "I did it to make you shut up."

"Oh."

Seeing the disappointed look on her face made him regret being so honest with her. But God help him, her incessant chatter drove him nuts.

Lucky squirmed out of Penny Sue's hold, leaned over and licked Vic in the face again.

He pulled the dog aside, patted him on the head, lifted him up and set him down on the floor.

When Penny Sue started to get up, he grabbed her around the waist and held her in place.

"What's your hurry?"

She sat there looking at him, not saying a word.

"I had another reason for pulling you down here," he told her.

She smiled.

"Want to know the other reason?"

She shrugged.

"Giving me the silent treatment?"

She nodded.

"Honey, there has to be a happy medium for you," he said. "Somewhere between non-stop yack-yack-yack and absolute silence."

She shrugged again.

Should he give up before he dug himself in any deeper? "The

complete truth of the matter is that I looked up and saw your beautiful face—" he let his gaze travel over her body neatly attired in gray slacks and a pale pink sweater set "—and the rest of you and I couldn't resist copping a feel." To emphasize his comment, he slid his hands down over her hips and caressed her buttocks. She sucked in a surprised breath.

"Your behavior is scandalous, Mr. Noble," Penny Sue told him, but made no attempt to leave his lap. "You're not acting like a gentleman, you know."

Keeping one hand resting on her hip, he lifted the other to stroke her neck. Their gazes met and locked. "I told you that I'm not a gentleman, honey. I'm just a man. You might want to keep that in mind for future reference."

A knock on Penny Sue's bedroom door alerted them half a second before Dottie Paine opened the door and came in, searching for her niece. When she immediately noticed the door between the two rooms was wide open, she peered inside and gasped when she saw Penny Sue sitting on top of Vic.

"Penny Sue Paine, what on earth do you think you're doing?"

Dottie wore a yellow silk negligee, the robe trimmed with black velvet, and a matching ribbon held her hair away from her face.

"I…we aren't doing anything." Penny Sue glanced from Dottie to Vic, silently pleading with him to reassure her aunt.

That was true enough. They hadn't been doing anything… much. Although if Vic had had his way, Penny Sue would have been naked and lying under him when her aunt walked in on them, after the fact, he hoped, and not in the middle. Vic's body responded to the thought of making love to Penny Sue.

"It's all perfectly innocent," Vic said.

"What if Ruby had seen you?" Dottie glanced at Vic's naked chest.

"Then I would have explained to her, just as I've explained to you, that nothing happened."

Penny Sue undoubtedly felt his arousal pressing against her backside because she gasped, snapped her head around and glared at him with wide eyes. He stared back at her and tried his best to look innocent.

As if just then realizing that she was still in bed with Vic, Penny Sue jumped up and onto her feet. Dottie shook her head and glared at her niece. The two women began a verbal sparring match, snapping back and forth at each other until the sound of their voices blended into one sing-song noise, which Vic tried to block out by humming in his mind.

Suddenly Lucky barked at Dottie, which immediately silenced both women.

"Hush up, Lucky," Penny Sue scolded. "It's just Aunt Dottie. Puff isn't with her."

"Perhaps we should leave and allow Mr. Noble to get dressed." Dottie hurriedly returned to Penny Sue's bedroom. Vic heard her say to her niece, "I thought he was staying in Percy's old room."

"He's Lucky's bodyguard, so he needs to be closer to Lucky at night," Penny Sue explained, then eased the door between her bedroom and the old nursery closed.

Vic threw back the covers, got out of bed and yanked off his pajama bottoms. After finding a pair of jeans in his bag, he put them on, along with a lightweight cotton sweater, a pair of cotton socks and his loafers. When he was fully clothed, he sat on the edge of the unmade bed, flipped open his cell phone and called Daisy at Dundee headquarters.

She answered on the third ring. "Daisy Holbrook."

"It's Vic."

"I still don't have an agent to replace you," she told him.

"That's not why I'm calling."

"Oh?"

"Penny Sue…Ms. Paine wants to hire another agent to come to Alabaster Creek to help with the investigation."

"And why is that? You haven't been there twenty-four hours yet, surely she didn't expect you to solve the mystery of who shot her dog that quickly."

"She isn't dissatisfied with me," Vic explained. "As a matter of fact, she's very pleased because I saved Lucky's life last night. Somebody torched the veterinary clinic where he was recuperating and I went into the burning building and brought him out safe and sound."

"Ah, so now you're the big hero."

Vic grunted. "After what happened, Penny Sue is more determined than ever to stop whoever is trying to kill Lucky. And she's right. Whoever set fire to the clinic not only didn't mind killing the animals, but they didn't care that those firemen risked their lives."

"I'd send another agent, if I could, but no one is available."

"Sawyer needs to hire some new agents."

"Funny you should mention that."

"Has he hired someone?"

"Two new someones," Daisy said.

"Is either one ready to jump in and go right to work?"

"You know the rules—everyone goes through a six-week training program."

"Just this once, Sawyer could bend the rules. If I stay on as Lucky's bodyguard until Dom or Lucie can take over for me, why couldn't one of the new guys do the investigative work?"

"I'm not sure Sawyer would agree, but I can contact him and see what he says."

"Do that." Vic paused, then asked, "Just who are the two new agents?"

"You remember the CIA guy we worked with on J.J.'s assignment to Mocorito?"

"Will Pierce?"

"That's the one. Well, Sawyer lured him away from the CIA and he starts Dundee indoctrination Monday morning."

"See if Sawyer will send him. He's qualified to do some investigative work. Or send the other guy. Either one."

"Sawyer definitely won't send the other guy," Daisy said. "He doesn't start with us for another couple of weeks."

"Hmm…then call Sawyer and ask him to send Pierce."

"Don't you want to know about the other new agent?"

He realized Daisy was dying to tell him. "Sure. So who is he?"

"Deke Bronson."

Had he heard her right? Deke Bronson? She couldn't mean that Deke Bronson. But what were the odds that there were two men in the business with the same name?

"Vic, are you still there?"

"Yeah."

"Sawyer said you two knew each other."

"Yeah."

"He's another former CIA operative, right?"

"Sort of." Only Deke Bronson, unlike Will Pierce and Vic, had been a freelance agent. Nobody at the company knew that much about Bronson, except that he'd worked as a mercenary in the past. As far as anyone knew, he was an American by birth, but where he'd been born and what his background was remained a mystery.

"Sort of?" Daisy asked.

"Yeah, he was an agent," Vic told her, his voice gruff. Changing his tone, he said, "Look, just see what you can do about getting another agent down here ASAP."

"Let me call Sawyer and see what I can set up. Okay?"

"Yeah, and in the meantime, give me Dom Shea's cell number."

"Any special reason you want to contact Dom?"

"Personal," Vic replied.

"Hold on, I'll look up his number."

Vic waited all of one minute before Daisy came back on the line, rattled off Dom's cell number and again promised Vic she'd call Sawyer. Vic said goodbye, then repeated Dom's number several times. He wouldn't forget it. He had a talent for remembering numbers. If Daisy couldn't finagle another agent for him by tomorrow, he'd give Dom a call. Of all the Dundee agents, Dom Shea was the one with whom he'd formed a tentative friendship. Maybe Dom could find a way to wrap up his latest assignment a little sooner than expected. Or if not, he might know how to get in touch with vacationing Geoff Monday, who'd gone off for two weeks of R & R a week ago, not leaving a number where he could be reached.

Vic was in hell. Pastel hell, surrounded by pale pink and blue and yellow and lavender. Half an hour ago, a huge shipment of Easter items had been delivered to Penny Sue's Pretties and the owner had commandeered his services.

"There's no reason you can't guard Lucky and help me unpack these boxes," she'd told him.

His first mistake this morning—after dragging Penny Sue into his bed—had been assuming he would stay at the house with Lucky all day today. But oh no. He was expected to babysit Lucky at Penny Sue's Pretties.

"Lucky goes to the shop with me," Penny Sue had told Vic. "He has his own little bed in the back and I keep a sack of his food there and some of his chew toys."

"Don't the customers mind your having a dog at the store?"

"Oh, no, he's well behaved and all my customers love him to pieces."

And so here he was—a highly trained professional bodyguard and former CIA hard-ass—surrounded by colorful Easter items, everything from cute little stuffed bunny rabbits to decorative glass Easter eggs. While Miss Eula attended to the morning customers, Vic assisted Penny Sue. They had already unpacked five of the ten boxes.

"Bring the box with the Easter baskets," Penny Sue said. "I want to put one in the window and then arrange the others throughout the store."

Like an obedient servant, Vic lifted the large box, carried it to the front of the store and walked around behind Penny Sue while she placed one basket after another in their chosen spots.

"Everybody is looking at me." Vic felt very conspicuous being the lone man in Penny Sue's Pretties. "I feel as if I'm on display."

"The ladies are just curious," she told him. "I'm sure everyone in town knows that not only are you Lucky's bodyguard, but that you're the man who saved Lucky and all the other animals from the fire at Doc Stone's last night. You should know that everybody loves a hero."

"I'm not a hero."

After placing an enormous pink-and-blue basket on her antique desk at the back of the shop, Penny Sue turned and faced Vic. "You're much too modest." She reached up and grasped his arms, just below his shoulders. "Not everyone would have done what you did. As far as I'm concerned, you're definitely a hero."

"I told you that I'm no hero. I'm trained to save lives, to protect people. And saving animals is pretty much the same thing."

"I suppose introducing you to all my customers today is out of the question?"

No way. Correction: no way in hell.

But when Penny Sue looked at him so pleadingly, he almost succumbed. After all, just how difficult would it be to say hello to the ladies meandering around in the shop?

Who was he kidding? He'd rather eat glass.

"I...uh...I'd rather not."

"What if I make it a mass introduction? You wouldn't have to meet each one individually. Please, Vic." When he frowned, she said, "I have twice as many customers as usual this early on a Thursday morning and Eula volunteered to work this morning and it's not even one of her days to work. They're all here to get a look at the big hero."

Vic groaned. "Make it quick, will you? Then I'm taking Lucky back to the storeroom with me and the two of us will find something to do back there until lunchtime."

Penny Sue slipped her arm through Vic's and smiled up at him as she batted those long dark eyelashes seductively. Not for the first time, he wondered if she realized exactly what she was doing. "Oh, thank you so much. You're an absolute sweetheart for doing this."

Before he had a chance to change his mind, she all but dragged him into the center of the shop and called in a loud voice, "Ladies, may I have your attention, please?"

Within two minutes, every customer in the shop had congregated within a few feet of Penny Sue and Vic and all eyes were focused on him. The last time he'd felt this cornered had been when he and a fellow agent had been surrounded by a band of guerrilla soldiers in Central America.

"Ladies, I'd like to introduce all of you to Mr. Vic Noble, Lucky's bodyguard and the man who saved all the animals at Doc Stone's clinic last night."

After several loud oohs and aahs, the ladies applauded.

If only a very large hole would open up and swallow me, Vic thought.

Penny Sue stood on tiptoe and whispered, "Try to smile, will you?"

He tried. And failed. Instead he glanced from woman to woman and nodded.

He leaned over and said in a hushed voice, "Get me out of here."

"Shop till your heart's content," Penny Sue told her customers. "We have bargains galore and new Easter items are coming in every day. If y'all would like refreshments, ask Eula. We have chocolate raspberry coffee and orange blossom tea today."

Yanking Penny Sue's arm, Vic turned them around and fled, stopping only to whistle to Lucky, who followed them into the storeroom. The minute Vic closed the door behind them, he grabbed her by the shoulders, intending to forcefully inform her that he wouldn't be making any more command performances today or anytime in the near future.

"What do you think you're doing? I can't have you manhandling me when I have a shop full of customers just dying to spend their money." She wriggled to free herself. "I'm sorry if you feel uncomfortable here, but you really shouldn't. There's no reason for—"

He brought his mouth down on hers, effectively stopping her from saying anything else.

The kiss quickly got out of hand and what started out as a means to silence her turned into a passionate moment that had Vic aroused and aching in no time flat. Penny Sue responded eagerly, opening her mouth for his invasion and pressing her body intimately against his.

Then, breathless and gasping for air, she pulled away from him and opened her eyes.

"Vic?"

Lucky pawed at Vic's leg. He petted the mutt on the head; apparently pacified, Lucky trotted across the room and curled up on his little bed.

Vic nuzzled Penny Sue's cheek and then her neck as his hands slid downward to her hips. "Who taught you how to kiss like that?"

"No one. I just did what you did, what felt right."

"I find it difficult to believe that you're not aware of what you're doing."

"I don't understand." She stared at him, genuine puzzlement on her face.

"Everything about you is sexy. The kind of sexy that turns a guy inside out." When she kept staring at him, her big brown eyes wide with wonder, he shook his head. "Honey, the way you walk is sexy. The way you talk is sexy. The way you bat those long eyelashes is sexy. The way you look at a man, as if he were the greatest thing since sliced bread, is sexy. And damn it all, the way you kiss is sexy."

"Is that bad?" she asked as innocently as a child.

"If you're just teasing a guy, it is."

"I do not tease," she said.

"I didn't say you did."

"You implied it."

"I'm sorry. I just said that if you know how sexy you are and use it against a guy without intending to follow through and give him what all that sexiness promises, then you're a tease."

She gasped indignantly. "And you are...you're a...a...a...a man!"

Vic snorted. "Meaning?"

"Meaning that I have never in my life deliberately tried to be sexy. I've never intentionally led a man on by the way I talk or walk or whatever. I'm just myself. No pretense. And if you or any other man chooses to read more into my being me, then you're an idiot. An idiot who lets his...his you-know-what...rule his actions instead of his heart or his mind."

Vic burst into laughter.

Penny Sue planted her hands on her hips and glowered at him. "What's so funny?"

It was all Vic could do to stop laughing, but he managed. By the way she was glaring at him, he figured Penny Sue was on the verge of hitting him.

"You're what's funny," he told her. "I swear I've never heard a grown woman call a man's penis his you-know-what."

"Well, excuse me for not being vulgar. But I was raised by two old-fashioned ladies and was taught that modesty and decorum were always expected of a lady." Tears welled up in her eyes.

Oh, God, he'd done it now. "Ah, honey, don't cry. I didn't mean to laugh at you."

When he took a step toward her, she backed up a couple of feet. "Don't touch me."

He rolled his eyes and groaned. Heaven help the man who wound up married to this woman. He'd have to have the patience of a saint. And being slightly deaf wouldn't hurt either.

He held up his hands in an I-surrender gesture. "Let's call a truce. Lucky and I will find something to do back here." He glanced at the dog who was lying on his dog bed, already half asleep. "Maybe take a nap, while you go do whatever it is you do out there in your shop."

With her arms folded over her chest, she stared at him for what seemed to him like a good five minutes, but which had probably been more like sixty seconds. Then she asked him, "Why did you kiss me?"

"What?"

"Why did you kiss me?"

He knew it was a trick question. No matter what he replied, he'd be damned. If he told her he'd kissed her because he couldn't keep his hands off her, she would accuse him of being "a man" and thinking with his you-know-what. So he went with what he thought might be the lesser of two evils. "I kissed you to keep you from talking."

"That's what I thought." Huffing loudly, she whirled around, opened the storeroom door and marched out into the shop.

Vic let out a sigh of relief, then eased down onto the floor beside Lucky. "She's going to torture me, isn't she?"

Lucky opened his eyes, looked up at Vic, then licked his hand.

"She's going to keep on batting those lashes at me and swaying those hips and flashing that million-dollar smile until I can't take it anymore."

Lucky cocked his head to one side, as if listening intently to what Vic said.

"Do you think it's too late for me to get the hell out of Dodge?"

Lucky lifted his head and laid it on Vic's thigh. "Yeah, that's what I thought. It was too late about half a minute after I met her."

* * *

Penny Sue avoided Vic the rest of the morning, then at lunchtime, she sent him and Lucky home. She did not want to see him, talk to him or think about him. But that had proven difficult when every customer who'd entered the store that afternoon had talked of nothing else but Mr. Noble, the town's hero. Even Doc Stone had telephoned, wanting to speak to Vic, to thank him personally. That's when Penny Sue's brilliant idea hit her. She supposed she should feel guilty for instigating something she knew Vic would hate with a passion, but it would serve him right after the way he'd treated her. He'd laughed at her, thought it funny that she didn't call a spade a spade, so to speak. No doubt he preferred women with potty mouths, women who could say the word…well, that word…as easily as they said good morning. Perhaps she was out of step with the times, much too old-fashioned for a woman of nearly thirty-three, but she had no intention of apologizing to Vic Noble or anyone else for the kind of genteel upbringing her aunts had given her.

"If you'd really like to thank Vic, you should throw a party for him and invite the owners of all the pets he saved last night," Penny Sue had told Doc Stone.

"What a great idea. I'll have Angela phone everyone and see if we can't set something up here at the house for tomorrow night."

Doc's wife Angela had called Penny Sue less than an hour ago to tell her that the party was on and Vic would be the guest of honor. Oh, how he'd hate that. Too bad. This would teach him not to laugh at her and to stop kissing her to prevent her from talking.

·She smiled to herself as she locked up the shop. With the time change, it was still daylight at five-thirty, so she could easily walk home before dark. Just as she dropped the keys into her shoulder bag and turned around, she saw Vic and Lucky coming up the sidewalk, Lucky quite content on his retractable leash.

"What are you doing here?" she asked.

"Lucky and I came to walk you home."

"That wasn't necessary." Didn't he know she was still angry with him?

"I stopped by the video store and picked up a couple of movies." He held up the plastic sack. "Your aunt Dottie told me she has dinner with her brother Douglas every Thursday night and Ruby and Tully will be at the rec center playing bingo until after eleven."

"So?" He really didn't have any idea that she was still very upset with him or that the Paine women's forgiveness couldn't be easily won.

"So, I thought we could pick up some burgers—" he glanced down at Lucky "—for the three of us and we could kick back, eat burgers and fries and watch these movies."

"What are the movies?"

"I wasn't sure what you'd like, so I asked the lady over at the video store if she knew your preferences in movies."

"Allie Stanfield?"

"Huh?"

"Allie Stanfield owns the video store and was probably the woman you spoke to," Penny Sue said.

"Hmm. Well, she suggested something called *Overboard*. She said it was a comedy. And the other one is something with *hawk* in the title. I figured it might be a Western."

"*Ladyhawk*?"

"Could be. I'm not sure."

Penny Sue tried not to smile. No need to forewarn Vic that Allie had rented him two chick flicks. It was her guess that he would hate both movies. Good. She'd make him sit through both of them. And then she'd spring her big surprise on him about the party at Doc Stone's tomorrow night. Ah, revenge was sweet.

"All right." She laced her arm through his. "Let's stop by the Alabaster Creek Café and pick up burgers. They make the best juicy burgers, thick home-style fries and to-die-for onion rings."

Vic's gaze narrowed. "Honey, you're the first woman I've ever known who wasn't worried about calories."

She almost stopped dead in her tracks. Was he implying that she was fat and therefore it didn't matter what she ate? If so, then he'd just added one more checkmark to the minus side of the scorecard she was mentally keeping. So far, he had several small checks in the minus column and one huge check in the plus column. No matter how upset she might be with him, she couldn't forget the fact that he was still a hero. In her eyes and in the eyes of the entire town.

"I don't think a woman should hide the fact that she has a healthy appetite," Penny Sue said.

Vic coughed a couple of times.

What was that all about? she wondered.

"You aren't coming down with a cold, are you?"

"Nope."

"Then why were you coughing?" she asked. "Were you just clearing your throat? Or did you want to make a comment about something I've said or done? You seem to have a definite opinion about me, so just come right out and say it. After all, you've told me yourself that you're no gentleman, so why spare my feelings?

"You think I talk too much, that I'm old-fashioned, sexually repressed and I'm fat! Well, you're not perfect yourself, you know. You form opinions much too quickly and based on very little evidence. You never smile and the only time I've heard you laugh was when you were laughing at me. And you probably think I'm crazy for hiring Lucky a bodyguard, don't you? Of course you do. And if you think you can buy my good opinion with a couple of movies and some hamburgers—"

Vic groaned, a rumble that began deep in his throat and erupted from his mouth like a spewing volcano. "For God's sake, woman, shut up!"

Feeling as if he'd slapped her, Penny Sue stopped dead in her tracks. Her bottom lip trembled and tears misted her eyes. How dare he speak to her in such a way.

He groaned again, but this time it was more of a mournful whine. "I didn't mean to say it like that and not in such a rough tone. But honey, you could drive a saint to murder."

She clenched her teeth in an effort not to cry, then snapped her head around and gave him a withering glare.

"That didn't make it any better, did it?" Totally perplexed, he huffed, then rubbed his hand over his chin.

After crossing her arms over her chest, she began patting her foot as she continued glaring at him. He was just digging himself in deeper and deeper, which meant it would take a great deal more penance before she would forgive him.

"I should have just kissed you again," he said.

"Is that your solution to every problem with a woman—just kiss her?"

"Not usually." He thought for a moment before saying, "Actually, only with you."

"Should I be honored?"

"You're really pissed, aren't you?"

She didn't think that comment required a response.

"Look, honey, you're not fat." His gaze drifted over her appreciatively. "You've got the kind of body that men have erotic dreams about."

"What!"

He shut his eyes, shook his head and groaned again. "It was a compliment. I swear. Penny Sue, you're a gorgeous woman."

That comment erased her frown.

"And?" she prodded.

"And there's nothing wrong with being old-fashioned. It's kind of…er…uh…" he struggled to find the right word. "It's endearing."

She stopped patting her foot. "What else?"

"We haven't had sex, so I can't make a judgment on that, but from the way you kiss, I doubt you're repressed in any way."

She sniffled, then brushed the teardrops from her eyelashes.

"I didn't mean to make you cry," he told her. "But you're much too sensitive about—"

Her bottom lip trembled again.

"Sensitivity is good…in a woman," he added hastily.

"But there's nothing good about my talking too much, is there?" She had just given him his final test. Let's see if he passes or fails.

Vic's cheeks puffed, filling with air, then he let out a long, whooshing breath. "You have a bubbly, outgoing personality and I'm sure most people aren't the least bit bothered by the fact that you talk a lot."

"But it bothers you?"

"I'm not going to win this one, am I?"

"Answer the question."

"Ah, honey, do we have to do this?"

He looked as if he were in pain.

Good!

"Just tell me the truth."

Vic glanced down at Lucky who had pulled ahead of them the entire length of his retractable leash, and was sniffing in the shrubbery in front of the local post office.

"Lucky's getting restless," Vic said. "We should probably get those burgers and head on home."

"No, not until you answer my question."

"You're not going to let it go, are you?"

She shook her head.

There was no pleasing this woman and certainly no way to make her see reason. Totally exasperated, Vic let his anger get the best of him.

"Okay, you want the truth—here it is. Penny Sue Paine, you are a royal pain in the ass."

## *Chapter 7*

Penny Sue hadn't said another word to him all the way home. When he had tried to apologize, she'd refused to even glance his way. And every once in a while during the six-block walk from her downtown shop to the old Paine mansion, he'd heard her sniffling and knew she was crying. Yes, he felt like the biggest heel of all time. But damn it, the woman had kept needling him until he'd lost his temper. And it wasn't as if he'd lied to her. She *was* a pain in the ass. A sweet, beautiful, sexy pain.

He wasn't used to dealing with women like Penny Sue, but he had no choice but to deal with her—he was her employee on this assignment and he'd just have to suck it up and find a way to make things right with her. But how?

The minute they got home, she'd gone running up the stairs and slammed the door to her room. So, here he was, standing at the bottom of the stairs, looking up and wondering, "Why me, God, why me?"

Lucky let out a yowl.

"What's the matter, boy?" Vic asked. "Worried about her?" He reached down, unleashed the dog and patted him on the head. "Yeah, me, too."

Vic snorted. He was talking to a dog and the crazy thing was he halfway expected Lucky to talk back to him.

"So, what do you suggest?" Vic asked. "You know her a lot better than I do. What can I do to get back on her good side?"

Lucky looked up the stairs for a half minute, then turned around and headed down the hall. Vic followed him straight into the kitchen. Lucky went over to his empty food bowl and sat down in front of it.

"You're hungry," Vic said. "That problem I can solve."

Vic picked up the empty bowl, then went into the pantry. He opened the bag of dog food and using the scoop inside, filled the bowl to overflowing. When he started to exit the pantry, he noticed a line of home-canned goods, each with a personal label that boasted, From the Kitchen of Ruby Cox. Homemade soups— vegetable, chicken noodle and beef stew. It was a chilly evening. Soup might hit the spot. Better even than the hamburgers he'd wanted and didn't get.

Lucky met him at the pantry door, obviously excited about the prospect of being fed. Vic placed the full bowl down beside the matching water bowl.

"Eat up, boy."

Lucky dove into the food, lapping greedily.

"What if I open some of Ruby's homemade soup and fix Penny Sue and me a bite of supper? Do you think that might soothe her ruffled feathers?" Maybe. It was worth a try.

Fifteen minutes later, with the kitchen table set with two large mugs of vegetable soup, plates with grilled cheese sandwiches and glasses of iced tea, Vic stood back and appreciated his handiwork. Just one more thing. He opened the bag of macadamia nut cookies and laid two on each napkin. There—protein, vegetables and dessert.

"Come on, Lucky. Go upstairs with me and see if you can help me persuade Penny Sue to come downstairs and have supper with me. After all, we guys need to stick together."

Lucky followed Vic out of the kitchen, down the hall and up

the stairs. Vic paused when he reached Penny Sue's room. Take a deep breath and knock, he told himself.

After knocking twice, he waited. No response. He knocked again. Still nothing.

"Penny Sue, I've fixed us some soup and grilled cheese sandwiches. We should eat supper while it's hot."

Dead silence.

Vic looked down at Lucky. "I think she's still angry with me."

Although Lucky wasn't capable of saying anything, Vic got the impression that if he could talk, he would have said, "She wants you to beg and plead, so just go ahead and do it."

"Penny Sue? Honey? Please, come downstairs and eat supper. I'm…we…Lucky's worried about you."

"I'm not hungry," Penny Sue said from the other side of the closed door. "Besides, skipping a meal won't hurt me. I need to lose weight anyway, don't I?"

"You don't need to change anything about yourself. You're perfect just the way you are." Vic had never sweet-talked a woman in his life, so he wasn't sure where that line of bull had come from or if he'd actually meant it.

The door cracked open a couple of inches and Penny Sue peeked out at him. "If I come downstairs and eat supper with you, will you watch both videos with me tonight?"

Vic let out a sigh of relief. That hadn't been too difficult. She had forgiven him a lot quicker than he'd thought she would. "Yeah, I'll watch the movies with you."

She eased the door open a little further. "You promise?"

"I promise."

She opened the door all the way, stepped out into the hall and offered him a sly smile that sent off a warning signal in his brain. He felt as if somehow he'd just been hoodwinked.

Penny Sue curled up on the sofa in the den, Lucky snuggled against her, halfway under the heavy cotton throw. Five minutes into *Overboard,* Vic had become restless and started giving her you-tricked-me glances, but it wasn't until three-quarters through the movie, when Kurt Russell kissed Goldie Hawn, that Vic voiced an opinion.

"Is the other movie an estrogen flick, too?" he asked.

She smiled at him and said, "*Ladyhawk* is an incredible love story about two doomed lovers. She is a hawk by day and a human by night. He is a human by day and a wolf by night. Only in those brief moments at sunrise and sunset are they both human. I cry every time I see the movie."

Vic groaned. "Oh, great. More tears."

"What did you say?"

"Nothing."

"You'll love the ending of this movie." She focused on the television screen. "It's just so sweet."

Vic forced a fake smile.

She had made him sit in the chair across from her. No way was she going to allow him to share the sofa with Lucky and her. Not yet. But later...

"Why don't I fix us some popcorn before we start the next movie," he said, already halfway to his feet.

She waved him down, then pointed her index finger directly at his chair, a nonverbal order for him to sit. "But you'll miss the end of this one and you don't want to do that. It's just so precious."

"I'll survive." He stayed on his feet.

"No, no. I insist you stay and see the end." Penny Sue smiled and deliberately batted her eyelashes. "Then we can fix the popcorn together and grab a couple of colas from the fridge."

Vic slumped down in his chair.

Oh, poor baby, Penny Sue thought when she looked at him. He's in misery.

*Serves him right!*

She forced herself not to glance his way until the very end of the movie, then she sighed dreamily, looked at him and said, "You can give me a little girl."

"What?" He practically jumped out of his skin.

"I love it when Kurt Russell asks her what he could possibly give her since she's so rich and she looks around at his four sons and says, 'You can give me a little girl.'" Penny Sue let out a very feminine sound of delight.

"What do you call that?" he asked.

"What?"

"That sound you just made. It was a cross between a squeal and a whine."

"Oh? Then it must have been a wheal," she told him jokingly.

"Must have been," he grumbled.

"Now for popcorn and colas before we watch *Ladyhawk*." She hopped to her feet. Lucky scrambled out from beneath the cotton throw, looked up at the two humans, then plopped back down on the sofa.

Vic glanced at her, hope in his expression. "Would you mind if I skipped—"

"You promised." She stopped and gave him a don't-you-dare-disappoint-me look.

"You're enjoying watching me suffer, aren't you?"

"Ah… How can you say that? Would someone as sweet as I am do such a terrible thing? And you did say I was sweet, didn't you?"

"I'm reconsidering the sweet part."

"Hmm… You probably should. After all, I'm not sure women who are pains in the…uh…the derriere can be considered sweet."

"Just how long will I have to do penance for that statement?"

She slipped her arm through his and, whistling all the way, led him into the kitchen. She had no intention of answering his question. Let him wonder. Let him worry. Let him suffer.

Two and a half hours later, they sat together on the sofa, Lucky nestled between them, and watched the happily-ever-after ending of *Ladyhawk*. Penny Sue had teared up several times and actually cried out loud during one scene. He'd found himself putting his arm around her and soothing her at that point and had been rewarded by her laying her head on his shoulder. Damn if he hadn't felt like a teenager on a date, sitting in his girlfriend's parents' den and expecting them to come barging in at any minute.

"Wasn't that the most romantic movie you've ever seen?" Penny Sue looked at him, sincerity in her eyes.

She actually wanted him to answer that question? Yeah, apparently she did. "Mmm...hmm," was all he could manage.

She snuggled against him, her body warm, her scent sweet and alluring. He'd been sitting here with a hard-on for the past thirty minutes.

He'd had his share of one-night stands, a few with women he barely knew. If the woman at his side was anyone on earth other than Penny Sue Paine, he'd take her here and now. Right on the sofa. But despite how much he wanted her, there were more reasons to avoid having sex with her than reasons to proceed. First of all, her aunt Dottie, not to mention Ruby and Tully, might walk in on them at any moment. Secondly, he didn't think Penny Sue had finished punishing him, so she was likely to say no to any proposition he made her tonight. And last and most important—if they had sex, Penny Sue was just the type who'd think she was in love and expect some sort of a commitment.

"You really aren't interested in romance, are you?" she asked him bluntly.

"Most men aren't."

"Just sex, huh?"

"I suppose to men sex *is* romance," he told her.

"It isn't to women."

"To some women it is."

"No, you're wrong there. It's just that some women pretend it is."

"I stand corrected."

"Vic?" She draped her arm across his waist and curled her hand softly into his side.

"Huh?" He swallowed. In his mind he heard her sultry, molasses-sweet voice telling him what he wanted to hear and using terminology he knew Penny Sue would never use.

"Have you noticed that I didn't talk your ear off while we were watching the movies?"

Reality was a major let-down from his fantasy.

If he were honest with her, he'd admit that he hadn't noticed, that he'd been torn between the sheer agony of being forced to watch back-to-back chick flicks and fighting the urge to jump her bones. Sometimes it just didn't pay to be honest.

"Of course I noticed," he lied.

She laughed. "Since you've been so good tonight, I'm thinking about forgiving you."

"I'd appreciate that."

"If I weren't a client, would you be so agreeable?"

You've already lied to her once, just do it again. "Maybe." When she frowned, he said, "Probably."

She smiled again, then reached over, speared her fingers through his hair at the back of his head and kissed him on the cheek. "I have a surprise for you. Something you're going to love."

He eyed her skeptically.

But before he could ask or she could explain further, her aunt Dottie breezed into the den, her spoiled-rotten cat, Puff, in her arms. "I just got home and thought I'd come in to say goodnight." She waved a hand at Vic. "No, no, don't get up. I'm off to bed. See y'all in the morning."

She floated out like a little fairy princess in her lightweight pink cape.

"Does she ever wear any other color besides pink?" Vic asked.

"Of course she does. Pink just happens to be her favorite and it's a big fashion color this year, too. Didn't you notice that I'm wearing pink?" She patted the left sleeve of her sweater.

"Oh." Naturally, Penny Sue would know what all of this year's big fashion colors were. "Uh, are you about ready to go upstairs?"

She lifted her shoulders and sighed. "I am getting sleepy."

"Why don't you go on up," he said. "I'll take Lucky out."

"I'll go with you and tell you all about the big surprise. And I'll give you a little hint right now. It's a way of thanking you for saving Lucky and the other animals last night."

He'd forgotten that she'd mentioned having a surprise for him. Something he'd like. It's not what you want, he told himself. It was probably something silly, like a key to the city or a certificate claiming him hero of the month. He could handle either just as long as he didn't have to make a public acceptance speech. Vic hated crowds almost as much as he hated being the center of attention. He'd always preferred keeping a low profile.

"Okay, come along," he said, then called out to Lucky, "Come on, boy. Time to get your job done for the night."

Vic followed Penny Sue and Lucky to the mud room, just off the kitchen, where he'd hung his coat and gun holster on one in a row of wooden pegs, before he'd fixed supper and fed Lucky.

Penny Sue watched him while he strapped on the holster. "Do you always carry a gun?"

"It's part of the job."

"And when you're not on an assignment?"

"I still carry it most of the time," he admitted.

"Why?" She handed him his coat, then pulled an oversized jacket, probably Ruby's, off another peg.

"I feel naked without one." He put on his sports coat, which neatly concealed the holster.

Penny Sue slipped on the old jacket, then removed Lucky's leash from the peg where Vic had hung it earlier. "What did you do before you became a Dundee agent?"

He took the leash from her, bent down and attached it to Lucky's collar, then opened the back door to let Lucky go outside. He followed directly behind the dog, but paused to hold the door open for Penny Sue.

"I worked for the U.S. government," he told her.

She stepped out onto the back porch. "FBI? DEA…?"

"CIA."

"Oh."

The crisp night air smelled of fruit-tree blossoms. He'd noticed the first time he came out here that there were apple, peach and pear trees in the backyard, just beyond the garage. Overhead the sky was clear and filled with stars. A half moon partially illuminated the yard, but dark shadows obscured the nooks and crannies around the backs of trees and shrubs and across the garage and gazebo.

"Did you work in an office?" she asked as they followed Lucky from the porch to the yard.

"Sometimes, but I worked outside the U.S., in the field, a great deal of the time."

"In dangerous places?"

"What is it that you really want to ask me, honey? Do you want to know if I've killed anyone, if I've used my gun to defend myself and others?"

"Have you?"

Lucky growled.

"What's the matter, boy?" Vic asked the dog.

"You didn't answer my question," Penny Sue said.

"The answer is yes."

"Yes, you have used your gun?"

"Yes, I have used a gun to protect myself and others. And yes, I have killed. More than once."

Lucky growled again and sniffed around in a circle.

"I wonder what's wrong with him." Penny Sue watched the dog's odd behavior. "I've never seen him act like this. What's the matter, Lucky? Did you hear something?"

Lucky barked. Then he barked again and again, taking a stance as if he'd treed something. He was focused on something at the back of the yard, something hiding in the dark.

Suddenly the back gate leading to the alley flew open and then shut. Lucky went wild, growling and barking, straining to go beyond the confinement of his leash. Then other growls and barks joined Lucky's, and two medium-size, four-legged silhouettes materialized from out of the shadows.

Penny Sue shrieked when the two snarling pit bulls raced toward Lucky. With no time to waste, Vic lifted Lucky, tossed him to Penny Sue and then drew his Glock from his holster.

"Run!" he told her.

"Vic?"

"Run, damn it."

She ran.

The pit bulls came toward him, their sharp teeth bared, and just as one hurled itself at him to attack, he shot the animal, aiming not to kill but to maim. The wounded dog howled and dropped just as the other dog snapped at Vic's leg. He felt the monster's teeth rip through his pants and into his flesh. He aimed straight down and fired.

Penny Sue called from the porch, "Vic, are you all right?"

He stood there staring at the two dogs, one wounded, the other possibly dead. His hand holding the Glock trembled ever so slightly. He hated harming dumb animals, ones that acted on instinct or as they'd been bred to act. It was easier to kill a person bent on doing you harm than an animal who would and could kill you.

"Call Doc Stone," Vic said. "One of them is still alive. Maybe both."

The police had come and gone, called by the neighbors when they'd heard the shooting. Penny Sue identified the two pit bulls as looking a great deal like dogs belonging to that good-for-nothing Freddy Long. For years, Freddy had been suspected not only of fighting his dogs, but of selling drugs and being a dope addict himself. "Nothing but trailer trash" was how her aunt Dottie referred to Freddy and people such as he.

"We'll talk to Freddy," Officer Kent had assured them. "If those were his dogs, we'll sure find out what they were doing loose in town."

Shortly after the police arrived, Doc Stone came and took the two animals away. Both still had been alive. Just barely. He'd told them that he would drive the dogs over to Minor Hill to the vet's there and assist his colleague in trying to save the animals' lives.

"You need to get that leg taken care of," Doc Stone had told Vic.

"I'll take him to the hospital," Penny Sue had said.

That had been over three hours ago, and she and Vic were just now returning home from the emergency room where the doctor on duty had sewn up Vic's ripped calf, given him several injections and a supply of pain medication.

Ruby met them at the back door. "We were beginning to worry."

"You know how it is at the emergency room," Penny Sue said. "It can take forever."

Tully stood just inside the kitchen, Lucky held securely in his arms. He had sworn to Vic that he wouldn't let Lucky out of his sight while they were at the hospital. And since Lottie had set up a trust fund pension for the Coxes, they were not heirs and therefore not suspects. Vic could trust them with Lucky.

"You should take him straight upstairs to bed." Aunt Dottie fluttered around them as they entered the kitchen. "You poor dear. It must hurt something awful. I was bitten by a dog once when I was a little girl and from that day forward I've preferred cats."

"Y'all didn't have to stay up and wait for us." Penny Sue figured that Vic would have preferred much less fanfare.

"We couldn't have gone off to bed and gotten any sleep," Ruby said. "The phone's been ringing off the hook. Half the town knows that a couple of Freddy Long's pit bulls attacked Mr. Noble in our backyard. Everyone's greatly concerned about Mr. Noble and about our Penny Sue and little Lucky."

"I'll come back down for Lucky once I get Vic settled," Penny Sue told Tully.

"I'm perfectly capable of walking upstairs and putting myself to bed without any help," Vic said. "Go ahead and take Lucky now."

"Is there anything we can do?" Tully asked.

Vic shook his head, then walked out of the kitchen. Tully put Lucky on the floor and when Penny Sue left the room, he followed her. By the time she reached her bedroom, Vic had already gone inside the nursery and closed the door halfway.

"Are you okay in there?" she asked.

"Yeah."

Lucky disregarded any need Vic had for privacy as he shoved open the door between the two rooms and ran straight to Vic. Penny Sue stood in the doorway, hesitant about approaching the wounded lion. Vic had been distant and cold on the ride to the hospital and no better on the drive home. He'd done little more than flinch when the doctor sewed up his leg and the wound had been deep and nasty. It must have hurt him terribly, but you'd never have known by the way he acted. Stoic. Expressionless. And quiet. Much too quiet.

After speaking quietly to Lucky, who lay down at his feet, Vic removed his bloody, torn slacks and tossed them aside, then took off his jacket and his empty holster. He'd left the gun on the back porch before they drove to the hospital. After taking off his shirt, he sat on the edge of the bed and reached down to remove his shoes. Penny Sue noticed him wince.

She rushed into the room, knelt down in front of him, beside Lucky, and removed his shoes.

"I don't need any help," he growled at her.

Lucky lifted his head and looked at Vic. Penny Sue stroked Lucky's back and patted him on the head, soothing his agitation. Then ignoring Vic's grumpiness, she yanked off his socks, then ran her fingertips in the air over his bandaged calf. "If it hadn't been for you, those dogs would have killed Lucky and possibly me, too."

"Yeah."

"Thank goodness you were here."

"And had my gun with me."

She nodded, then still on her knees, gazed up at him. "You had no choice but to shoot them. Those poor animals were bred to be killers. That Freddy Long should be hung by his private parts from the highest tree in the state of Alabama."

Vic's lips twitched as if he was amused.

"You certainly have a way with words, honey."

"Everybody knows that man is worthless trash, but how he could allow those dogs to get loose in town and—"

Vic placed his index finger over her lips. "Stop and think about exactly what happened tonight." When she looked at him, puzzled by his statement, he continued. "Don't you remember the back gate opening and closing quickly?"

Oh, mercy! In all the hullabaloo, she'd forgotten about it. "Yes. You're right."

"Someone opened the back gate and let those pit bulls loose in your backyard when they knew Lucky was outside."

"Someone put those dogs in the backyard to kill Lucky, didn't they?"

"And whoever did it either didn't stop to consider the fact that you or I could be harmed or they simply didn't care."

## Chapter 8

$V$ic finished off his third biscuit, then downed his fourth cup of coffee. If he stayed in Alabaster Creek much longer and kept eating Ruby's big Southern breakfasts, he'd put on ten pounds by the end of a month. He wasn't accustomed to eating eggs, sausage, hash browns and grits every morning. And Ruby's huge buttermilk biscuits were irresistible, as were her homemade jellies and preserves. Grape, strawberry, peach and pear.

Penny Sue sat across from him, sipping coffee laced liberally with cream and sugar. She alternated between tossing Lucky what she referred to as "last bites" and gazing out the floor-to-ceiling bay window in the breakfast room.

"You're awfully quiet this morning," he said.

She focused her gaze on him. "You men are all alike." Her smile told him that she was teasing instead of scolding. "You can't be satisfied, can you? If I talk too much, you want me to shut up and if I'm quiet, you think something's wrong."

His mind wandered off into dangerous waters, concentrating on the "you can't be satisfied, can you?" comment. He knew exactly what would satisfy him.

Get your mind off sex.

"You've had to deal with some difficult things and it's understandable that you'd be worried," Vic told her. "Someone is trying to kill Lucky and whoever that person is, he or she apparently doesn't care who else gets hurt."

"I can't believe a member of my family could be so ruthless and cold-blooded. It was bad enough when Lucky was shot, but the fire could have killed numerous other animals and it completely destroyed Doc Stone's clinic. That's unforgivable. And then to make matters worse, they set two vicious pit bulls loose to attack Lucky and one of them attacked you. What sort of person could be capable of such horrible things?"

"A greedy person," Vic said. "Maybe a desperate person."

"Speaking of your being attacked…" Ruby poured Vic a fresh cup of coffee. "How's the leg this morning?"

"It's okay," he said.

"It must be." Penny Sue gave him a condemning glare. "He refused to take any of the pain pills the ER doctor gave him. Of course, you know how these macho men are. They don't feel any pain the way we mere mortals do."

Vic frowned, remembering how Penny Sue had hovered over him last night after they'd returned from the emergency room. His refusal to take the prescription pain medication had nothing to do with machismo. Years ago, on one of his first assignments, he'd been captured and held prisoner in a godforsaken country half a world away from the United States. Having been tortured mercilessly before being rescued, he'd found it all too easy to become addicted to pain medication when he later recuperated in an army hospital.

"Whoever this person is, he or she is not a Paine by blood. I refuse to believe that any blood relative of mine would intentionally harm a pet dog," Dottie said as she appeared in the doorway, dressed this morning in a pair of black slacks and a frilly, hot-pink blouse. At eight in the morning, the elderly woman had her makeup on and her hair fixed, just as Penny Sue did. Even Ruby sported a touch of rouge and lipstick.

As Dottie walked into the room, her black high heels tapped against the hardwood floor.

"I agree with you," Penny Sue told her aunt. "At least in theory. My mind tells me that the evidence points to one of the heirs and my heart tells me that it cannot be one of the people we know so well and love so dearly."

After sitting, Dottie motioned to Ruby, then looked at Vic. "Of course, shooting those wild beasts last night was entirely justifiable. Animals who have been trained to kill are a menace. The law should have done something about Freddy Long's inhumane treatment of those animals long before now."

Ruby put a plate of scrambled eggs, sausage and two buttered biscuits in front of Dottie. Within half a minute, she poured coffee into Dottie's cup and added a dollop of cream.

"Before I came downstairs this morning, I phoned my boss, Sawyer McNamara, and explained what happened last night," Vic said. "He's going to do his best to get another agent sent in to help me with the investigation as soon as possible since guarding Lucky has turned out to be a little more complicated than we first thought. Whoever the perp is, he or she doesn't seem to be afraid to risk human lives in order to get to Lucky. I hope we'll have another agent here as early as tomorrow."

"Good," Dottie said emphatically. "We need to put a stop to these attempts on Lucky's life; they're now endangering others. And apparently, the only way to do that is to apprehend the culprit."

"You're right." Penny Sue looked directly at her aunt. "You don't object to my spending more of Lucky's inheritance on hiring another Dundee agent?"

"No, of course not. At least not now, after everything that's happened." Dottie opened her already sliced and buttered biscuit and smeared a liberal amount of pear preserves on both pieces. "We can narrow down the field of suspects by eliminating all blood relatives."

"Miss Dottie, I don't think I can do that," Vic said. "As much as you'd like to believe none of your immediate kin are responsible, we can't be a hundred percent sure."

"And as much as I hate to agree, he's right, Aunt Dottie. We can't eliminate anyone until we're sure—"

"Am I a suspect?" Dottie dropped her biscuit onto her china plate.

"Of course not," Penny Sue said.

"If you can't eliminate Douglas and Eula and the others, then you can hardly eliminate me. After all, if Lucky dies, I stand to gain as much as Douglas does and a bit more than all the others."

Penny Sue reached over and patted her aunt's hand. "You don't have a mean bone in your body. And you're certainly not greedy. You're one of the most generous people I've ever known. Besides that, you love animals."

"So does Douglas. He loves Lucky and Puff," Dottie said. "Percy and Douglas always had a dog when they were boys, and we all had ponies. I had a cat and Lottie had a dog, and we raised baby chicks once and Percy raised rabbits, and there were the love birds my daddy bought my mama for their anniversary one year.

"Mercy me, I'll never forget the sight of Mama crying and then kissing Daddy when he gave her those birds. It was the one and only time I ever saw them openly affectionate, you know. People of their generation weren't much into kissing and touching and such in front of others. Besides, our daddy was a very reserved gentleman. He never once told us he loved us, but he showed us in countless ways." Barely taking a breath, Dottie continued, "Douglas reminds me a lot of Daddy, just as Percy reminded me so much of Uncle Henry. That was my Daddy's brother, Cousin Eula's father. Such a dear, kind man. And the epitome of Southern manhood at its best."

What was it with these Paine women? Vic wondered. Had they all been born talking non-stop? Had they popped out, said hello to the doctor and told everyone in the delivery room about their experiences before, during and immediately after birth?

Penny Sue patted her aunt's hand again. "Yes, I know how impossible it is to think Uncle Douglas could be behind the attempts on Lucky's life. It's not as if we're accusing him or anyone else of the crimes," Penny Sue tried to explain. "But someone has tried to kill Lucky three times and there's no reason for anyone, other than someone with something to gain, to want Lucky dead."

"Then it must be Douglas's wife Candy or Clayton's wife Phyllis," Dottie said. "Or what about Dylan? I'd think after what he did to you, you'd have put him at the head of any suspects list. He pretends to like Puff and Lucky, but it's all an act. I can see through that young man, despite the way he has always acted like such a gentleman around Lottie and me."

"You're probably right about the culprit being one of the in-laws." Penny Sue squeezed her aunt's hand reassuringly. "Vic will start the investigation with Dylan and Phyllis and Candy, won't you, Vic?"

"Sure, why not," he said. "We have to start somewhere." Vic would begin by checking the in-laws' alibis for the time when the fire at the clinic had been set. Then he'd check everyone else's alibis. But she didn't need to know that—not yet.

Dottie sighed dramatically, apparently satisfied with her niece's promise and Vic's agreement, then resumed eating her breakfast.

Vic glanced at Penny Sue and noted the relieved expression on her face. Was this what her entire life had been like? he wondered. Placating her elderly aunts, trying to please them and her father, keeping the family content? If so, then he understood why Lottie Paine had made Penny Sue executor of her will, other than the fact she was probably the only relative the old woman had trusted completely. Lottie must have thought that if anyone could keep peace in the family, protect Lucky and manage to fulfill her dying wishes, Penny Sue could. He might be wrong of course, but he suspected that she had been playing the role of family diplomat all her life. Seeing this gorgeous, chatty Southern belle in a new light made him wonder if he had misjudged her. Women with bubbly personalities are often thought of as airheads, and he had to admit that originally he'd pegged Penny Sue for just such a woman. Silly, flirtatious, clinging, helpless. Had he mistaken gentleness for weakness?

Penny Sue offered Vic a pleasant smile, one that said everything was going to be all right. He gave her a hesitant, closed-mouth smile—the best he could manage—somehow sensing that she needed his support and approval.

"I'll be ready to go to the shop as soon as I brush my teeth and grab my purse," Penny Sue said. "It's looking overcast this morning, so it could be raining later. Would you prefer taking the car instead of walking?"

"Whatever you'd like," Vic replied.

"We could walk into town this morning and if it's raining this evening, I'll call and ask Tully to pick us up."

"Okay."

She scooted back her chair and stood. "Lucky and I will meet you on the front porch in ten minutes."

Vic set his cup on the matching porcelain saucer. "Wait and I'll go up with you two. I need to get my laptop and take it with me so I can do some investigative work while keeping an eye on Lucky today."

"Aren't computers marvelous things?" Dottie paused her coffee cup in mid-sip. "I've made numerous friends online. I simply don't know what I did before e-mail."

Although totally surprised that such an old-fashioned lady would own a computer, let alone know how to use one, Vic just nodded as he rose from his chair and followed Penny Sue out of the kitchen. That was another thing about these Paine women—they constantly surprised him.

As they started up the back stairs, Vic clutched Penny Sue's arm to halt her. She turned and smiled, her gaze questioning him. Lucky stopped beside her and looked up at Vic.

"Tell me something," he said.

"If I can."

"Does the burden of looking after the entire Paine family ever become too heavy on those beautiful little shoulders?"

Her smile vanished, replaced with a bewildered expression. "How did you know…I mean is it all that obvious? You're the first person who has ever said anything."

"Just a wild guess. I've noticed the way you handle your aunt Dottie. And it's apparent that Ruby and Tully look to you for their orders. And there's your cousin Eula, who retired with a good pension, right?" Penny Sue nodded. "But you gave her a job at your shop to keep her from being bored. And despite the fact that your cousin Valerie stole your fiancé, you're civil to her. And your aunt Lottie probably had come to depend on you long ago, which is one of the reasons she made you executor of her will."

"It seems odd to me that you actually looked beyond the obvious," she said.

"Which is?"

"I talk and laugh too much. I'm old-fashioned and my thinking tends to be illogical more often than not. I'm pretty much ruled by my emotions. I get my feelings hurt easily, I cry easily and I can throw a hissy fit with the best of them." She sucked in a deep breath, then huffed quietly. "But from the time I was a little girl, I refereed spats between my aunts and did my best to keep them both content. And my father...well, he told me himself that if it hadn't been for me, he might have killed himself when my mother died. You see, he loved her terribly."

Vic cringed. How dare a grown man tell a child such a thing? How dare he put such a burden of emotional responsibility on her shoulders?

"And what did you do when Dylan Redley ran off with Valerie?"

"I threw a royal hissy fit." She frowned sadly, obviously remembering that unhappy time. "Then I got on with my life."

"And when they came back to town, Redley and Valerie, what did you do?"

She gave him a puzzled look. "I don't know what you mean."

"When Valerie and her husband moved back to Alabaster Creek and started sucking up to your aunt Lottie, did you tell your aunt she shouldn't trust them? Did you remind her of what they'd done?"

"She knew they were sucking up," Penny Sue said. "Aunt Lottie was a shrewd lady. And I didn't have to remind her that Valerie had disgraced the family. But in the long run, Valerie is family and—"

"And because she's your cousin, you forgave her and everyone welcomed her back into the bosom of the family?"

"That's the way families are." Penny Sue walked up several

steps, then paused and glanced over her shoulder at Vic. "I really haven't forgiven Valerie completely, although seeing what a good-for-nothing Dylan turned out to be has made me realize she did me a favor by stealing him from me."

Vic followed her when she continued up the stairs, Lucky on her heels. The little mutt seemed devoted to Penny Sue. No doubt after Lottie Paine died, he had gradually bonded with his new care-taker. As Vic had recently learned, bonding with Penny Sue wasn't all that difficult. In fact it was downright easy.

"Do you think Valerie and Dylan could be behind the attempts on Lucky's life?" Vic asked.

"You want the truth? There's a tiny, vengeful part of me that would like to think they're the guilty parties, but…"

"But?"

"But just because Valerie is a slut and Dylan is an idiot, that doesn't make them cruel or vicious. And whoever is behind these attempts on Lucky's life is an evil person."

Mean as the devil and greedy as hell, Vic thought. But evil in the truest sense of the word, probably not. However, Penny Sue had no means of comparison. In her world, shooting a dog or torching a vet clinic was evil. In his world, torturing, killing and maiming innocent human beings was evil. If she had seen the slaughter he had… Thank God she hadn't. Thank God not many people had.

"Vic? Vic, are you all right?"

"Huh?" What had just happened? Had he faded out of reality there for a second?

She clasped his hand in hers. Lucky lifted his head and sniffed as if sizing up the situation. "You had the most peculiar look on your face. Is your leg hurting? If it is, you should take one of those pain pills and lie down for a while. I can take Lucky to the shop with me and keep an eye on him until you're feeling better. And if we get really busy today, which I doubt we will, I'll just call in extra help. I have several part-time employees, so it shouldn't be a problem to—"

He grabbed her. She gasped. He kissed her, thereby silencing her.

Lucky whined a couple of times, probably his way of asking his mistress if she was all right or if he should attack the guy who'd grabbed her.

But Penny Sue didn't seem to be in trouble, judging by the way she responded to him. She had the sweetest lips. Warm, soft, pliable. And heaven help him, when she returned his kiss, her mouth eager and hungry, he couldn't stop himself from taking things a step further than he'd intended. When his tongue probed, she opened up to him without hesitation. Her eager response brought him to his senses quicker than any hesitation on her part would have. It told him that she wanted him.

He ended the kiss abruptly, then lifted his head slowly. She gazed up at him with half-closed eyes and sighed.

"Vic?" When she spoke his name, it sounded like a sultry invitation.

He stepped back away from her, cleared his throat and squared his shoulders. "We have to stop doing that."

"Why?" She batted her eyelashes at him flirtatiously. "I rather like it. Don't you?"

"Yeah, honey, I do. And that's exactly why I can't let it happen again."

She leaned toward him, lifted her right hand and laid it on his shoulder. "Do you believe in love at first sight?"

Every nerve in his body froze. This couldn't be happening. Not to him. He'd made a rule of staying away from good girls as if they were a plague.

"Don't go there," he told her, then turned and walked down the hall ahead of her. "I'll get my laptop and be ready to leave whenever you are."

"Vic Noble!" She called his name in a don't-you-turn-your-back-on-me tone.

Vic paused. "Let's not do this. It was just a kiss."

"It was an incredible kiss."

"I kissed you to shut you up."

"That seems to be becoming a habit with you."

When he heaved a deep sigh, his shoulders lifted and dropped. With his back to her, he said, "I don't believe in love at first sight. I don't even believe in love. Not the kind of love you're talking about."

"Oh."

She uttered that one word with such disappointment that even Lucky picked up on it and started whimpering.

"It's all right, sweetie," Penny Sue said to the dog. "I'm fine."

Vic glanced over his shoulder for half a second, just in time to see her lift Lucky into her arms. While the getting was good, he walked hurriedly down the hall and into her bedroom, leaving the door wide open for her. By the time she and Lucky reached the bedroom, he'd already gone into the adjoining room and had closed the door behind him. Standing there in the sitting room-cum-nursery, he closed his eyes, took a deep breath and called himself every kind of fool known to man.

Hell fire! He was Vic Noble, a former CIA operative who had a heart of stone. He was a highly trained professional who didn't let emotions enter into any assignment. So what had happened to him? How was it possible that some woman he barely knew had turned him inside out and had him acting totally out of character?

Whatever voodoo spell Penny Sue had cast on him wasn't going to work. All he had to do was hang in there, treat her like any other client and do his job. And when the other Dundee agent showed up, he could hand over the personal bodyguard duties to him and he would be free to do the investigative work. That way, he wouldn't be spending twenty-four/seven with temptation.

Lucky lay at Vic's feet—actually he lay *on* Vic's feet. The pooch was definitely spoiled and needed to be around people to be content. While Penny Sue handled the daily chores of running a business, Vic set up shop in a back storage room that held several odds and ends of furniture, including a table he was using as a desk. He had hauled in a chair from the store, one that looked sturdy enough to support a man of his size, and placed his laptop on the desk. For the past three hours he had been in touch with Daisy, via e-mail and cell phone. He had compiled a suspects list that included every heir to Lottie Paine's fortune, and despite

Penny Sue's promise to Aunt Dottie, he was investigating all the heirs, including the blood relatives. Just because they didn't want to believe that a relative was capable of the crimes that had been committed didn't mean someone with the last name of Paine wasn't the perpetrator. These people had a warped sense of family loyalty. He had learned long ago that relatives were as likely, if not more likely, to screw you as anyone else. Of course, he had developed a cynical view of the world, whereas Penny Sue and Miss Dottie tended to be optimists. Both of them were still looking at life through rose-tinted lenses.

From headquarters in Atlanta, Daisy had instigated an initial search for information on all the suspects. He needed to know everything he could find out about each one, things most people would consider insignificant. But you never knew when an apparently insignificant tidbit of info would prove useful.

Of course, he needed to know if anyone had a criminal record or a history of mental illness or violent behavior. And he needed to find out who did and who didn't have alibis for when Lucky was shot and for when the clinic fire was set. The police had dismissed Lucky's shooting as an accident, but they could not readily dismiss a deliberately set fire.

Vic grunted.

God knew that even from his brief acquaintance with the Paine family, he'd lay odds that there was more than one nut hanging on the family tree.

Did any of the heirs own pets? He couldn't see an animal lover shooting Lucky or setting fire to a veterinary clinic.

Was one of the heirs in debt and desperate for money? Normal greed didn't usually prompt someone to commit a crime, but desperation could and often did.

There were numerous little telltale signs that a person could be guilty. Vic needed to find out who among the suspects was the most likely not only to have a motive, but to be capable of the crimes that had been committed.

His cell phone rang half a minute before someone knocked on the closed door.

"Yeah," he called.

Penny Sue opened the door. "Time for lunch." She eyed the cell phone in his hand and mouthed, "Sorry."

Vic flipped open his cell phone. "Noble here."

"Vic, it's Daisy."

"Yeah, honey, hold just a sec, will you?" He focused on Penny Sue. "I need to take this call. Give me a couple of minutes, okay?"

She nodded. "I ordered lunch from the Country Kettle and they just delivered it." She held up the large plastic bag containing two covered foam plates. "While I have two part-timers here today, I can take a whole hour for lunch and I thought it would be nice for the two of us—" she glanced at Lucky who had raised his head and was looking at her "—the three of us to have a sort of picnic back here.

"I'll be quiet as a mouse while I'm setting things up. You go right ahead with your phone call. You won't even know I'm here. And if Lucky follows me back into the shop when I go get a few other things, don't worry about him. I'll keep an eye on him."

Vic stared at her. She stared back at him.

"What?" she asked.

"Are you finished?"

"Huh?"

He held up his hand and flapped his fingers against his thumb in a talk-talk-talk gesture.

"Oh, you meant was I finished talking?"

He nodded.

"Yes, I'm finished. For now. So go ahead and take your call. You're keeping your *honey* waiting."

"My honey?"

"That's what you called her."

Vic groaned. "I call all women honey."

"Oh."

He held up his cell phone. "Daisy Holbrook is the Dundee office manager. This is a business call." Why had he bothered explaining to Penny Sue that this call wasn't personal?

Doing his best to ignore Penny Sue, Vic returned to his telephone call. "Sorry to keep you on hold. What's up?"

"Miss Paine seemed concerned that you'd received a call from another woman," Daisy said.

He could hear the laughter in Daisy's voice and could imagine the smile on her face.

"Why did you call?" he asked. "Do you have something for me already?"

"Several somethings as a matter of fact."

"Shoot."

Penny Sue set the lunch sack from the Country Kettle on a partially empty shelf, then headed out the door, pausing only long enough to smile at him and mouth the words, "Be right back." Lucky rose up and off Vic's feet and meandered to the open door, but he didn't leave the safety of the storeroom.

"First of all, Candy Coley Paine has a rap sheet about half a mile long," Daisy said. "Back in Vegas, she worked as a call girl and apparently that's where she met Douglas Paine. But before that, she was picked up in various places across the country not only for solicitation, but a couple of times for shoplifting and once for stabbing her boyfriend. He lived and didn't press charges."

"Interesting, but it doesn't make her a dog killer."

"No, but it does imply she'd do anything for money. And that she's capable of violence."

"That it?"

"Reverend Clayton Dickson's wife Phyllis has a problem. The lady writes bad checks. On four different occasions, the good reverend has paid off her bills to keep her out of jail."

"Hmm…"

"And last, but not least, we have Chris Paine, Douglas Paine's son." Daisy paused for effect. "Chris is a gambler. In the past year, he had to sell his Corvette and take a second mortgage out on his house to pay off gambling debts."

"So, the guy could be desperate for money."

"Could be."

"Okay, let's start with these three. I want an in-depth profile on each of them. But keep digging up dirt on all the others, too."

"Will do. Talk to you soon…honey."

Before Vic could think of an appropriate comeback, Daisy

hung up. And Penny Sue sailed into the room, carrying a quilt, several decorative pillows and a couple of large, fat candles.

She paused in the middle of the storeroom and glared at him. "What makes you think there is any dirt to be dug up on the members of my family?"

"It's just an expression," he assured her. "I'm not accusing anyone of anything. But if there is any dirt to be dug up, then I need to know. It can help me focus on the right person and eliminate others."

Penny Sue stuck her nose in the air disapprovingly and busied herself by spreading the quilt on the floor and adding the pillows. Then she placed the candles in the center of the quilt, pulled a lighter from her pocket and lit the candles.

"What are you doing?" he asked.

"I should think that would be obvious. We're having an indoor picnic."

Yes, of course they were. She had spoken to him as if she doubted his sanity. People had picnics in storerooms all the time, didn't they?

But he didn't get a chance to say anything before Penny Sue hurried out again, this time with Lucky following. Vic rubbed the back of his neck. Where was she going? Their food was on the shelf here in the storeroom.

Several minutes later, she returned carrying lace place mats and matching napkins and real silverware. After arranging everything to her satisfaction, she got the plastic bag containing their lunch off the shelf, removed each item and put their food and drinks neatly on the place mats.

"There," she said, studying her handiwork. "Doesn't that look nice?"

Was that a rhetorical question or did she expect an answer? With Penny Sue, he could never be certain. To be on the safe side, he said, "Yes, it looks...nice." He wasn't sure he'd ever used the word *nice,* so it kind of stuck in his craw.

"Guess what I bought for dessert?" She looked at him as if he was supposed to know.

He shrugged. She smiled. He did his best to smile and found

that it was getting easier. Penny Sue's smiles were infectious, as was her perky, sparkling personality. There was something about her that made others feel good when they were around her. A phrase his grandmother had used in his boyhood came to mind. *A joyful soul*. That's what Penny Sue had, what she was— a joyful soul.

"Can't you guess?" she asked.

"What?"

"The dessert."

"Oh, I...er...pie?"

She frowned.

"Cake?"

"What kind of cake?" she asked.

"I don't know."

"Oh, Vic, you should know that I'd get chocolate. It's my favorite." She laughed. "Well, actually anything chocolate is my favorite. We need to learn these things about each other, you know."

"We do?"

"Of course we do."

He didn't dare ask why because he was pretty sure what she'd say. Hadn't she asked him only this morning if he believed in love at first sight? He should say something to clear up any misunderstandings right here and now. "Look, honey, we need to—"

"Is that a generic honey or a specific, meaningful honey?"

"What?"

She reached out, grasped his hands and urged him to follow her down onto the quilt. Lucky was already lying there, on his tummy, his nose pointing and his black eyes glued to their covered plates of food.

"I ordered iced tea," she told Vic. "Wine would have been better, I suppose. But I don't usually drink this early in the day. Not even wine. Actually, to be honest, I seldom drink alcoholic beverages. Only on special occasions."

Vic sat, crossed his legs and looked over the perfectly laid-out indoor picnic. How many women would have used cloth place mats—lace at that—and napkins, and real silverware for an impromptu lunch on the floor?

"Iced tea is fine," he told her.

"You didn't answer my question."

"Which question was that?"

"You said you call all women honey. So when you just called me honey was that the generic, one-size-fits-all honey or was it a personal honey, just for me? If it was the generic honey, then I'd prefer you call me something else. Maybe sweetheart or dear or darling or sugar. I kind of like sugar. It suits me, don't you think? I mean I am sort of sweet, aren't I? And if you're sweet on me—"

"I'm not going to call you sugar," he said emphatically. "And when I called you honey it was the generic honey. I'm not *sweet* on you. There is nothing personal between us and you know it. I'm your temporary employee. That's all. Got it?"

"My goodness, Vic Noble, what a fuss you're making. You know what they say, don't you, about protesting too much." Penny Sue removed the lids from the covered foam plates and slipped the straws out of their wrappers.

"I'm not protesting," he told her. "I'm simply stating facts." Yeah, for all the good it would do him. Talking to this woman was like talking to a brick wall.

She stuck the straws through the holes in the lids of their foam cups. "Pot roast. Lots of meat, potatoes and carrots. The Country Kettle has great food. You'll love it. It's not quite as good as Ruby's, but close." Penny Sue winked at Vic. "Now, don't you go telling Ruby I said that. It might hurt her feelings, and Lord knows I'd never intentionally hurt anyone's feelings. Not that I'm Miss Perfect, you understand. I'm sure that I have—unintentionally— hurt people's feelings. But never on purpose.

"I'm very sensitive myself. All the Paine women are. We're very emotional. We care deeply about things. And most definitely about people. It could be that's one of the reasons so many of us die old maids. We scare men off just by caring way too much. Do I scare you, Vic?"

A soft rapping on the closed door saved Vic from having to respond. God only knew what he would have said. What man would admit to a woman half his size that he actually was afraid of her? But damn it all, Penny Sue scared the living daylights out of him. He'd never dealt with a woman who drove him nuts and yet at the same time made him want to drag her off to the nearest dark corner and—

"Penny Sue," Eula said through the closed door. "Telephone for you. It's Doc Stone."

"Oh!" Penny Sue jumped up, almost knocking over her tea. "I'll be right there." She glanced at Vic. "Go ahead and eat. I won't be long."

She left in a flash and returned in a few minutes. He hadn't had a chance to do more than taste the sweet tea and spear a gravy-rich potato with his fork. When she reentered the storeroom, he glanced up and the instant he saw her, he knew something was wrong.

He lowered his fork back to the foam plate. "What is it? What's wrong?"

She stood in the doorway, wringing her hands nervously and forcing a smile. "Nothing's wrong. Everything's fine."

A knot formed in the pit of his stomach. "You're acting mighty peculiar."

She came over, sat down beside him and batted her eyelashes. Again. He honestly didn't think she realized what she was doing, batting her eyelashes in a flirtatious way. Her feminine mannerisms were completely natural.

"That was Doc Stone on the phone," she said.

"Yeah. And?"

"And we're invited to a party at his house tonight. You and me and Lucky."

"What kind of party?" He'd never heard of a party where pets were invited, but then he'd never been personally acquainted with a veterinarian.

"Well, you see, that's the thing." She batted her eyelashes at him again and reached out and caressed his arm. "It's a party for you," she told him in a rush, then followed with, "to thank you for saving Lucky and all the other animals at the clinic the night before last. Everyone who had a pet at the clinic will be there, plus a lot of other folks who just want to show their appreciation."

Instant rage hit Vic like a tidal wave. He had to get out of Alabaster Creek, away from Penny Sue and back to some sort of normalcy. He hated parties, hated being in a crowd of strangers to whom he'd have to be pleasant and make idle chitchat. He'd rather walk over hot coals.

"I appreciate the sentiment," he said. "But call Dr. Stone back and tell him that a party isn't necessary."

"Of course it's necessary. Oh, Vic, you can't disappoint all those people. And Doc Stone and his wife Angela are the sweetest people on earth. They'll be terribly hurt if you don't go. And I just know you would never—"

"I'm not going."

"Please."

"No."

She puckered her soft pink lips. Her chin quivered.

He narrowed his gaze and gave her a warning glare. "Don't you dare cry."

"We won't have to stay for long. Just thirty minutes. Please."

She looked at him with those big brown eyes, misty with tears, and God help him, he knew he couldn't refuse her. What was it with her anyway, being able to cry on cue? Any other woman and he'd have ignored her feminine ploys, but with Penny Sue, her actions seemed genuine.

"Thirty minutes," he said. "And that's it."

"Oh, thank you, Vic. Thank you." She leaned over and kissed him on the cheek.

His body tensed immediately. Don't touch her. Don't kiss her. Do not react in any way, he warned himself.

Penny Sue gathered Lucky up in her arms and hugged him. "Isn't our Vic the absolute sweetest man on earth?" She stroked Lucky's head, then released him before picking up a dinner roll from her plate, breaking off a piece and giving it to him.

Had he heard her right? Had she said he was sweet? And what was this "our Vic" business?

"Penny Sue…?"

"Yes, sugar?"

He groaned.

She smiled innocently. "Well, you just said you weren't going to call me sugar. You never said a word about my calling you sugar."

Vic grimaced. Apparently, trying to reason with Penny Sue was a losing battle.

## Chapter 9

Penny Sue put on her new silk party dress. The form-fitting design and the coral-red color did wonders for her. It not only made her auburn hair appear darker, but it made her brown eyes look black and her pale-olive complexion shimmer. Every hourglass-shaped woman should own at least one décolleté dress that exposed some cleavage and hugged her waist and hips. After sitting on the bed to slip into her coral high-heeled sandals, she reached over and picked up the gold pendant necklace that had been an eighteenth birthday present from her aunts. The delicate oval pendant had belonged to her Grandmother Paine. She wore it only on special occasions. And she knew, with absolute certainty, that tonight was going to be special.

Thinking about Vic, she sighed. If she had ever seen a man in desperate need of love and affection, it was Vic. He tried to act as if he was immune to the basic human needs, that he felt nothing romantic for her. But she knew better. Oh, he might be telling himself that he was simply sexually attracted to her, but eventually, he would realize that sex wasn't all he wanted from her. He said he didn't believe in love at first sight, that he didn't even believe in love.

Penny Sue laughed. Had it been only a few days ago that she'd felt the same way, that she had believed there would never be true love and exhilarating passion for her?

She had never dreamed she could fall head over heels for someone she barely knew, a man who hadn't been a part of her life until three days ago. Now, she knew better. She was in love with Vic. No doubt about it. She could deny it all she wanted— and she had—but it didn't change the fact that she was in love. It was one of those crazy, irrational things that didn't make any sense whatsoever. But there it was—true love. And a love stronger and more powerful than anything she could have imagined. Having been in love only once before in her entire life— with Dylan Redley—she knew all the signs. Butterflies in the tummy. Thinking of the other person all the time. Longing to be with him. Filled with happiness the moment he walked into a room. Wanting his kisses, his touches. But with Vic, there was more. A passion afire deep inside her, a longing that urged her to take action.

She rose from the bed, picked up her beige shawl and beige purse and walked across the room. After knocking on the closed door to Vic's room, she waited for a response.

"Be there in a sec," he said.

"Ruby has Lucky downstairs. She's fed him his supper and put on his new blue collar that matches his new leash. So, we're ready whenever you are."

Penny Sue knew that Vic didn't want to attend this party at Doc Stone's in his honor. He seemed reluctant to accept his hero status. Why was that? she wondered. It was apparent that he wasn't a people person and in that respect they were exact opposites. Actually, they seemed to be poles apart in almost every way. Except when it came to duty…to responsibility.

Vic opened the door. Penny Sue let out a long, appreciative sigh.

"You look very handsome," she told him. He wore brown dress slacks, a brown tweed sports coat and an open-collar, beige shirt. No tie.

He surveyed her from head to toe. "You look hot, Miss Penny Sue."

"Thank you, kind sir."

He took her arm and laced it through his. "Let's get this show on the road. We put in an appearance and then leave in thirty minutes. Right?"

"Certainly," she replied. "*If* after we get there, you still want to leave that soon."

He eyed her suspiciously. "Don't do any finagling to try to make me stay longer. And don't you dare use any feminine wiles on me."

"Whatever are you talking about?" She gazed at him innocently.

"You know what I'm talking about. No batting your eyelashes. No puckered lips and quivering chin. And absolutely no crying."

"Whyever would I do any of those things when I know they have no effect on you?"

Vic growled, then, without responding, led her out of the bedroom, down the stairs and into the kitchen to pick up Lucky.

She had promised Vic that she wouldn't force him to stay at the party longer than he wanted, but she had a feeling that once they were there, he'd be willing to prolong their stay. After all, she would be at his side every minute, taking care of him, helping him feel at ease. And what man could resist all that adulation? Besides, tonight was a good time for him to learn that not only could he fit into her world, but that he'd actually like it.

Dottie had read the e-mail over and over again and each time her heart fluttered maddeningly. Tonight was the night. In only a few minutes, she would meet the man with whom she'd been carrying on a cyberspace love affair for the past few months. Hal was a lonely widower with no children, just two cats, Hansel and Gretel. They corresponded on a daily basis, sharing so much of themselves, their innermost feelings and desires. Hal was a romantic. He knew how to use words to sweep a woman off her feet.

Dottie was in love.

Perhaps some people would think it foolish for an old woman in her seventies to want love and romance. And yes, even sex. But what did she care what others thought? Penny Sue was right. They were Paines and people expected the Paines to be eccentric.

She had met Hal in an online grief workshop, where those who had lost loved ones could come and share their pain. Hal had been participating for over a year, ever since his wife's death. And when Dottie joined the group only weeks after Lottie's death, he was the one who had offered her the most comfort, the kindest solace.

Not until a few days ago had they exchanged addresses and they had been delighted to discover that they lived within easy driving distance of each other. He was less than a hundred and fifty miles away, in Birmingham.

It had been Hal's idea to come to Alabaster Creek and rent a motel room for several days so that they could become acquainted face-to-face. She had been the one who'd arranged for them to meet for the first time at the Castle, a renovated building that housed a drugstore in one side and an ice cream parlor in the other. The Castle provided them with a public place for their first meeting, and Dottie had always thought a replica of an old-fashioned malt shop was rather romantic.

Dottie didn't usually drive after dark. Her eyesight wasn't what it used to be. But she certainly hadn't wanted Tully to drive her and ask all sorts of questions. She'd told the Coxes and Penny Sue that she was meeting Evelyn O'Brien to discuss the Easter-egg hunt held each year at the Paine mansion, outside in pretty weather, inside if it rained. She had told only a tiny white lie—she and Evelyn were going to meet tomorrow for lunch.

After carefully parking her 1957 T-bird, a car she had bought new, she stepped out onto the sidewalk. Although she always prided herself on her appearance, tonight she'd wanted to look spectacular. Younger and more vibrant. Of course, not even with plastic surgery and dieting had she been able to maintain the beauty of her youth, but for a woman her age, she looked darn good.

She wasn't the type to go for understated. Leave simple and plain to other women. Lottie had always dressed conservatively, as did Eula. But not Dottie. And not Penny Sue. They liked color and never shied away from reds and yellows. And they loved jewelry. Even Lottie had had a weakness for gold and diamonds.

Tonight Dottie had chosen one of her favorite new outfits. A short black skirt—short enough to show that she still had a great pair of legs—and a yellow jacket with small black polka-dots. Her shoes were black leather, with cute little yellow bows attached.

As she neared the entrance to the Castle, she paused to re-arrange the cluster of gold bangles on her right wrist and the two diamond bracelets and watch on her left wrist. After putting the bracelets in order, she straightened two of the six rings that adorned her fingers.

She flung open the door to the Castle and breezed into the malt shop, confident that she looked absolutely stunning.

"Look for the eager man carrying a bouquet of red roses," Hal had told her in his last e-mail this morning, sent before he left Birmingham.

Dottie glanced around the malt shop, from table to table. Then she saw him. Her heart skipped a beat. All alone at a table near the row of side windows sat a white-haired gentleman wear-ing a navy-blue suit. Lying on the table in front of him was a bou-quet of red roses.

My, he's handsome, Dottie thought. He had a mane of snowy white hair, neatly styled, and sparkling blue eyes. And he was a dapper dresser, too. But best of all, he was probably somewhere between sixty-five and seventy-five years old. It was difficult to tell. At least he wasn't twenty years younger than she, something that had recently crossed her mind because they had never dis-cussed their ages.

When she approached the table, he rose to his feet, a hesitant smile forming on his clean-shaven face. "Miss Dottie Paine?"

"Yes." She bestowed a glowing smile on him. "And you must be Hal Esmond."

"Your servant, ma'am." He bowed. He honest to goodness bowed. Then he took her hand, lifted it to his lips and kissed it.

Dottie giggled like a schoolgirl. Indeed, she felt like a school-girl. Not a day over sixteen. "I'm so pleased to finally meet you." The man was a dream come true, a prince charming if she'd ever met one.

"The pleasure, my dear Dottie, is all mine." He pulled out her chair and gallantly assisted her. "I am hoping that tonight is only the first of many lovely nights we'll share."

Dottie sighed as she gazed up into his true-blue eyes. "I'm sure it will be."

"I'd like to meet your family while I'm in town," he said. "I very much want their approval."

"Yes, of course. You'll meet everyone."

What would Penny Sue say when she found out that Dottie had been having a secret cyberspace romance? Would she approve? Or would she caution Dottie, as Lottie had done in the past, that she shouldn't put her trust in a stranger? Yes, once, long ago, she'd been badly hurt when her fiancé had swindled her out of a sizable amount of money and left her high and dry. And yes, a couple of other times, she had trusted the wrong man despite her family's dire warnings. But Hal was different. She knew he was someone trustworthy, someone who wouldn't break her heart.

Doc and Angela Stone lived in a renovated Craftsman-style house originally built in the early 1920s. The rooms were large and one flowed into the other, making the place perfect for entertaining. The house was filled to capacity with families and their pets, as well as a host of people who'd shown up for various reasons, but mostly to meet Vic Noble, hero. Every time Penny Sue introduced Vic to someone new and they referred to him as a hero, he cringed. Even a nearsighted monkey would have realized how uncomfortable Vic was with all the fawning and oohing and aahing. Doc had set up a makeshift clinic in his sunroom. Angela had told everyone that she'd moved her furniture out of that room and put it in storage, so that her husband could bring in an array of pet carriers to house his patients.

Penny Sue had been reluctant to leave Lucky, but when Doc assured her that his receptionist, Tanya, had volunteered to animal-sit the guests' pets tonight, she had agreed to leave him. Vic, on the other hand, had questioned just how safe Lucky would be since at least sixty people had access to the sunroom tonight. Guests included members of Penny Sue's family, all heirs to Lottie's fortune: Valerie and Dylan Redley, Uncle Douglas and Candy as well as Stacie and Chris.

Doc had slapped Vic on the back and said, "Tanya will keep a close watch over Lucky. This is your night, Mr. Noble. We don't want you worrying about anything. Just have a good time and let all the folks show you how much they appreciate what you did for their pets."

"I can't leave Lucky alone," Vic said. "It's my job to protect him."

"Doc's right." Penny Sue placed a hand on Vic's arm. "Lucky will be just fine with Tanya. She'll keep an eye on him."

Shaking his head, Vic stood his ground. "My leaving him is not a good idea."

"I promise he'll be safe," Doc Stone insisted.

"I'm you boss," Penny Sue told Vic, "and I'm telling you—no, I'm ordering you—to leave Lucky with Tanya."

Even if she had originally concocted tonight's event to punish Vic, she now realized that she wanted the townspeople to meet him, like him and approve of him. And she wanted Vic to receive the homage a true hero deserved.

With a fierce frown on his face, Vic groaned, then reluctantly turned Lucky over to Doc Stone's receptionist and followed Penny Sue into the fray.

They hadn't been there five minutes when she saw Wayne Boggus heading their way. Oh, my. She'd forgotten all about Wayne. However could she make him understand that their budding relationship was over now that she was in love with Vic? The last thing she wanted to do was hurt Wayne's feelings, but she couldn't lead him on.

"Evening, Penny Sue." Wayne glared at Vic. "Mr. Noble."

Vic nodded.

"Lovely party," Penny Sue said.

"Quite a shindig. Doc and Angela are mighty grateful to you, Mr. Noble, for saving all those animals. Everybody here thinks you're a real hero."

"He *is* a real hero," Penny Sue said. "He has saved Lucky's life twice and even saved my life last night."

"Yeah, I heard about that. Damn shame you had to kill those dogs." Wayne looked directly at Vic.

"He had no choice. Besides, you know as well as I do that the police would have had the dogs put to sleep because they attacked us."

"You're right." Wayne shuffled his feet and looked downright uneasy. "I sure hope Mr. Noble finds out who's been trying to kill Lucky." He focused on Vic. "Wonder about how long that'll take?"

"I have no idea," Vic replied.

Wayne turned back to Penny Sue. "Well, since Lucky's in good hands with Mr. Noble, there's no reason for you to be tied down at the house tomorrow night, is there?" Before she could stop him, he went on. "There's a new romantic comedy playing at the movies. I thought maybe we could go see it and then eat a late supper."

"Oh, Wayne. I—I can't."

Vic put his arm around Penny Sue's shoulders. "I'm afraid she'll be busy this weekend helping me with the investigation."

"Is that a fact?" Wayne's expression hardened.

"I'm so sorry," she said. "But Lucky comes first."

"Another time, then." Wayne grumbled to himself as he walked away, not looking back when Penny Sue called his name.

"Let him go," Vic told her. "The guy needs to save a little of his pride."

"Meaning?"

"Meaning the fire chief is a lot more interested in you than you are in him, and your being kind to him won't soothe his feelings any."

"Oh. I suppose you're right."

After they had mixed and mingled for twenty minutes, Vic maneuvered Penny Sue through the crowd and out onto the patio where less than a dozen people congregated, most of them smokers who couldn't go another minute without a cigarette. Neither Doc nor Angela smoked and Angela didn't allow anyone to smoke in her home.

Vic tapped his wristwatch. "Twenty-three minutes and counting."

"You're really going to hold me to that thirty-minute time frame, aren't you?"

"Sure am."

"We haven't even had a drink or eaten a bite," she reminded him. "Couldn't we at least have a glass of wine or a beer or a cola before we go?"

Vic huffed. "Okay. You stay here and I'll get us something to drink. Then as soon as we finish our drinks, we're leaving."

How long could she make a glass of wine last? she wondered. It wasn't that she wanted to prolong Vic's agony, but if they were going to be a couple, he'd have to become accustomed to parties because she loved to entertain. And she didn't want him to be rude to these people. She wanted them to like him since many of them would become his friends once she and he were married.

Oh, my! The *M* word. And she couldn't take it back.

"Agreed?" he asked.

"Huh?"

"After we finish our drinks, we'll leave."

"Of course, sugar. Whatever you want."

He glowered at her, then turned and headed back inside to search for drinks. Penny Sue gazed up at the night sky, inky-black vastness sprinkled with tiny shimmering lights. As a child she had made wishes on the first star she saw at night, but as she grew older, she began making wishes on all the stars. Actually her wishes were often more like prayers and directed as much to the good Lord as to one of His most dazzling creations—the stars in the heavens. Over the years, she had wished and prayed for many things. Sometimes her prayers were answered with a resounding "yes" and she got her wish. Other times, the answer was a flat-out "no". Her average was pretty good, especially when she asked for things for others.

When her father had become ill, she had prayed that he would live, but that if it was meant for him to go and be with her mother, then she asked that he not suffer. Although her daddy had died, he had not lingered. And she had asked the same for Aunt Lottie.

How about letting whoever is trying to harm Lucky have a change of heart? Penny Sue prayed.

And then she closed her eyes and made her wish. In a way the wish is for me, but it's as much for Vic as it is for me, she rationalized. Let him realize that he loves me, too, that he needs me in his life as much as I need him in mine.

"Stargazing?" a familiar voice asked.

She opened her eyes and looked right at Dylan Redley.

"Something like that."

Dylan had been the catch in high school and every girl had wanted him. But he'd been hers. Just not exclusively. She'd found out later, after he ran off with Valerie, that he'd never been faithful to her. Dylan wasn't all that good-looking anymore and everybody knew he was just about worthless. She'd heard that he hadn't held down a steady job in years and he and Valerie were in debt up to their eyeballs. But despite knowing all this, she couldn't believe that Dylan was behind the vicious attacks on Lucky. He might not have been a faithful boyfriend and he certainly wasn't all that smart, but he really wasn't a bad person.

"You sure do look pretty tonight, Penny Sue."

His gaze raked over her in a rather lascivious manner that made her feel downright uncomfortable.

"Thank you."

Dylan inched closer to her. Too close. His arm rubbed against her shoulder and she could smell liquor on his breath.

"I think you're even prettier now than when you were head majorette at Alabaster Creek High." Dylan slipped his arm around her waist and yanked her to his side.

"I must have been a fool to let you go. You have no idea how much I've regretted walking out on you."

"That's the liquor talking," she told him, doing her best to untangle herself from his tenacious hold. "You and Valerie were obviously meant for each other."

"Val's a bitch. A first-class, money-grubbing bitch. She's made my life a living hell." He leaned down and nuzzled Penny Sue's neck. "She makes me sleep on the sofa half the time."

"Please, let go of me," she told him in the sternest tone possible.

"Penny Sue, sweetheart…it could be so good for us. Remember what it was like?"

She remembered that their lovemaking hadn't been anything spectacular. And if she hadn't been young-love crazy about him, she'd have found him a very disappointing lover.

"Dylan, you're drunk and I'll make allowances for that, but if you don't release me this instant, I'll—"

Suddenly Vic appeared from out of nowhere, grabbed Dylan by both shoulders and yanked him away from Penny Sue. The two men stood there glaring at each other, Dylan breathing hard and Vic tense with rage.

"I won't make allowances for the fact that you're drunk," Vic said. "Penny Sue asked you to release her, but you didn't. You had no right to touch her. And if you ever come near her again or even think about putting your hands on her, I'll break you in two. Do I make myself clear?"

Penny Sue's heartbeat accelerated. She hadn't had two guys fighting over her since she was in kindergarten and Bobby Joe Morris and Tim Blevins got in a fistfight to decide who was going to be her boyfriend.

Dylan growled drunkenly and shook a weak fist at Vic. "She was my girl once, before I made a terrible mistake. But she still loves me. You do, don't you, Penny Sue?" He looked at her with pathetic hope in his eyes.

"Oh, Dylan…" She glanced from Dylan to Vic, who narrowed his gaze and flared his nostrils. Then she looked at Dylan again. "I'm sorry. I don't love you. I haven't loved you in a long, long time."

Dylan's face fell, his shoulders slumped. The poor guy looked like a whipped dog. Then suddenly his entire demeanor altered. He lumbered toward Vic, anger in his eyes and a snarl on his lips.

"I had her first. And you know they say a girl never forgets her first." Dylan tapped Vic in the center of his chest.

Vic swiped Dylan's hand away and grunted. "Being a girl's first lover isn't all that important. It's not the first she never forgets, it's the best that she always remembers."

A small crowd had gathered nearby and to a person they held

their breath until Vic grasped Penny Sue's arm and said, "I'm ready to leave now. How about you, sugar?"

Warmth spread through her like butter melting on hot toast. He'd called her sugar. She took his arm and smiled at him. "I'm ready." I'd go anywhere with you, Vic, she thought. Anywhere on earth.

As they made their way through the house, several people stopped them to ask if they were leaving. Her response was the same for everyone. "I'm afraid so. We hate to rush off, but Vic's recovering from that nasty dog bite, you know."

"Let's get Lucky and leave before someone else waylays us." Vic kept his arm securely around her waist.

"We have to say goodnight to Doc and Angela."

"Why?"

"Why? Well, it's simply good manners, that's all, to say good-bye to your host and hostess and thank them for a lovely party."

"For once could you forget about good manners."

Penny Sue gasped. "Never! Generations of Paines would roll over in their graves if I did such a thing."

Vic laughed.

"You're laughing."

"Sorry," he told her. "And I'm not laughing at you. I swear I'm not. It's just that you're one of a kind, Penny Sue. I find you very amusing."

"That's good. A sense of humor in a relationship is very important. Not necessarily the most important, but in the top five."

"The top five?"

"Yes, you know—love, sex, commitment, faithfulness, sense of humor."

"I don't suppose it would do any good to remind you that we don't have a personal relationship."

She shook her head. "Good heavens, Vic, what a thing to say only minutes after practically thrashing a man for putting his arm around me."

"I would have done the same thing for any woman who was being harassed by an old boyfriend."

"Aren't you just the sweetest thing." She cuddled against him, rose on her tiptoes and kissed his cheek. "But you wouldn't have told Dylan in front of everyone out there on the patio that you were going to be my very best lover if we didn't have a relationship."

Vic stared at her quizzically. "I told Dylan what? I never said I was going to be—"

"Yes, you did. You told him in no uncertain terms that a woman's best lover is the one she always remembers. You were talking about yourself and everybody knew it."

"Everybody?"

Smiling like a Cheshire cat, she nodded.

"Let's get Lucky and go home," he said.

"Not yet. We haven't—"

"All right, all right. Let's find Doc and Angela, say thank you and then get Lucky and go home."

Twenty minutes later, after being coerced by Angela Stone into eating "just a bite" before leaving, Penny Sue and Vic headed toward the sunroom to pick up Lucky.

"Weren't those crab cakes divine?" Penny Sue said. "I have to ask Angela for her recipe."

"The way you devoured those fudge brownies, I wasn't sure you even tasted anything else on your plate."

She stopped outside the sunroom, planted her hands on her hips and glared at Vic. "A gentleman should never remind a lady that she's eaten too much of anything, especially chocolate."

"Who says?"

"The Southern Women's Code."

"The what?"

"The Southern Women's Code," she repeated. "Section Six, paragraph five plainly states that a gentleman must not comment on a lady's eating habits, especially when it comes to eating chocolate."

"You're kidding."

"I never kid about chocolate or the Southern Women's Code."

Vic eyed her skeptically. "Someday you'll have to show me a copy of this code."

"Oh, I can't do that. It's forbidden for a man to see a copy of the code."

"I'll bet it is." Vic laughed again.

She loved the sound of his laughter, especially because she suspected he hadn't done much laughing in his life, at least not since he'd been a kid. She intended to change all that.

Vic opened the closed sunroom door and waited for Penny Sue to enter first. Training him to be a gentleman wouldn't be all that difficult. He seemed to have really good instincts.

Vic came inside behind her and then headed toward Lucky's pet taxi.

"Where's Tanya?" Penny Sue scanned the room. "I can't believe she left Lucky alone. Not after she promised Doc—"

"Lucky's not in his pet carrier," Vic said.

"What?"

"His pet carrier is empty."

"Maybe he needed to do his business and Tanya took him out."

"I don't think so."

"Why do you say that?"

Vic hauled Penny Sue around in front of him and pointed down to the floor between two wicker chairs that had been pushed to the side of the room. There lay Tanya, face down on the tile floor.

"Oh, no." Penny Sue gasped. "You don't think she's dead, do you?"

Vic knelt down beside Tanya and felt for a pulse. "She's still alive." He gave her a quick once-over and brought his hand up to show Penny Sue the blood on his fingers. "Looks like somebody hit her on the head."

"They knocked Tanya out and stole Lucky."

"Go get Doc and tell Angela to phone the police and have them send an ambulance."

Penny Sue hesitated before leaving the sunroom. "Will Tanya be all right?"

"Probably. But we need to get her to the hospital ASAP."

Penny Sue rushed out of the room, then paused in the doorway. "Do you think whoever kidnapped Lucky will kill him?"

"I don't known, sugar. Maybe not."

He knew that she knew he'd just said what she needed to hear, not what he truly believed.

## Chapter 10

Vic had three objectives. First was to keep Penny Sue calm and reassured. Second was to find Lucky as soon as possible, preferably before whoever kidnapped the little pooch killed him. And third was to stop beating himself over the mistake he'd made in agreeing to leave Lucky in the hands of the vet's receptionist. What was done was done. The truth of the matter was that he'd screwed up by allowing whatever the hell was going on between Penny Sue and him to interfere with his normally astute judgment.

But she had ordered him to leave Lucky. And she was his boss.

They had been delayed in leaving Doc and Angela's because, since they were the ones who had discovered the unconscious Tanya, they'd had to wait for the police to arrive and provide statements. That was thirty-five minutes lost in the search for Lucky. Thirty-five minutes that might mean the difference between life and death for the dog. But Vic hadn't wasted the time simply waiting. He had examined the scene for any evidence, but there was none. And he had questioned all the guests. No one had seen anything suspicious.

"This is all my fault." Penny Sue sat beside Vic in her black SUV as he started the engine and backed out of the driveway. "Oh, Vic, what are we going to do?"

"We're going to question each one of the suspects…each one of Lottie's heirs," Vic said. "My guess is that one of them either kidnapped Lucky or hired someone to do it."

"And what makes you think they'll admit anything?"

"I don't think they will," Vic said. "But we have to start somewhere and there's always a chance that whoever took Lucky still has him."

She uttered a trembling groan. "We've got to find him before…" Her teary voice trailed off into silence.

Keeping his eyes on the road as he steered the SUV toward town, Vic reached across the console and grasped Penny Sue's hand. "We'll find him." He sure as hell hoped they'd find Lucky alive. If not… He didn't even want to think about it.

Penny Sue squeezed Vic's hand, then released it so that he could put both hands on the wheel. "Should we rule out Dylan, Valerie and Uncle Douglas since they're still at the party?" she asked.

"Not necessarily. But we'll start with those who were at the party earlier but left before we discovered Lucky was missing."

"That would be Candy and Stacie and Chris."

"Yes, it would. So, let's start with Candy. Give me directions to your uncle's house."

"I'm certain Uncle Douglas would never be involved in—"

"But his wife might," Vic said. "And Angela Stone mentioned that Candy left early, claiming she had a headache, and that your uncle was going to catch a ride home with neighbors who live close by."

"Anne and Steven Hollis?"

"Yeah."

"You don't really think anyone would be stupid enough to keep Lucky at their house, do you? I mean…" She gulped down the tears lodged in her throat. "Oh, Vic, this is all my fault. If I hadn't insisted we go to the party…" she whimpered. In his peripheral vision, he caught a glimpse of the misery on her face.

"It's not your fault," he told her, wishing he could wrap his arms around her. "It's mine."

"No, it's not your fault at all. It's totally my fault. You see...well, I'm the one who suggested to Doc that he might want to throw a party for you to thank you for saving all the animals at his clinic."

"You what? Why would you do something like that? You had to know that I'd hate it." Her eyes widened with guilt. "Oh, don't tell—you did it to punish me, didn't you?"

"Maybe," she admitted. "You were terribly ugly to me about...well about several things. And it's within a woman's rights to retaliate when the man in her life doesn't treat her the way she deserves to be treated."

Vic clenched his teeth and counted to ten. "Of all the idiotic nonsense! Where did that rule come from anyway—straight out of the Southern Women's Code?"

Penny Sue crossed her arms over her chest, squeezed her thighs together and sat straight as a board, her chin tilted upward. "Section Ten, paragraph eleven."

Vic groaned. How was it that she could act like the offended party, when she was in the wrong? But a man knew when he couldn't win a battle. Better to cut his losses and live to fight another day.

"Let's call a truce for now," he suggested.

"All right," she agreed. "But only until we find Lucky."

"Yeah, okay." If we find Lucky, he thought. If we find him alive. "Now give me directions to your uncle's house."

How was it possible to be madly in love with such an infuriating man? Penny Sue asked herself. He had absolutely no right to be upset with her about instigating the party at Doc Stone's, not after the way he'd treated her. He'd accused her of being old-fashioned, of talking too much and had even implied she was plump. She hated the word *fat* and seldom used it. *Plump* sounded so much nicer. Anyway, turn about was fair play, wasn't it? Vic had deserved to suffer just a little.

But he was right about their calling a temporary truce until after they found Lucky. And they *would* find him alive and well. She refused to think otherwise. Every time a negative thought entered her mind, she pushed it aside.

She knew Vic was frustrated and angry with himself for leaving Lucky in Tanya's care, but how could either of them have known someone would do something so ruthless? So unpredictable? Of course, it was all her fault. She had ordered Vic to leave Lucky with Tanya. Poor Tanya! She had regained consciousness just as the paramedics had arrived, but she couldn't tell the police anything about who had knocked her on the head. She swore she hadn't seen a thing.

"Is this your uncle's house?" Vic asked. It was the first thing he'd said to her since they'd called a temporary truce.

"Yes, the brick house with a circular drive," Penny Sue told him.

Vic pulled the SUV into the drive in front of the large, one-story colonial. He parked behind a silver Mercedes and killed the motor, then turned to Penny Sue and said, "Is that your uncle's car?"

"Yes, but I don't understand why Candy didn't pull into the garage. Her headache must have been really bad, and she just rushed inside to take some aspirin or something."

"Hmm…"

"What does that 'hmm' mean?"

"Nothing. Just hmm."

"You think she had Lucky with her and was hurrying to get into the house before anyone saw her?"

"Possibly."

"Then what are we waiting for? Let's go." Penny Sue grasped the door handle.

He reached over and grabbed her hand. "I don't guess it would do any good to ask you to stay here, would it?"

"None whatsoever."

After releasing her, Vic opened his door and got out. She swung open her door, got out and followed Vic, catching up with him just as he peered into one of the front windows where the plantation blinds had been left open.

"See anything?" she whispered.

"Not a thing." He turned around and glanced at the front door. "Any chance it might be unlocked?"

Penny Sue shrugged. "I doubt it. Lots of people leave their doors unlocked in the daytime, if they're at home, but not at night. We don't have a lot of crime in Alabaster Creek, but in this day and age, it pays to be safe rather than sorry."

Vic grasped the front doorknob, twisted it and grinned when the door opened. "Your aunt Candy must have been in a really big hurry. She left the door unlocked." Vic pushed the door, which opened into a dimly lit foyer.

"She is not my aunt!" The very idea that a woman as young as Candy, who looked and acted like the floozie she was, could be Penny Sue Paine's aunt was ludicrous. Aunt-by-marriage was bad enough. That her uncle had brought such a woman into the family was a disgrace. A part of Penny Sue hoped that Candy had kidnapped Lucky so maybe Uncle Douglas would, once and for all, realize what type of person she was.

"Shh…" Vic glared at Penny Sue. "Not so loud."

Penny Sue snorted indignantly. "Sorry. I forgot we were breaking and entering."

Vic stepped over the threshold and into the foyer, Penny Sue following. He paused, glanced from side to side and whispered, "Technically, we didn't break in, so we're just entering."

"That's simply a technicality," she told him in a soft voice.

"If Candy took Lucky, where would she put him?" Vic asked.

"I have no idea."

"Let's say that she kidnapped him and intends to have someone else get rid of him for her, what would she do with him in the meantime?"

"Put him in the laundry room maybe?" She headed down the hallway toward the kitchen. "Or she could have—"

"Listen." Vic grabbed her hand to halt her. "Do you hear that?"

She stopped and listened. Voices. Whimpers. Moans? "What is that? Sounds as if someone is in pain."

Vic's lips twitched.

"What's funny?"

"Nothing."

"Maybe that's Lucky whimpering." Penny Sue pulled away from Vic and headed straight down the hall toward the master bedroom, the room from where all the noise was coming.

"I don't think it's Lucky," Vic called after her in a hushed tone.

"Well, we'll soon find out." Penny Sue broke into a run.

"Wait!" Vic said in a loud whisper.

He caught up with her just as she flung open the bedroom door and shouted, "Aha, we caught you red-handed."

The naked couple in the bed sprang apart, their motions comical as they tried to disengage their tangled limbs and at the same time cover themselves with the sheet.

Oh my God! Penny Sue froze for a second when she realized what was happening in her Uncle Douglas's bed. Then she backed up slowly until she ran smack dab into Vic's chest.

"Oh...er...I—I don't think Candy kidnapped Lucky."

Vic chuckled. "It appears not."

"Penny Sue, what on earth are you doing here?" Candy demanded. "How did you—"

"Don't you dare question me! I've done nothing wrong, whereas you're committing adultery. And in my uncle's bed." Suddenly Penny Sue realized who the man was in bed with Candy. She gasped. "And with Tommy Rutland!"

"Now, Penny Sue, this isn't what it looks like." Tommy gazed at her pleadingly.

"Oh, get real." Penny Sue propped her hands on her hips. "This is disgraceful. Both of you are married to other people. I'm not surprised in the least by your actions, Candy. The family has been expecting something like this ever since you married Uncle Douglas.

"But you, Tommy. You're a pillar of the community. A deacon in your church. And you're a candidate for mayor." But not for long, Penny Sue thought. "You'll withdraw your candidacy, of course."

"Please, Penny Sue, you can't tell anyone about this," Tommy pleaded. "It would kill Cherie if she knew and it would ruin me in this town."

"Cherie! Oh, your poor wife. She's the sweetest person ever. You scoundrel. You good-for-nothing, two-timing scoundrel. If you think for one minute that I'll keep quiet about this, then you'd better think again. The both of you should be ashamed of your-selves.

"Just how long has this been going on? Weeks? Months? Years? Uncle Douglas will be devastated." Penny Sue held up a restraining hand. "No sirree, don't think for one minute that he's not going to learn about this. I will not keep your dirty secret. I will—"

Vic grasped her shoulder, leaned down and whispered in her ear. "Let's leave these two to stew in their own juices. You can take an ad out in tomorrow's paper, but for now, we need to find Lucky."

"Oh! Oh my goodness." She glared at the couple who sat cring-ing in the bed. "I'll deal with you two later!"

For the next ten minutes while Vic drove to Chris Paine's house—the one he'd taken out a second mortgage on to pay off gambling debts—Penny Sue ranted and raved about her uncle's wife and Tommy Rutland. Vic let her talk to her heart's content. The only way he could have stopped her was if he kissed her or gagged her. At present, he didn't have time for either.

"There's Chris's place." She pointed to the forties-style bunga-low in the middle of a row of similar houses on Milton Street. "All the lights are off and his car isn't in the drive. He did have a cute little sports car, but he sold it recently and now he's driving an older model Chevy."

"You stay in the car this time," Vic told her as he pulled up in front of the house and parked the SUV by the curb. The words were barely out of his mouth when he realized his mistake and tried to backtrack. "Let me rephrase that. Penny Sue…sugar…will you please stay in the car and let me check things out?"

"I might," she said. "Since you put it so nicely."

He grinned and mentally patted himself on the back. He was learning.

Vic opened the door and got out, but before closing it, he looked right at Penny Sue. "Please, don't get out and follow me. I'm a big boy. I don't need help. If I find Lucky, I'm capable of rescuing him without you."

"I don't think Chris is at home anyway, so I doubt you'll find anything."

"You'll stay here?"

She nodded.

Just as he started to close the door, she said, "Be careful."

He shut the door and headed up the driveway toward the dark house.

Penny Sue hated waiting. It wasn't that she thought Vic needed her help. He didn't. But sitting idly by while someone else handled things and took all the risks wasn't her usual style. For as long as she could remember—ever since her mother had died and she and her daddy had moved in with Aunt Dottie and Aunt Lottie, she'd been handling things. Making Daddy smile had not been easy in those first few years, but eventually he'd lit up every time she came into a room.

"You remind me of your mother," he'd always told her. "Same beautiful hair and same lovely smile."

And as time went on, she had made a point of helping Aunt Lottie keep an eye on Aunt Dottie, who was the most impractical, illogical woman in the world, God love her. Then before long, Penny Sue had realized how alone Aunt Lottie was in her family responsibilities, so she'd done her best to help shoulder the load, eventually taking it over completely. That was one of the reasons—other than the fact she loved Lucky—she just had to find the dog. To save him. For Aunt Lottie.

Penny Sue watched Vic's dark shadow until he disappeared into the backyard. Minutes ticked by. She glanced at her wristwatch. He'd been gone only four minutes, but it seemed much longer. Maybe she should go check on him. Just to make sure he was all right.

You told him you'd stay in the car, she reminded herself. But you didn't promise. You said you might.

She opened the passenger door and got out, but just as her feet hit the ground, Vic came striding up the driveway. She stretched and yawned.

"It won't work," he told her as he approached.

"What won't work?"

"Pretending you were just stretching your legs."

"I was."

"No, you weren't. You were coming to look for me."

"So what if I was?"

Vic huffed. "Let's go."

"You didn't find anything, did you? I told you I didn't think Chris was here."

"He's not. And neither is Lucky."

"So, what's next? Stacie's house?"

Vic nodded, then opened the SUV's front passenger door and helped Penny Sue up and inside the vehicle. "How far does she live from here?"

"Two blocks over on North Woodland Avenue. She owns a duplex, lives in one and rents out the other."

Vic jumped in the SUV, strapped on his seatbelt and started the engine. "Go up two blocks and turn right or left?"

"Left."

They arrived at Stacie's in less than three minutes flat. Once again, Vic parked by the curb. Before getting out, he turned to Penny Sue and said, "Come on. You might as well go in with me now instead of sneaking up on me later."

She smiled triumphantly. Damn the woman. She knew she'd won another battle without him even putting up a fight. Sometimes winning just wasn't worth the effort, especially not with Penny Sue.

Stacie Paine's duplex was ranch-style with a white brick facade, black shutters and separate porches for each unit.

"Hers is the one on the right," Penny Sue said.

Vic nodded. "The lights are on, so she's probably home."

"Her car's in the drive," Penny Sue said. "And Chris is here. That's his old Chevy."

"Okay, here's what I want you to do. Go ring the doorbell and—"

"You want me to announce myself? Why aren't we snooping around the way we did—"

"Because someone is looking out the window and has already seen us," Vic told her. "Now go ring the doorbell and tell Stacie that Lucky was kidnapped and you need her help. Tell her you're forming a search party, which is something that actually might become necessary if Lucky's not here and we don't find him soon."

"Okay. And while I'm doing that, what are you going to do?"

"Nothing, except stand at your side and pat my foot."

She looked at him and frowned.

"Just get us inside the house, okay? And keep talking. If Lucky's there, he'll hear your voice and let us know where he is."

"Aren't you brilliant."

"Sometimes I can be," he told her. "But this is just common sense."

He urged her into motion, staying at her side while she stepped onto the porch and rang the doorbell. Within seconds, Stacie opened the door and smiled. Nervously? Or was it just his imagination that the young woman seemed slightly rattled.

"Why Penny Sue, what are you doing coming by so late?" Stacie asked, then glanced at Vic. "And you've brought Mr. Noble with you."

Penny Sue grabbed Stacie's hands, pushed her back into her house and said, "Oh, Stacie, the most awful thing has happened. Someone's kidnapped Lucky."

Stacie's face turned pale. "How awful."

"We're afraid for Lucky's life. We simply must find him, so Vic thought it wise to form a search party. I need your help. Yours and Chris's." Penny Sue peered around Stacie, into the living room and down the hall. "Chris *is* here, isn't he? We saw his car parked outside."

"He—he's in the bathroom. I'll go get him."

Penny Sue grasped her cousin's arm and all but dragged her into the living room. "Why don't you let Vic go get him while you help me decide who else we can contact to join the search party?"

"No, no, I'll get him." Stacie pulled loose from Penny Sue's hold and rushed out into the hall.

"She's acting strange," Penny Sue said.

"You stay here," Vic told her.

"Where are you going?"

"Outside. Just in case Chris is making a fast getaway."

"Oh. You think...?"

"Just keep talking as if I'm still here."

Vic hurried to the front door, went onto the porch and off into the yard. Suddenly, the back door creaked, then footsteps padded around the house. Vic crept slowly along the side of the duplex and waited in the shadows.

Chris Paine came into view when he neared his car, illumination from a nearby streetlight revealing his presence. There, tucked under Chris's arm, was something wiggling and whimpering.

Vic stepped out of the shadows. "Going somewhere?"

Chris froze. Lucky barked.

Stacie came running out of the house, Penny Sue behind her.

"We weren't going to hurt Lucky," Stacie cried. "I swear we weren't."

Vic walked over, took Lucky from Chris and handed him to Penny Sue.

"Why did you take him?" Penny Sue asked.

"Because we had to do something," Stacie said. "We don't want Lucky dead, but we need our inheritance from Aunt Lottie and as long as Lucky is—"

"I can't believe you're capable of killing a poor defenseless little dog." Penny Sue glared at her cousin through a mist of tears. "Or did y'all intend to have someone else do the dastardly deed?"

"We weren't going to kill him," Chris said. "We were just going to take him off somewhere out of state and give him away to somebody who'd take care of him."

"That way everyone would think he was dead and then all of us would be entitled to our inheritances from Aunt Lottie," Stacie explained.

"Don't blame Stacie." Chris hung his head. "It's totally my fault. I'm the one who kidnapped Lucky. I did it on the spur of the moment. Just a harebrained scheme. And then I realized what a crazy thing I'd done and panicked, so I brought him here to my sis's house."

"You knocked Tanya unconscious." Penny Sue glared accusingly at her cousin.

"Is she all right?"

"We think so, but the paramedics took her to the ER."

"I didn't mean to hurt her. I didn't mean to hit her so hard. But I'm desperate, Penny Sue," Chris admitted. "I'm the one who needs my inheritance now, and not years from now. I'm sorry about…" His voice cracked. "I'm in big trouble. My life is in danger."

"What are you talking about?" Penny Sue cuddled Lucky close, soothing him with her touch.

"Your cousin Chris owes a lot of money to a bookie," Vic said. "That's why he sold his car and why he took out a second mortgage on his house. He's desperate for money to pay off his gambling debts."

"Is that true?" Penny Sue penned Chris with her condemning glare.

"Yes, it's true."

"Uncle Douglas doesn't know, does he?" Penny Sue asked.

"Don't tell Daddy," Stacie pleaded. "It'll break his heart."

"I really don't know what I'm going to do," Penny Sue said. "I'll let y'all know—"

"Please…" Chris's voice trembled.

"What you need, Chris Paine, is a good thrashing. And if I was a man…" Penny Sue blew out an angry breath. "Just be glad I'm not. You have disgraced the Paine name and I really don't know any way to keep the truth from Uncle Douglas. At least not for long."

"Just don't tell him tonight," Stacie said. "Let Chris tell Daddy himself."

"Yes, that would be best, but if he doesn't tell Uncle Douglas, I will. Tomorrow. For now, all I want to do is take Lucky home." She turned to Vic. "Call Doc and Angela for me, will you? Tell them we found Lucky, but don't mention anything about Chris and Stacie."

"The police will have to be notified," Vic told her. "Remember, Tanya was injured. She could bring Chris up on assault charges."

Penny Sue's shoulders slumped. "Oh, dear. I don't know what to do."

"You don't have to do anything," Vic said. "I'll handle this. You take Lucky and get in the car."

She looked at him, uncertainty in her eyes, then she nodded, hugged Lucky close and walked down the drive to her SUV.

Vic studied the two criminals and couldn't help feeling sorry for them, especially Stacie. "Ms. Paine, why don't you go on into the house. I think your brother is man enough to take the blame for what he did without involving you any further." He glanced at Chris. "Isn't that right?"

"Yes, that's right." Chris gulped.

"If you need me…" Stacie left her sentence unfinished as she turned and ran into her house.

"What now?" Chris asked.

"You're going to get into your car and drive down to the police station, where you'll confess what you did. It's up to you whether or not you tell them why you did it."

"Daddy will be so—"

"He'll be proud of you for taking responsibility for your own actions. And if it helps any, my guess is a smart lawyer can keep you from serving a prison sentence."

"Oh, God!"

"Believe me, if you ever cause Penny Sue another minute of worry, going to jail will be the least of your concerns. Do I make myself clear?"

Wringing his hands, Chris nodded. "Yes. I—I understand."

"Let's go," Vic said. "Penny Sue and I will follow right behind you."

"You don't trust me?"

"Fellow, I don't know you, so why would I trust you?"

"But I'm Penny Sue's cousin. I'm a Paine."

Vic snorted. "If being a Paine is such an all-fired big deal, then straighten your shoulders, suck in your stomach and act like a man. Act like somebody worthy of being Penny Sue's cousin."

"I… Yes, I will." Chris climbed into his old Chevy, grasped the steering wheel and laid his head down on his hands.

Hating to see a grown man cry, Vic walked up the sidewalk and got in the SUV.

"Is Lucky all right?"

"He's fine." Penny Sue glanced out the window at her cousin's car. "How's Chris?"

"He'll be all right. He's going to the police station to turn himself in and we're going to follow along behind him. I'm sure they'll want to ask him some questions about the fire and Lucky's shooting."

Penny Sue whipped around and stared at Vic. "This was your idea—for him to turn himself in to the police?"

"Yep."

"And he agreed?"

"Yep."

"What about Stacie?"

"She didn't do anything except try to protect her brother."

Penny Sue sighed heavily. "I don't know how Uncle Douglas is going to handle so much bad news all at once. He's not a young man, and finding out what Chris did, and that he's in debt to a bookie, is bad enough. But then learning that his wife is having an affair with another man—with Tommy Rutland, of all people. I'm not sure what to do, but I'll think of something. I'll hire Chris a good lawyer, of course. And I'll pay off his gambling debts to save his life. But what can I do about Candy? Uncle Douglas has to know the truth, but—"

Vic reached over the console, grabbed her face between his hands and kissed her.

When he finally let her come up for air, she looked at him and asked, "Did you do that to make me shut up?" When Lucky nudged her arm, she lifted him and hugged him close.

"No, sugar, I did it because I've never known anyone who cares so damn much about other people. Who wants to fix everybody's problems." Still cupping her face in his hands, he smiled at her, then eased his hands over her cheeks, down her neck and onto her shoulders. "How on earth do these small shoulders carry such a heavy load?" He caressed her tenderly. "Why don't you let some-one take care of you for a change?"

"And just who would that someone be?"

"It would be me, sugar. It would be me."

## Chapter 11

Vic had kept Lucky in the room with him while Penny Sue took a bath and got ready for bed. Then she'd suggested he use her bathroom for his shower instead of going down the hall to the one he'd being using, adjacent to her father's old room. At this time of night—past midnight—he wasn't going to argue with her. Once they had deposited Cousin Chris at the police station—where he would be staying overnight—they'd had to come home and face all the questions from Aunt Dottie, Ruby and Tully. If he'd thought for one minute that by the time they arrived home the whole town wouldn't know about Lucky's kidnapping, then he'd have been dead wrong. But what he hadn't been able to figure out at first was how Aunt Dottie knew that Chris had been the kidnapper. Not until she explained that her friend, Lorraine Thrasher, had a son who was a policeman and had been on duty when Chris had turned himself in.

"That boy should be ashamed of himself," Ruby had said.

"Poor Douglas." Dottie had shed a few tears, then asked Penny Sue, "You will help Chris, won't you, dear? You know I would, if I had the money, but I don't."

Tully had grumbled something barely intelligible under his breath, something that had sounded a great deal like, "Expect her to take care of the whole damn lot."

Penny Sue had adamantly refused to even discuss the possibility that Chris might be responsible for both Lucky's shooting and the clinic fire. If he'd thought he could reason with her, Vic would have insisted that she face that possibility. But Penny Sue knew her cousin far better than Vic did, so maybe she was right to believe in him, to think him incapable of setting fire to the clinic or of shooting Lucky.

"I know one of my blood relatives might turn out to be guilty," she'd told Vic. "But I just can't bear the thought of it."

Vic stepped out of the warm shower, dried off and after slipping into his pajama bottoms, wiped off the mirror over the vanity and took a look at himself. He needed a shave, but it could wait until morning. It wasn't as if anyone would complain about his beard stubble tonight. After dumping his towel in the laundry basket inside the linen closet, he eased open the door to Penny Sue's bedroom. All quiet. The room lay in semidarkness, illuminated only by the light from the bathroom and the shimmering moonlight dancing in through the sheer curtains on the windows that overlooked the backyard. He turned off the bathroom light and walked out into the room, pausing briefly at Penny Sue's bedside. He had thought maybe she'd still be awake. She wasn't.

She lay there on the massive antique canopy bed, only her legs covered with the light cotton sheet. Curled up in the curve of her body, Lucky nestled against her, his head resting on her arm. He opened his black eyes and looked up at Vic, but didn't stir. Who could blame him? If Vic were lying there, so close to Penny Sue's warm, luscious body, he wouldn't let anything or anyone disturb him either.

Vic studied her, so serene in sleep. So quiet. He chuckled softly to himself, which garnered another glance from Lucky. As he watched her sleeping, a sensation of longing combined with possessive concern overcame him completely. He wanted Penny Sue. What man wouldn't? But he also cared about her. He wanted to take care of her and protect her from all harm.

What is it about you, Penny Sue Paine, that makes me feel things I've never felt before, things I don't want to feel?

At thirty-nine, he'd known a number of women, in the biblical sense. And he'd thought he was in love at least once. He didn't count any teenage romances that had been dictated solely by raging hormones. But what he'd felt for Lyssa had been deeper than anything he'd ever felt, more centered on pleasing her than pleasing himself. He'd been employed by the CIA for ten years when he'd met her on their first of several joint assignments. She was new to the agency, twenty-eight to his thirty-two. Long, lean, black-haired and blue-eyed. They had become lovers within six weeks and were engaged within six months. He had shared a part of himself with her that he'd never shared with anyone else.

They hadn't gotten around to setting a wedding date or talking much about the future—leaving the CIA, having kids, stuff like that. In retrospect, he realized that on some gut level he'd probably known things between them wouldn't work. What he hadn't known was how badly it would end. Or that he would be the one to end it.

Vic closed his eyes as memories bombarded him. Not the good memories of the times when things had seemed right between them. No, his memories were of the last time he'd seen Lyssa. God help him, would he ever be able to erase the look on her face when she'd realized that he knew the truth about her, and that he was the agent who had been assigned to eliminate her?

Vic opened his eyes and forced the painful thoughts away as he looked down at Penny Sue again. What would you think of me, if you knew everything about me? Would you hate me if you knew that I had terminated my own fiancée?

Penny Sue was so gentle and kind, so loving and giving. She would never be able to understand the world he'd lived in when he'd worked for the CIA. She could not imagine the things he'd done, the things he was capable of doing.

There's no reason for you to ever share those things with her, he told himself. She never has to know.

Vic couldn't take his eyes off her, couldn't walk away. Not

yet. Maybe he was a glutton for punishment, but God help him, he needed to look at her. She wore a short-sleeved, pale yellow silk pajama top that gaped open a fraction across the buttoned top because of the way she was lying on her side. The top was open just enough to reveal a sneak-peak of her breasts. He swallowed hard, the thought of touching her, of running his thumbs over her nipples and taking her into his mouth driving him crazy. It aroused him unbearably. Everything male in him urged him to reach out and take what he wanted. His erection strained against his pajama bottoms.

His gaze traveled over her. Her long, auburn hair. Her soft, creamy skin. Her hourglass body, half hidden beneath the sheet. He wanted to rip the sheet away, lie down beside her and take her into his arms. And then he wanted to—

Stop doing this to yourself! Stop drooling over something you can't have, shouldn't want and don't deserve.

Vic forced himself to walk away and go into the adjoining room. He flopped down atop the covers on the daybed and lay there looking up at the ceiling. Moonlight mixed with the blackness of night and created dark, oddly shaped shadows. As a general rule, he didn't require more than five hours of sleep in order to function well, and he could get by on less. As a boy he'd had to get up early and do chores before going to school—feed the chickens, milk their one cow and bring in wood for the fireplace to supplement their small gas furnace, which didn't heat the entire four-room shack. At night, after chores were done and supper finished, he'd stay up late doing his homework and reading past midnight. He'd been hungry for knowledge, knowing that a good education was his key out of poverty.

He had worked his way through college, some days eating only one meal because it was all he could afford, and occasionally skipping an entire day when his money ran out. He hadn't dated much because he couldn't afford the luxury of taking a girl out on the town. But there had been a few girls who hadn't minded skipping dinner and a movie…the ones who'd wanted to go straight from hello to "let's screw."

Why was he thinking so damn much about the past? His childhood, his college days, his career with the Company. And Lyssa. It wasn't as if he was the kind of guy who allowed his past to haunt him. He'd learned a long time ago to take one day at a time, put the past behind him and let the future take care of itself.

Okay, so Penny Sue Paine had his guts tied in knots, had him thinking all kinds of stupid thoughts about things that should be of no interest whatsoever to him. Things like settling down, getting married, raising kids. Things like love and commitment. Things he knew weren't for him.

He was here in Alabaster Creek on a Dundee assignment. Tomorrow, another agent would join him and within a week—two, tops—they'd find out who was trying to kill Lucky and then he could leave this town, the millionaire dog and Penny Sue behind. But between now and then, he had to keep his hands off Penny Sue because as much as he wanted to make love to her, he knew that if she gave herself to him, she would expect more from him than he had to give.

*Is it that you don't have it to give or that you're just afraid to give it?*

Was he afraid he'd hurt Penny Sue, disappoint her, break her heart? Or was he afraid that if she knew the real Vic Noble, she wouldn't want him?

Penny Sue woke abruptly, coming out of a dream that had been both exhilarating and unnerving. When she roused, Lucky didn't even move. In her dream state, she had shoved most of the cover off her and it now lay wadded near the foot of the bed. Although the room was reasonably warm, there was a slight chill in the air. Spring nights tended to be cool, and old houses were always drafty.

After lying there for several minutes, she managed to vividly recall her dream, at least parts of it. She and Vic had been running, but she wasn't sure if they'd been chasing someone or running from someone. But she had known that there was great danger surrounding them. Suddenly, it had thundered and lightning had ripped across the sky. Within minutes, it had started raining and they were caught outside and were soon drenched to the skin. He had led her off the street and into an alley doorway, then they had taken off their clothes and...

Penny Sue gasped. A cold shiver rippled through her.

She had never—ever—dreamed about having sex with a man!

Lucky shifted from one side to the other. She reached out and stroked him tenderly, then slipped out of bed as quietly as possible. Once on her feet, she glanced down at her bedside clock to check the time. Four fifteen.

Padding barefoot into the bathroom, she closed the door behind her and flipped on the light, which nearly blinded her. She groaned and shut her eyes.

Try to forget about that dream, she told herself. Try to forget about how it felt to be in Vic's arms, the two of you naked.

But her traitorous body wouldn't let her forget. Her face was flushed and warm to the touch where she pressed her open palms against her cheeks. Her nipples were tight and hard, the points pressing against the soft silk of her pajama top. And her femininity was moist and pulsating.

She couldn't deny the effect of the erotic dream. Her body showed all the signs of arousal, of a woman on the brink of an orgasm.

Opening her eyes, Penny Sue turned on the tap's cold water faucet, cupped her hands to catch the flow and doused her face. After shaking her head and rubbing the clinging droplets of water into her skin, she stared at herself in the mirror. Then she groaned.

What was she going to do? She had fallen in love with a man she barely knew, wanted him so badly that she dreamed of making love with him and all the while she knew, soul-deep, that she and Vic were two very different people, from two very different worlds. In his world, having sex with a woman didn't come with any strings attached. It was physical gratification and nothing more. But in her world, sex meant love and commitment.

But Vic cares about you, maybe even loves you. He just doesn't know it or if he does, he hasn't admitted it to himself. Not yet.

Wide awake, sexually aroused and emotionally torn, Penny Sue didn't know what to do with herself. She could go to Vic and tell him she wanted to make love. She could take Lucky and go downstairs, prepare herself some coffee and get an early start on her day. Or she could go back to bed and try to sleep another hour or two.

If she went to Vic, would she regret it later? If she went back to bed, she was unlikely to go back to sleep. And if she went downstairs, unless she was exceedingly quiet, she was likely to wake Ruby and Tully, who'd both want to know what was wrong with her.

Deciding to return to bed so as not to disturb anyone, she flipped off the light and opened the bathroom door, then gasped when she ran smack-dab into Vic.

He grabbed her shoulders to steady her.

"Are you all right?" he asked.

"I'm fine," she said breathlessly.

"You sound odd," he told her, tightening his hold on her shoulders.

She shivered.

"You're cold," he said.

"Chilly."

"You need to get back into bed under the covers, or put on a robe."

"I don't think I can go back to sleep." Her eyes began to adjust to the semidarkness and she was able to make out his shadowy facial features. "Did I wake you? If I did, I'm sorry. It's just that I had this dream that woke me and—"

"Was it about me?" He eased his hands across her shoulders and up her neck. She shuddered when his thumbs skimmed along her jawline.

"What makes you think it was about you?"

He lifted one hand from her face and cupped the back of her head, forcing her to look up at him. "Because I was dreaming about you, sugar."

"You were?" She gulped.

"Yeah, and it was a hell of a dream."

"It was?"

"In my dream, your cheeks were flushed." He caressed her cheek with his fingertips. "And your nipples were hard." He glanced down at her peaked nipples. "And you were wet and hot and—"

She placed her index finger over his lips. "You know that if I let you…that if we…it will mean more to me than just sex."

He shut his eyes as if in pain.

"Vic?"

His hand cupping her head quivered ever so slightly as he pressed her toward him until their lips almost touched. "Yeah, sugar. I know…I know."

And then he kissed her. Kissed her like she'd never been kissed. Not even by him.

Her toes curled, her head spun and a hundred crazed butterflies did a happy dance in her belly. She was so ready for this.

He deepened the kiss, all the while holding her head in place as if he wanted to get her as close as possible, wanted to shove her into him until they didn't know where one of them began and the other ended. Feeling as if the whole world had tilted on its axis, Penny Sue gave herself over to the moment, to this man and the feelings he evoked within her. If this wasn't love, she didn't know what was. Love and lust. Sex and forever after. Physical and emotional passion. All these things and more. Fully participating in the kiss, she opened her mouth for his invasion and gave as good as she got. Every nerve in her body screamed for more, more. And every muscle tensed with anticipation.

Her breasts felt heavy and achy, longing for his touch, yet supersensitive, her silk pajama top feeling like sandpaper against her pebble-hard nipples. And her core tightened and released in preparation, flooding with moisture.

Still kissing her, Vic picked her up in his arms. She clung to him, lifted her head and laid it on his shoulder. He carried her over to her bed, then laid her down and straddled her. She gazed up into his eyes and smiled.

Lucky roused, came to his feet and stared at Vic. As if sensing they needed privacy, he jumped out of bed, trotted across the room and curled up on the area rug in front of the fireplace.

"Are you sure?" Vic asked her.

"I'm sure," she told him.

"Be very sure," he said.

She caressed his face, then slid her hand down his throat, over his chest and down to the waistband of his pajama bottoms. When she eased her hand inside and covered his erection with her palm, he shuddered and groaned.

Maneuvering himself down and to her side, he slowly unbuttoned her pajama top, exposing more and more of her flesh to the cool morning air and to his hungry gaze. He spread the top apart, then lowered his mouth to one breast while he curved his hand around the other breast and squeezed gently. When his tongue flicked one nipple while his finger and thumb pinched the other, she cried out with intense pleasure and pain, and bucked her hips up in invitation.

In this situation, turnabout was indeed fair play. She circled his sex with her hand. He growled, then easing from her grasp, he did wicked things to her with his mouth, going from one breast to the other and then down over her belly to her navel. When he encountered her pajama bottoms, he slipped his hands beneath her hips, lifted her and yanked the bottoms over her hips and down her legs. She assisted him in every way possible and within a few seconds, she kicked the pajamas off her feet and onto the floor.

Vic kissed a path over her belly, down her right thigh and calf to her foot, then moved over to her left side and came all the way back up to her hips. Penny Sue sighed and shivered and grabbed at him, trying to touch him, hold him, control him. But he was wild and there was no controlling him. Before she realized what he intended, he spread her thighs and positioned himself between them, then lowered his head and kissed her mound. She trembled.

"Vic…?"

"Sh…" He spread her feminine lips apart and inserted his tongue.

She cried out with shock. And with sheer delight.

He made slow, sweet, torturous love to her with his mouth, taking her where she'd never been, giving her a pleasure she'd never known. And all the while his mouth worked magic below her waist, his fingertips worked their own magic on her breasts. Her entire body came alive with his touch and soon the pleasure reached an unbearable point. One final stroke of his tongue sent her toppling over the edge, and her tightly wound core exploded with fulfillment.

While the aftershocks of release rippled through her, Vic lifted himself up and over her. He entered her with one swift, hard thrust and brought his mouth down on hers with equal passion. Her senses at full alert, she experienced several things at once. She saw stars in the darkness behind her closed eyelids. She smelled the scent of hot, moist flesh and the muskiness of sex. She heard Vic's labored breathing and her own whimpering sighs. She felt him inside her, stretching her, filling her completely. And she tasted herself on his lips as he devoured her mouth.

He made love to her again, this time with more urgency as he sought to fulfill his own needs. But with every lunge, every kiss, every caress, he intensified her pleasure, and when he seemed on the verge of release, he slowed, pulled back and focused on her again. Completely. Until she caught up with him and she, too, was ready.

He made sure she reached fulfillment a second time before he climaxed, so that she unraveled beneath him only moments before he came. When he was spent, he rolled off her and onto his side while wrapping his arms around her and keeping her close.

Lying in his arms, sated and happier than she'd ever been in her life, Penny Sue kissed Vic's neck and whispered, "I love you."

And in the stillness of predawn, in the utter quiet of her dark bedroom, Vic's silence was deafening.

## Chapter 12

Penny Sue and Vic slept for nearly two hours, then woke and made love a second time. That loving had been even better than the first time because the hunger was less ravaging, the tenderness greater, with moments of lingering passion that built and built and built. And it was with the second loving that she realized Vic had used a condom, that he'd actually used one the first time, too, but she had been so caught up in the fantasy that reality had played only a minor part in what had transpired between them.

He had said some rough, crude things to her in the throes of passion, and his words had excited her, stimulated her in a way that made her feel almost ashamed. Almost.

Sitting at her dressing table in the corner of her big bathroom, Penny Sue brushed her hair as she gazed into the mirror. It was not her face's reflection she saw, but Vic's. He stood behind her, a cockeyed grin on his face.

"I'm sorry I didn't shave last night," he said. "I'm afraid my beard stubble scratched you."

She sighed. "I didn't mind in the least. And what my clothes didn't cover, makeup did." Glancing over her shoulder, she smiled at him. "Are you ready to—"

"No, I'm not. If I had my way, we'd never go downstairs," he told her. "We'd stay up here and make love all day, every day for at least two weeks."

"As nice as that sounds, I'm afraid—"

"Nice?" He swooped down, grabbed her shoulders and kissed her on the neck.

"More than nice—wonderful, fabulous," she corrected herself as she laid her hairbrush on the dressing table. Making love with Vic had been incredible experiences for her. She knew what they had shared was the kind of thing that made people rave about sex. "But if we don't go down to breakfast soon, Aunt Dottie will be banging on my bedroom door wanting to know what's wrong."

"We can't have that."

"No, we can't." She tilted her neck and lowered her head, then kissed the top of his hand, which rested on her left shoulder. "If Aunt Dottie knew we had slept together, she'd be looking at wedding invitations by this afternoon."

Vic's hands tensed on her shoulders. "Penny Sue, we need to talk about—"

"No, we don't." When she jumped to her feet, his hands fell away from her shoulders and he took a step back, away from her.

She turned around and kept smiling at him, wanting to reassure him. After all, if he felt roped and hog-tied by what they'd shared, he might bolt and run. She couldn't risk that happening. Not when she had big plans for Vic Noble, plans she intended to ease him into gradually. "You're not ready to make a commitment. I understand."

"I may never be ready." He looked down at the floor instead of at her.

She reached out, clasped his hands in hers and said, "Then what's there to talk about? You didn't lie to me or make me any promises. I had my eyes wide open. I knew what I was getting myself into. But you didn't, did you, my darling? You still have no idea that you're mine completely, do you? But you will. It's only a matter of time."

"Even so, I—"

Standing on tiptoe, she kissed him. "There, I kissed *you* to shut you up this time."

Chuckling, he lifted his gaze to meet hers and almost wished he hadn't. As much as she tried to hide the rejection she felt, Vic was too astute not to pick up on her emotions. He gave her a questioning look, concern in his expression.

"Stop feeling guilty. I wanted you as much as you wanted me." She wrapped her arms around his waist and cuddled against him. "I want you right now."

He groaned. "Keep that up and we won't make it downstairs until after Aunt Dottie walks in on us."

After pulling away from him, she motioned for him to follow her. "When we get downstairs, try to act natural. Tell them we both overslept." She whistled to Lucky, who rose from his comfy position on the bedroom rug and followed her out into the hall.

Once in the hall, she whispered to Vic, "And whatever you do, don't touch me. Don't even look directly at me. I'm liable to melt into a puddle if you do."

"Ah, sugar, what a thing to say to a man."

"It's the truth."

"I guess you know you've given me a hard-on."

"Vic Noble, hush your mouth. What if someone overhears you?"

When she moved ahead of him, Lucky on her heels, he reached out and swatted her playfully on the behind. Giggling, she didn't turn around or comment on what he'd done. Instead, she bounded down the back stairs ahead of him, humming softly to herself. Lucky rushed ahead of her straight into the kitchen.

She entered the kitchen, an explanation of her tardiness on her lips, but abruptly skidded to a halt in the doorway. Sitting there at the breakfast table with Aunt Dottie was a man. A young man. Young in comparison to her aunt, that is. The man couldn't be much over forty, if that. Broad and sturdily built, like a massive bulldog, with wide shoulders and huge arms, the blond-haired man wolfed down scrambled eggs and sausage while Penny Sue watched.

Aunt Dottie glanced up and smiled pleasantly. "Come in, dear, and meet Mr. Monday."

Vic came up behind Penny Sue and stopped.

"You got here bright and early," Vic said to the man, as he nudged Penny Sue in the back, urging her to move. "I assume you introduced yourself to Ms. Paine."

With his mouth full of food, the man wasn't able to respond before Aunt Dottie replied for him. "He most certainly did. Mr. Monday showed up about half an hour ago and told Tully who he was, and Tully brought him straight back here to the kitchen for a nice, big breakfast." She glanced from Penny Sue to Vic, her keen brown eyes revealing her curiosity. "I told Mr. Monday—"

"Geoff," he said.

"Oh, yes." Aunt Dottie smiled. "I told Geoff that I had no idea why you two hadn't come down for breakfast, that undoubtedly you'd both overslept." She eyed them speculatively, as if studying them closely might reveal some deep, dark secret they were keeping from her.

"We overslept," Penny Sue and Vic said in unison.

Geoff strangled on a sip of coffee.

Aunt Dottie cleared her throat and said, "Yes. Well, like I said, I assumed as much."

Ruby looked right at Penny Sue and shook her head.

Smiling, Penny Sue tried her best to look totally innocent.

"I put everything in the oven to keep it warm. It'll just take a minute to get it on the table." Ruby glanced at the coffeemaker on the counter. "And I just put on a fresh pot of coffee."

Penny Sue felt as exposed as if she had walked into the room naked as a jaybird. Was it her imagination or did everyone—Aunt Dottie, Ruby, Tully and even Mr. Monday—know that she and Vic were now lovers?

"Coffee—" Once again Penny Sue and Vic spoke at the same time, saying the same word.

Knowing everyone was looking at her and that her cheeks were flushed, Penny Sue tittered. Ignoring the curious stares, she headed straight for the coffeemaker. But so did Vic, and the two collided, then jerked apart and stared at each other. Oh, lordy, lordy. This wouldn't do. If she kept acting as if she was guilty of some secret sin, then if everyone didn't already know what she'd done, they soon would.

Penny Sue laughed. Vic grinned.

"Excuse me," he said.

"It was my fault entirely."

"Sit down, both of you," Ruby said. "I'll get the coffee."

"That's not necessary," Penny Sue told the housekeeper, but when Ruby cocked one eyebrow and gave her a sit-down-young-lady look, Penny Sue pulled out a chair and sat. "Thank you, Ruby."

Vic followed Penny Sue's lead and sat down beside Geoff. "How was the flight from Atlanta?"

"I didn't fly," Geoff said. "I drove. We left at about three this morning and came through Chattanooga. I had to drop Dom off. He's starting on a new assignment today."

"I didn't know he'd finished up his last job." Vic frowned. "I thought there were no other agents available."

Geoff popped the last bite of buttery biscuit into his mouth, chewed and swallowed. "I love Southern cooking." He glanced at Ruby. "And this is some of the best food I've eaten since coming to the U.S." Geoff turned to Vic. "Dom and I both just completed our assignments. I arrived back in Atlanta yesterday morning and Dom flew in last night. He didn't even have time to unpack."

"It's a good thing Sawyer hired a couple of new recruits," Vic said. "We've been working shorthanded for months."

"The bodyguard business must be so exciting," Dottie said. "Traveling all over the world, protecting interesting people." She sighed, then reached across the table and patted Vic's hand. "Being here in Alabaster Creek to protect Lucky must be boring for you."

"Not at all, Miss Dottie," Vic replied, his gaze lifting to meet Penny Sue's. "I've found this assignment to be very…stimulating."

Geoff made a noise, something that sounded like a cough mated with a laugh.

"I'm going to have to hurry to make it to the shop on time," Penny Sue said, deliberately taking the focus off Vic. "Ruby, don't bother with more than coffee for me." She glanced at Vic. "Why don't you and Lucky stay here this morning and you can do whatever you need to do to bring Mr. Monday up-to-date on the case."

"Please, call me Geoff," the big blonde said in a distinctive British voice, with just a hint of a Scottish brogue.

When she looked at him, he smiled, and she thought that although he wasn't really handsome, he was extremely masculine in a Viking-raider kind of way. "And you must call me Penny Sue."

Vic glowered at Geoff, which made Penny Sue very happy. A little jealousy was good for a man's soul. And very good for a woman's ego. Hmm…that bit of perceptive reasoning should be added to the Southern Women's Code, for future use.

"You shouldn't have called me at home," Tommy Rutland whispered into the phone.

"This can't wait," Candy told him. "I need to know if you're going to tell Cherie about us."

"I—I don't know. To be honest, I was hoping we could figure out a way to persuade Penny Sue not to expose our dirty little secret."

"Is that the way you think of our affair—as something dirty?"

"Don't go getting upset," Tommy said. "You know I didn't mean it that way. But if Penny Sue tells Douglas about us, then it's bound to get out and I'll be ruined politically in this town, not to mention that Cherie will divorce me. God, Candy, I can't let that happen."

"Then what are you going to do about it?"

"I don't know, but I'll think of something. I have to. We have to stop Penny Sue and that bodyguard fellow from ruining everything."

"I have an idea," Candy told him. "But you're not going to like it."

Geoff Monday joined Vic in the backyard when he took Lucky out to do his business. Ever since the incident with the pit bulls, Vic had kept Lucky on a leash, even in the fenced yard. Considering how many times the little mutt had come close to death, it paid to be extra careful. After all, not only would he be a laughingstock at Dundee if he failed to keep Lucky safe, it would break Penny Sue's heart if anything happened to her dog. And the last thing he wanted was to see Penny Sue's heart broken.

Then why did you make love to her? She thinks she's in love with you. When you leave her, you'll break her heart.

"Ms. Paine is a beautiful woman," Geoff said. "Why is it that since I came to work at Dundee, I haven't been given the opportunity to guard someone like her?"

"Luck of the draw," Vic said. "I was the only agent available at the time."

Geoff chuckled. "Guarding a dog has to be a low point in your career, but considering how chummy you are with his owner, I'd say it's well worth the embarrassment."

"What makes you think I'm chummy with Penny Sue?"

Geoff slapped Vic on the back. "Even the old auntie knows what's going on between you and her niece."

"Did she say—"

"She didn't say anything. She didn't have to. Everyone sensed something the minute you two walked into the kitchen doing your best not to look at each other or touch each other. But the thing no one knows for sure is whether or not you've shagged her yet." Geoff clamped his hand down on Vic's shoulder. "Want to share the details with Uncle Geoff?"

Vic slung off Geoff's hand and walked away, following Lucky as he sniffed around the back fence. What had happened between Penny Sue and him had been private, not something to be shared with anyone else.

"Wait," Geoff called. When he caught up with Vic, he said, "Sorry, old chap. I didn't realize that you were serious about the lady."

Vic clenched his teeth tightly, not wanting to lose his temper and say something he would regret later. Changing the subject, he asked, "I assume you came with information I need, right?"

Falling into step alongside Vic, Geoff told him, "So I have. First of all the blood on the toy dog left on Ms. Paine's front porch was cow's blood, from a fresh cut of beef. And the stuffed toy dog was one sold at many retail stores nationwide. It would probably be difficult if not impossible to find out who bought it, especially if they didn't buy it locally."

"I figured as much. What about the butcher knife?"

"It's one you can pick up just about anywhere and there were no fingerprints on it. So that leaves the bullet that the vet dug out of Lucky. It was a 32-20, commonly used years ago, especially in Winchester rifles. We should find out if one of the heirs owns an old Winchester."

"Hmm… I doubt anyone is going to volunteer that information."

"Well, we've still got the fire at the clinic and the pit bull attack. If we can come up with a lead on either of those—"

"Add kidnapping Lucky to that list," Vic said.

"When did this happen?"

"Last night."

"Maybe I should ask how it happened, but since you obviously recovered your client—" Geoff glanced at Lucky who was busy hiking his leg on a nearby tree "—a better question is who dognapped the little bugger?"

"Penny Sue's cousin, Chris Paine. Long-story-short, Chris Paine owes a bundle to a local bookie, so he stole the dog and says he planned to give the dog away, out of state, then Lucky would have been presumed dead and the heirs could have collected their inheritance."

"Do you believe the guy?" Geoff asked. "I mean, about him planning to give the dog away and not kill him? If he meant to kill the dog, then he could well be the one who shot—"

Vic shook his head. "He's not the type. The guy was a basket case when we caught him. And I don't think he'd burn down a clinic or let pit bulls loose on his cousin."

"Well, somebody sure wants Lucky dead. Three attempts on his life, if you don't count the kidnapping. We're looking for someone capable of shooting Lucky, of torching a veterinary clinic and killing a dozen or more animals, and of setting pit bulls loose on Lucky, Ms. Paine and you."

"We don't have much to go on," Vic said. "No one saw anything when Lucky was shot. And learning the bullet was used in an old rifle won't help us unless we can find out who owns the rifle. Other than the fact the fire at the clinic was deliberately set, the fire chief hasn't shared any other info with me. And as far as I know, the police can't do anything to the owner of the pit bulls because he claims someone stole his dogs."

"Looks as if we have quite a mystery on our hands. You should concentrate on protecting Lucky and let me take over working the investigation. And if at any time, you want to swap jobs, just let me know." Geoff winked at Vic.

Vic resisted the urge to sock Monday in the jaw. He knew the burly Brit was kidding him about getting in over his head with Penny Sue, which was a major no-no in their business.

"I'll fill you in on everything I've learned about this case and I'll work with you today," Vic said. "I'll phone Penny Sue and tell her that I'm keeping Lucky here at the house all day so we can concentrate on the investigation."

"Tell me something—going strictly on gut instinct, which one of the suspects would you say did it?"

Vic took a deep breath and released it. "By process of elimination, I'd say Valerie and Dylan Redley, or Douglas Paine, or his wife Candy. And even possibly Reverend Clayton Dickson."

"You think a minister could have—"

"Dickson is also a man," Vic said. "A man with a wife who writes a lot of bad checks. And after seeing the guy only twice, I don't like him. He's got phony written all over him."

"Okay, so going by your gut instincts, we can rule out Miss Dottie, Chris and Stacie Paine and Eula Paine."

"No, we shouldn't rule them out. It's just my gut feeling that those people aren't capable of committing any of the life-threatening crimes against Lucky."

"Where do you suggest we begin?"

"We begin by finding out who owns a rifle that uses 30-20 ammo."

"Phone call for you," Ruby told Dottie as she handed her the portable telephone. "It's a man. Said his name is Hal Esmond. Do we know him?"

"Hal? Oh, my…" Dottie giggled. "You don't know him. But Mr. Esmond is a friend of mine. A new friend."

Ruby rolled her eyes heavenward.

"There's no need for you to act like that," Dottie said, placing her hand over the telephone receiver to block her conversation from the caller. "I'll have you know that Hal Esmond is a true gentleman."

"Yeah, and so were Howard Yarborough, Edward Terrell and Lawrence McDaniel. And all three men broke your heart. And Edward Terrell swindled you out of a small fortune."

"Hush up," Dottie scolded. "Don't remind me of unhappy times. That's all old news. Hal is nothing like Howard or Lawrence and he's most certainly a far better man than Edward ever thought of being."

"If you say so."

"I do say so!"

Dottie tossed her head high, cut her eyes to give Ruby a sidelong, condemning glance and then rushed into the front parlor, seeking privacy. As soon as she was alone, she put the phone to her ear and said, "Hello, Hal. So sorry to have kept you waiting."

"Is everything all right?" he asked.

"Everything is just fine."

"Do we still have a date for a ride out in the country this afternoon?"

"We certainly do. I'll be ready for you to pick me up at two."

"I can hardly wait."

"Neither can I." Dottie knew in her heart that this time things would be different. Hal *was* a true gentleman and he wouldn't disappoint her.

"I have a little surprise for you," he told her. "I believe it's something that will please you. And if it does, then your pleasure will make me the happiest man in the world."

"Oh…oh, my…" He was going to ask her to marry him. She just knew he was. He had hinted of a future for the two of them several times in various e-mails during the past month.

"Hal, I—I'd like for you to come to church with me tomorrow for Palm Sunday services, and then come home with me for dinner."

"Why, Dottie, my dearest, I'd be honored."

"I want you to meet my family," she told him. "Everyone's been invited so they can all meet you at the same time. I know they're going to love you." Just as I do.

Business at Penny Sue's Pretties had been brisk. Everyone was gearing up for Easter, which was only a week away. And half the customers had been bold enough to ask her about Chris's arrest last night. Since word had spread around town quickly this morning, everyone who'd heard the news assumed Chris had not only cold-cocked Tanya and kidnapped Lucky, but that he was responsible for all the other crimes committed against Lucky. If Penny Sue had said once, she'd said a hundred times, "But Chris didn't shoot Lucky and he didn't torch the clinic and he didn't set the pit bulls loose." She truly believed her cousin was innocent and that his kidnapping Lucky had been a spur-of-the-moment, desperate act.

By lunchtime, she and Eula were both ready for a break—more from answering questions than making sales. At Eula's suggestion, they had ordered in and when lunch arrived, they'd left the part-time workers, Mary and Kira, to handle the customers.

Hiding away in the storeroom, they spread out their bagged lunches on a table and closed out the inquisitive world of Alabaster Creek.

"We've been so busy since I came in that I haven't had a chance to tell you that Douglas phoned me this morning and asked for a loan," Eula said.

"Oh, dear. Then it's true that he's spent every dime he has on Candy and he's flat broke." Penny Sue had heard the rumors, of course, but had hoped they weren't true.

"He wanted the money to post Chris's bail." Eula sipped her tea through a straw.

"Did you loan him the money?"

Eula nodded. "Enough for bail, but Chris is going to need a

good lawyer. I expect Douglas will be coming to you, hat-in-hand."

"I wish to goodness that Aunt Lottie hadn't left her money to Lucky. Surely she knew I would take good care of him. It would have made more sense for her to take care of the family by giving them their inheritances, and not making them wait for Lucky to go to puppy-dog heaven."

"Lottie was a shrewd woman," Eula said. "No doubt she knew that you'd take care of Dottie and handle any financial crises that came up in the family. But she also knew that if she left everything outright to her heirs, most of them would squander the money. Dottie would just have had more plastic surgery, bought herself more expensive jewelry she doesn't need and probably wasted a great deal on some gigolo. Chris would have gambled away his share and Candy would have spent every dime of Douglas's share. And Clayton—that nutcase—he'd have donated every last cent to that weird church he belongs to. And considering the fact that Valerie and Dylan are in debt up to their eyeballs, I dare say they'd have gone through their inheritance within a year or less."

"What about you, me and Stacie?"

Eula laughed. "Well, you and I don't need the money. I'm not as rich as you by any means, but I've socked away quite a bit over the years. And Stacie, bless her, would probably have wound up giving Chris and Douglas most of her share."

Penny Sue groaned. "I suppose I should call Uncle Douglas and tell him I'll pay for Chris's lawyer."

"That would be very kind of you." Eula unwrapped her sandwich and took a bite.

"Eula?"

"Hmm…?"

"I need to ask your opinion about something."

Eula swallowed, washed her food down with a sip of tea and said, "You sound very serious."

"I have to swear you to secrecy."

"Oh, my. Yes, of course."

"Last night when Vic and I were searching for Lucky, we…we

found Candy in bed with Tommy Rutland." There, she'd said it out loud and the heavens hadn't come crashing down on her.

Eula's eyes widened in surprise, then she burst out laughing. "Well, I imagine you'll win the mayoral race hands down."

Penny Sue whimpered. "This isn't funny."

Eula sobered, but couldn't wipe the grin off her face. "Serves Douglas right for marrying a woman younger than his daughter. And an ex Vegas showgirl at that."

"It'll break his heart when he finds out."

"He'll survive. Besides, he'll be better off without her."

"Should I tell him?"

"Oh, now there's the rub." Eula patted her fingers on her lips as she thought. "Someone will have to tell him."

"There's no need," a man's voice said.

The door they had thought was closed was now open and Douglas Paine stood there with a stricken look on his face. Oh, dear Lord, how much of their conversation had he heard? Penny Sue wondered.

"Uncle Douglas, how long—"

"Long enough," he replied.

Penny Sue rose to her feet. "I'm so sorry you found out this way."

Leaving the door wide open, Douglas entered the storeroom. "I knew before I came here. Candy told me this morning. She was under the impression she had no choice in the matter, that if she didn't tell, you would."

"Are you all right, Douglas?" Eula asked.

"No, I'm not all right," he said, "but I will be. However, I didn't come here to discuss my wife's infidelity. I came here to ask Penny Sue to pay for a decent lawyer for Chris and plead with her to do all she can to help him out of this terrible trouble he's in."

Just as Penny Sue opened her mouth to respond, her uncle continued, "Remember that Chris didn't intend to hurt Lucky. And he is your cousin. He's family. And if Lottie hadn't done such a darn fool thing, leaving her money to a dog, none of this would have happened."

Penny Sue put her arm around her uncle's shoulders. "How much does Chris owe this bookie?"

"Fifty thousand." Douglas hung his head in shame.

"I'll take care of it," she promised. "And I'll pay for a lawyer, too, of course. But after this, don't come to me for any money for Chris. Do you understand?"

Douglas nodded. "I need to ask one more favor."

Penny Sue took a deep breath. She had spent years helping Aunt Lottie care for the family, doing them favors, keeping them out of trouble. "What's the favor?"

"Please don't tell anyone else about Candy's indiscretion. She doesn't want word of it to get back to Tommy's wife, and she and I... Well, we want to try to work things out."

"Oh, Douglas, really." Eula moaned, then murmured under her breath, "No fool like an old fool."

Patting her uncle on the back, Penny Sue assured him, "I won't tell another soul. I promise."                    .

"Somehow, someway, I'll pay both of you back." Douglas glanced from Penny Sue to Eula. "And that's a solemn vow."

Business had been steady all afternoon. Hectic really. And Penny Sue hadn't had a minute to herself or a chance for her and Eula to talk over what had happened with Douglas.

She had taken a few minutes to phone Vic, and told him everything about her morning, especially Uncle Douglas's visit.

"Your uncle is a fool to forgive her and think they can salvage that marriage."

"Love makes fools of all of us," Penny Sue had said.

"Yeah, and so does senility," Vic had replied.

"I miss you," she'd told him.

"Lucky and I miss you, too, sugar."

"But you're getting more work done there at the house, with Mr. Monday, than you would here with me, aren't you?"

"Sure am. But later on, what do you think about Lucky and me coming to the shop to meet you and walk you home?"

"I think it's a wonderful idea," she'd told him.

That had been right after lunch and she'd been watching the

clock ever since, counting the minutes until she and Vic would be together again.

While Penny Sue carefully wrapped the cloisonne Easter eggs Stella Lowrance had just purchased, a new customer entered the shop. Glancing at the front door when the bell chimed, she gasped softly when she saw Wayne Boggus. It wasn't that he'd never been in her shop. He had. But since they were no longer dating, she'd hardly expected him to show up out of the blue.

*But he doesn't know you two won't be dating anymore. You haven't told him.*

She hurriedly put the carefully wrapped eggs in a box and handed the box to Stella, along with her receipt. "I know you're going to love these."

"I'm sure I will." Stella looked at Wayne when he approached. "Good afternoon, Chief Boggus."

He nodded. "Ma'am."

Stella turned back to Penny Sue. "We'll see you at church tomorrow, won't we? And you'll bring that handsome Mr. Noble with you, of course." Stella smiled innocently, tucked her box of cloisonne eggs under her arm and walked away.

"Hi, Wayne," Penny Sue said. "What brings you to Penny Sue's Pretties this afternoon? If you want to buy your nieces and nephews something for Easter, we have an entire children's section." She came out from behind the checkout counter. "They're right over—"

He grasped her arm and jerked her close, then said in a quiet, hard voice, "Is it true that there's something of a personal nature going on between you and Mr. Noble?"

Penny Sue's heart sank. "Wayne, I—I don't know what to say."

"Just tell me the truth. Are you still my girl or…" He lowered his voice to a whisper. "Everyone is talking about what happened last night at Doc and Angela's. That man practically told everyone that you two were lovers."

"He did no such thing!"

"Didn't he and Dylan Redley nearly get in a fight over you? And didn't Mr. Noble tell Dylan that it's not a woman's first lover that she never forgets, but it is the best lover she always remembers?"

"For goodness sake, Wayne, lower your voice. People are staring at us." Indeed, half the customers had stopped shopping and were doing their best to overhear her conversation with the fire chief.

"My relationship with Vic Noble has nothing to do with you and me." Lord, help me be kind to this dear man. I don't want to hurt Wayne, but it would be cruel for him to think we have a future together.

"Then there is nothing but business between the two of you?"

She reached out and took Wayne's hand. "I'm very fond of you."

He looked hopeful. "And I am of you, too."

Try again, she told herself, and just get straight to it. Be tactfully honest. "I don't love you, Wayne, and there's no point in our dating any longer," she whispered. "You should be free to find someone who truly deserves a wonderful man like you."

His face fell. Penny Sue felt just awful.

"Is it Mr. Noble? Are you in love with him?"

Penny Sue didn't know how to respond honestly without causing more harm to Wayne's ego.

"You barely know the man," Wayne reminded her. "He came to town only a few days ago. And he'll leave again just as soon as his job is finished. He'll walk away from you and never look back. Surely you know that."

She squeezed Wayne's hand. "Whatever does or doesn't happen between Vic Noble and me doesn't change the fact that you need to find someone else, someone who'll want you the way you want them."

"And you don't want me any longer, do you?"

Before she could respond, he yanked his hand from hers, turned and left the shop. Curious stares followed him until the door closed, then they focused on Penny Sue. She forced a smile, then crept over to Eula and spoke to her in a hushed voice.

"I thought everyone in town was talking about Chris kidnapping Lucky, but that hasn't been the only thing they've been gossiping about, has it? They've been talking about what happened between Vic and Dylan last night at the party, haven't they?"

"Oh, Penny Sue, I thought you knew." Eula glanced around and smiled at the customers within earshot. "The whole town believes you and Mr. Noble are lovers."

A flush crept up Penny Sue's neck and spread to her cheeks. Merciful heavens. She was the talk of the town and hadn't even known it.

As if on cue, the front door opened and in walked Vic, Lucky several feet ahead of him, his retractable leash secure in Vic's big hand. Was it closing time already? Or had Vic arrived a bit early? What did it matter? She was glad to see him. And there was nothing she wanted more than to run into his arms and tell him.

Why not? a devilish inner voice asked. If the good citizens of Alabaster Creek wanted something to gossip about, she'd give them something.

Without a logical thought in her head, Penny Sue ran across the shop, stopped, knelt down and patted Lucky quickly and then threw herself at Vic. He opened his arms and grabbed her. Smiling at him, she stood on tiptoe and whispered against his lips, "I'm so glad you're here." Then she kissed him. A good old wet, tongue-thrusting kiss.

## *Chapter 13*

"That was quite a welcome back there," Vic said, smiling. Actually grinning like an idiot. "Aren't you concerned about your reputation? After all, you *are* running for mayor, aren't you?"

Hand in hand, Penny Sue and Vic strolled along on their walk from her shop to her home, Lucky leading the way several feet ahead of them. She shook her head. "I believe Tommy Rutland will withdraw from the race very soon, and he was the only real opposition I had. As far as my kissing you—"

"You practically jumped on me, right there in Penny Sue's Pretties, with all your customers watching."

Totally unperturbed by his comment, she replied, "Sometimes a woman doesn't think her actions through thoroughly, she just does what she feels like doing."

"And you felt like throwing yourself into my arms and kissing me in front of at least two dozen customers?"

"Yes, I did. Besides, it seems everyone already assumes we are lovers."

Pausing, Vic inadvertently clamped down on Lucky's retractable leash, halting the dog in mid-sniff. Sensing something was wrong, he growled, then looked back at Vic.

"How is that possible?" Vic asked. "Was someone peeking in your bedroom window early this morning?"

"No, of course not. It has nothing to do with the fact that we actually made love this morning." Her cheeks flushed a very becoming shade of pink. "It's about what happened at the party last night. What you said to Dylan."

"What I said to Dylan?" Vic mentally went over the events of the previous evening, starting with the moment he had jerked Dylan Redley away from Penny Sue. Recalling his exact words brought a chuckle to Vic's throat, one he tried to suppress because he didn't think Penny Sue found it humorous. "Exactly what did I say?"

"You remember what you said and don't deny it. I can tell by that smirk on your face. And you think it's funny, don't you? You implied that you were the lover I would always remember, so everyone assumed we're involved."

"Sugar, we *are* involved."

"I know that, but we weren't last night when you said what you did to Dylan."

"So it's all my fault that the whole town knows we're lovers?"

"You're missing the point entirely."

Uh-oh, she had that look in her eyes again. The one that warned him she was either going to quote from the Southern Women's Code or she was devising a plan to punish him.

Penny Sue's thought processes were totally illogical sometimes, especially when she dealt with emotional situations. But the strange thing—the scary thing—was he found that quality not only amusing but downright sweet.

You've got it bad, buddy boy, he told himself. You're so hung up on this woman that you think even her flaws are wonderful now.

"Will it save me a lot of grief if I just go ahead and say I'm sorry?" he asked. "Or would you prefer I do penance?"

She stared at him, a puzzled expression on her face. "What are you talking about? Oh, you think I'm angry with you because of what you said to Dylan and because everyone thinks we're lovers." She laughed. "If we weren't lovers, I'd be upset that the rumor was floating around town that we were."

Okay, he needed to backtrack a little because somewhere in this conversation, he'd gotten derailed. Hadn't she been accusing him of having done something wrong when he'd made his possessive comment to Dylan last night?

"You're confusing me," he admitted.

"How's that?"

"Are you upset with me because of what I said to Dylan?"

"Certainly not." She wrapped her arm through his and snuggled up to him. Right there on the street, where any passerby could see them. "I thought what you said to Dylan was chivalrous. Don't you know that you're my white knight?"

Vic couldn't keep his smile from expanding from ear to ear. He liked the idea of being Penny Sue's white knight. "Actually, I'm more of a black knight."

"You say that because of your background, don't you? You've taken part in some rather terrible things, haven't you? No, don't answer that. The way I look at it, everything that's happened in your life up to this point has helped create the man you are now." She rose up on her toes and kissed his cheek. "And I, for one, think the man you are right now is pretty wonderful."

"Penny Sue—"

She kissed him on the lips. And he returned her kiss. God, how he loved the taste of this woman, the feel of her in his arms.

Lucky barked. Vic ended the kiss, glanced down at the dog and grinned. "You'd better get used to that, little fellow, because I'm going to be kissing her every chance I get from now on." Where the hell had that come from? Vic wondered, two seconds after the words came out of his mouth. He had practically made a vow of commitment.

"Someday, when you're ready to tell me about your past—if that day ever comes—I'll be ready to listen," she told him. "And even if some of the things you tell me are difficult for me to understand, I promise I won't judge your actions by my small-town, Pollyanna standards."

An overwhelming sense of relief spread through him, as if

somehow, in some way, Penny Sue had absolved him of his sins, of any and all crimes he had committed in the name of safeguarding his country. It wasn't that he felt any great sense of guilt, not even about Lyssa, but in the real world—outside top-secret, covert operations—killing another human being was a crime. He couldn't imagine someone like Penny Sue ever understanding how a man could kill a woman he had thought he loved, even if her actions had threatened the lives of numerous others.

"Maybe someday," he told her. "For now, you've got enough problems without listening to me bare my soul."

She heaved a deep sigh. "Speaking of my problems—did you and Geoff work out a battle plan? And did y'all come to any conclusions about who might be trying to kill Lucky?"

Vic released his tight hold on Lucky's leash and the three of them continued their stroll up the street. "Since you mentioned it, I did want to go over a few things with you."

"We've got four more blocks until we reach the house, so start talking."

Before he got a chance to say a word, a lady wearing a floral caftan waved at them from her front porch and called out, "Yoohoo. How are you, Penny Sue?"

Penny Sue waved back at the lady. "Just fine, Miss Cora. How are you this evening?" Penny Sue nudged Vic in the ribs and whispered, "Just wait, she'll tell me all about her arthritis and her migraines and her bad knee."

"Tolerable," Cora replied. "Of course my bad knee is acting up. You know it hasn't been right since Clarence and I were in that bad wreck back in '92." The woman rubbed her left temple. "And I think I have another killer migraine coming on. It's all the stress I live with, what with Clarence thinking about retiring and cutting our income in half, and that brother of his living here and freeloading off us."

"How's your arthritis?" Penny Sue asked.

"Oh, child, it's awful. Let me warn you, the body starts falling apart after you hit forty. Just you wait and see."

"Forty?" Vic murmured. "She hasn't seen forty in twenty years."

Smiling, Penny Sue nudged him in the ribs again, then said to her neighbor, "You take care, Miss Cora. We've got to get on home. You know how Aunt Dottie likes to have supper on time."

"Give Dottie my love, will you, and tell her to stop by sometime." Cora looked pointedly at Vic. "Penny Sue, aren't you going to introduce me to your young man? I've heard all about him, you know."

"Oh, forgive me. Miss Cora, may I introduce Vic Noble, from Atlanta. Vic, this is Mrs. Cora Wilbanks. Her mama's granddaddy fought at Shiloh with my granddaddy Paine's grandfather and the two men came home from the war and married cousins. So, you see, Miss Cora and I are dog-tailed kin."

"It's a pleasure to meet you, Mr. Noble." Cora ran her gaze over him, sizing him up. "I guess you know you've got the pick of the litter with Penny Sue. You treat her right, you hear me, or you'll have half the town coming after you with tar and feathers."

"Yes, ma'am."

Penny Sue waved goodbye to her distant relative and hurried Vic along. Once they were half a block away, she said, "You do realize she was joking about the tar and feathers?"

Vic grunted. "I'm not so sure about that. You seem to have quite a fan club in this town. And that half the town Miss Cora was referring to—I think they're all your cousins, aren't they? No wonder you're running for mayor, sugar. You're sure to win by a landslide."

"I think you're right."

They both laughed.

Keeping her arm laced through his and meandering along at a leisurely pace, she asked him, "So what was it you wanted to discuss with me?"

"First of all, do you know anyone in the family—one of the heirs—who owns an old Winchester rifle?"

"Uncle Douglas does," she replied. "Actually, since it belonged to my granddaddy Paine, it's a family heirloom. Why did you— oh, no, don't tell me that the bullet Doc Stone took out of Lucky came from that old Winchester."

Vic nodded. "We can't prove it came from your uncle's rifle without checking the rifle."

"We'll have to ask Uncle Douglas to see the rifle. But even if the bullet was fired from Granddaddy's old Winchester, I refuse to believe that Uncle Douglas shot Lucky."

"Would anyone else have access to the rifle? Does he keep it under lock and key or—"

"Not that I know of. I believe he keeps it in a cedar chest in his attic."

"Does everyone in the family know where he keeps the rifle?"

"Probably." She frowned. "That means anyone could have used it."

"And that's what we'll tell your uncle when we ask to take a look at the rifle."

"I'd appreciate your taking that approach. Uncle Douglas has enough to deal with right now without being accused of shooting Lucky."

Vic paused, looked at Penny Sue, and shook his head. "Were you born this way or—"

"Born what way?"

"So caring and kind and loving."

Instantly, tears glistened in her eyes. "What an incredibly sweet thing to say."

"You're not going to cry, are you?"

She batted her eyelashes and several teardrops adhered to the tips. "You know there is such a thing as happy tears."

He caressed her cheek. "Doesn't take much to make you happy, does it, sugar?"

"Sometimes it's the little things that matter the most."

Their conversation was getting a little emotionally heavy for him. He cleared his throat and grunted. "Some other things Geoff and I discussed were the toy dog and the blood that was smeared on it. The blood was cow's blood, from a fresh piece of beef. Both the toy and the blood are items anyone could have—"

"Phyllis collects toy animals," Penny Sue said. "I don't know why I hadn't thought of that before now. Her house is filled with them. They're on every bed, in several curio cabinets and she even has a couple of stuffed toy birds in a cage in her kitchen.

"Of course, that doesn't necessarily mean the toy dog that was left on my front porch belonged to Phyllis. I really can't see her doing something as gruesome as stabbing one of her prized stuffed animals and smearing it with blood."

"I think I should question Mrs. Dickson, see if any of her toy animals are missing. It could be that another member of the family stole the toy dog from her collection."

"I don't think anyone else, other than Clayton, could have taken it," Penny Sue said. "I doubt another member of the family has been in their house in years, not since Clayton became such a religious fanatic. And if Clayton did it, that means a member of my family—a blood relative—is the guilty party."

"I hate to say it, but the guilty party might well turn out to be a blood relative. You can't be certain that it's not, just because you don't want to believe it."

"You're pooh-poohing my instincts, aren't you? You think I'm silly to listen to what my heart tells me." Her bottom lip trembled.

"Don't do it," he told her. "Don't cry. And don't blame me for daring to consider that someone you're blood related to might be capable of committing all the crimes against Lucky."

"In your line of business, I'll bet you rely on your gut instincts all the time, don't you?" Penny Sue pulled away from him, planted her hands on her hips and issued him a challenging glare. "So why are your instincts better than mine? Because they're male?"

"No, sugar, because they're logical."

Her lips puckered.

"Penny Sue…" Why was it that a woman's tears had never affected him before, never garnered the least bit of sympathy from him, and all Penny Sue had to do was look like she was going to cry to have him on his knees, begging?

"You just wait and see, Vic Noble—whoever the culprit is, he or she will turn out *not* to be a Paine blood relative."

"Are you forgetting that Chris kidnapped Lucky last night?"

He could see the wheels turning furiously in her mind and

knew she would come up with an explanation that made perfect sense to her. "Chris didn't harm Lucky."

"He knocked Tanya over the head and rendered her unconscious."

"I'm sure he didn't mean to hit her so hard. Besides, if Tanya's skull is as fragile as her brain, then even a light tap would have knocked her out."

"Why, Miss Penny Sue, what an unkind thing to say about someone." Vic grinned.

Penny Sue's lips twitched, then curved into a smile. "See, I'm not always sweet. I can be rather catty at times."

He reached out and laced his arm through hers. "Why don't we shelve this discussion until after supper. If we're not home soon, Miss Dottie will send out a search party for us. Right before Lucky and I left to come to the shop to meet you, she informed me that she had something very important to tell you this evening."

"I wonder what it could be. The thought of Aunt Dottie having important news to share unnerves me just a little. With her, you never know."

Like aunt, like niece, Vic thought. He figured if he spent a hundred years with Penny Sue, she'd still say and do things that both unnerved and surprised him.

The minute she finished eating her banana pudding, Dottie Paine glanced around the table at each person—Geoff Monday, Vic Noble and Penny Sue—then with a wide smile on her face, she said, "If y'all are finished with dessert, I'd like to share my wonderful news with you."

Penny Sue pushed aside her half-eaten pudding. Vic had already finished his and was drinking the last drops of his iced tea. Geoff hurriedly gulped down the final spoonful from his bowl.

"We're all finished," Penny Sue said, her stomach tied in knots. Please, Lord, let this really be good news and not something that will mean Aunt Dottie has set a new blazing fire that I'll have to put out.

Dottie reached inside the pocket of her frilly white blouse and pulled out a ring, then hurriedly placed it on the third finger of her left hand. As she held out her hand and dangled her fingers in a look-at-this gesture, she announced, "I'm engaged to be married."

Geoff grinned. Vic's eyes widened. Penny Sue's mouth dropped open.

"Well, somebody say something." Dottie looked directly at Penny Sue.

Ruby, who had just come into the dining room with the silver coffeepot, said, "Give 'em a minute to recover from the shock." She went from person to person, pouring after-dinner coffee into their demitasse cups.

"Who? When? Aunt Dottie...?" Penny Sue couldn't quite wrap her mind around the news. Dottie Paine engaged? Again? At seventy-five?

"His name is Hal Esmond. He's a widower from Birmingham. And he's a totally charming gentleman." Dottie wiggled her fingers again. "Isn't this ring to-die-for? Two carats. Hal's a retired banker. He's loaded. Imagine me marrying a rich man, someone who could care less that I don't have a dime to my name."

"Hal Esmond? I don't know him, do I?" Penny Sue asked. "How did you meet him? How long have you known him? Why haven't you ever mentioned him to me?"

"I'll reply in reverse order," Dottie said. "We were keeping our romance a secret, that's why I didn't tell anyone about him. And I've known him for months. We met shortly after Lottie died and..."

"You've known him for only two months?" Penny Sue realized that she, of all people, shouldn't be criticizing her aunt for falling in love so quickly. It had taken her days, not months, to know that Vic was the man with whom she wanted to spend the rest of her life.

"Two hours, two days, two months, two years, what's the difference?" Dottie sighed. "Falling in love is just one of those unpredictable things, isn't it? I mean, just look at you and Vic."

Geoff Monday cleared his throat. Vic gave him a harsh glare. Geoff shrugged. Penny Sue glanced from one man to the other, settling her gaze on Vic. He looked downright uncomfortable.

"How did you meet Mr. Esmond?" Geoff asked.

Dottie flopped her right hand in a limp wave. "Oh, that's the most exciting part. Hal and I met online, in a chat room. We've been e-mailing for two months and falling more and more in love with each message. Finally, we decided we should meet in person, so he came to Alabaster Creek last night and I met him downtown at the Castle. Then this afternoon, we went for a ride out in the country and he popped the question.

"He's coming for Sunday dinner tomorrow and I'm introducing him to the rest of the family. Won't everyone be surprised? Hal and I want a May wedding. At our age, you don't want to put things off. Neither of us is getting any younger."

"Congratulations, Miss Dottie," Geoff said.

"Congratulations go to the groom," Dottie corrected. "You must offer me your best wishes."

"Oh. Yes, ma'am." Geoff grinned. "May I offer you my best wishes."

"Thank you."

"I hate to ask this, but—does Mr. Esmond know you're one of the heirs to your sister's twenty-three-million-dollar fortune?" Vic asked. "And does he know that Lucky is the only thing standing between you and your inheritance?"

Gasping, Dottie clutched her throat. "You're implying something unthinkable. I told you that Hal is a very wealthy man. If you have any doubts, feel free to check him out." Shaking her head, Dottie whimpered. "I'm surprised that you, of all people, would ask such questions."

"Why is that?" Vic looked at her curiously.

"Well, I'd think it's obvious. You're in love with our Penny Sue and no doubt plan to marry her, so what if I were to imply that you were interested in her simply for her money? Can't you see how insulting that would be?"

Geoff covered his mouth with his hand, but the action did little to muffle his chuckle.

Penny Sue looked nervously at Vic. Oh, my. What must he be thinking? She offered him a smile that she hoped conveyed a message—my aunt's just a silly old woman, please ignore her. Then she turned to Aunt Dottie. "Of course we all wish you every happiness. But it's only natural that Vic…that anyone…would be concerned, considering how you met Mr. Esmond, and because none of us know him personally."

"As I said, he'll be coming for Sunday dinner tomorrow, along with the rest of the family. Once you meet my Hal, you'll adore him. Simply adore him."

Penny Sue hoped and prayed, for her aunt's sake, that Hal Esmond was who and what he professed to be. But the odds were not in Dottie's favor. After all, her track record with men was dismal. Three engagements before this one, and not one had ended at the altar.

"You've met the other members of the Paine family, haven't you?" Geoff Monday asked as he stood on the front porch with Vic, the two of them looking out over the yard bursting with springtime blossoms. The scent of flowers hung heavily in the evening air. "What's your take on things?"

"I've met with all of them only once and got the impression that they're pretty much your typical eccentric Southern family."

Geoff's brow wrinkled. "You might want to clarify that for me a bit. Is that a good thing or a bad thing?"

Vic grinned. "Neither. All I meant was that there's a mixture of oddballs in the family, so trying to zero in on one who might be just a little too far over the edge isn't easy."

"You think they're all peculiar, even Penny Sue?"

"Oh, most definitely Penny Sue."

"But I thought you two…well, you know." Geoff studied Vic for a moment. "It's not as if you and I know each other all that well, but we've been around each other enough that I've noticed you seldom smiled and never laughed. Since I arrived in Alabaster Creek this morning, I've seen you smile and heard you laugh, both in the same day."

"Penny Sue has that effect on me. It's impossible to be around her and not… It's just that I find her… She's different, in a good kind of way."

"You find her delightfully amusing."

Vic chuckled. "Yeah, to say the least."

"Hmm…"

"Look, it isn't that I'm not enjoying our little chat, but you didn't ask me to come out here on the porch to inquire about my intentions toward Penny Sue, did you?"

"Sorry, old man. I got sidetracked." Geoff braced his backside against the banister railing and crossed his arms over his chest. "Miss Dottie told me that her brother owns an old Winchester rifle, one that belonged to their father."

Vic nodded. "Penny Sue told me the same thing."

"Then we need to get our hands on that rifle. If we ask the uncle for it, he could refuse, but if he does that, it's as good as admitting he's guilty."

"So, tomorrow, after Sunday dinner, we'll take him aside and ask him."

"Miss Dottie gave me another interesting bit of information," Geoff said.

"When did you have such a lengthy conversation with Penny Sue's aunt? She was gone nearly the entire afternoon."

"We chatted while you went to meet her niece. The old bird is a chatterbox. All I had to do was ask this and that and she couldn't stop talking."

"About?"

"The brother and their father's old Winchester rifle, for one thing," Geoff said. "And about her cousin Clayton, the minister. Seems his wife owns a collection of toy animals."

"Penny Sue told me about Phyllis Dickson's collection, but she's convinced the woman isn't capable of committing most of the crimes against Lucky."

"Have you ever considered the possibility that we have more than one culprit?"

"It crossed my mind." Vic mulled over Geoff's comment. The more he thought about it, the more sense it made. Chris Paine had kidnapped Lucky and his sister Stacie had protected him. But Chris had not shot Lucky or torched the clinic. He'd been able to prove his whereabouts on both occasions. "It's a reasonable hypothesis. It could be that Phyllis Dickson or her husband left the bloody toy dog on the porch, but didn't do any of the other things."

"More than one of the heirs is in need of their inheritance now, so it's possible several different ones have taken a turn trying to do away with Lottie Paine's dog."

"If Douglas shot Lucky, that would give us three culprits."

"I think perhaps we have a fourth," Geoff told him.

"And that would be?" Vic asked.

Geoff uncrossed his arms and placed his hands on the banister railing, at either side of his hips. "Miss Dottie also told me that their cousin Valerie's husband, Dylan Redley, used to be a big high-school football star."

"So?"

"One of his teammates was Freddy Long, the chap who owns the pit bulls."

"Are the two men still friends?"

"I don't know, but I think we should find out."

The front door opened and Penny Sue stood in the doorway. "What is it that y'all should find out?"

Geoff slid off the banister railing, slapped Vic on the shoulder and said, "I'll leave it to you to tell Penny Sue about our theory." He nodded and smiled at her, then paused when he reached her side. "I'll go in and keep an eye on Lucky. You two stay out here as long as you'd like." He went into the house, closing the door behind him.

When she approached Vic, he turned to greet her. "You should have put on something heavier than that sweater. It's getting pretty chilly out here."

"Don't change the subject. What theory have you and Geoff come up with?"

"Nothing much. Just the idea that it's possible more than one person is behind what's been happening to Lucky."

Penny Sue looked out over the front yard, took a deep breath and exhaled. "I love this old house and the big yard and this quiet street. It's like a page out of an old magazine, depicting life years ago, when things were far more simple. How did everything get so complicated?" She stood at his side, breathing softly. He knew she was considering the possibility that he and Geoff were right about the attempts on Lucky's life. "Do you really think that several members of my family have banded together in an effort to kill Lucky?"

"No, we don't think several of them have banded together," Vic told her. "We think maybe several have acted independently, the way Chris did. The ones who are desperate, for whatever reason, to get their hands on their inheritance now. Maybe one person shot Lucky, another left the bloody stuffed dog on the porch as a warning, then another set fire to the clinic and yet another—"

"Counting letting the pit bulls loose, that's five separate incidents." Penny Sue moaned softly. "For your theory to be correct, that would mean five members of my family are criminals."

Seeing the hurt and disillusionment in her big brown eyes, he said, "It's just a theory, sugar."

"But you and Geoff both think it's possible, don't you?"

Vic took her hands in his and led her across the porch to the big white swing in the corner. Thickly padded floral cushions hung from the back and rested across the seat. He sat and pulled her down beside him, then draped his arm across her shoulders and snuggled her against him.

"Are we going to put on a show for the neighbors?" she asked.

"I'm game if you are." He winked at her.

"I guess you know that you're a very bad influence on me."

He leaned down and nuzzled her neck. She giggled and swatted at him.

"You're trying to distract me and it's almost working." She laid her hand on his knee.

"Only almost?"

"Be serious with me for a minute, okay? I need to know if you and Geoff have any suspects, any that you feel reasonably certain about."

He took a deep breath. "Your uncle owns an old rifle that uses the kind of bullet the vet dug out of Lucky. Your cousin Clayton's wife collects toy dogs, and someone left a bloody toy dog on this very porch. Your cousin Chris kidnapped Lucky, and all we have is his word that he wasn't going to kill him." When Penny Sue opened her mouth to speak, Vic tapped her on the lips with his index finger. "And your former fiancé used to play high-school football with the guy who owned those pit bulls. That's four possible suspects right there. Douglas Paine, Phyllis Dickson, Chris Paine and Dylan Redley."

"Hmm… I'll buy Phyllis leaving the toy dog and *maybe* Dylan 'borrowing' those pit bulls from Freddy, but Uncle Douglas would never shoot Lucky. And I believed what Chris said about not intending to hurt Lucky. So that narrows it down to two probable suspects."

"No, sugar, what you just did was eliminate your blood relatives. You can't do that."

"Why can't I? They're my relatives. I know them a lot better than you do and I'm telling you that neither Uncle Douglas nor Chris is capable of hurting Lucky."

Vic groaned. "You're not being logical. You're letting your emotions overrule your common sense."

"I have plenty of common sense, thank you very much." She snatched her hand off his leg, then sat up ramrod straight, her whole body going stiff.

"I didn't say you don't have any common sense, I just said you weren't using it in this case. Why you think your blood relatives aren't as capable of murder and mayhem as the rest of this town's population doesn't make any sense. It's ridiculous."

"So now you think I'm ridiculous!" She stuck out her bottom lip. Her chin quivered.

"Honey, you have a way of twisting what I say—"

"You called me honey!"

"It was a slip of the tongue. I meant to say sugar."

God help him, she was pouting. And about what? Nothing. Absolutely nothing.

"Penny Sue…sugar…" He tightened his hold around her shoulders. "You have loads of common sense. And you're not ridiculous. I never said you were. And if you believe your uncle and your cousin would never hurt Lucky, then maybe you're right. Maybe Geoff and I should concentrate on the in-laws first. Phyllis, Dylan and Candy."

There in the twilight shadows, a cool evening breeze wafting around them, Penny Sue smiled, then turned and laid her head on Vic's shoulder. "Whatever you think best, Vic."

Whatever he thought best? If he wasn't so crazy about this woman, he'd strangle her. But he was crazy about her. Or maybe he was just crazy.

"Am I going to have to talk you to death to get you to kiss me?" she asked.

"The neighbors might see us."

"Yes, they might." She lifted her head and smiled. "Let's give them something to talk about at church in the morning."

Vic grinned, then lowered his head and took her mouth. His brain turned to mush and his body went rock hard. He should have put more effort into fighting his attraction to her, should have followed through with his initial resolve to get out of this assignment while he still could. But it was too late now. He had to hang in there and let this thing run its course.

He ended the kiss, and when she opened her eyes and looked at him, he said, "Can I interest you in turning in early tonight?"

"Why, Mr. Noble, what a marvelous idea."

Vic started to get up, but before he got halfway out of the swing, he heard a familiar sound and then something hit the back of the swing and splintered the wood. Instinctively, he grabbed Penny Sue. Another shot rang out as he threw Penny Sue to the floor. Then a third shot hit the wall behind them just as he covered her body with his. The squeal of brakes and the roar of a car's engine told Vic that their shooter was escaping.

He rolled off Penny Sue, but kept down, just in case.

"When I tell you to, I want you to get up, run inside and call the police," he told her.

She didn't respond.

"Penny Sue, did you hear me?" He looked over at her and saw that her eyes were closed and she wasn't moving. "Penny Sue? Sugar?"

He grabbed her and shook her. She moaned. Then he saw the red liquid staining the side of her white cashmere sweater and knew she'd been hit.

## Chapter 14

Geoff Monday barreled through the front door and onto the porch like a raging bull. With gun in hand, he surveyed the area and assessed the situation. "What happened? I heard shots." He glanced down at the floor where Vic held Penny Sue in his arms. "Is she hit?"

"He's getting away," Vic said. "He must have been parked across the street."

Dottie Paine came to the door. "Oh, dear God, what happened?"

"I can still see a car's red taillights down the street." Without wasting another minute, Geoff ran off the porch and straight to his rental car parked in the driveway.

Vic heard rather than saw Geoff back out of the drive and head off down the street after the shooter. Whoever the son of a bitch was, Vic would see to it that he paid dearly for what he'd done. If Penny Sue was badly hurt, if she died…

"What's wrong with Penny Sue?" Wringing her hands, Dottie ventured onto the porch, Ruby and Tully right behind her. Dottie held Puff in her arms and Ruby held Lucky, who was whimpering and straining to get free.

"Call 911," Vic shouted at them.

Tully turned back into the house immediately.

"Penny Sue," Vic called her name as he eased her sweater apart to examine the wound.

She moaned and opened her eyes. "I think I fainted."

Didn't she realize she'd been shot? Wasn't she in pain?

"Sugar, I've got to check your side," Vic told her. "If I hurt you, tell me. Okay?"

"Okay." She smiled at him. "But why are you checking my side?"

Suddenly the front porch light came on and Tully returned. "They're on their way. An ambulance and the police."

Penny Sue tried to sit up, but Vic kept her pinned down and on her back. Dottie, Ruby and Tully hovered nearby. He knew they were as concerned as he was.

"Stay still," Vic told her.

Then he focused on the profuse amount of red staining on both her sweater and the black-and-white polka-dot blouse beneath, searching for the entrance wound. But there wasn't a hole in either her sweater or her blouse, only a ragged tear across the top side pocket of the sweater. After inspecting the red liquid visually, he touched a spot, brought his finger to his nose and smelled. No odor whatsoever. Odd. Then he tasted the liquid.

It wasn't blood.

"Did you find what you were looking for?" Penny Sue asked.

"Yeah, I did." He lifted her up off the floor as he got to his feet. "How do you feel?"

"Silly," she replied. "I've never fainted in my entire life, but then I've never had anyone shoot at me before tonight."

"What did you have in the pocket of your sweater?" Vic asked.

She glanced down at the red liquid covering her sweater and blouse, then groaned. "Oh, my goodness. This sweater and blouse are ruined. That red egg dye will never come out of either. I'll have to throw them away. And this sweater was one of my favorites."

Egg dye? She'd had red egg dye in her pocket. If he hadn't been so glad she wasn't hurt, that one of the bullets hadn't hit her, he would have choked her.

"What the hell were you doing with red egg dye in your pocket?"

"Do not swear at me, Vic Noble."

"I thought it was blood. I thought you'd been hit."

"Oh." Her mouth formed a surprised oval. "You thought the red dye was blood? My blood? It wasn't. I'm fine. I just fainted from all the excitement." She reached out and caressed his face. "Poor darling. You were worried about me, weren't you?" She glanced over at her aunt and the Coxes. "Stop looking so concerned. It's nothing, really. I'm fine." Then hearing Lucky whimper, she focused on him. "Oh, Lucky, sweetie, I'm all right. Ruby, bring him over here so I can show him that—"

Vic grabbed her shoulders and shook her. Quieting immediately, she stared at him with a startled expression in her eyes. "Damn it, woman, don't you realize that someone shot at you, at us, and—" he yanked up the tattered edge of the pocket on her damp sweater "—my guess is that one of the bullets barely missed you. See this tear—"

She looked at the ripped pocket. "Oh. Oh, dear. The bullet ripped the edge of my sweater and cut a hole in the plastic dye bottle." She turned pale and swayed unsteadily.

"You aren't going to faint again, are you?"

"I—I don't think so."

Vic swept her up in his arms and, practically shoving the others aside, carried her into the house. Once inside the parlor, he placed her on the sofa, then turned and issued orders. "Ruby, get her some water…no, some brandy or whiskey. Tully, put Lucky upstairs and then go outside and wait for the police and the ambulance to arrive. Aunt Dottie, sit down and take a few deep breaths before you pass out. I can't handle two unconscious Paine women at one time."

When Dottie slumped into the nearest chair, Puff zipped out of her arms and raced off toward the stairs. "Someone shot at Penny Sue? But who would do such a thing? And why?"

"Good question." Vic swept Penny Sue's hair away from her face and grasped the side of her neck gently.

Ruby returned with whiskey in a small glass and handed it to Vic. He lifted the tumbler to Penny Sue's lips. "Take a few sips."

She did as she was told. When she swallowed the liquor, she shook and coughed, then glared at Vic. "That's awful. How do people drink that stuff?"

If he hadn't been so concerned about who had shot at them and why, he would have laughed. His sweet little Penny Sue. "Take just a couple more sips."

She shook her head.

"It'll help calm your nerves."

"My nerves are just fine, thank you. But maybe you'd better drink the rest. I think you're the one who needs it."

"You could be right." Vic lifted the glass to his lips and downed the entire contents.

"You're used to drinking, aren't you?"

He nodded. "One of my many bad habits."

Penny Sue looked at him with those big, soulful brown eyes and said, "What I really need is chocolate."

"Chocolate?"

"Chocolate is very soothing to the nerves," she told him.

Vic glanced at Ruby, who nodded and disappeared down the hall. "Ruby's gone to get you something."

Penny Sue smiled. Within minutes, Ruby returned with a piece of chocolate candy nestled inside a paper wrapper.

Just as Penny Sue popped the candy into her mouth and sighed, the wail of sirens gained everyone's attention. Within minutes, two police cars stopped in front of the house and an ambulance pulled into the driveway.

"Oh, Ruby, go outside and tell them that we don't need an ambulance," Penny Sue said. "And apologize for having bothered them."

"Why not let the medics check you over?" Vic set the empty glass down on a coaster atop the side table to his left.

"There's no need for that. I'm fine." She looked down at her ruined clothing. "I'm a mess, though. I should go upstairs and change before the police question me."

When she started to get up, Vic stood and pushed her back onto the sofa. "Stay put. First things first. You can change after we talk to the police."

Frowning, Penny Sue placed her hands in her lap. Vic gave her a don't-you-dare-move glare before he headed to the front door to meet the officers.

Fifteen minutes later, with the ambulance dismissed, the police interview complete and four officers now outside checking the yard and house for evidence, Penny Sue excused herself and went upstairs.

"I'll need to soak in the tub for a while," she told Vic. "That red dye probably went all the way through to my skin."

"Want to explain to me what red egg dye was doing in your sweater pocket?" Vic asked.

"I put it in my pocket the other day when I wore the sweater to work. I intended to use the dye to color some Easter eggs. I always do a basket filled with pink eggs for our church's big Easter-egg hunt every year and I remembered we didn't have any red dye here at the house. I just forgot to take the dye out of the pocket and put it up in a kitchen cupboard."

Vic's cell phone rang. He hesitated.

"Go ahead and take that call," Penny Sue said. "If you need me, you know where to find me."

"I'll go up with you, dear." Dottie sighed. "I'm simply exhausted and completely unnerved. I'll have to take a sleeping pill tonight if I want to get even a wink of sleep."

"I'll fix you some herbal tea and bring it up," Ruby said, then glanced at Vic. "Would you like Tully to take care of Lucky until things have settled down? I'm sure you'll want to talk to the police again before they leave."

"Thanks." Vic removed his phone from the belt clip. "I'd appreciate Tully looking after Lucky." He flipped open his phone and said, "Noble here."

"Vic, this is Geoff."

"Yeah?" He looked around the room and found it empty.

"How's Penny Sue?"

"She's fine. She wasn't hit."

"She wasn't?"

"No, she had a bottle of red dye in her sweater pocket that she planned to use to dye Easter eggs," Vic said. "The bullet ripped through the pocket, hit the bottle and the dye leaked out onto her clothes."

Geoff chuckled.

"Laugh all you want, but at the time, in the dark, it looked like blood."

"I'd have made the same mistake. Anybody would have."

"Maybe."

"As they say, I have good news and bad news," Geoff told him.

"Give me the good news first."

"I have your shooter."

"You've got him?"

"Right here," Geoff said. "We've been having a chat. He's pretty torn up about what he did. Says he doesn't know what got into him, doing something so stupid."

"Who is he?"

"He says he's the local fire chief, a chap named Boggus."

"Wayne Boggus?"

"He says he wasn't shooting at Ms. Paine. He was shooting at you, but only to scare you, not to harm you."

Vic groaned. "Haul his ass down to the police station."

"He wants to talk to Penny Sue before he turns himself in."

"No way."

"He says either he sees Penny Sue first or he's not cooperating."

"You caught him, I assume he has the rifle with him and he's confessed to you that he's the one who took those pot shots at us. Penny Sue's been through enough without having to listen to Boggus try to talk his way out of this."

"I don't disagree," Geoff said. "But are you sure Penny Sue will understand if she finds out he wanted to talk to her and you wouldn't let him?"

"Damn!" Vic was tempted to tell Geoff to go ahead and take Wayne Boggus to the police station and he'd deal with Penny Sue later. But in this instance, Geoff was right. "She's upstairs. I'll take my phone to her and—"

"He wants to see her in person."

"I don't like this," Vic said. "Oh, all right. Bring him here. I'll go up and tell Penny Sue."

After checking with the police, who said they'd dug two slugs out of the side of the house and one from the swing, Vic retrieved the box of chocolates that Ruby kept in the pantry and headed upstairs. If he had a lick of sense, he'd have told Officer Gibbs, the policeman in charge of the investigation, that his fellow Dundee agent had captured the shooter. But he didn't. And all because he didn't want Penny Sue to be upset with him.

Idiot. That's what he was—an idiot.

When he opened Penny Sue's bedroom door, he found the room empty, but he noted the bathroom door stood ajar and heard the sound of running water.

"Penny Sue? Sugar?"

She appeared in the doorway, wearing only her bra and a pair of red-stained white panties. He sucked in his breath. Did she have any idea how sexy she was?

"What have you got there?" she asked, eyeing the box of candy.

"Medication to calm your nerves." He held the box out in front of him. "I thought you might need more chocolate."

"Maybe just one more piece. For my nerves." Smiling, she came to him, lifted the box's lid and retrieved a piece of candy. "You should try one. They're a lot better than whiskey to soothe the nerves."

"I'll stick with whiskey," he told her as he watched her bite into the dark chocolate nugget. "I...uh...I need to tell you something."

She looked at him, her expression serious. "All right. What is it?"

"Geoff Monday followed the shooter only minutes after you were...well, after I thought you were hit. And Geoff just called to tell me that he's captured the guy."

Penny Sue's eyes widened. "Who—?"

"Promise me you aren't going to get upset. Promise me that you'll react in a rational—"

"It wasn't a member of my family, was it?"

He hated the worried look in her eyes.

"No, it was Wayne Boggus."

"Wayne? But why would he try to shoot me?"

"He says he wasn't shooting at you. He was shooting at me, to try to scare me."

"Oh, my goodness."

"He's willing to turn himself in to the police and tell them the truth, but he wants to talk to you first. Geoff is bringing him here. Do you want to see Boggus? Do you want to hear what he has to say?"

"Of course I do." Penny Sue popped the rest of the candy into her mouth, then rushed back into the bathroom. She called out, "Have the police left yet?"

"Yeah, they're gone. Why?"

She emerged from the bathroom wearing a black silk robe. "Did they find any evidence?"

"All three bullets."

"Hmm…poor Wayne. He must have been out of his mind to have done something so foolish. But no real harm was done. No one was hurt."

"If for one minute you think I'm going to let this guy get away with what he did—"

She stood on tiptoe and kissed him. "Before we make any decisions, let's hear what Wayne has to say."

They sat at the kitchen table—Penny Sue, Vic and Wayne Boggus. Geoff and Tully stood by the back door, drinking coffee and staying out of the way. Lucky lay at Penny Sue's feet, content just to be near her.

"Can you ever forgive me?" Wayne asked, his voice quivering.

Penny Sue patted his trembling hand. "If I understood why—"

"I wanted to scare him off." Wayne glared at Vic. "You were my girl. I thought we had something special, and then this guy shows up and sweeps you off your feet and…the whole town's laughing behind my back. Even the men at the station. I'm their superior and they're making fun of me, saying I can't hold on to my woman."

"Oh, Wayne, I'm sure that's not true."

"Yes, it is. I overheard a couple of my guys talking about it to-night and I saw red. I don't know what happened to me. I guess I just went berserk. I wasn't thinking straight. I got in my truck and headed over here, intending to talk to you, to make you see how wrong this guy is for you." Wayne sneaked a sidelong glance at Vic, but quickly returned his full attention to Penny Sue. "Then I saw the two of you on the porch swing, all lovey-dovey, kissing and…and I took my rifle and… I just wanted to scare him. I thought…I don't know what I was thinking."

"Oh, Wayne, I'm so sorry." Penny Sue patted his hand again. "Of course, you weren't thinking straight. You did something to-tally out of character for you."

"Thank you for understanding. I just had to clear things up with you before I turned myself in to the police."

"You'll do no such thing," Penny Sue said.

"What!" Vic yelled.

Geoff and Tully glanced from Vic to Wayne to Penny Sue.

"No one was hurt. We were just startled," Penny Sue said. "I see no reason for you to lose your job and possibly go to jail for—"

"The man shot at us—at me," Vic said. "One of the bullets came damn close to hitting you. We are not letting him get off scot-free."

"He's said he's sorry and I know he'll feel guilty about it till his dying day," Penny Sue said. "I don't see why you can't be rea-sonable about this."

"Reasonable?" Vic groaned. She was the one not being rea-sonable, once again thinking with her heart and not her head. "I'm sorry, sugar, but you're not going to get your way about this." Vic turned to Wayne. "Do you want Geoff to drive you to the police station or do you want us to call and have them come pick you up?"

"I'd appreciate it if Mr. Monday would drive me," Wayne said.

"You don't have to do this, does he, Vic?" Penny Sue looked pleadingly at Vic.

Ignoring her, Vic said, "Geoff will drive you to the police station."

Penny Sue shot up out of her chair so quickly that she toppled it over. Lucky jumped up, his hackles raised, and growled menacingly. Penny Sue glared at Vic, balled her hands into fists and groaned, then ran out of the kitchen and up the back stairs. Lucky followed her, but paused before going up the steps. He turned around and growled at the four men, as if warning them to leave his mistress alone.

"Anytime you're ready," Geoff said to Wayne.

Wayne stood. "I'm ready now."

When Vic was alone in the kitchen with Tully, he looked at the older man and said, "I'm right about this and she's wrong. So, why am I the one who'll have to grovel?"

"You expect an answer to that question, don't you?" Tully asked.

"You're older and wiser and have experience," Vic said. "You and Ruby have been married a long time. Surely you've learned something about how to handle a woman."

"Yeah, I have," Tully told him. "I've learned that no matter who's right and who's wrong, if a man wants his meals cooked, his shirts ironed and his bed warmed, he apologizes and takes all the blame. He tells his woman whatever she wants to hear."

Vic heaved a deep sigh. "I was afraid that was what you were going to tell me."

Tully laid his hand on Vic's shoulder. "Better get on up there and do a little damage control before she works herself up into a royal snit. The longer you let 'em fume, the more you have to grovel."

Vic found the bathroom door locked and when he knocked and called her name, she didn't answer.

"Penny Sue, I'm sorry. I just did what I thought was right."

No response.

He heard splashing water.

"Shouldn't we talk about this?"

More splashing.

"You're going to give me a chance to apologize, aren't you?"

Silence.

"Okay, sugar, you think about it while you take your bath," he said through the closed door. "I'm going down the hall to take a shower, but I'll be back in a few minutes so we can make things right between us."

Vic went into his bedroom, gathered up his shave kit and pajama bottoms, then traipsed off down the hall. He showered, shaved and returned to Penny Sue's bedroom in less than ten minutes, wanting to be there waiting for her when she emerged from the bathroom. He barely made it in time and had just sat down in one of the chairs flanking a table under the windows when the bathroom door eased open and Penny Sue walked into the room. She wore a demure, long-sleeved, white cotton gown that came to her ankles. A row of tiny pink silk roses covered the neck-to-hem buttons. Lucky came bounding out alongside her, then stopped and stared at Vic, as if trying to decide whether he was friend or foe.

Penny Sue took one look at Vic, turned up her nose and ignored him. Taking his cue from his mistress, Lucky did the same.

"I guess both of you are upset with me," Vic said.

Penny Sue turned down the covers, smoothing them with the palm of her hand.

"Did you hear something, Lucky?" she asked. "I think it's a pesky mosquito."

Vic rose from his chair. "Just tell me what my penance is and I'll—"

"Just ignore that incessant buzzing and the mosquito will go away." When Penny Sue sat on the side of her bed, Lucky jumped up right beside her. She stroked him lovingly.

"Don't you think Boggus would have done the right thing and turned himself in regardless of what I said?" Vic walked toward the bed.

When Lucky settled his head on the opposite pillow, Penny Sue lay down, turned over and pulled the covers up to her neck, for all intents and purposes dismissing Vic.

He stood by the bed and looked at her back. "I'm willing to say or do anything you want, you know. Just name it and it's yours."

Her shoulders trembled. Oh, God, she's crying. How the hell had he gotten himself into such a mess? Here he was all torn up because this woman was upset with him. And without a good reason. Just because he'd done the right thing instead of what she'd wanted him to do.

He eased down onto the bed and reached out to touch her back. She jerked away from him. "Don't cry, sugar. I know you've been through a traumatic experience and that finding out your former boyfriend was the one who shot at us—at me—had to have upset you even more. And...and I guess I could have handled the situation better."

He scooted up to her and draped his arm over her. She quivered.

"Penny Sue...?"

She trembled even harder and made an odd noise that sounded like laughter. Laughter?

He yanked the covers off her and flipped her over. She looked up at him and he saw that she was laughing so hard she had tears in her eyes.

"Why you little fake!" Vic grabbed her by the shoulders.

Lucky lifted his head and stared at Vic, then at Penny Sue. Since she was laughing, he probably assumed everything was all right, so he laid his head back down on the pillow.

Vic shook her none too gently. "Did you enjoy listening to me grovel?"

Barely managing to stop laughing, she replied, "As a matter of fact, I did."

"I thought you were angry with me." He released her shoulders.

"I was."

"But you're not now?"

Smiling, she shook her head. "No, not since you showed me how far you were willing to go to appease me."

Groaning, Vic tightened his hold on her. "Are you willing to admit that I was right and you were wrong?" When her smile vanished, he wondered if he'd just made another mistake. "Let me rephrase that." He ran his hands down her arms, then released her.

She sat up beside him. "You don't have to rephrase anything. Yes, you were right. Wayne should turn himself in, but… I wish there had been some other way to handle things. He'll lose his job and his good reputation, and have to go to prison."

"He should have thought about all that before he started shooting at us." When her frown deepened, Vic slipped his arm around her waist and nudged her toward him. "So hire him a good lawyer."

"I intend to, if he'll let me."

"If we don't press charges, a good lawyer can probably plea bargain and get him off with probation." Vic placed his other hand just above her knee and caressed her thigh.

"Since I already hired a Birmingham lawyer for Chris, I suppose I can have him represent Wayne, too."

"Kill two birds with one stone." He leaned over and kissed her ear.

She shivered. "I feel like I'm partly to blame for what happened."

Vic nuzzled her neck. "You are not to blame because your former boyfriend let his jealousy override his common sense."

"Yes, I know, but I should have explained to him that…well, that even if you hadn't come into my life, I wouldn't have continued dating him."

Vic grasped her chin between his thumb and forefinger and forced her to look directly at him. "You can't take responsibility for the actions of your entire family and all your friends. It's too heavy a burden for one person to bear."

He lowered his head and kissed her. Sweet and gentle. A loving, undemanding kiss.

She sighed against his lips and closed her eyes. Without her saying a word, he understood that she was giving herself over to his safekeeping, that she was surrendering to her own needs, allowing him to give her what she needed.

Vic tossed the covers to the foot of the bed, then shooed Lucky off the pillow. Lucky hesitated for a minute, then when Penny Sue told him to go, he hopped down and found his favorite spot on the rug in front of the fireplace.

"Close your eyes again," he told her. "And think of me."

"Where are you going?"

"To get something out of my shave kit."

"Oh."

It took him less than a minute to run into his bedroom, unzip his shave kit and retrieve a couple of condoms. Okay, so maybe he wouldn't need both, but he brought two back with him, just in case.

He stripped off his pajama bottoms.

She opened her eyes and peeked at him. "You're awfully sure of yourself, aren't you?"

He ripped open the packet, removed the condom and sheathed his sex. "I'm sure that I want you."

She stared at his erection. "That's rather obvious."

He crawled into bed with her, slid his hand up under her gown and between her thighs. When her legs parted of their own volition, he slipped two fingers up inside her and found her hot and wet. "It's obvious that you want me, too."

She squirmed against his hand.

"Tell me exactly what you want," he said.

Snuggling against him, she reached out and circled his straining sex. He groaned.

"I want this," she told him.

"Never let it be said that Vic Noble didn't aim to please."

After he yanked her gown up to her hips, she lifted herself just enough so that he could pull the gown all the way up over her head and off. He came down on top of her, bracing himself with his elbows as he looked at her.

"What *have* you done to me, sugar?"

"All I've done is fallen in love with you," she told him.

He kissed her, and what started out as a tender moment quickly turned passionate. His lips moved over her face, down her neck and to her breasts, then went back up to take her mouth again. After wrapping her arms around him, she raked her fingers down his back and clutched his tight buttocks.

Moaning deep in her throat, she bucked up, pressing her mound against his sex. All his good intentions—his plans to make love to her with slow, precise deliberation—vanished in that instant. Next time, he told himself. Next time.

Cupping her hips, he lifted her up to meet his deep, powerful thrust. She clung to his shoulders, whimpering, shivering, and when he was buried to the hilt within her, she murmured his name.

Their mating was fast and hard, she as eager as he to reach fulfillment as quickly as possible. She came first. He kissed her hungrily and captured her cry. Feeling her unraveling, crying, coming apart beneath him sent him over the edge. His release hit him like a tidal wave, exploding inside him, turning his body into sheer sensation. His climax raced through him, shattering him, rendering him depleted and totally satisfied.

As he rolled off her and onto the bed, dragging her beside him, keeping her close, he whispered against her ear, "You're mine, sugar. All mine."

## Chapter 15

On Sunday morning, the entire household went to church, leaving Vic and Geoff alone with Lucky and the elusive Puff, who was seldom seen or heard. Penny Sue had asked Vic to go to church with her, but he had declined and to his surprise, she hadn't pressed him to change his mind. He would have felt as out of place sitting beside Penny Sue at Sunday school as the proverbial whore in church. He hadn't been inside a house of worship, except for several funerals, since he was sixteen. From birth, his mama and grandma had taken him to church on a regular basis, for all the good it did him. In the end, the heathen tendencies he'd inherited from his father had won out.

Granny had "gone to Jesus" when he was twelve, and then four short years later, his thirty-six-year-old mother had died suddenly from a brain aneurysm. A great deal of whatever goodness and kindness he'd had in him as a boy had died the day his mama had died and left him with his hard-drinking, emotionally withdrawn father.

As Vic walked Lucky in the backyard, he noted how pleasantly warm it was this morning, with bright sunshine and an almost cloudless sky. Perfect weather for Palm Sunday. Next Sunday, it would probably rain, ruining people's Easter plans. In his experience, that was usually the way things went.

After Lucky did his job, he followed Vic to the back porch. When Vic sat on the steps, Lucky curled up in the grass beside his feet. Absently, Vic reached down and stroked the little dog's back. Despite every effort not to care, Vic found that he'd become quite fond of his client. And of his client's mistress.

As he sat quietly, soaking up the sun's warmth and mulling over his personal situation with Penny Sue, Vic's cell phone rang. Lucky lolled his head to one side and glanced up at Vic, who removed his phone from the belt clip and flipped it open, while continuing to pet Lucky with his other hand.

"Noble here."

"Good morning," Daisy Holbrook said. "How are you today?"

"For a man who was shot at last night, I'm doing remarkably well."

Daisy laughed. "Good thing Ms. Paine's boyfriend was shooting only to scare you off and not to kill."

"I suppose Geoff gave you all the details when he spoke to you last night."

"Every juicy tidbit. So, considering how chummy you've gotten with Ms. Paine, I don't suppose you'd be interested in a replacement."

"Do you have someone in mind?"

"Lucie's flying in from Europe this evening," Daisy said. "I could ask her if she'd be willing to take over for you."

Do it, Vic's logical mind advised him, but his gut told him that he couldn't leave until the job was done, until Lucky was safe. Until he was certain that Penny Sue would be all right.

"I'd hate to ask Lucie to replace me before she's had a chance for some downtime. Besides, Geoff's here and we're beginning to put the puzzle pieces together."

"That's fine by me, and I'm sure Lucie will be glad, but since you'd been so insistent that you wanted out of Alabaster Creek and off this assignment ASAP, I thought I'd make the offer."

"That was then, this is now."

"Hmm…"

Geoff opened the back door and walked out onto the porch. "Vic, Officer Gibbs just called—" He glanced at the cell phone Vic held to his ear. "Sorry, didn't see you were on the phone."

"It's Daisy," Vic said.

Geoff nodded.

"Is there anything else?" Vic asked Daisy. "I don't suppose Geoff remembered to ask you to run a check on a guy named—"

"Hal Esmond," Daisy said. "As a matter of fact he did, and I'll e-mail the initial report to you when I get back from church. But I can hit the highlights for you right now."

"Do that."

"Hal Esmond is a widower, no children, a retired banker worth in the neighborhood of five to six million. He owns a house in Birmingham, a vacation cabin in Gatlinburg, Tennessee, and a beach house on the Gulf. He's a staunch Republican, a lifelong Presbyterian and he's never gotten so much as a parking ticket."

Vic sighed with relief. "Well, that's one problem Penny Sue won't have to deal with."

"Did she think the man was a shyster?"

"It crossed her mind."

"Well, he's not. Like I said, I'll e-mail the report to you later and when we get a detailed report, I'll send that along, too. Anything else you need?"

"Not this morning, but I'll be in touch."

Vic closed his phone and clipped it to his belt. "What's up?" he asked Geoff.

"I just got off the phone with Officer Gibbs." Geoff sat down on the steps with Vic. "He had some rather interesting information for us."

"About last night's shooting?"

"No, nothing new there. Boggus is still in jail, waiting for a hearing so he can post bond," Geoff said. "This is information about the pit bulls you had to kill…or rather, it's about their owner's wife."

"Freddy Long's wife?"

Geoff nodded. "It seems Freddy not only abuses animals, but he's been known to brutalize his wife and kids, too. Around midnight last night, Mrs. Long—Heather—showed up at the hospital with a broken nose and two black eyes. She had both of her children with her, and she told the ER staff that her husband beat the hell out of her and she wanted to press charges. And when the police showed up to take her statement and arrange for her to go into the local women's shelter, she told them all sorts of interesting things about her husband."

Vic smiled. "Go on, I'm listening."

"It seems that, according to Heather Long, Freddy sold those two pit bulls to an old friend of his on the same day the animals showed up in this very backyard."

"Would the old friend's name happen to be Dylan Redley?"

"Indeed it would."

Laughing, Vic slapped his knee. "Now, we're getting somewhere." He glanced over at Geoff. "I don't suppose there's any documentation of the sale, is there?"

"I'm afraid not. Mrs. Long said it was a cash transaction."

"Then we don't have anything that would hold up in a court of law, do we? It would be her word against her husband's word and Dylan Redley's word."

"Officer Gibbs said that they intend to question Redley sometime today."

"He's not likely to admit what he did."

"We can lean on Redley," Geoff said. "I dare say you and I could persuade him to confess."

"We can talk to him and put the fear of God in him, but Penny Sue wouldn't approve of the type of methods you're talking about."

"Penny Sue doesn't have to know."

"This isn't an SAS or a CIA operation," Vic said.

Geoff shrugged. "Redley is coming to dinner today, isn't he?"

"Yeah, he'll be here. The whole Paine clan has been invited so that Miss Dottie can make her big announcement and introduce her fiancé to the family."

"Then, after dinner, I say we escort Redley outside and explain why it would be a good idea for him to admit what he did."

"It sure would be sweet if we could pin everything else on him, too." Vic would like to prove that Dylan Redley was behind all the attempts on Lucky's life, despite the fact that his instincts told him otherwise. "I think we'd better let the police handle Redley. Why don't you give Officer Gibbs a call and let him know Redley will be here this afternoon and—"

"So, are we or are we not going to talk to Redley first?" Geoff asked.

"We're not," Vic replied. "Not today. We need to question Douglas Paine first about the rifle and find out if he's willing to allow us to have a ballistics test run on it."

Geoff smiled. "My money's on the uncle for shooting Lucky and on the minister's wife for leaving the bloody dog on the porch. As for the clinic fire—maybe Redley was behind that, too. If not, we'll have to consider all the other relatives."

"If all your theories are correct and if Redley didn't set the fire, then we're going to wind up with five different felons. And if even one turns out to be a blood relative, it'll break Penny Sue's heart."

Geoff cleared his throat. Vic glanced at him and noted the odd expression on his face.

"Have you got something you want to say?" Vic glared at his fellow Dundee agent.

"It's none of my business, but—"

"Then stay out of it."

Vic knew exactly what Geoff was thinking, what he'd come close to voicing aloud. If anything or anyone would wind up breaking Penny Sue's heart, it would be Vic Noble, the son of a bitch who couldn't keep his hands off her.

Penny Sue drove home from church alone since Aunt Dottie had ridden with her fiancé. Hal Esmond seemed like a very nice man. He was well-dressed, well-spoken and appeared to be genuinely besotted with her aunt Dottie. Since they didn't intend to announce their engagement until after Sunday dinner, Aunt Dottie hadn't worn her engagement ring this morning, but Penny Sue suspected it had been tucked away in her purse.

Vic had promised her he would have the Dundee office run a check on Mr. Esmond. She hoped the results would be favorable, that the man would turn out to be who and what he proclaimed himself to be. If that were the case, then Aunt Dottie need never learn that the Dundee agency had compiled a report on her fiancé. On the other hand... No, she wasn't going to think about any other possibility. Not today. There would be time enough to deal with other problems later.

When she pulled into the garage, she saw Vic standing there, apparently waiting for her. Every time she saw him, her stomach fluttered and her heartbeat accelerated. And whenever he touched her, she felt giddy and light-headed and...aroused. Being in love was exhilarating.

Vic opened the driver's door and helped her out, then pulled her into his arms and kissed her. She didn't think she'd ever get enough of him. The more they were together, the more she wanted to be with him. But she couldn't tell him that what she wanted most of all was a lifetime with him. Marriage, children, growing old together. The whole nine yards. He just wasn't ready. She had to give him time.

"Did you miss me?" She slipped her arms around his neck.

"What do you think?"

"I think I'd better get in the house and help Ruby before the horde descends on us."

"Ruby has everything under control." Vic cupped her buttocks as he nuzzled her neck. "Geoff and I helped Tully put the two extensions in the dining-room table and Ruby's got the table set for fifteen. And by the delicious aroma coming from the kitchen, I believe dinner is probably ready, or soon will be."

"You'd better let go of me. If you don't...well, we certainly don't want anyone catching us making out here in the garage, do we?"

"I don't mind," he told her teasingly.

She pulled away from him and swatted his chest playfully. "You're just awful, Vic Noble. Have you no shame?"

"None whatsoever," he told her. "But I do have some good news about Aunt Dottie's fiancé."

"What? Tell me."

"From the initial report Geoff asked Daisy to compile, it seem Hal Esmond is just what he represents himself to be—a childles millionaire widower."

Penny Sue threw her arms around Vic and hugged him "This is wonderful. Finally, Aunt Dottie has found a man wor thy of her." She drew back from Vic, but grabbed his hand "This day may turn out to be not so bad after all. I've bee dreading it so much."

"You haven't forgotten that Geoff and I have to speak to you uncle about his Winchester rifle, and to Phyllis Dickson abou the toy dog."

Penny Sue's smile vanished. "No, I haven't forgotten. But w know at least one thing will turn out right. And I'm convinced tha Uncle Douglas is innocent, and even if Phyllis is guilty, she real didn't commit a crime. Not a real crime."

Vic grumbled under his breath.

"Well, she didn't."

"I didn't say a word."

"Then you were thinking out loud," Penny Sue told him.

"Okay, so I was thinking out loud." He squeezed her hands. " have to tell you something you're not going to like. We know wh set those pit bulls loose in the backyard."

Her heart stopped for half a second. "Who?"

"According to Freddy Long's wife, Freddy sold both of the dog to Dylan Redley a few hours before they showed up in your back yard."

"Dylan! Are you sure?"

"I'm sure. Why are you having a problem believing Redle would set a couple of vicious attack dogs loose on Lucky and us?

She heaved a deep sigh. "I don't know. Maybe because I re member Dylan the way he was in high school. That Dyla wouldn't have put another person's life in danger. But I suppos I don't really know the man Dylan has become."

"We don't have any proof, so it will be Heather Long's wor against her husband's and Redley's. Unless we can wrangle a con fession out of him before the police question him."

"What do you mean by wrangle?" Surely Vic wasn't implying that he and Geoff Monday would beat a confession out of Dylan.

"We won't lay a finger on him."

"Good. I think there's been enough violence as it is, don't you? Perhaps if I spoke to Dylan alone, he might—"

Vic grabbed her by the shoulders. "No way in hell. Do you hear me? If you want me to treat Redley with kid gloves, then you stay away from him, because I'm telling you, sugar, if he lays one finger on you, he's a dead man."

A shiver raced up Penny Sue's spine. "I—I'll leave the interrogation to you and Geoff."

"Good." Vic loosened his tenacious hold on her and looked her right in the eyes. "Try to remember this—if it turns out that one or more of your blood relatives is guilty—"

"They aren't!"

"All I'm saying is *if*," he told her. "If they are, then you can't protect them. You can't wave a magic wand and make it all go away."

"I know that. But don't you think that losing their inheritance would be punishment enough? Anyone who tries to harm Lucky can't inherit. Aunt Lottie put that stipulation in her will."

"Do you really want the person who shot Lucky to go unpunished? And what about whoever set the clinic on fire?"

"You're right, of course," she told him. "It's just that whatever happens, it's going to tear our family apart."

As soon as Ruby finished serving after-dinner coffee to the Paine clan, including Wilfred Hopkins and his wife, Pattie, Dottie scooted back her chair from the huge dining-room table and stood. While everyone continued talking, sipping on coffee and moaning about the fact that they had eaten too much, Dottie pulled her engagement ring from the pocket of her suit jacket and slipped the ring on her finger. Then she motioned for Hal Esmond to stand and come to her, which he did instantly.

Dottie cleared her throat. "May I have everyone's attention, please."

All eyes focused on the elderly couple.

"I have an announcement to make," Dottie said. "You've all met Hal Esmond from Birmingham. But what you don't know is that Hal has been courting me for several months and he's asked me to marry him." She held up her hand and flashed the diamond. "And I've said yes."

"Lord help us," Eula moaned.

"Oh, Aunt Dottie, that's wonderful." Stacie stood and walked over to her aunt and hugged her.

Following his sister's example, Chris did the same, then shook hands with Hal. Douglas glanced at Candy, who smiled at him, then he, too, got up to congratulate the happy couple.

"What do you think about this engagement?" Valerie asked Penny Sue. "Do you suppose he's another swindler out to get his hands on Dottie's money?"

"Dottie doesn't have any money," Penny Sue reminded her cousin.

"She will have, when she inherits her share of Lottie's fortune."

"Which won't be anytime soon."

"Well, no, of course not, but—"

"I have it on good authority that Mr. Esmond is quite wealthy in his own right."

Valerie's eyes widened in surprise.

While the family began to disperse, some going into the front parlor, others remaining in the dining room, Vic leaned over and said to Geoff, "As much as I hate to ruin Miss Dottie's celebration, I think it's time you and I started asking questions."

"Who's going to be first?" Geoff asked.

"Let's start with the first crime. We'll ask Douglas Paine about his father's Winchester and see what he says."

Douglas had sat back down and was drinking his coffee when Vic and Geoff approached him, each taking a seat on either side of him.

"Mr. Paine, we'd like to ask you a few questions," Vic said.

Douglas faced Vic. "About what?"

"About an old Winchester rifle that once belonged to your father," Vic told him. "Do you still have the rifle in your possession?"

"Why yes, of course. It's up in the attic, stored away with several other items that belonged to my daddy."

"Would you allow us to borrow the rifle in order to run some ballistics tests on it?" Geoff asked.

Suddenly the room quieted. Vic glanced at Penny Sue, who stood at her aunt's side.

"Why would y'all need to run tests on Daddy's old rifle?" Dottie asked.

"Do you think it might have been the weapon used to shoot Lucky?" Douglas asked calmly. Much too calmly.

"We have every reason to think it's possible," Vic replied.

"Oh, I see." Douglas's face fell, and tears gathered in his eyes.

"This is nonsense," Dottie said. "Douglas would no more shoot Lucky than I…" She stared at her brother, who had bent his head and covered his face with his hands. "Douglas didn't shoot Lucky. I did. I—I knew where he kept Daddy's old rifle and I went to his house and got it, and I shot Lucky."

"Aunt Dottie!" Penny Sue wrapped an arm around her aunt's frail, trembling shoulders. "Why on earth would you confess to a crime we know you didn't commit? You don't know the first thing about shooting a rifle, and besides that, you would never harm Lucky."

Douglas lifted his head. He stood and looked at his niece and then at his sister. "She's trying to protect me." He turned to Vic and held out his hands in a gesture of surrender. "I'm the guilty party. I shot Lucky."

## Chapter 16

The shock in Penny Sue's eyes quickly vanished and was replaced with disbelief. "I don't believe you, Uncle Douglas. You would no more shoot Lucky than I would. You love animals."

"Of course...he didn't...do it," Dottie said, her voice quivering. "I told you that...I did it."

"This is utter nonsense." Penny Sue looked from her aunt to her uncle. "Why are you two lying? Who are you trying to protect?"

Hearing the pain in her voice, Vic came up beside Penny Sue, but didn't touch her, despite his primitive male instincts telling him to wrap her in his arms and protect her.

She turned to Vic and looked at him pleadingly. "You mustn't believe either of them. They're lying."

Hal Esmond put his arm around Dottie's waist and whispered something to her. She shook her head. With tears streaming down her face, she went into his arms and laid her head on his chest.

Pattie Hopkins glared at her husband. "Willie Hopkins, shouldn't you be speaking up about now and telling Douglas to keep his mouth shut? After all, you are the lawyer for the Paine family, aren't you?"

"My dear, I'm afraid that I can't advise Douglas, considering the fact that I represent Penny Sue and Lucky in this matter," Wilfred said.

Giving her husband a condemning glare, Pattie snorted indignantly and marched hurriedly from the room.

Penny Sue cried, "Please, Uncle Douglas, if you're trying to protect someone—"

"I'm sorry that I've disappointed you, Penny Sue, but I did it. I shot Lucky," Douglas practically shouted, then choked back tears as he hung his head.

Apparently alerted by Pattie Hopkins that something of great interest was occurring, the family members who had gone into the front parlor returned to the dining room, one by one. First Eula, then Chris and Stacie, followed by Valerie and Dylan. Candy Paine came into the room last and stayed near the door, nervously watching the others.

"What's going on in here?" Eula asked. "We heard Douglas shouting, and then Pattie came rushing in and told us to come into the dining room immediately." She focused on Douglas. "Just what were you shouting about?"

"I—I'm the one who shot Lucky," Douglas said, his head bent, his eyes downcast.

Lifting her head from Hal's chest, Dottie whimpered, then re-affirmed her confession. "I tried to tell them that I was the one who shot Lucky, but they won't believe me."

"No wonder," Chris said. "Everyone knows you'd never harm Lucky or any animal for that matter, Aunt Dottie. And neither would my father." He looked pointedly at Vic. "I did it. I shot Lucky. They're trying to protect me."

"Chris!" Douglas shook his head. "No, son, don't."

Vic and Geoff exchanged what's-going-on-here glances.

"And I helped him," Stacie chimed in as she came over and stood by her brother's side.

Douglas groaned. "Please, don't do this. Allow me to make a full confession. I'm guilty on all counts. I shot Lucky. I left the bloody toy dog on the porch. I—"

"Stop right this minute!" Phyllis Dickson, who had been standing on the far side of the dining room with Pattie Hopkins when Douglas made his initial confession, came forward and patted Douglas on the back. "You mustn't take the blame for something I did. It's not right. I—I committed a grievous sin." She looked at Penny Sue. "Please, forgive me. I'm the one who put that butcher knife in one of my toy dogs and smeared the blood from a beef roast all over the dog."

Clayton Dickson hurried to his wife, took her in his arms and consoled her as if she were a frightened child. "Now, now, my love, all is forgiven." He glanced around the room at the others. "Y'all must understand the pressure Phyllis has been under lately. You see, she and I desperately need the money we thought Lottie would leave us."

"No, that's not true. *We* don't need the money, only *I* need it," Phyllis admitted, entwining her hands in a prayer-like gesture as she turned to face the family. "I have a sickness, you see. I buy things. I can't stop myself. And sometimes…sometimes I write checks that aren't any good."

The others grumbled and mumbled and started looking at one another with accusatory glances.

Penny Sue grabbed Vic's arm. "Please, do something," she said in a quiet voice.

"Folks, let's everybody calm down," Vic told the Paine family. "We seem to have multiple confessions and some doubts as to who the guilty parties are."

Suddenly everyone started talking louder, jabbering about who was guilty and who was innocent and who would still inherit and who wouldn't. Vic let out a long, loud whistle. Immediately the room quieted and everyone stared at him.

"Mr. Monday will keep watch at that door." Vic nodded to the open pocket doors that led into the hall. "And Tully—" he shouted the man's name and within seconds Tully appeared in the doorway between the dining room and kitchen "—will keep watch at that door."

"What's going on?" Valerie asked. "Do you intend to keep us hemmed up in the dining room against our will?"

"Yes, ma'am," Vic replied. "That's exactly what I'm going to do."

"I must protest this treatment," Clayton said.

"We have a mystery on our hands," Vic told them. "Several mysteries in fact. And since everybody seems to be in a confessing mood, I believe now just might be a good time to solve a few of the mysteries surrounding the recent attempts on Lucky's life."

"I should think it's obvious that none of us want to believe that a member of our family would do anything to harm Lucky." Penny Sue clutched Vic's arm. "But we have to face facts. Someone shot Lucky, someone torched Doc Stone's clinic, someone left a bloody toy dog on the porch, someone set pit bulls loose in the backyard and someone kidnapped Lucky." She turned to her uncle. "You didn't leave the toy dog on the porch, did you?"

Douglas shook his head.

"Phyllis, did you do it?" Penny Sue asked.

Phyllis nodded. "I'm so sorry. It was such a silly thing to do, but I thought…I hoped perhaps you would take it as a warning and…oh, I don't know what I thought. God forgive me, but we need our inheritance, and I actually had thoughts of killing Lucky. Of taking that butcher knife and stabbing the poor little thing."

"Oh, Phyllis!" Dottie Paine's eyes glistened with tears.

"I think maybe I stabbed the toy dog as a warning to myself, too. I don't know. It doesn't make sense, and I'm so very, very sorry. Please—" She looked directly at Penny Sue "—forgive me. You know if I can't pay off my debts, it will become public knowledge that I wrote bad checks. Just think how that will affect Clayton's ministry."

No more so than the whole town knowing that Clayton Dickson was married to a certifiable fruitcake, Vic thought.

"It'll be all right," Penny Sue told her cousin's wife. "I have no intention of pressing charges against you and there's no reason why anyone outside this room should ever know what you did. As for making good on those bad checks—just how much do you owe?"

Vic rolled his eyes toward the ceiling. If he thought warning Penny Sue not to waste her concern or her money on any of these people would do any good, he'd speak up. But he knew better. Her heart was far too generous and forgiving.

"Fifteen thousand dollars." Weeping uncontrollably, Phyllis covered her face with her hands and not even Clayton could console her.

"If you'll get the professional help you need, I'll pay off your debts," Penny Sue said.

"Cousin Penny Sue, how generous of you." Clayton rushed over and hugged her. "God will bless you for this."

Vic cleared his throat. "All right, that's two crimes solved. We already knew that Chris kidnapped Lucky and now we know that Phyllis left the bloody dog on the porch."

"But Lucky wasn't hurt in either incident," Stacie said. "And even if y'all hadn't caught up with Chris at my house, you know he would never have harmed Lucky. He meant it when he said he had planned to find a good home for Lucky."

"We believe Chris." Penny Sue gazed sympathetically at Stacie.

Vic groaned. This had to be the neediest bunch of loonies he'd ever seen. And Penny Sue had to be the most understanding person on earth.

"We still have three unsolved crimes," Vic said. "The shooting, the fire and the pit bulls." Penny Sue could absolve everyone of their crimes, she could forgive, forget and spend money on this worthless lot, but two of the three unsolved mysteries were crimes the police would not overlook—the fire and the pit bulls.

"I told you, I shot Lucky." Douglas confessed once again.

Before Dottie or Chris or anyone else could once again confess to the crime, Vic spoke up. "We have three people who claim they shot Lucky. Would any one of you like to recant your confession?"

Silence.

Vic focused first on Dottie. "Tell me the truth, Miss Dottie. Do you know the first thing about guns? Have you ever shot a rifle before in your entire life?"

Dottie's face flushed. "Well…I…er…uh…"

"No, of course she's never shot a rifle, and she knows nothing about guns. She hates guns," Penny Sue said.

Vic nodded, then looked at Chris. "Did you shoot Lucky?"

Chris hesitated, then said, "I could have."

"But you didn't," Vic said.

"And neither did Uncle Douglas," Penny Sue added, then walked over to her uncle and draped her arm around his shoulders. "You didn't shoot Lucky, but you know who did, don't you?"

Douglas trembled as he wept silently.

"Oh, for goodness sakes, leave him alone." Candy came forward and confronted Vic. "I'm the one Douglas is trying to protect and God knows I don't deserve his loyalty, not after…well, let's just say that I haven't been a very good wife to him."

"Did you shoot Lucky?" Vic asked.

"Yes," Candy admitted. "I learned how to shoot a rifle when I was just a kid. My old man used to take all us kids hunting with him. And as far as shooting Lucky, I suppose it's no secret that I married Douglas for his money, only he turned out not to be as rich as I'd thought he was. If that crazy sister of his hadn't left all her money to that damn dog, none of this would have happened. No one would have been forced to go to such extreme measures to get rid of Lucky. Everything that's happened is Lottie Paine's fault."

"Candy, honey…" Douglas gazed lovingly at his wife. "You—you didn't do any of those other things, did you? You didn't set fire to the clinic or release those pit bulls on Lucky, did you?"

"Would anyone believe me if I said that I didn't?" Candy surveyed the room, studying everyone's reaction.

"I believe you," Douglas told her.

"I believe you, too," Penny Sue said. "It won't be easy to forgive you for shooting Lucky, but for Uncle Douglas's sake, I won't press charges."

"Does this mean that Douglas won't inherit his share of Lottie's fortune?" Candy asked.

Douglas gasped.

"No." In the utter stillness of the dining room, Wilfred Hopkins's voice seemed louder than it actually was. "If Douglas didn't harm Lucky or assist you in harming Lucky, then his inheritance is secure."

"He didn't help me and I had no idea he knew I'd shot Lucky," Candy said.

"Does that mean Clayton won't be penalized because of what I did?" Phyllis asked hopefully.

"Mercy no," Wilfred replied. "You didn't harm Lucky in any way. What you did was little more than a practical joke. Besides, Clayton wasn't a party to your silly stunt, was he?"

Phyllis shook her head. "No. No, of course not."

"What about Chris?" Stacie asked.

"He didn't harm Lucky either," Wilfred said. "So, his only real concern is the charges against him for hitting Tanya on the head."

"Since so many of you are in the mood to confess and clear your consciences, we have two other crimes against Lucky that no one has taken the blame for, at least not yet. Do I have any takers?" Vic asked. "Would anyone like to own up to releasing those pit bulls or to torching the clinic?"

Silence once again.

Each person looked at the person next to them and then glanced around the room. A soft rumble rose slowly and spread quickly until the whole group was talking all at once.

Vic checked the exits, making sure Geoff and Tully had the doors blocked. It wasn't that he actually believed Dylan Redley would confess to having set the pit bulls loose, but since they were expecting the police to arrive at any moment, the guy could easily bolt and run when he saw the first uniformed officer.

Penny Sue tugged on Vic's arm, then asked in a whisper, "Do you know something I don't know?"

Vic glanced at his wristwatch and replied in a low voice, for her ears only, "Officer Gibbs is supposed to show up at two o'clock to question Redley, and it's one minute till."

"I hate this," she said. "I hate all of it. In a way, Candy is right. This is all Aunt Lottie's fault. If she hadn't left Lucky her millions, none of this would have happened."

"An inheritance often brings out the worst in people," Vic told her. "And it's not just your family. I've seen families fight over who's going to get Grandma's iron skillet or Uncle Joe's collection of comic books."

Penny Sue sighed. "We can't keep them in here for very long. If no one else makes a grand gesture of confessing, or Officer Gibbs runs late for some reason—"

As if on cue, the doorbell rang. Everyone froze.

"I'll go," Penny Sue said.

Geoff stepped out of the way to allow her into the hall, then quickly blocked the exit again. The sound of voices coming from the foyer echoed down the corridor, but the conversation was unintelligible. A few minutes later, Penny Sue reappeared, Officer Gibbs with her. Geoff stepped aside once again, this time to allow them entrance.

"For those of you who might not know him, this is Officer Gibbs of the Alabaster Creek police department," Vic said.

"Am I under arrest?" Candy clutched Douglas's arm.

Officer Gibbs gave Candy a puzzled look. "No, ma'am. I'm here to question Mr. Redley—" he zeroed his gaze in on Dylan "—about a recent purchase he made."

Valerie gasped, then deliberately put some distance between herself and her husband before she demanded, "What have you done, you idiot?"

Dylan's face turned beet-red as he backed up against the wall, looking very much like a guilty man. He glanced jerkily from Officer Gibbs to Vic, and then to Penny Sue. "That damn stupid ass Freddy told you, didn't he? I knew I couldn't trust him. I paid him five hundred dollars for those two dogs and he swore he'd never tell a soul."

"Mr. Long didn't tell us anything." Officer Gibbs removed a pair of handcuffs from his belt and walked toward Dylan. "Mrs. Long told us."

"Damn it, you tricked me," Dylan shouted, and tried to make a break for it.

Dylan shoved past Valerie, then knocked Eula to her knees before reaching the door to the kitchen. Chris and Stacie rushed to help Eula, who yelled at Dylan and waved her fist at him.

What the hell did the guy think he was doing? Vic wondered. There was no way he could escape.

When Dylan grabbed Tully, apparently intending to shove him

aside, Tully balled his right hand into a fist and punched Dylan in the stomach. Bellowing, Dylan doubled over in pain, and before he could lift his head, Vic grabbed his arms, brought them behind him and held him in place until Officer Gibbs cuffed him.

The policeman led Dylan from the dining room, reading him his Miranda rights. Dylan halted just over the threshold and cried, "Valerie! Get me a lawyer."

"Get yourself a lawyer," his wife told him.

"You'd better take care of me or I'll tell the whole world that buying those pit bulls and setting them loose was your idea."

"You good-for-nothing, lying swine," Valerie shouted. "I made the biggest mistake of my life when I left my first husband and married you."

Officer Gibbs paused by Geoff before leaving and said something to him, then herded his prisoner down the hall and out the front door.

Penny Sue made the rounds, going from one family member to the other, making sure everyone, especially Eula, was all right. To a person, the entire group became unnaturally quiet. Shock, Vic thought. Everyone was in shock. Everyone except Penny Sue.

"I think maybe all of you should go home, now," Penny Sue said, then glanced at Vic. "That is, if it's all right with you."

Vic hesitated for a minute, then said, "Yeah, it's fine if everyone wants to leave." He was ninety-nine percent sure no one was going to admit to torching the clinic, and as of right now, they didn't have a suspect.

As if he'd known why Vic had hesitated, Geoff came over to him and said, "No one's going to confess to setting the veterinary clinic on fire because none of them did it."

Vic snapped his head around and stared at Geoff. "And you're sure of this because?"

"Officer Gibbs just informed me that they caught the arsonist. It seems the clinic here in Alabaster Creek was only one of three recently torched within a hundred-mile radius. They caught the man in the act over in the next county late last night."

"They're sure he's the one who set fire to Doc Stone's clinic?" Vic asked.

"They're sure. The man even confessed. And according to Officer Gibbs, the lunatic actually bragged about it."

Vic should feel relieved. After all, with very little effort, he and Geoff had solved all the mysteries and had revealed the identities of all the culprits. This meant his job was over and by this time tomorrow, he could be back in Atlanta and away from the nutty Paine family and their crazy high jinks. All he had to do was tie up a few loose ends.

Was that what Penny Sue was—a loose end?

He looked at her. That she was beautiful went without saying. But she possessed the kind of beauty that was more than skin-deep. Penny Sue had a beautiful heart. A beautiful soul. And she deserved a man worthy of her. He sure as hell wasn't that man.

Wilfred Hopkins went up to Penny Sue, his wife at her side. "I can't say any of this surprised me. I tried to warn Lottie when she insisted on leaving her entire twenty-three-million-dollar estate to Lucky, that it would end badly."

"There isn't any way we can overturn the will, is there?" Penny Sue asked.

"I'm afraid not."

"Then there's only one thing for me to do, Uncle Willie." She pulled him aside and while they talked privately, Vic watched them and wondered just what elaborate scheme she had concocted. Something totally illogical, no doubt.

"Are you sure you want to do this?" Wilfred asked, loud enough for everyone to hear.

"I'm sure. I'll come to your office tomorrow and we'll make everything legal."

Wilfred kissed Penny Sue on the cheek, then clasped his wife's arm and led her out of the dining room and down the hall. You could hear Pattie asking, "Just what was that all about?" and him replying, "Lawyer/client privileged information, my darling."

When the entire group had dispersed, leaving only Penny Sue and Dottie, along with the Coxes, Vic, Geoff and Hal Esmond, Penny Sue put her arm around her aunt.

"I'm so sorry your big day was ruined."

"It's not your fault, sweet girl," Dottie said. "But it has been rather exhausting, hasn't it?" She turned to her fiancé. "Does what happened here this afternoon change anything between us? Do you want to run for the hills while you still can?"

Hal smiled warmly, lifted Dottie's frail hand and kissed it. "Of course not, my love. All families have their squabbles, but I must say the Paines do things in a big, overly dramatic way, don't they?"

Dottie sighed. "Yes, we do tend to be a little melodramatic."

"A little?" Penny Sue groaned.

"Just what did you tell Willie?" Dottie asked.

"I told him I thought I had a solution to the problem of keeping Lucky safe."

"And just what would that be?"

"I intend to provide any of the heirs who badly need money an advance on their inheritance, up to five hundred thousand dollars," Penny Sue said. "I'll provide the funds for them whenever they need the money. And years from now, when Lucky goes to puppy-dog heaven and they receive their share of the inheritance, they can repay me."

"Oh, Penny Sue, that could add up to several million dollars. Do you have that much?" Aunt Dottie's black eyes widened with concern.

"I have just enough so that if each heir takes five hundred thousand, I can provide it."

"Then you'd be completely broke, wouldn't you?" Dottie clung to Hal's hand.

"Of course not. I have this big old house and an allotment to maintain it and to care for Lucky, and don't forget that I own a very successful business and—"

"I won't take a red cent." Dottie turned to her fiancé. "If that's all right with you, Hal?"

"Of course it's all right with me," he replied. "I'm perfectly capable of providing you with everything you'll ever need."

"I dare say Eula won't take any money, nor will Stacie," Dottie said. "Chris, of course, will need enough to pay off his debts, as will Phyllis. But I suppose Valerie will jump at the chance to get her hands on as much cash as possible, and unless Douglas divorces that tramp he's married to, she'll persuade him to grab as much as you'll give him."

"Let's not worry about any of this today," Penny Sue said. "Why don't you and Hal go for a lovely Sunday-afternoon drive and put all this out of your minds? This should have been your day."

"That's an excellent idea," Hal said as he urged Dottie toward the door.

"Are you sure you'll be all right?" Dottie called from the hallway.

"I'll be fine. Now go on, you two."

As soon as Dottie and Hal left, Ruby came bustling into the dining room. "Everybody get out of here so I can clean up this mess." She shooed her hands at them until they walked out of the dining room and into the hall.

Geoff paused and smiled at Penny Sue. "Well, I'd say my job here is done, unless you think you'll need two Dundee agents to wrap things up."

"Oh, no, I—I'm sure Vic can handle tying up all the loose ends." Penny Sue held out her hand to Geoff. "Thank you so much."

"You're quite welcome." Geoff shook her hand and then turned to Vic. "I'll go up and pack my bag now. If I head out soon, I can make it back to Atlanta by late this evening. You take care of things here—" he looked pointedly at Penny Sue "—and I'll report in to Daisy, let her know this case is closed. Take as long as you need to settle everything."

Vic nodded. "Yeah, thanks. I...uh...I'll see you back in Atlanta, then."

"Sure thing."

Penny Sue stood there in the hallway, her hands clutched together in front of her and her gaze downcast. "When will you be leaving?"

He would rather walk over hot coals than answer her question. "I thought...well, there's not much else to do here, so—" He cleared his throat. Trying to think of the best way to handle the situation, he reached out and took both her hands in his. "If you want me to, I can stay until tomorrow. That would give us one more night together."

Her head snapped up, her eyes wide, her chin quivering. She jerked her hands from his and glared at him. "One more night? Do you think that's all I want from you?"

"I didn't mean it that way. I just thought maybe…"

"As far as I'm concerned, you can go pack your bag and drive back to Atlanta this afternoon, with Geoff."

"Penny Sue…sugar…"

"Don't you sugar me," she replied. "If you think for one minute that I'm going to have sex with you again as a way of saying goodbye, then mister, you'd better think again."

"I never said—"

"Leave! I want you to leave today. And don't you ever come back—not unless you decide you want to marry me. Then maybe, just maybe, I'll consider forgiving you."

"You don't want to marry me," he told her. "I'd make a really bad husband. You think you know me, but you don't. There are things about me…about my past—"

"You're just making excuses. If you loved me the way I love you, nothing else would matter. But I was a fool to think you actually cared about me."

"I do care about you." He cared too much, and that was the problem. It would be so easy for him to accept what she was offering, to reach out and grab her and never let go. But it wouldn't be fair to her. He could no more change who he was, who he had been, than she could change from being the sweet, loving, gentle woman she was.

"But you don't love me, do you?" she asked.

Tell her what she needs to hear, an inner voice urged him. End it here and now before you admit that she's everything you have ever wanted and more. "No, I don't love you."

Tears filled her eyes. Her chin quivered. Penny Sue ran from him, into the foyer and up the stairs. He stood there in agony until Lucky appeared out of nowhere and licked his hand. He figured Tully must have released the dog from wherever he'd been keeping him. Lucky was indeed a lucky dog. He would get to spend the rest of his life with Penny Sue, sleep by her side each night and wake to the sight of her beautiful face every morning.

Vic glanced at Lucky, then reached down and patted him on the head. "You'll take care of her for me, won't you?"

The past week had been, without a doubt, the most difficult six days of Penny Sue's life. And despite the fact that she had cried herself to sleep every night, she'd managed to fill her days with the things that needed to be done. Besides helping Aunt Dottie make plans for a small, private wedding in May, dealing with one of the busiest weeks of the year at Penny Sue's Pretties and preparing two dozen baskets for today's Easter-egg hunt sponsored by the church, she had written out one five-hundred-thousand-dollar check—to Valerie. Her cousin had packed up and left town, taking her son and her money with her and leaving her husband behind to rot in jail. Penny Sue had gotten Uncle Willie to hire a lawyer for Dylan and told him to explain to her former fiancé that she would pay for his defense, with one stipulation—that no matter what happened, he would leave Alabaster Creek and never return. Dylan had readily agreed.

Chris had accepted the money to pay off his gambling debts and the fees his lawyer charged, and swore he would repay her. Fortunately, Tanya hadn't been seriously injured and decided not to press charges against Chris.

Uncle Douglas asked Candy for a divorce, and since she agreed to leave town immediately, Penny Sue hadn't pressed charges against her for shooting Lucky. And although everyone who knew about Candy's involvement with Tommy Rutland promised him they wouldn't tell his wife, he decided to bare all and plead for mercy. Cherie and Tommy had begun marriage counseling this past Thursday. On Friday, he had officially withdrawn from the mayoral race.

Wayne Boggus was out of jail on bond and his trial date was not yet set. But Penny Sue had talked to him on the phone and promised to speak on his behalf when he was tried for reckless endangerment, a charge that his lawyer had plea-bargained to get him.

A little tattered and torn, a few hearts broken and dreams unfulfilled, she supposed the Paine family was pretty much back to normal. Penny Sue smiled at the thought of her family being in any way normal.

Today had been warm and bright, perfect weather for Easter-egg hunts. This year, as with every year in Penny Sue's lifetime, the big church egg hunt was held at the Paine mansion, outside on the nearly two-acre lawn if the weather was good, and inside the house if the weather turned nasty. Forty children, ranging in ages between one and thirteen, had shown up at one o'clock today for the festivities. And now, at a little past four, parents and children began leaving. She watched them with a heavy heart, wondering if this was to be her fate. Would she spend the rest of her life watching other people's children grow up, while she remained unmarried and childless?

When she'd fallen in love with Vic…

I have to stop thinking about him. He's gone. Whatever we had together is over.

"Penny Sue," Aunt Dottie called from the front porch. "Why don't you come in and rest for a while before you start the clean up?"

"You and Hal go on in," she said. "I'd like to sit in the swing for a bit."

"Would you like Ruby to bring you out something to drink?"

"Yes, some iced tea would be nice. Thank you."

Penny Sue walked up onto the porch and over to the swing. She shoved the swing gently back and forth. After she slowed the swing's movements, she sat, closed her eyes and leaned her head back.

Suddenly, feeling something cold against her cheek, she reached up and her hand encountered a frosty glass pressed against her warm skin. She opened her eyes, turned and clasped the glass. She blinked her eyes several times. What was the matter with her? She thought she saw Vic standing there beside the swing. It's just a hallucination, she told herself. But no matter how hard she tried to vanquish the image, it wouldn't go away.

"Vic?"

"Hello, sugar."

The iced tea slipped from her fingers and hit the porch, the glass shattering and sending liquid and ice cubes over the floor.

She jumped out of the swing and straight into Vic's arms.

"It's really you," she cried.

He lifted her off the ground, then swung her around and around before easing her to her feet and kissing her. Several minutes later, breathless, her head spinning and her heart bursting with joy, Penny Sue laid her hands on his chest and looked up into his hazel-blue eyes.

"You've come back to stay?" she asked.

He nodded.

"You love me?"

"More than you'll ever know."

"Then why did you leave me? Why did you let me suffer for six whole days before—"

He grabbed her and kissed her again.

When the kiss ended, she looked up at him and said, "Why did you leave?"

"I thought I could live without you. I was wrong. I can't," he told her. "I have to believe that you'll be able to understand certain things about me, about my past. If you'll let me, I'll tell you about—"

She placed her index finger over his lips. "Not now. One day, when you're truly ready. And I promise you that no matter what you tell me, it won't change the way I feel about you."

"Then will you forgive me for leaving you last Sunday?" he asked.

"I'll forgive you, on one condition."

"And that would be?"

"If you ask me the right question."

Vic knelt on one knee, took her left hand and said, "I love you, Penny Sue. And if you'd do me the great honor of consenting to be my wife, I'll spend the rest of my life utterly and completely devoted to you." He dug in his jacket pocket and brought out a jeweler's box.

Penny Sue laughed, her heart bursting with happiness, as Vic flipped open the box and removed a sparkling, emerald-cut diamond flanked by two smaller diamonds set in platinum. When she held out her left hand, he slipped the ring on her finger, then rose to his feet and took her into his arms.

The front door burst open and out came Dottie and Hal, Puff tucked under Dottie's arm and Hal's two calico cats, Hansel and Gretel, curling about his legs. Behind them, Ruby and Tully stood in the doorway, wide smiles on their faces. Lucky ran over to Vic and pawed his leg. Vic picked up Lucky and he and Penny Sue nestled the little dog between them.

Penny Sue gazed up at Vic. "How does a June wedding sound to you?"

## *Epilogue*

And so we were married in June, I got pregnant in July and was elected mayor in November. All in all, not a bad year. Vic resigned from Dundee and bought the local hardware store when Buster Johnson retired and moved to Florida to live with his daughter. He seems perfectly content living in Alabaster Creek, and although I know at times my family gets on his last nerve, he tolerates them because he loves me. And he truly enjoys small town life, and says being married to me is all the excitement and adventure he needs.

And this morning I took the oath of office with my husband at my side and surrounded by family, friends and loyal supporters. I'm now officially the mayor of Alabaster Creek. If Daddy were here, he'd be so proud of me. After Tommy Rutland dropped out of the mayoral race, I didn't face any party opposition and the other party's vote had been split between two candidates whose combined votes hadn't come close to equaling my landslide victory. Aunt Dottie and Uncle Hal drove in from Birmingham just for today's festivities. The crowd moved from the courthouse to the Country Kettle for a celebratory lunch and ended up at the Paine mansion this evening. Now, the group has dwindled down to family only. Aunt Dottie and Uncle Hal, Uncle Douglas and his new girlfriend, Amanda—an attractive divorcée only three years his junior—Chris and Stacie, Clayton and Phyllis, and Eula.

When Aunt Dottie married, she'd wanted Ruby and Tully to move with her to Birmingham, but they chose to stay on with Vic and me, much to my delight. What with my being elected mayor and still managing Penny Sue's Pretties, I don't know how I'd manage when the baby comes if I didn't have Ruby and Tully. Of course, Vic swears he's going to be a hands-on daddy and I don't doubt that he'll be a wonderful father, because he's been a model husband these past seven months.

I suppose it should be illegal or immoral or downright sinful for one woman to have been given so much happiness, but I don't question fate. After all, fate brought Vic into my life. When I hired a Dundee agent to come to Alabaster Creek to act as Lucky's bodyguard, I had no idea that the person who would show up would turn out to be the love of my life.

"Penny Sue, I think it's time you said goodnight to everyone," Vic said to me. "You've been on your feet all day." He placed his arm around me and laid his hand over my slightly protruding belly. I'm six months along and started showing only a few weeks ago.

"Everyone, please stay as long as you'd like. But Vic's right. I'm worn to a frazzle," I said.

He's so protective of me, and was even before I got pregnant. But the way he's treated me since the moment I told him I'd taken a home pregnancy test and it was positive, you'd think I was made of spun glass. Not that I'm complaining, mind you.

He draped his arm around my shoulders and led me away from the others, out into the foyer and up the stairs, Lucky following right behind us.

"I'll draw you a warm bath," he said. "And I'll wash your hair and afterward, give you a nice, soothing massage."

"That sounds heavenly."

When we reached our bedroom, I grabbed his hand and brought it to my lips and kissed it. "Have I told you today how much I love you?"

He wrapped me in his arms and nuzzled my neck. "Not half as much as I love you, Mrs. Noble."

Cupping his chin between my thumb and index finger, I lifted his face. "Do you suppose Lucky will be jealous of the baby?"

Lucky looked up from where he was lying on the rug in front of the fireplace, knowing full well that we were talking about him.

Vic caressed my cheek. "Nope. Lucky's too good-natured to be jealous. Besides, he and Paine are going to be best buddies. Every boy needs a dog and our son will have one from the moment he's born."

"You aren't too disappointed that the baby's a boy, are you? I know you said you wanted a little girl who looks just like me."

"I do," he said, then kissed me. "We'll have a girl next time."

"Next time?"

"You do want at least two children, don't you? Maybe three."

"You know I do."

"Then it will be my pleasure to do everything I can to help you achieve that goal."

He removed my suit jacket, then unbuttoned my silk blouse and slipped it down my arms, pausing to kiss my shoulder. "I think we should knock out the wall between the back storerooms at Penny Sue's Pretties and Noble's Hardware. That way we can set up a nursery between your place of business and mine so that we can take Paine to work with us every day."

"You're just full of all kinds of good ideas, aren't you?"

"Yes, I am. As a matter of fact, I have several really good ideas, and I'd like to try a few of them out tonight, if you're not too tired, Mrs. Mayor."

"I'm never too tired to try out something new."

He finished helping me undress, then peeled off his clothes and led me into the bathroom. After reaching inside the shower to turn on the water, he leaned down and whispered in my ear, telling me exactly what he had planned.

"You devil, you." I swatted him playfully.

He pulled me into the shower, both of us laughing, and then cradled my face in his hands. "And you, Penny Sue, are an angel. My angel."

"Ooh, we've never played angel and devil before. I think I'm going to like this game."

"I promise you, you will."

And Vic Noble keeps his promises. Always.

\* \* \* \* \*

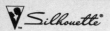

# INTIMATE MOMENTS™

**Paranormal Allied eXperts—
genetically enhanced
superagents leading the
world into a new era of defense**

After her twin vanishes, evidence leads
Sienna Parker to the deep blue waters
off the Florida Keys. Hot on her trail is
PAX agent Cade Brock, and he claims
only Sienna can prevent a potentially
devastating terrorist attack!

# *Deep Blue*
## by **Suzanne McMinn**

(Silhouette Intimate Moments #1405)

*Available February 2006
at your favorite retail outlet.*

If you enjoyed what you just read,
then we've got an offer you can't resist!

# Take 2 bestselling
# love stories FREE!
# Plus get a FREE surprise gift!

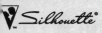

# INTIMATE MOMENTS™

Bad-boy government officer Simon Byrne
avoids relationships. By-the-book tech
officer Janna Harris won't get involved.
Pairing these two could only lead to
trouble and a passion so strong it
could risk their lives.

# *Breaking All the Rules*

## by Susan Vaughan

(Silhouette Intimate Moments #1406)

*Available February 2006
at your favorite retail outlet.*

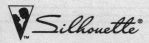

# COMING NEXT MONTH

SIMCNM0

customed to take their orders from the magistrates are not ready in these emergencies to obey his, and he will always in difficult times lack men whom he can rely on. Such a prince cannot base himself on what he sees in quiet times, when the citizens have need of the state; for then every one is full of promises and each one is ready to die for him when death is far off; but in adversity, when the state has need of citizens, then he will find but few. And this experience is the more dangerous, in that it can only be had once. Therefore a wise prince will seek means by which his subjects will always and in every possible condition of things have need of his government, and then they will always be faithful to him.

## Chapter X

### HOW THE STRENGTH OF ALL STATES SHOULD BE MEASURED

IN examining the character of these principalities it is necessary to consider another point, namely, whether the prince has such a position as to be able in case of need to maintain himself alone, or whether he has always need of the protection of others. The better to explain this I would say, that I consider those capable of maintaining themselves alone who can, through abundance of men or money, put together a sufficient army, and hold the field against any one who assails them; and I consider to have need of others, those who cannot take the field against their enemies, but are obliged to take refuge within their walls and stand on the defensive. We have already discussed the former case and will speak of it in future as occasion arises. In the second case there is nothing to be said except to encourage such a prince to provision and fortify his own town, and not to trouble about the surrounding country. And whoever has strongly fortified his town and, as regards the government of his subjects, has proceeded as we have already described and will further relate, will be attacked with great reluctance, for men are always averse to enterprises in which they foresee difficulties, and it can never appear easy to attack one who has his town stoutly defended and is not hated by the people.

The cities of Germany are absolutely free, have little surrounding country, and obey the emperor when they choose, and they do not fear him or any other potentate that they have about them. They are fortified in such a manner that every one thinks that to reduce them would be tedious and difficult, for they all have the necessary moats and bastions, sufficient artillery, and always keep food, drink, and fuel for one year in the public storehouses. Beyond which, to keep the lower classes satisfied, and without loss to the commonwealth, they have always enough means to give them work for one year in these employments which form the nerve and life of the town, and in the industries by which the lower classes live. Military exercises are still held in high reputation, and many regulations are in force for maintaining them.

A prince, therefore, who possesses a strong city and does not make himself hated, cannot be assaulted; and if he were to be so, the assailant would be obliged to retire shamefully; for so many things change, that it is almost impossible for any one to maintain a siege for a year with his armies idle. And to those who urge that the people, having their possessions outside and seeing them burnt, will not have patience, and the long siege and self-interest will make them forget their prince, I reply that a powerful and courageous prince will always overcome those difficulties by now raising the hopes of his subjects that the evils will not last long, now impressing them with fear of the enemy's cruelty, now by dextrously assuring himself of those who appear too bold. Besides which, the enemy would naturally burn and ravage the country on first arriving and at the time when men's minds are still hot and eager to defend themselves, and therefore the prince has still less to fear, for after some time, when people have cooled down, the damage is done, the evil has been suffered, and there is no remedy, so that they are the more ready to unite with their prince, as it appears that he is under an obligation to them, their houses having been burnt and their possessions ruined in his defence.

It is the nature of men to be as much bound by the bene-fits that they confer as by those they receive. From which it follows that, everything considered, a prudent prince will not find it difficult to uphold the courage of his subjects both at the commencement and during a state of siege, if he possesses provisions and means to defend himself.

## Chapter XI

### OF ECCLESIASTICAL PRINCIPALITIES

It now only remains to us to speak of ecclesiastical prin-cipalities, with regard to which the difficulties lie wholly before they are possessed. They are acquired either by ability or by fortune; but are maintained without either, for they are sustained by ancient religious customs, which are so powerful and of such quality, that they keep their princes in power in whatever manner they proceed and live. These princes alone have states without defending them, have sub-

jects without governing them, and their states, not being
defended, are not taken from them; their subjects not being
governed do not resent it, and neither think nor are capable
of alienating themselves from them. Only these principalities, therefore, are secure and happy. But as they are upheld
by higher causes, which the human mind cannot attain to,
I will abstain from speaking of them; for being exalted
and maintained by God, it would be the work of a presumptuous and foolish man to discuss them. However, I might
be asked how it has come about that the Church has reached
such great temporal power, when, previous to Alexander
VI, the Italian potentates—and not merely the really powerful ones, but every lord or baron, however insignificant—
held it in slight esteem as regards temporal power; whereas
now it is dreaded by a king of France, whom it has been
able to drive out of Italy, and has also been able to ruin the
Venetians. Therefore, although this is well known, I do not
think it superfluous to call it to mind.

Before Charles, King of France, came into Italy, this
country was under the rule of the Pope, the Venetians, the
King of Naples, the Duke of Milan, and the Florentines.
These potentates had to have two chief cares: one, that no
foreigner should enter Italy by force of arms, the other
that none of the existing governments should extend its
dominions. Those chiefly to be watched were the Pope and
the Venetians. To keep back the Venetians required the
alliance of all the others, as in the defence of Ferrara, and
to keep down the Pope they made use of the Roman barons.
These were divided into two factions, the Orsini and the
Colonna, and as there was constant quarrelling between
them, and they were constantly under arms, before the eyes
of the Pope, they kept the papacy weak and infirm. And although there arose now and then a resolute Pope like Sextus,

yet his fortune or ability was never able to liberate him from these evils. The shortness of their life was the reason of this, for in the course of ten years which, as a general rule, a Pope lived, he had great difficulty in suppressing even one of the factions, and if, for example, a Pope had almost put down the Colonna, a new Pope would succeed who was hostile to the Orsini, which caused the Colonna to spring up again, and he was not in time to suppress them.

This caused the temporal power of the Pope to be of little esteem in Italy. Then arose Alexander VI who, of all the pontiffs who have ever reigned, best showed how a Pope might prevail both by money and by force. With Duke Valentine as his instrument, and seizing the opportunity of the French invasion, he did all that I have previously described in speaking of the actions of the duke. And although his object was to aggrandise not the Church but the duke, what he did resulted in the aggrandisement of the Church, which after the death of the duke became the heir of his labours. Then came Pope Julius, who found the Church powerful, possessing all Romagna, all the Roman barons suppressed, and the factions destroyed by the severity of Alexander. He also found the way open for accumulating wealth in ways never used before the time of Alexander. These measures were not only followed by Julius, but increased; he resolved to gain Bologna, put down the Venetians and drive the French from Italy, in all which enterprises he was successful. He merits the greater praise, as he did everything to increase the power of the Church and not of any private person. He also kept the Orsini and Colonna parties in the condition in which he found them, and although there were some leaders among them who might have made changes, there were two things that kept them steady: one, the greatness of the Church, which they

dreaded; the other, the fact that they had no cardinals, who
are the origin of the tumults among them. For these parties
are never at rest when they have cardinals, for these stir up
the parties both within Rome and outside, and the barons
are forced to defend them. Thus from the ambitions of
prelates arise the discords and tumults among the barons.
His holiness, Pope Leo X, therefore, has found the pontifi-
cate in a very powerful condition, from which it is hoped
that as those Popes made it great by force of arms, so he
through his goodness and infinite other virtues will make
it both great and venerated.

## Chapter XII

### THE DIFFERENT KINDS OF MILITIA AND MERCENARY SOLDIERS

HAVING now discussed fully the qualities of these principalities of which I proposed to treat, and partially considered the causes of their prosperity or failure, and having
also showed the methods by which many have sought to
obtain such states, it now remains for me to treat generally
of the methods, both offensive and defensive, that can be
used in each of them. We have said already how necessary
it is for a prince to have his foundations good, otherwise he
is certain to be ruined. The chief foundations of all states,
whether new, old, or mixed, are good laws and good arms.
And as there cannot be good laws where there are not good
arms, and where there are good arms there must be good
laws, I will not now discuss the laws, but will speak of the
arms.

I say, therefore, that the arms by which a prince defends
his possessions are either his own, or else mercenaries, or

auxiliaries, or mixed. The mercenaries and auxiliaries are useless and dangerous, and if any one supports his state by the arms of mercenaries, he will never stand firm or sure, as they are disunited, ambitious, without discipline, faithless, bold amongst friends, cowardly amongst enemies, they have no fear of God, and keep no faith with men. Ruin is only deferred as long as the assault is postponed; in peace you are despoiled by them, and in war by the enemy. The cause of this is that they have no love or other motive to keep them in the field beyond a trifling wage, which is not enough to make them ready to die for you. They are quite willing to be your soldiers so long as you do not make war, but when war comes, it is either fly or decamp altogether. I ought to have little trouble in proving this, since the ruin of Italy is now caused by nothing else but through her having relied for many years on mercenary arms. These did indeed help certain individuals to power, and appeared courageous when matched against each other, but when the foreigner came they showed their worthlessness. Thus it came about that King Charles of France was allowed to take Italy without the slightest trouble, and those who said that it was owing to our sins, spoke the truth, but it was not the sins they meant but those that I have related. And as it was the sins of princes, they too have suffered the punishment.

I will explain more fully the defects of these arms. Mercenary captains are either very capable men or not; if they are, you cannot rely upon them, for they will always aspire to their own greatness, either by oppressing you, their master, or by oppressing others against your intentions; but if the captain is not an able man, he will generally ruin you. And if it is replied to this, that whoever has armed forces will do the same, whether these are mercenary or not, I would reply that as armies are to be used either by a prince or by a republic, the prince must go in person to take the position of captain, and the republic must send its own citizens. If the man sent turns out incompetent, it must change him; and if capable, keep him by law from going beyond the proper limits. And it is seen by experience that only princes and armed republics make very great progress, whereas mercenary forces do nothing but harm, and also an armed republic submits less easily to the rule of one of its citizens than a republic armed by foreign forces.

Rome and Sparta were for many centuries well armed and free. The Swiss are well armed and enjoy great freedom. As an example of mercenary armies in antiquity there are the Carthaginians, who were oppressed by their mercenary soldiers, after the termination of the first war with the Romans, even while they still had their own citizens as captains. Philip of Macedon was made captain of their forces by the Thebans after the death of Epaminondas, and after gaining the victory he deprived them of liberty. The Milanese, on the death of Duke Philip, hired Francesco Sforza against the Venetians, who having overcome the enemy at Caravaggio, allied himself with them to oppress the Milanese his own employers. The father of this Sforza, being a soldier in the service of Queen Giovanna of Naples, left her suddenly unarmed, by which she was compelled, in order not to lose the kingdom, to throw herself into the arms of the King of Aragon. And if the Venetians and Florentines have in times past increased their dominions by means of such forces, and their captains have not made themselves princes but have defended them, I reply that the Florentines in this case have been favoured by chance, for of the capable leaders whom they might have feared, some did not conquer, some met with opposition, and others directed their ambition elsewhere. The one who did not conquer was Sir John Hawkwood, whose fidelity could not be known as he was not victorious, but every one will admit that, had he conquered, the Florentines would have been at his mercy. Sforza had always the Bracceschi against him which served as a mutual check. Francesco directed his ambition towards Lombardy; Braccio against the Church and the kingdom of Naples.

But let us look at what occurred a short time ago. The Florentines appointed Paolo Vitelli their captain, a man of great prudence, who had risen from a private station to the highest reputation. If he had taken Pisa no one can deny that it was highly important for the Florentines to retain his friendship, because had he become the soldier of their enemies they would have had no means of opposing him; and if they had retained him they would have been obliged to obey him. As to the Venetians, if one considers the progress they made, it will be seen that they acted surely and gloriously so long as they made war with their own forces; that it was before they commenced their enterprises on land that they fought courageously with their own gentlemen and armed populace, but when they began to fight on land they abandoned this virtue, and began to follow the Italian custom. And at the commencement of their land conquests they had not much to fear from their captains, their territories not being very large, and their reputation being great, but as their possessions increased, as they did under Carmagnola, they had an example of their mistake. For seeing that he was very powerful, after he had defeated the Duke of Milan, and knowing, on the other hand, that he was but lukewarm in this war, they considered that they would not make any more conquests with him, and they neither would nor could dismiss him, for fear of losing what they had already gained. In order to make sure of him they were therefore obliged to execute him. They then had for captains Bartolommeo da Bergamo, Roberto da San Severino, Count di Pitigliano, and such like, from whom they had to fear loss instead of gain, as happened subsequently at Vailà, where in one day they lost what they had laboriously gained in eight hundred years; for with these forces, only slow and trifling acquisitions are made, but sudden and miraculous losses. And as I have cited these examples from Italy, which has now for many years been governed by mercenary forces, I will now deal more largely with them, so that having seen their origin and progress, they can be better remedied.

You must understand that in these latter times, as soon as the empire began to be repudiated in Italy and the Pope to gain greater reputation in temporal matters, Italy was divided into many states; many of the principal cities took up arms against their nobles, who, favoured by the emperor, had held them in subjection, and the Church encouraged this in order to increase its temporal power. In many other cities one of the inhabitants became prince. Thus Italy having fallen almost entirely into the hands of the Church and a few republics, and the priests and other citizens not being accustomed to bear arms, they began to hire foreigners as soldiers. The first to bring into reputation this kind of militia was Alberigo da Como, a native of Romagna. Braccio and Sforza, who were in their day the arbiters of Italy were, amongst others, trained by him. After these came all those others who up to the present day have commanded the armies of Italy, and the result of their prowess has been that Italy has been overrun by Charles, preyed on by Louis, tyrannised over by Ferrando, and insulted by the Swiss. The system adopted by them was, in the first place, to increase their own reputation by discrediting the infantry. They did this because, as they had no country and lived on their earnings, a few foot soldiers did not augment their reputation, and they could not maintain a large number and therefore they restricted themselves almost entirely to cavalry, by which with a smaller number they were well paid and honoured. They reduced things to such a state that in an army of 20,000 soldiers there were not 2,000 foot. They had also used every means to spare themselves and the soldiers any hardship or fear by not killing each other in their encounters, but taking prisoners without expectation of ransom. They made no attacks on fortifications by night; and those in the fortifications did not attack the tents at night, they made no stockades or ditches round their camps, and did not take the field in winter. All these things were permitted by their military code, and adopted, as we have said, to avoid trouble and danger, so that they have reduced Italy to slavery and degradation.

## Chapter XIII

### OF AUXILIARY, MIXED, AND NATIVE TROOPS

WHEN one asks a powerful neighbour to come to aid and defend one with his forces, they are termed auxiliaries and are as useless as mercenaries. This was done in recent times by Julius, who seeing the wretched failure of his mercenary forces, in his Ferrara enterprise, had recourse to auxiliaries, and arranged with Ferrando, King of Spain, that he should help him with his armies. These forces may be good in themselves, but they are always dangerous for those who borrow them, for if they lose you are defeated, and if they conquer you remain their prisoner. And although ancient history is full of examples of this, I will not depart from the example of Pope Julius II, which is still fresh. Nothing could be less prudent than the course he adopted; for, wishing to take Ferrara, he put himself entirely into the power of a foreigner. But by good fortune there arose a third cause which prevented him reaping the effects of his bad policy; for when his auxiliaries were beaten at Ravenna, the Swiss rose up and drove back the victors, against all expectation of himself or others, so that he was not taken prisoner by the enemy which had fled, nor by his own auxiliaries, having conquered by other arms than theirs. The Florentines, being totally disarmed, hired 10,000 Frenchmen to attack Pisa, by which measure they ran greater risk than at any period of their struggles. The emperor of Constantinople, to oppose his neighbours, put 10,000 Turks into Greece, who after the war would not go away again, which was the beginning of the servitude of Greece to the infidels.

And one, therefore, who wishes not to conquer, would do well to use these forces, which are much more dangerous than mercenaries, as with them ruin is complete, for they are all united, and owe obedience to others, whereas with mercenaries, when they have conquered, it requires more time and a good opportunity for them to injure you, as they do not form a single body and have been engaged and paid by you, therefore a third party that you have made leader cannot at once acquire enough authority to be able to injure you. In a word, the greatest danger with mercenaries lies in their cowardice and reluctance to fight, but with auxiliaries the danger lies in their courage.

A wise prince, therefore, always avoids these forces and has recourse to his own, and would prefer rather to lose with his own men than conquer with the forces of others, not deeming it a true victory which is gained by foreign arms. I never hesitate to cite the example of Cesare Borgia and his actions. This duke entered Romagna with auxiliary troops, leading forces composed entirely of French soldiers, and with these he took Imola and Forlì; but as they seemed unsafe, he had recourse to mercenaries as a less risky policy, and hired the Orsini and Vitelli. Afterwards finding these uncertain to handle, unfaithful, and dangerous, he suppressed them, and relied upon his own men. And the difference between these forces can be easily seen if one considers the difference between the reputation of the duke when he had only the French, when he had the Orsini and Vitelli, and when he had to rely on himself and his own soldiers. His reputation will be found to have constantly increased, and he was never so highly esteemed as when every one saw that he was the sole master of his forces.

I do not wish to depart from recent Italian instances, but I cannot omit Hiero of Syracuse, whom I have already mentioned. This man being, as I said, made head of the army by the Syracusans, immediately recognised the uselessness of that militia which was organized like our Italian mercenary troops, and as he thought it unsafe either to retain them or dismiss them, he had them cut in pieces and thenceforward made war with his own arms and not those of others. I would also call to mind a symbolic tale from the Old Testament which well illustrates this point. When David offered to Saul to go and fight against the Philistine champion Goliath, Saul, to encourage him, armed him with his own arms, which when David had tried on, he refused saying, that with them he could not fight so well; he preferred, therefore, to face the enemy with his own sling and knife. In short, the arms of others either fail, overburden, or else impede you. Charles VII, father of King Louis XI, having through good fortune and bravery liberated France from the English, recognised this necessity of being armed with his own forces, and established in his kingdom a system of men-at-arms and infantry. Afterwards King Louis his son abolished the infantry and began to hire Swiss, which mistake being followed by others is, as may now be seen, a cause of danger to that kingdom. For by giving such reputation to the Swiss, France has disheartened all her own troops, the infantry having been abolished and the men-at-arms being obliged to foreigners for assistance; for being accustomed to fight with Swiss troops, they think they cannot conquer without them. Whence it comes that the French are insufficiently strong to oppose the Swiss, and without the aid of the Swiss they will not venture against others. The armies of the French are thus of a mixed kind, partly mercenary and partly her own; taken together they are much better than troops entirely composed of mercenaries or auxiliaries, but much inferior to national forces.

And let this example be sufficient, for the kingdom of France would be invincible if Charles's military organization had been developed or maintained. But men with their lack of prudence initiate novelties and, finding the first taste good, do not notice the poison within, as I pointed out previously in regard to wasting fevers.

The prince, therefore, who fails to recognise troubles in his state as they arise, is not truly wise, and it is given to few to be thus. If we consider the first cause of the collapse of the Roman Empire we shall find it merely due to the hiring of Goth mercenaries, for from that time we find the Roman strength begin to weaken. All the advantages derived from the Empire fell to the Goths.

I conclude then by saying that no prince is secure without his own troops, on the contrary he is entirely dependent on fortune, having no trustworthy means of defence in time of trouble. It has always been held and proclaimed by wise men 'quod nihil sit tam infirmum aut instabile quam fama potentiae non sua vi nixae.' One's own troops are those composed either of subjects or of citizens or of one's own dependants; all others are mercenaries or auxiliaries. The way to organise one's own troops is easily learnt if the methods of the four princes mentioned above be studied, and if one considers how Philip, father of Alexander the Great, and many republics and sovereigns have organised theirs. With such examples as these there is no need to labour the point.

## Chapter XIV

### THE DUTIES OF A PRINCE WITH REGARD TO THE MILITIA

A PRINCE should therefore have no other aim or thought, nor take up any other thing for his study, but war and its organisation and discipline, for that is the only art that is necessary to one who commands, and it is of such virtue that it not only maintains those who are born princes, but often enables men of private fortune to attain to that rank. And one sees, on the other hand, that when princes think more of luxury than of arms, they lose their state. The chief cause of the loss of states, is the contempt of this art, and the way to acquire them is to be well versed in the same.

Francesco Sforza, through being well armed, became, from private status, Duke of Milan; his sons, through wishing to avoid the fatigue and hardship of war, from dukes became private persons. For among other evils caused by being disarmed, it renders you contemptible; which is one

of those disgraceful things which a prince must guard
against, as will be explained later. Because there is no comparison whatever between an armed and a disarmed man;
it is not reasonable to suppose that one who is armed will
obey willingly one who is unarmed; or that any unarmed
man will remain safe among armed servants. For one being
disdainful and the other suspicious, it is not possible for
them to act well together. And therefore a prince who is
ignorant of military matters, besides the other misfortunes
already mentioned, cannot be esteemed by his soldiers, nor
have confidence in them.

He ought, therefore, never to let his thoughts stray from
the exercise of war; and in peace he ought to practise it
more than in war, which he can do in two ways: by action
and by study. As to action, he must, besides keeping his
men well disciplined and exercised, engage continually in
hunting, and thus accustom his body to hardships; and
meanwhile learn the nature of the land, how steep the moun-
tains are, how the valleys debouch, where the plains lie,
and understand the nature of rivers and swamps. To all
this he should devote great attention. This knowledge is
useful in two ways. In the first place, one learns to know
one's country, and can the better see how to defend it. Then
by means of the knowledge and experience gained in one
locality, one can easily understand any other that it may be
necessary to observe; for the hills and valleys, plains and
rivers of Tuscany, for instance, have a certain resemblance
to those of other provinces, so that from a knowledge of
the country in one province one can easily arrive at a knowledge of others. And that prince who is lacking in this skill
is wanting in the first essentials of a leader; for it is this
which teaches how to find the enemy, take up quarters, lead
armies, plan battles and lay siege to towns with advantage.

Philopœmen, prince of the Achaei, among other praises bestowed on him by writers, is lauded because in times of peace he thought of nothing but the methods of warfare, and when he was in the country with his friends, he often stopped and asked them: If the enemy were on that hill and we found ourselves here with our army, which of us would have the advantage? How could we safely approach him maintaining our order? If we wished to retire, what ought we to do? If they retired, how should we follow them? And he put before them as they went along all the contingencies that might happen to an army, heard their opinion, gave his own, fortifying it by argument; so that thanks to these constant reflections there could never happen any incident when actually leading his armies for which he was not prepared.

But as to exercise for the mind, the prince ought to read history and study the actions of eminent men, see how they acted in warfare, examine the causes of their victories and defeats in order to imitate the former and avoid the latter, and above all, do as some men have done in the past, who have imitated some one, who has been much praised and glorified, and have always kept his deeds and actions before them, as they say Alexander the Great imitated Achilles, Cæsar Alexander, and Scipio Cyrus. And whoever reads the life of Cyrus written by Xenophon, will perceive in the life of Scipio how gloriously he imitated the former, and how, in chastity, affability, humanity, and liberality Scipio conformed to those qualities of Cyrus as described by Xenophon.

A wise prince should follow similar methods and never remain idle in peaceful times, but industriously make good use of them, so that when fortune changes she may find him prepared to resist her blows, and to prevail in adversity.

*Core of Machiavellian Philosophy*

## Chapter XV

### OF THE THINGS FOR WHICH MEN, AND ESPECIALLY PRINCES, ARE PRAISED OR BLAMED

It now remains to be seen what are the methods and rules for a prince as regards his subjects and friends. And as I know that many have written of this, I fear that my writing about it may be deemed presumptuous, differing as I do, especially in this matter, from the opinions of others. But my intention being to write something of use to those who understand, it appears to me more proper to go to the real truth of the matter than to its imagination; and many have imagined republics and principalities which have never been seen or known to exist in reality; for how we live is so far removed from how we ought to live, that he who abandons what is done for what ought to be done, will rather learn to bring about his own ruin than his preservation. A man who wishes to make a profession of goodness in everything must necessarily come to grief among so many who are not good. Therefore it is necessary for a prince, who wishes to maintain himself, to learn how not to be good, and to use this knowledge and not use it, according to the necessity of the case.

Leaving on one side, then, those things which concern only an imaginary prince, and speaking of those that are real, I state that all men, and especially princes, who are placed at a greater height, are reputed for certain qualities which bring them either praise or blame. Thus one is considered liberal, another *misero* or miserly (using a Tuscan term, seeing that *avaro* with us still means one who is ra-

Must learn how not to be good
To maintain position
THE PRINCE 57

paciously acquisitive and *misero* one who makes grudging use of his own); one a free giver, another rapacious; one cruel, another merciful; one a breaker of his word, another trustworthy; one effeminate and pusillanimous, another fierce and high-spirited; one humane, another haughty; one lascivious, another chaste; one frank, another astute; one hard, another easy; one serious, another frivolous; one religious, another an unbeliever, and so on. I know that every one will admit that it would be highly praiseworthy in a prince to possess all the above-named qualities that are reputed good, but as they cannot all be possessed or observed, human conditions not permitting of it, it is necessary that he should be prudent enough to avoid the scandal of those vices which would lose him the state, and guard himself if possible against those which will not lose it him, but if not able to, he can indulge them with less scruple. And yet he must not mind incurring the scandal of those vices, without which it would be difficult to save the state, for if one considers well, it will be found that some things which seem virtues would, if followed, lead to one's ruin, and some others which appear vices result in one's greater security and wellbeing.

## Chapter XVI

### OF LIBERALITY AND NIGGARDLINESS

BEGINNING now with the first qualities above named, I say that it would be well to be considered liberal; nevertheless liberality such as the world understands it will injure you, because if used virtuously and in the proper way, it will not be known, and you will incur the disgrace of the contrary vice. But one who wishes to obtain the reputation of liberality among men, must not omit every kind of sumptuous display, and to such an extent that a prince of this character will consume by such means all his resources, and will be at last compelled, if he wishes to maintain his name for liberality, to impose heavy taxes on his people, become extortionate, and do everything possible to obtain money. This will make his subjects begin to hate him, and he will be little esteemed being poor, so that having by this liberality injured many and benefited but few, he will feel the first little disturbance and be endangered by every peril. If he recognises this and wishes to change his system, he incurs at once the charge of niggardliness.

A prince, therefore, not being able to exercise this virtue of liberality without risk if it be known, must not, if he be prudent, object to be called miserly. In course of time he will be thought more liberal, when it is seen that by his parsimony his revenue is sufficient, that he can defend himself against those who make war on him, and undertake enterprises without burdening his people, so that he is really liberal to all those from whom he does not take, who are infinite in number, and niggardly to all to whom he does not give, who are few. In our times we have seen nothing great done except by those who have been esteemed niggardly; the others have all been ruined. Pope Julius II, although he had made use of a reputation for liberality in order to attain the papacy, did not seek to retain it afterwards, so that he might be able to wage war. The present King of France has carried on so many wars without imposing an extraordinary tax, because his extra expenses were covered by the parsimony he had so long practised. The present King of Spain, if he had been thought liberal, would not have engaged in and been successful in so many enterprises.

For these reasons a prince must care little for the reputation of being a miser, if he wishes to avoid robbing his subjects, if he wishes to be able to defend himself, to avoid becoming poor and contemptible, and not to be forced to become rapacious; this niggardliness is one of those vices which enable him to reign. If it is said that Cæsar attained the empire through liberality, and that many others have reached the highest positions through being liberal or being thought so, I would reply that you are either a prince already or else on the way to become one. In the first case, this liberality is harmful; in the second, it is certainly necessary to be considered liberal. Cæsar was one of those who wished to attain the mastery over Rome, but if after attaining it he had lived and had not moderated his expenses, he would have destroyed that empire. And should any one reply that there have been many princes, who have done great things with their armies, who have been thought extremely liberal, I would answer by saying that the prince may either spend his own wealth and that of his subjects or the wealth of others. In the first case he must be sparing, but for the rest he must not neglect to be very liberal. The liberality is very necessary to a prince who marches with his armies, and lives by plunder, sack and ransom, and is dealing with the wealth of others, for without it he would not be followed by his soldiers. And you may be very generous indeed with what is not the property of yourself or your subjects, as were Cyrus, Cæsar, and Alexander; for spending the wealth of others will not diminish your reputation, but increase it, only spending your own resources will injure you. There is nothing which destroys itself so much as liberality, for by using it you lose the power of using it, and become either poor and despicable, or, to escape poverty, rapacious and hated. And of all things that a prince must guard against, the most important are being despicable or hated, and liberality will lead you to one or other of these conditions. It is, therefore, wiser to have the name of a miser, which produces disgrace without hatred, than to incur of necessity the name of being rapacious, which produces both disgrace and hatred.

## Chapter XVII

### OF CRUELTY AND CLEMENCY, AND WHETHER IT IS BETTER TO BE LOVED OR FEARED

PROCEEDING to the other qualities before named, I say that every prince must desire to be considered merciful and not cruel. He must, however, take care not to misuse this mercifulness. Cesare Borgia was considered cruel, but his cruelty had brought order to the Romagna, united it, and reduced it to peace and fealty. If this is considered well, it will be seen that he was really much more merciful than the Florentine people, who, to avoid the name of cruelty, allowed Pistoia to be destroyed. A prince, therefore, must not mind incurring the charge of cruelty for the purpose of keeping his subjects united and faithful; for, with a very few examples, he will be more merciful than those who, from excess of tenderness, allow disorders to arise, from whence spring bloodshed and rapine; for these as a rule injure the whole community, while the executions carried out by the prince injure only individuals. And of all princes, it is impossible for a new prince to escape the reputation of cruelty, new states being always full of dangers. Wherefore Virgil through the mouth of Dido says:

> Res dura, et regni novitas me talia cogunt
> Moliri, et late fines custode tueri.

Nevertheless, he must be cautious in believing and acting, and must not be afraid of his own shadow, and must proceed in a temperate manner with prudence and humanity, so that too much confidence does not render him incautious, and too much diffidence does not render him intolerant.

From this arises the question whether it is better to be loved more than feared, or feared more than loved. The reply is, that one ought to be both feared and loved, but as it is difficult for the two to go together, it is much safer to be feared than loved, if one of the two has to be wanting. For it may be said of men in general that they are ungrateful, voluble, dissemblers, anxious to avoid danger, and covetous of gain; as long as you benefit them, they are entirely yours; they offer you their blood, their goods, their life, and their children, as I have before said, when the necessity is remote; but when it approaches, they revolt. And the prince who has relied solely on their words, without making other preparations, is ruined; for the friendship which is gained by purchase and not through grandeur and nobility of spirit is bought but not secured, and at a pinch is not to be expended in your service. And men have less scruple in offending one who makes himself loved than one who makes himself feared; for love is held by a chain of obligation which, men being selfish, is broken whenever it serves their purpose; but fear is maintained by a dread of punishment which never fails.

Still, a prince should make himself feared in such a way that if he does not gain love, he at any rate avoids hatred;

for fear and the absence of hatred may well go together, and will be always attained by one who abstains from interfering with the property of his citizens and subjects or with their women. And when he is obliged to take the life of any one, let him do so when there is a proper justification and manifest reason for it; but above all he must abstain from taking the property of others, for men forget more easily the death of their father than the loss of their patrimony. Then also pretexts for seizing property are never wanting, and one who begins to live by rapine will always find some reason for taking the goods of others, whereas causes for taking life are rarer and more fleeting.

But when the prince is with his army and has a large number of soldiers under his control, then it is extremely necessary that he should not mind being thought cruel; for without this reputation he could not keep an army united or disposed to any duty. Among the noteworthy actions of Hannibal is numbered this, that although he had an enormous army, composed of men of all nations and fighting in foreign countries, there never arose any dissension either among them or against the prince, either in good fortune or in bad. This could not be due to anything but his inhuman cruelty, which together with his infinite other virtues, made him always venerated and terrible in the sight of his soldiers, and without it his other virtues would not have sufficed to produce that effect. Thoughtless writers admire on the one hand his actions, and on the other blame the principal cause of them.

And that it is true that his other virtues would not have sufficed may be seen from the case of Scipio (famous not only in regard to his own times, but all times of which memory remains), whose armies rebelled against him in Spain, which arose from nothing but his excessive kindness, which allowed more licence to the soldiers than was consonant with military discipline. He was reproached with this in the senate by Fabius Maximus, who called him a corrupter of the Roman militia. Locri having been destroyed by one of Scipio's officers was not revenged by him, nor was the insolence of that officer punished, simply by reason of his easy nature; so much so, that some one wishing to excuse him in the senate, said that there were many men who knew rather how not to err, than how to correct the errors of others. This disposition would in time have tarnished the fame and glory of Scipio had he persevered in it under the empire, but living under the rule of the senate this harmful quality was not only concealed but became a glory to him.

I conclude, therefore, with regard to being feared and loved, that men love at their own free will, but fear at the will of the prince, and that a wise prince must rely on what is in his power and not on what is in the power of others, and he must only contrive to avoid incurring hatred, as has been explained.

## Chapter XVIII

### IN WHAT WAY PRINCES MUST KEEP FAITH

How laudable it is for a prince to keep good faith and live with integrity, and not with astuteness, every one knows. Still the experience of our times shows those princes to have done great things who have had little regard for good faith, and have been able by astuteness to confuse men's brains, and who have ultimately overcome those who have made loyalty their foundation.

You must know, then, that there are two methods of fighting, the one by law, the other by force: the first method is that of men, the second of beasts; but as the first method is often insufficient, one must have recourse to the second. It is therefore necessary for a prince to know well how to use both the beast and the man. This was covertly taught to rulers by ancient writers, who relate how Achilles and many others of those ancient princes were given to Chiron the centaur to be brought up and educated under his discipline. The parable of this semi-animal, semi-human teacher is meant to indicate that a prince must know how to use both natures, and that the one without the other is not durable.

A prince being thus obliged to know well how to act as a beast must imitate the fox and the lion, for the lion cannot protect himself from traps, and the fox cannot defend himself from wolves. One must therefore be a fox to recognise traps, and a lion to frighten wolves. Those that wish to be only lions do not understand this. Therefore, a prudent ruler ought not to keep faith when by so doing it would be against his interest, and when the reasons which made him bind himself no longer exist. If men were all good, this precept would not be a good one; but as they are bad, and would not observe their faith with you, so you are not bound to keep faith with them. Nor have legitimate grounds ever failed a prince who wished to show colourable excuse for the non-fulfilment of his promise. Of this one could furnish an infinite number of modern examples, and show how many times peace has been broken, and how many promises rendered worthless, by the faithlessness of princes, and those that have been best able to imitate the fox have succeeded best. But it is necessary to be able to disguise this character well, and to be a great feigner and dissembler; and men are

Since others are bad, good people must become bad to defend themselves so simple and so ready to obey present necessities, that one who deceives will always find those who allow themselves to be deceived.

I will only mention one modern instance. Alexander VI did nothing else but deceive men, he thought of nothing else, and found the occasion for it; no man was ever more able to give assurances, or affirmed things with stronger oaths, and no man observed them less; however, he always succeeded in his deceptions, as he well knew this aspect of things.

It is not, therefore, necessary for a prince to have all the above-named qualities, but it is very necessary to seem to have them. I would even be bold to say that to possess them and always to observe them is dangerous, but to appear to possess them is useful. Thus it is well to seem merciful, faithful, humane, sincere, religious, and also to be so; but you must have the mind so disposed that when it is needful to be otherwise you may be able to change to the opposite qualities. And it must be understood that a prince, and especially a new prince, cannot observe all those things which are considered good in men, being often obliged, in order to maintain the state, to act against faith, against charity, against humanity, and against religion. And, therefore, he must have a mind disposed to adapt itself according to the wind, and as the variations of fortune dictate, and, as I said before, not deviate from what is good, if possible, but be able to do evil if constrained.

A prince must take great care that nothing goes out of his mouth which is not full of the above-named five qualities, and, to see and hear him, he should seem to be all mercy, faith, integrity, humanity, and religion. And nothing is more necessary than to seem to have this last quality, for men in general judge more by the eyes than by the hands,

if everybody did it
no one would
have to ...

for every one can see, but very few have to feel. Everybody sees what you appear to be, few feel what you are, and those few will not dare to oppose themselves to the many, who have the majesty of the state to defend them; and in the actions of men, and especially of princes, from which there is no appeal, the end justifies the means. Let a prince therefore aim at conquering and maintaining the state, and the means will always be judged honourable and praised by every one, for the vulgar is always taken by appearances and the issue of the event; and the world consists only of the vulgar, and the few who are not vulgar are isolated when the many have a rallying point in the prince. A certain prince of the present time, whom it is well not to name, never does anything but preach peace and good faith, but he is really a great enemy to both, and either of them, had he observed them, would have lost him state or reputation on many occasions.

## Chapter XIX

### THAT WE MUST AVOID BEING DESPISED AND HATED

But as I have now spoken of the most important of the qualities in question, I will now deal briefly and generally with the rest. The prince must, as already stated, avoid those things which will make him hated or despised; and whenever he succeeds in this, he will have done his part, and will find no danger in other vices. He will chiefly become hated, as I said, by being rapacious, and usurping the property and women of his subjects, which he must abstain from doing, and whenever one does not attack the property or honour of the generality of men, they will live contented; and one will only have to combat the ambition of a few, who can be easily held in check in many ways. He is rendered despicable by being thought changeable, frivolous, effeminate, timid, and irresolute; which a prince must guard against as a rock of danger, and so contrive that his actions show grandeur, spirit, gravity, and fortitude; and as to the government of his subjects, let his sentence be irrevocable, and let him adhere to his decisions so that no one may think of deceiving or cozening him.

The prince who creates such an opinion of himself gets a great reputation, and it is very difficult to conspire against one who has a great reputation, and he will not easily be attacked, so long as it is known that he is capable and reverenced by his subjects. For a prince must have two kinds of fear: one internal as regards his subjects, one external as regards foreign powers. From the latter he can defend himself with good arms and good friends, and he will always have good friends if he has good arms; and internal matters will always remain quiet, if they are not perturbed by conspiracy and there is no disturbance from without; and even if external powers sought to attack him, if he has ruled and lived as I have described, he will always if he stands firm, be able to sustain every shock, as I have shown that Nabis the Spartan did. But with regard to the subjects, if not acted on from outside, it is still to be feared lest they conspire in secret, from which the prince may guard himself well by avoiding hatred and contempt, and keeping the people satisfied with him, which it is necessary to accomplish, as has been related at length. And one of the most potent remedies that a prince has against conspiracies, is that of not being hated by the mass of the people; for whoever conspires always believes that he will satisfy the people by the death of their prince; but if he thought to offend them by doing this, he would fear to engage in such an undertaking, for the difficulties that conspirators have to meet are infinite. Experience shows that there have been very many conspiracies, but few have turned out well, for whoever conspires cannot act alone, and cannot find companions except among those who are discontented; and as soon as you have disclosed your intention to a malcontent, you give him the means of satisfying himself, for by revealing it he can hope to secure everything he wants; to such an extent that seeing a certain gain by doing this, and seeing on the other hand only a doubtful one and full of danger, he must either be a rare friend to you or else a very bitter enemy to the prince if he keeps faith with you. And to express the matter in a few words, I say, that on the side of the conspirator there is nothing but fear, jealousy, suspicion, and dread of punishment which frightens him; and on the side of the prince there is the majesty of government, the laws, the protection of friends and of the state which guard him. When to these things is added the goodwill of the people, it is impossible that any one should have the temerity to conspire. For whereas generally a conspirator has to fear before the execution of his plot, in this case, having the people for an enemy, he must also fear after his crime is accomplished, and thus he is not able to hope for any refuge.

Numberless instances might be given of this, but I will content myself with one which took place within the memory of our fathers. Messer Annibale Bentivogli, Prince of Bologna, ancestor of the present Messer Annibale, was killed by the Canneschi, who conspired against him. He left no relations but Messer Giovanni, who was then an infant, but after the murder the people rose up and killed all the Canneschi. This arose from the popular goodwill that the house of Bentivogli enjoyed at that time, which was so